THE
LAST
ONE
HOME

THE
LAST
ONE
HOME

VICTORIA HELEN
STONE

LAKE UNION
PUBLISHING

Published by Lake Union Publishing, Seattle

www.apub.com

Amazon, the Amazon logo, and Lake Union Publishing are trademarks of Amazon.com, Inc., or its affiliates.

ISBN-13: 9781542014427
ISBN-10: 1542014425

Cover design by Damon Freeman

Printed in the United States of America

THE
LAST
ONE
HOME

CHAPTER 1

LAUREN

The heat of this place grew serial killers.

Not that everyone born here became a murderer, but the Sacramento area had more than its fair share. Lauren Abrams had been raised with that truth, always aware of her own faint brush with darkness and destruction. Something dangerous vibrated in the air of this place, though most people never registered the thrum of it.

When outsiders set foot here, the thing they noticed was the heat. Something about it haunted them until it was all they could mention when Lauren said she was from Sacramento. *What a hellhole. It's so hot! Who could live there?*

And why? It was hardly the hottest place in California. So maybe it was that low register of danger they felt.

Lauren had felt it the first time she'd come, but she'd been primed for it. Warned about what would happen if she ever returned to this place. She'd ignored the predictions, and she'd returned, terrifyingly untethered from the first decade of her life.

She'd learned herself here. She'd let this place mold her into the person she was today, and she could feel the city sink into her as she drove through the flat river plain of the town toward the hills beyond.

When she spotted the exit that would take her to the hospital where her grandmother lay, guilt tugged at her. She desperately wanted to veer to the right and race toward the big gray building, but the visit could wait one hour. The stroke had happened two days earlier, and Grandma's doctors said she was improving and even recovering well from the concussion she'd sustained when she'd fallen.

If Lauren barged in wearing rumpled clothes dusted with the snacks she'd munched on during her drive from LA, her grandma might have another stroke. Elizabeth Abrams had always held a firm belief in putting your best foot forward. She'd worn ranch clothes while working outside, but she'd never, ever worn them around the house.

Right now Grandma was stable, and there was no danger in waiting a few more moments. She was on the mend, so Lauren was there to help with the mending. Her grandmother's, but maybe her own too.

This move wasn't permanent, but she'd still packed up nearly her entire life when she'd left Bastian's condo that morning. She'd have to find her own place when she returned. But she didn't need to think about that yet. For now she would watch over her grandma's home and get it cleaned and ready before her release from rehab, and that was more than enough to worry about.

The sprawl continued along the highway much farther out than it used to, but Lauren finally exited and pushed her little red hatchback up into the hills. Before she was quite ready, she'd turned onto a narrow paved road with ditches on either side, and then she was slowing for the gravel drive she'd been aiming for these past eight hours.

Home.

It felt strange to approach and know that the screen door wouldn't open to reveal her grandmother stepping onto the porch. Then again, Grandma was ninety now, so Lauren tried to count her blessings as she opened the car door and pushed to her feet.

She stretched hard to loosen up her lower back and flexed the poor fingers that had clutched the steering wheel, choking it in grief and anger. What the hell was she going to do after this visit? She had nothing. No boyfriend. No home.

Stop, she told herself. Her grandma wouldn't tolerate wallowing, and Lauren had no right to be worried about herself in the face of that stroke. She would be fine. She'd help her grandmother get back on her feet, and then . . . then she'd be free. She could take her graphic design work anywhere. Live anyplace she wanted. But the freedom of that left too much space around her when all she craved was a safe nook. After her childhood she'd learned to treasure security over anything.

Turning in a lazy circle, she soaked in the sight of the rolling gold hills around her and tried to let some peace seep into her. The afternoon was warm, nearly hot, but some of the trees had lost their leaves already, and Lauren couldn't wait for the cool bite of the autumn night, reminding her of the holidays she'd spent here. All the trees she'd climbed. The endless adventures and explorations. As a child Lauren had thought this property as vast as a continent.

She took in another breath of peace before confronting what she'd come to do. She forced herself to hurry up the steps so she wouldn't notice how chilling it was to see the door locked up tight behind the screen. She reached around the porch light and found the key her dad had told her to look for. She'd never been here without her family before.

Reminding herself it was only temporary, she kept moving, propping the screen open so she could unlock the door and push inside. When she stepped in, Lauren inhaled. Despite the closed doors and drawn curtains, the house still smelled of the last flowers in the garden. One scent was missing, though: lemon polish. It had been replaced by dust.

Grief tugged like a burr inside her heart. Grandma had always kept this place polished to a shine, but now, even in the dimness, Lauren could see signs that her grandmother had been slowing to a stop. Several old newspapers were piled on the parlor table next to a glass, and a blanket and pillow lay crumpled on the sofa.

She'd never given any indication that she wasn't feeling well, and Lauren had called her every two weeks like clockwork.

Blinking back tears, she pulled a set of curtains open and watched dust dance in a swirl of sunlit air before it joined the layer accumulating on a shelf of keepsakes. The ceramic topper that had graced her grandparents' wedding cake, two pale figures with faded faces and linked arms. A beautiful glass horse pawing at the ground. A black-and-white photo of this very house from nearly a hundred years ago.

These small treasures had seemed so strange and elegant the first time Lauren had seen them. She could vividly remember every moment of that first visit because after all the years of scary stories her mother had whispered in the dark, Lauren had walked into her grandmother's home in absolute terror. She'd been shaking and scared, sure that she would be killed or kidnapped or something worse that a ten-year-old couldn't even imagine.

And then, despite so many years of swelling horror . . . her dad and his mother had been utterly, impossibly *normal*. Warm. Loving. Tidy and attentive. They were like every solid sitcom family Lauren had watched on crappy fuzzed-out TVs her whole life.

Those families had been a fantasy that Lauren had wholeheartedly indulged in from her earliest moments. Carefree children riding bikes and kicking balls, no traffic in sight. Houses grouped around green lawns as if they were protecting each other, gathering close, whispering good morning and good night to the occupants.

Family life had looked like a fairy tale, a faraway land where other people lived, not Lauren, not her mom.

Not until she'd come here and discovered a cozy heaven: Waffles for breakfast, made in an honest-to-God cast-iron waffle maker. Fresh whole milk. Warm cookies in the afternoons. Pot roasts for dinner.

Hand-squeezed lemonade. Beautiful flower gardens shaded by the biggest trees Lauren had ever seen.

For a girl who'd lived in cramped city apartments her whole life, she'd been happy to be seduced into what her mother had called a cult. It was a cult of security and love and a father who was dying to get to know his little girl and didn't blame her for any of the bad things that had happened. His eyes hadn't glowed with the feverish vengeance she'd been promised. They'd glowed with love.

Lauren swiped at her tears and nodded. She'd clean this place up, and her grandmother would come back, and everything would be good here again. A touchstone she could always return to.

"Time to buckle down," she said aloud, just as her grandma had said in this room a hundred times. "Hard work is the best medicine."

So she set her shoulders and hurried out to the car for her bags. She'd have time for melancholy later. Right now her family needed her.

Fifteen minutes later she'd brushed her teeth, combed her hair back into a neat ponytail, and changed into clean clothes. Her bags were stowed in the small bedroom she'd used since childhood, and Lauren was back in her car and on her way.

Every ache she'd accumulated on the drive from LA returned with a vengeance as she wound her way down the rural roads to the highway beyond. By the time she reached the hospital over thirty minutes later, her neck screamed with tension, but she pasted a smile on her face and hurried up to the third floor.

The door to room 326 stood open in the quiet hallway, and Lauren took that as a good sign. Things were normal and calm. Her grandmother was doing well.

But then she walked in. Her grandma, normally so dignified and crisp, lay in a tiny bundle on the bed, eyes closed, mouth gaping, her silver curls distorted into strange whorls on the pillow. She looked dead or dying, a flattened animal on the side of the road. "Oh no."

At that slight whisper the old woman's eyes fluttered open, and when she spotted Lauren, she stirred and tried to push herself higher up the angled mattress.

"Grandma!" Lauren cried, rushing forward. "Let me help!"

She hooked her hands beneath her grandma's arms and shifted her up, then rearranged the pillows and smoothed down her thin curls. She pressed a kiss to her grandmother's head and wrapped her arms around her. Grandma still smelled of the shampoo she'd always used, but she felt as fragile as an antique doll.

"It's so good to see you," Lauren murmured.

"Sit down," her grandma responded, the words a little thicker than they should've been. "Sit down. I wish I could make you some lemonade."

Lauren huffed out a laugh. "I should be making you lemonade, silly. I'm here to take care of you."

"Nonsense." She waved her right hand, but her left arm lay limp on the mattress, and that side of her face sagged in matching tragedy. She could still talk, at least. And surely she'd be good as new in no time. "You look beautiful, my dear."

"Thank you. You look great too."

Her grandmother rolled her eyes. "Funny, I feel like I've had a stroke."

"Oh, Grandma." Though she laughed, tears pooled in her eyes as she took her grandmother's limp hand and squeezed.

A nurse bustled in, though she only smiled as she quietly checked a couple of machines and then picked up the chart to make a note.

"What happened?" Lauren asked her grandmother.

"I'm not exactly sure . . ."

"She's had a bit of memory loss," the nurse said, her voice a husky drawl from somewhere in the Deep South. "A minor concussion. Lost about a week of memory, we think."

"That's awful. Dad said you hit your head."

"I don't remember that at all, and I feel just fine."

"Mrs. Abrams," the nurse said brightly, "the physical therapist will be by in an hour or so."

"That's good news," Lauren said. "They'll get you back to normal in no time." She looked down at her lap as the nurse left. "I'm sorry it's been so long since I've visited. I feel terrible. Things have just been . . ."

Her grandma gave a weak, lopsided smile and reached to cover Lauren's hand with her right one. "You have a whole life to live down there in the big city."

"Well. Not so much anymore. I guess you might not remember, but Bastian and I . . . we broke up."

"I do remember, and it was bull hockey," her grandma scoffed, surprising Lauren into a laugh. "That boy was a worthless specimen if he couldn't see what was right in front of his face. I said it all along, didn't I? You deserve better, my girl. You deserve everything."

Lauren kissed her grandmother's cheek, holding back a bitter laugh. She didn't even want *everything*. She just wanted *something*. A home. Love. Family.

"Well, it's all one big silver lining because here I am to help. I can stay as long as you need me now!" That was a good spin on having nowhere else to go.

"Yes. Well," her grandmother said, "about that help . . ."

Lauren had never heard this note of hesitation in her voice before. Grandma Abrams was strong as steel and always had been. Lauren's dad was charming and confident, but even he sat up straight and paid attention when his mother's voice cracked with command.

"Things have changed, and I've spent the past two days thinking. You know how I am. I believe in making firm plans for life, and this thing"—she tipped her chin toward the TV on the wall—"is nothing but mindless drivel. No distraction at all."

"Can I bring you a newspaper? A book?"

"I'm fine. I have a lot to think about. And I think maybe you should consider moving here. To the house."

"The house? I can't . . . No, I'll find something. I'll be just fine."

"I know you're fine. You're strong and smart."

"I'll stay as long as you need me to, so please don't worry about that. But I can't really move in with you permanently." That would be admitting defeat, wouldn't it? And it would be so, so humiliating, especially after Bastian had told her she was afraid to put herself out there, afraid to take chances.

"We wouldn't be roommates," her grandma said, but oh God that was exactly what they'd be.

The worst part was she wasn't even sure she'd hate it. She'd hate only the idea of Bastian finding out. "Grandma, I really appreciate the offer, but once you're on your feet, I have to look for a place on my own and . . . I don't know. Get back out there, I guess. Move on."

"Move *up*," she insisted.

"Yes. Move up. Find someone ready to settle down."

"Exactly. You want to build a life. That's what you told me. And you're a single young woman. You need your own space."

Yes, she definitely wanted to have sex again someday.

"But the thing is, my dear, they're not sure I *will* be back on my feet."

Lauren cringed, her eyes sliding down the insubstantial hills of her grandmother's legs beneath the blankets. "Don't say that!"

"Oh, I'll work as hard as I can at the therapy, but they say a two-story house is out of the question." Her right shoulder rose in a shrug. "They're sending me to a rehabilitation facility for a week or so, but after that . . . They left a lot of pamphlets."

For the first time Lauren noticed the rolling table pushed to the other side of the bed. There were in fact quite a few brochures on them. She glimpsed the phrase *Fantastic senior living in the Folsom foothills!* in white script.

"I'll talk to them," Lauren promised. "Maybe we could get one of those chairlifts for the staircase. Or even convert the parlor into a bedroom. If we—"

"I'm not sure it feels safe anymore," her grandmother said softly.

Lauren snapped her mouth shut as her throat tightened.

"I don't remember the fall or the stroke. Or the week leading up to it. But I do remember the after. Just *lying* there. And, oh Lauren, it took me such a very long time to make it to the phone."

"Oh, Grandma." She lifted the clawed, precious hand and pressed her lips to it. "I'm so sorry." She didn't want to cry. Her grandma had always kept her own feelings private, and Lauren didn't want to weep over her when she looked so calm and stoic. Still, the idea of her trying to drag herself along the floor to call for help . . .

They should have known. She and her father should have made accommodations for a ninety-year-old woman living on her own. Instead, they'd selfishly ignored the looming issue.

Her grandmother sighed. "I'm glad I sold off the rest of the grazing land. I made a pretty penny on that sale, and I'm going to need it. Did I tell you those developers are subdividing now? Thank God I forced them to put those tracts on the far reaches where there's no sign from the house. It would drive me mad to see that!"

"You said it was quieter this month," Lauren reminded her. "The dust has died down."

"It has." She sighed again. "My point is that everything changes. Even our Abrams land. And the house is just too much for me now."

"Oh," Lauren breathed, realizing now what was really happening. It made sense. It did. But it still hit her as a terrible blow, the force of it whooshing all the air from her lungs.

She thought of stories she'd heard of being stabbed. How it felt as though you'd only been punched until you realized the life was falling out of you through an open wound, and then the true pain started.

But no. This wasn't that. This was just a life change that anyone might go through. Her grandmother was selling Lauren's childhood. She had every right. Lauren wasn't a child anymore, and no one could stop time. This wasn't a blow. Just a blip.

Right.

The tears finally spilled over, and Lauren hurried to wipe them away.

She cradled her grandmother's slender fingers, the cool skin. "I want whatever is best for you. I always do. I'll do everything I can to help, absolutely anything you need. I'll stay for as long as you need me, and we'll get this place ready in no time."

Her grandmother's face folded into a half frown that revealed a hundred chasing lines on her face for a brief moment before she smoothed it out again, never one for showing vulgar emotion. "Ready for what?"

"For the market."

"The market? No! I don't want a stranger living there! That's our home. Yours. Mine. Your father's. I could *never*. I want to sell it to *you*, Lauren. I want you to live there. I want you to own our land and carry on, just as Abramses have been doing for a hundred and thirty years."

A strange sizzle went through her. A zing that warmed her skin and muffled her hearing like she'd tugged down a knit cap. *"Me?"*

"Yes."

Lauren shook her head automatically. "The house should go to Dad. It belongs to him. And his kids—"

"You're his child too. Don't be silly."

"But there are three of us now." She'd been the only grandchild for so long. The only daughter. But now he had another daughter. One he could spend an entire life with, not pick up halfway through. Plus the son he'd always wanted. He'd started talking about Little League the moment the sonogram showed a tiny penis. A *son*. He'd been desperate for someone to carry on the line even though Lauren had taken his name when she'd turned fourteen.

Then there was the unavoidable fact that his two younger children had no connection at all to the woman who'd sent him to prison for murder.

But that was good. He deserved a happy life after everything he'd been put through. She craved that for him with all her heart.

"Lauren," her grandmother sighed. "I'd do anything for your father, but he would sell my home for a profit in a heartbeat. Men don't care about the heart of a place, not like women do. And of course I love Grace and Cody, but they have busy lives in Menlo Park. Suki and your dad have careers and a house and that darn sailboat, and the kids have five hundred ridiculous after-school activities. They don't want a home out here, and they never have. But I think you do, sweetheart. Don't you?"

"Grandma—" she started, and it was all she could get out. She shook her head and pressed her lips tight together in a vain attempt to control herself.

"Your father was always too big for this place, anyway."

Meaning that Lauren was small enough to stay. The idea didn't even prick her because it was true. That home had been her biggest dream, her wildest fantasy, and she'd already lived it. Why not admit as much and return to the one spot where she'd been happy?

She swallowed a half-dozen times until the pressure in her throat eased and she knew she wouldn't embarrass herself with a sob. Her grandmother would not approve.

Lauren had been raised by a mother who yelled and spat and fought her way through life, throwing her every volatile emotion into the world like a battle to be won. When Lauren had shown up on her father's doorstep at age ten, she'd been too scared to say much, so she'd ducked her head and observed. There had been no yelling in her grandmother's house. There had been cool and calm. *Control.* Lauren didn't come by it naturally, but she'd learned.

She pulled in a quiet breath and let it out as slowly as she could.

"I can't afford it," she managed to say, "but I can't tell you how grateful I am for the offer, Grandma. I feel so . . ." What did she feel? Loved. Cared for. Enveloped. All those things.

But most of all, biggest of all, she felt *accepted*.

That had never been a given. Even now she still quietly waited for her dad's family to wise up. After all, her mother's lies had put her father in prison, torn him from his family in an act of vengeance that was meant to be permanent. So Lauren had waited for them to change their minds about loving her, and she made sure never to give them a reason to. Even today. But now this. Proof that it was all real. That she truly was his daughter no matter what her mother had done.

She held her grandmother's hand in both of hers and squeezed gently. "I love you so much," she rasped. "And I love that place. I just don't have the money."

"It's only the house and ten acres now. It needs a new air conditioner, and the roof will only last another two years, maybe three. Anyone else who buys it will gut it and tear everything apart so they can have vaulted ceilings and skylights like all those places on cable. Double ovens and brick walls. They'll tear down the last of the outbuildings and sell the wood to some restorer who'll turn it into a floor for a rich family. I've watched those shows with Suki, you know. And I don't want that, sweetheart. Not for my home. You know that place means everything to me. If I can't live there, I want my own blood to carry on. My own lovely little girl. We fought so hard for you, you know."

Lauren smiled past her tears.

"You're a single young woman. I understand that you can't afford to purchase a big estate outright. I'll sell it to you in a private deal, and we'll work out a monthly payment. No mortgage approval involved. Two hundred thousand over twenty years. How's that sound?"

The laugh caught her by surprise, and she accidentally snorted, then covered her nose in horror. "It's worth three times that, at least!"

Her grandmother's delicate shoulders rose in the briefest shrug. "It's my home. The selling price is up to me. Who's going to even know?"

"But Dad . . . and Grace and Cody."

"Oh pshaw. Your dad will get his fair share. But your share will be the house. He would much rather live in a condo in the city when he fully retires. Somewhere near his boat and all those restaurants. We both know that. He finally got away, and he's not coming back to the country."

Hope was beginning to fizz up inside her. "But maybe you can still come home," she protested.

Her grandma leaned forward, one side of her mouth curving up in a rueful smile. "I'll tell you a secret, but you can't tell anyone."

"I promise."

"For the last six weeks, I was sleeping on the sofa downstairs."

"No."

"It's true. I couldn't bear the thought of coming down that long flight of stairs in the middle of the night for the bathroom. I can't live in that house anymore, sweetheart. I think I've known that for quite a while, and I just didn't want to admit it. But this . . ." She gestured toward her left side.

"But you're so strong. You can get better."

"Oh, I *will* get better. I promise you that. But I think my next ten years will involve listening to old biddies gossip instead of tending that big garden. I let it go to heck this year, my love. I really did." She shook her head in disapproval of her own fallible body. "What a shame."

"I don't have much of a green thumb, but I'll work on it if you come home. I'll help. I was serious about building you a bedroom downstairs! What if we—"

"You don't want the house?"

"It's not that, I swear. But, Grandma . . . it's *yours*."

Her grandma tilted her head, and suddenly her expression didn't look quite so crooked. It looked as straight and strong as it ever had.

"Maybe I'll like the change. Do you know that some of these communities have monthly trips to the Sacramento opera? And real crystal in the dining room? My mother would have loved that. She believed in nice things. She *insisted* on them. Even on the ranch my father always cleaned up and wore a jacket to dinner. Granted, it was worn brown corduroy, but my mother maintained standards. We had a family name. A place of honor in the community . . ." She trailed off.

Lauren had heard the stories, paged through all the ancient photo albums. The men posing in hats and shiny boots, the women in delicate printed cotton and heeled shoes with little straps across the instep.

Lauren had never met Grandfather Abrams, but she had secretly wondered if Grandma had married him only because he was a second cousin. Being able to keep the Abrams name may have been the only wedding gift she'd wanted. She was an Abrams through and through. She'd gotten the name and the son, and when her much older husband had died, she'd been left with the home she'd always known. Certainly she'd never spoken of love or romance. Just the land.

And now it could belong to Lauren.

She did not plan on marrying a second cousin, but she'd keep her last name if she got married. She'd worked hard for the right to it, after all.

"Are you serious?" she pressed. "You'd sell me your house?"

"I'm serious," her grandma said firmly, and her right hand reached for Lauren's wrist, latching on with a surprising amount of force. "I want you in that house, my girl. I've dreamed of this for you since before you were born."

Before she was born. When her father had been married to another woman and her mother had been the spurned, pregnant lover . . .

Lauren didn't like to think about that time, so she smiled instead. "This is a huge step. I'll have to give it some thought."

"Of course."

She felt slightly alarmed by the offer, but she had no idea why. Of course she wanted to live in that house. She wanted it with all her heart. She was a freelance artist, and she could live anywhere, so why was she hesitating?

Something felt scary about this. Some instinct raised the hair on the back of her neck and whispered warnings.

But then Lauren recognized the doubtful voice. She heard it murmuring, telling her to think, to be cautious, to forge her own life away from this place. To run fast and get as far away from these people as she could and hide, for God's sake, *hide*.

That voice was her mother's.

"Actually, no," she heard another voice say now, and it was her own, strong and a little too loud. "No, I don't need to think about it. This has always been my home, and now it always will be. There's nothing that would make me happier, Grandma. Thank you. It's all I've ever wanted."

Her mother's lies be damned.

CHAPTER 2

DONNA

1985

Blowing air through her teeth, she tapped the cigarette pack hard against her hand. When the perfect scent of fresh tobacco hit her, Donna reached automatically for one of the slim cigarettes that emerged, and slid it free before she even realized what she was doing. She held it between two fingers, rolling it slightly, considering, *wanting*.

"Damn it," she muttered, pushing the cigarette back into place so she could shove the pack deep into her bag. She felt ashamed at the action, happy no one could see her. Why was she bothering being cautious about nicotine? What was the point of denying herself when there was no lasting reason?

Stepping out the front door to the walkway overlooking the court-yard, she told herself to calm down. To take it all in. If she could show this view to her teenage self, that girl would be screaming and jumping up and down at the thought that one day she'd live in an apartment in LA with a pool and palm trees and flowering vines climbing up the wall. Hollywood, baby. She'd made it. And she'd made it as an artist.

All right. Not quite as an artist.

She barked out a laugh. She was an artist in that she still practiced painting, but she supported herself with an office job at a midlevel public relations firm. Still, PR was art in its own way, wasn't it?

"Fuck yeah," she whispered into the ticking leaves of the nearest palm. "Living the dream, baby."

But the sad truth was that her dreams had been small and desperate. All she'd wanted was freedom, and freedom as a kid was just . . . adulthood. As if all adults were footloose and fancy free.

It somehow never occurred to a fifteen-year-old that the cool apartment in LA came with cockroaches, creepy landlords, an old convertible that fit her image but needed thousands in repairs, and, most screwed up of all, a boyfriend in Sacramento who hadn't wrapped up his drawn-out divorce yet.

She patted her pockets, looking for a cigarette again, restless and lost. "Jesus, I've got to get out of here," she muttered. It was only 7:00, but someone was partying somewhere, right? It was Hollywood on a Friday night, and she was young and single.

Was she actually still young, though? "Young enough," she grouched.

Donna changed into her favorite tight black bodysuit, the one with the perilously low neckline; then she tugged on a pair of baggy jeans that made her slim waist look even slimmer. May as well show it off while she still had it. She laced up her scuffed boots and slicked back her short hair. She might be thirty-five, but she was still punk enough to show these kids a thing or two. None of them had ever lived on the streets of San Francisco in the late '70s. Most had never lived on the streets at all. Half of these assholes were just trying to put a good scare into Daddy before they got a respectable haircut and a real job and could brag about their days of banging around the darkest clubs of LA with bleached hair and a nose ring.

Not that she was heading anywhere dangerous. She'd spent way too many years truly roughing it to be interested in some broken-ass unlicensed club with just one filthy urinal and no working toilet. She'd take a bar with a women's room and a health inspection certificate every day. One round of hep A was enough to last anyone's whole lifetime. She'd been lucky compared to a lot of her friends. She'd somehow managed to avoid hep C so far. And AIDS. And she had firm plans to keep avoiding them if she could. There was living rough and then there was beat the hell up and gasping for air.

Clawing out a life on the street was far behind her. Almost twenty years now. She had no idea why she was thinking of that life tonight, ass-kicking boots or not.

But that wasn't true. She knew exactly why she was thinking of it. She hadn't felt this desperate in a long while.

She set her jaw and drew on thick black eyeliner and put the past out of her mind. She was going to head to a bass-booming club with wonderful friends and let the strobe lights and dance music fry every thought from her head until all she felt was peace. It was always the perfect solution for what ailed her.

~

Two hours later Tom and Tom were walking her home, each of them with a tight arm around her waist to support her. But for the first time it wasn't because she was drunk. She was stone-cold sober and wiping endlessly falling tears from her cheeks. "I'm sorry," she blurted for the third time. "I really wasn't going to tell you tonight. Now all of our nights are ruined."

"Do not apologize. We'll both go to the abortion clinic with you, girl. You do not have to freak out."

"No," she said. "That's not it. I've done that before. It's no big deal. I have a doctor who prescribes *great* pain meds."

Tom Number One—Tomás, her best friend—guided her carefully up the walk through the courtyard while the second Tom—Tommy—let go of her to unlock the door to their downstairs apartment. It was so much nicer than her place. Two bedrooms and bright corner windows shaded from the worst of the sun by thick fronds of green. The place was always filled with the absolutely delicious scent of food made by Tomás's mother, who was the reason for the second bedroom. She was also the reason for the warm aura that bathed the place. It felt like home because it was a home.

"I'll be fine," Donna insisted.

"Then why is there snot straight up running out your nose?" Tommy asked in his smooth Louisiana drawl.

"I hate you," she muttered, but she gratefully snatched the wad of tissues he offered once they were inside.

Donna blew her nose and collapsed onto their couch, sure the tears were done. But they kept dripping down her cheeks as if she'd sprung an unfixable leak. And she never cried. Never. "This is so stupid. I'm so stupid."

"You're not stupid," Tommy said with a sigh.

"Yes, I am. I'm an idiot."

"No, you're a person with a uterus, and I hear this can happen when a dick gets too close to one. Danger, Will Robinson. Get far away from that penis."

"Speaking of, is that dick still married?" Tomás asked as he lit a cigarette and took a deep drag.

"Jesus, give me that," Donna muttered, stealing it to finally get a hit of nicotine after a long day of resisting.

Tomás snatched it back after she managed one long, delicious draw. "Cut it out. You're smoking for two now, apparently."

"Oh God," Donna groaned, letting her head fall back so that the tears snaked over to her temples. "Oh God, there's just no way."

"Again, you have a uterus, so there's—"

"I know how it happened, Tom, I just don't know how I can let it *continue*. Why am I even thinking about this? It's ridiculous. What the hell am I doing?"

Tommy placed a very careful hand on her knee. "So . . . you *are* thinking about it? Like, seriously?"

"God, I don't know! I'm thirty-five! Jesus, when the fuck did I get old? But yeah, I'm thirty-five and I'm knocked up, and for some reason that feels really . . . *real*. It feels like some sort of ridiculous *possibility* when it didn't feel that way at all at twenty-two. Is that the dumbest thing you've ever heard?"

"No," he answered simply, and her tears turned to a choked sob. He pulled her to his chest. "It's not dumb, sweetheart. It's just scary."

"It is scary!" she wailed. "And I hate being scared. I'm not afraid of anything. I'm a tough bitch."

"The toughest bitch," he agreed, and she cried harder.

"Have you told him yet?" Tomás asked once she quieted down.

"No. I'll decide whatever I'm going to decide, and then I'll let him know."

"Good," he said shortly. Tommy liked Michael, but Tomás didn't trust him. Which was fair because that fully summed up Donna's ambiguous feelings too. She loved the asshole. He was funny and cute, and he gave her the freedom she craved, but she'd never trusted a man in her life. She wasn't going to start with a guy who'd dated her for a full year without ever managing to finalize his divorce. It was contentious, he said. Complicated. His nearly ex-wife kept drawing things out.

"It's none of his business," she said quietly. "It's not like I want to get married and start a little family."

Tommy let loose a soft hiss of disapproval. "You're going to have a baby and *not* get married?"

"Oh, come on," Tomás countered. "This isn't the 1950s. You're such a little Catholic boy, Tommy."

"I'm just saying, what's the point of all that work if you don't get the man too? And the house. The financial protection. You're just going to do it all on your own? Why?"

"Listen to you." Tomás shook his head. "She doesn't need a man."

"I don't. But how the hell *am* I going to do this by myself? I don't know the first thing about kids."

Tomás cocked his head. "You know . . . my mother loves babies. I mean, it's the only reason she still calls Tommy my roommate."

"True," Tommy agreed. "She calls me her son and she knows damn well we're gay, but she still thinks Tomás might accidentally get married to a woman and make her a grandmother one day."

Tomás waved a hand. "My sister finally graduated college, so she's getting all the pressure now. I bring it up myself every day just to be sure the focus is on Luce."

Donna managed a watery snort. "I think it would be weird if I just let you guys have my baby. I'd be living right upstairs."

"Not that! I don't want a baby! I meant you could hire my mom as a babysitter so you can keep working. Do you know how much she'd love that? She hates being retired, and she's making us fat with all her cooking." Tomás patted his perfectly flat stomach.

"I don't know," Donna groaned.

"In a few years, the kid would be in school. How hard could it be? Five years and you're home free."

She suspected it would be really, really hard. After all, she'd had a mother and a father, a family picture complete with a green lawn and decent schools, and her childhood had been a cold mess.

"It's just one little baby, and you're a tough-ass bitch, remember? You can do it."

Tommy rolled his eyes. "Don't write your man off just yet. He's cute and he makes a ton of money. He should be around. Or he should be responsible, at least. Let him help. Maybe you'll like it so much you'll end up waddling down the aisle in a long white gown."

"Yeah, imagine me in white lace, Tommy."

"We could tear some holes in it, give it a little Madonna vibe."

She felt a pang in her heart and ruthlessly smashed it down. "First things first. Let's see how Michael reacts to the idea of this bundle of joy. *If* I decide to keep it. And that's a big if."

"I don't know, girl. You're glowing."

"Fuck off. My nose is red from crying for an hour."

Tomás patted her shoulder. "We're here for you no matter what."

"We are," Tommy agreed. "This is exciting. We don't get many pregnancy scares among our friends. I feel like I'm in a TV movie! If only you were a worried teenage girl instead of a terrified middle-aged woman. The stakes would be so much higher."

Donna banged her knee hard into his and gave him the finger. But he wasn't wrong. She wasn't quite middle-aged, but she was damn sure terrified, and when she told her boyfriend, he'd likely abandon her to a home for unwed mothers, so maybe it would make a good movie.

Picturing herself stealing cigarettes from rebellious pregnant teenagers in the basement of some institutional Catholic laundry, Donna finally laughed. Even if that's what she felt like on the inside, the truth was that she was an adult, if not a responsible one. She could do whatever she wanted. The question was, what did she want?

CHAPTER 3

LAUREN

Her grandmother looked so small sitting in the new recliner, her khaki slacks blending in with the tan leather. She was dressed like herself again, at least, in those creased pants and a white cotton blouse, her hair neatly curled, though more white threaded through the silver now.

It had taken two weeks of full-time work to sort through her grandmother's home to decide what to move to the assisted-living apartment and what to throw out or save. Not that Lauren was finished yet, but the main bedroom was clean and nearly empty, at least.

"Dad should be back with the last box in a minute!" Lauren said as she put a few more pieces of her grandmother's favorite china in the cabinet. "You look pretty settled, Grandma."

Her smile was still crooked, and it might stay that way forever, but Lauren was more worried about how easily she tired. She'd spent a week in a rehab facility; then Lauren had driven her to look at two different senior communities. She'd liked this one for the views of the hills she loved so much, and she'd chosen a roomy one-bedroom apartment.

"Are you sleeping well here?" Lauren asked, dusting off her hands on her jeans before she sat in a kitchen chair pulled close to the recliner.

"Oh sure. I'm so happy to be in a place where I can have all my things. But what about you, my dear? Do you have enough furniture at the house?"

"It's wonderful. Don't worry for a moment."

Her grandma patted her hand. "I won't. This is what I've dreamed of for so long—you living there."

It hadn't been something Lauren had imagined—not as an adult, at least—but it felt natural. As if she'd returned to a summer holiday. She'd been lonely these last two weeks, but there had been loneliness back then too. She'd spent many of her childhood days alone, reading and exploring. It had usually been a sweet solitude, though sometimes she'd missed her mother, and sometimes she missed Bastian now. She tried to force herself to forget her loss just as she had then.

Those were the kinds of choices people made in life. A bit of loneliness in place of chaos or heartache. "It means so much to me, Grandma," she said. "I can never repay you."

"It's where you belong. It brings me joy to think of you there. Another generation of Abramses on the Abrams ranch, just as it should be."

Lauren glanced at the door. "I just keep worrying about Dad . . ."

"I've been planning this for a while, and if your father doesn't like it, he can take it up with me. That man would sell the ranch and move on without another thought. I know him as well as I know myself." With those words, Lauren remembered all the hints her grandmother had dropped over the years. Little digs about her son thinking he was too good for the family home. About men being inconstant and unreliable.

She should have listened to Grandma.

"But you, Lauren, you let the land soak into you even before you were born. When you finally came home, it was like you remembered."

Her heart swelled so big that it clogged her throat. She'd heard a lot of stories about that time, all of them from her mother. Scary stories told with wild eyes and clenched teeth. She wished she could ask her

grandmother more about them, but they never, ever spoke of those terrible days that had led to her dad's unjust imprisonment.

"This is a few years sooner than I planned, I suppose," her grandma
continued. "But now I'm glad it's happened. Better that I'm still here to
see another generation settled on the land. I want you to make it your
home now, you know. Truly yours."

"I will."

"You promise?" Her grandma actually wagged a finger.

"I do."

"Put in a new kitchen!"

It wasn't the first time she'd said it in the past two weeks. Lauren
shook her head. "I'm not going to put in a new kitchen. Heck, everyone
is dying for a farmhouse sink these days, and you've had one for decades.
I love your kitchen."

"Fine, but at least promise to put in a bathroom upstairs. I would've
set fire to those darn stairs if I could have. All that up and down. You'll
still be there fifty years from now, and you don't want that problem for
yourself."

Would Lauren really be there fifty years from now? It hit her suddenly what she'd taken on. The family legacy. Forever. But what if she
met someone with a career somewhere else? What if she and Bastian
got back together?

She sensed the ties around her pull tighter, but the restriction felt
comforting instead of confining. She wanted to be tied down. Wanted
to be part of something permanent and unmovable.

"I think I'll start with the floors. They're so beautiful."

"Good idea! I've been thinking about pulling up that carpet. It
seemed like a good idea back then, but now . . . Anyway, the floors will
be a good start. That's all hardwood under there."

Then what? A bathroom? She'd been working as a graphic artist
for a big printing company for two years, and she'd despaired of being
able to afford a solo life in Los Angeles on her income, but here? Here

she could afford the mortgage and day-to-day expenses. But surely a bathroom renovation would cost too much. Maybe if she did a lot of the labor herself? She tried to ignore the excited response her brain returned: a major renovation would give her a reason to contact Bastian.

He'd worked for a contractor through high school and college while studying to be an architect. She could at least ask his advice. She could reach out and pretend it was all practical, when the truth was that she desperately wanted to hear his voice.

"I've been thinking, Grandma, that if I put a bathroom upstairs, you'd be able to come visit. Or we could convert the front parlor into a bedroom! You could stay for the holidays, at least. Or during the summer. Remember when we'd all come for two weeks every summer? Dad and I? Then Suki and the kids? Wouldn't that be nice?"

"Oh yes," she responded, though her head sagged a bit, as if she were slipping into a nap.

"Should I help you with the recliner?" she offered, reaching for the throw blanket folded on a side table.

"Not yet. Your father will be back, won't he?"

As if summoned, her dad pushed through the door with a big box labeled PHOTO ALBUMS. "Here it is," he said. "Last of the old house. Your eviction is complete, Mom."

Lauren winced but ignored the barb. "I was thinking maybe you could all come out for dinner this weekend. A little housewarming! I'd cook, obviously. It would be nice to spend a little family time. Grandma, too, of course."

"I'd love to, pumpkin, but we're sailing this weekend," her dad said. "The forecast is perfect."

"Oh. Sure. Just . . . come visit anytime, okay?"

"Plus it'd be a strange housewarming, wouldn't it? It's my old house."

"I guess so," she murmured as he disappeared into the bedroom with the box. But it was her old house too.

Her dad had moved back to his childhood home for a year after he'd been exonerated and released from prison. Lauren had met him for the first time in that house. She'd lived there on the weekends she'd visited him. Then he'd gotten a nice apartment for himself when he'd finally landed a job in Stockton, but just as often as not, they'd stayed at his mom's house during Lauren's visits. They'd been a tight little trio into Lauren's college years, when he married Suki, who was twenty years younger and made a quarter million a year at a tech company. The past decade had been a slow-moving wedge of distance and distraction pushing their trio apart.

But that was fine. He deserved peace. He deserved this new life that had nothing to do with his painful past. He'd given Lauren stability and love and a whole new family, and she could let him have that for himself too. He was seventy-one and thriving, teaching his new kids how to sail now that they were ten and eleven, attending fancy parties with his accomplished, willowy wife. But it must be strange to think the house that should have been yours was going to your child.

He emerged from the bedroom, dusting off his hands.

"You know it's still your home," Lauren blurted out, infusing the words with truth and warmth so he wouldn't feel rejected. "It still belongs to all of us."

"Not really. Not at all when you think about it." He hid whatever he meant by that behind a charming smile.

"Daddy, if I thought . . ."

"It's fine, pumpkin. We're all happy for you."

"That's right," her grandmother declared. "And that's the way I want it."

"I know, Mom."

"I hope you and Suki will still come every July," Lauren said. "Everything will be the same. We'll all get together for Thanksgiving too! It will be so fun. Grandma, you won't have to do any work for once."

"Sure," he said absently, looking at his phone. "You and Suki talk about it. I've got to head out. Love you."

"I love you," she responded as he hugged her and gave her a kiss on the head. He hugged his mother goodbye too, and then he was gone, pulled back to his life in Silicon Valley.

Crap. Not exactly the reassurance she'd been looking for from him. All his words had been . . . *fine*, but they'd also been honed to a sharp edge of irritation. Whether he'd wanted the estate or not, he'd still expected to get it.

She glanced over to see her grandmother nodding off. "Grandma, let's put your recliner back. The nurse said she'd be by at five to take you to dinner. That's still an hour off."

"Oh, if you think that would be all right."

"You've got your call button?" Lauren settled her back with the blanket and set a glass of water on the table. "Call me if you need anything at all. I'm half an hour away if I speed."

"Don't speed!" she scolded before Lauren let herself quietly out.

Her stomach tied itself in knots as she drove home, and she hated herself for that. She didn't need a housewarming party to feel good about this. Grandma had wanted her to have the house, and she had it.

By the time she got home, her shoulders ached with tension, and for a moment the windows of her house spoke of loneliness instead of progress. She needed someone to talk to. Someone who would hear her stress and tell her it was stupid, so she could laugh and move on.

She parked in the gravel driveway and pulled up her FAVORITES screen. There were only four people: Dad. Bastian. Grandma. Jill.

Four people she was close to.

Christ, Bastian was right. She didn't put herself out there. She'd always been afraid to. After all, who could you trust after you discovered the dark and terrifying truths your mother had raised you with were all lies? When your own mother made you believe your dad was a horrible monster?

Third grade had been the worst, when her class had filled out a simple family tree at the start of the school year. Lauren had felt frozen and panicked. She recognized the blank nervousness in another girl's eyes, but even at age nine Lauren had known that girl's response wasn't hers. That girl didn't know who her father was, most likely. But Lauren had the opposite problem. She'd known too well.

Hands shaking, she'd made up a name for her father, then written Grandma and Grandpa in the spaces above. After glancing at a boy's paper, she'd added Nana and Papa above her mother's name, and the rest had been easy. There were no siblings to account for. Not even a family pet to add in the square in the bottom corner.

The whole time she'd been scared she would be pressed on the issue and had already resolved to tell her teacher that her father was dead. He'd been as good as dead, anyway. Every grandparent too—all of them forbidden topics that would only make her tired mother sigh and shake her head. On a good day, anyway. On a bad day any reference to family would bring a lecture about watching out for evil people in the world.

Was that how her mother moved through life? Always watching out for the imaginary danger other people brought?

Bastian had called her a calming presence when they'd met and fallen in love. He'd liked her self-contained quiet. But quiet twisted into boring after a few years, didn't it?

She held her breath as she touched Jill's name.

Lauren had moved to LA for Bastian, which meant she'd moved into his home and his life with his friends. That had felt wonderfully convenient considering she'd left her little Sacramento apartment behind for a big new city full of strangers.

It had worked out perfectly. With Bastian she wasn't a stranger there, and she and Jill had quickly fallen into a comfortable friendship. Brunch every other week. Girls' nights out. A fun and welcoming face at every party when Lauren would've otherwise floated at the edges, uncertain. Jill and Bastian had gone to college together, and once Lauren had been embraced, Jill had felt like a lifelong friend as well. It had been so easy. No taking chances with the unknown. No risk of rejection or not being good enough.

Her pattern of serial monogamy hadn't often come with friends included, so she'd never considered that adopting *his* friends meant he would get custody of them in a breakup. But guess what? That was the way things worked. Jill hadn't answered any calls from Lauren in the past few weeks, and her texts were short and full of excuses for how busy she was.

Lauren closed the screen with a curse and threw open the car door. She rarely had a cell signal here anyway. Luckily, she'd already invested in her first home improvement: high-speed internet. A woman had installed the antenna on the roof yesterday, and it was working perfectly. The world was her oyster!

By the time she got out of the car, the sun was already melting away and the house was a silhouette of grays against an orange glow. The warm light filled her up, and suddenly everything felt possible.

"This is mine," she said aloud. Then she tipped her head back to yell, *"It's mine!"*

She'd signed the papers the day before, but today it was real. The house was hers. Forever, just as her grandma had said. The world was a magical, hopeful place, and she would make magic in it, damn it.

Tonight she'd cook pasta primavera with real semolina noodles because Bastian wasn't here to frown at the processed flour. And she'd turn up the music loud because her grandmother wasn't here to complain about the noise. And she'd dance and drink too much because she didn't have to worry about being the perfect daughter so her father would never reject her.

And most of all, she'd be fucking ecstatic without her mother's dark voice saying it was all wrong, wrong, wrong. Yes, she would be here for the next fifty years. She was an Abrams, and this was where she belonged.

~

Two hours later, she was full and her thighs ached from dancing. She was also drunk enough to look up do-it-yourself home improvements on YouTube. "Girl power!" she cheered as she started the second video about refinishing wood floors. That definitely seemed doable.

Installing her own bathroom upstairs, though? That wasn't going to happen. She could probably manage to replace an existing sink or toilet, but plumbing out the second floor? Nope. Still, she could shop for fixtures. She could use software to plan the layout. Hell, she could even lay tile after everything else was in place!

Probably.

"Definitely," she answered herself.

In fact, this would be a blast. It would also be a lot of hard work, but she could practically touch the absolute satisfaction she'd feel after each project.

"Make it your home now," she said, repeating her grandma's words. Not with destruction and erasure but by building on what was already here. Pull up all the downstairs carpet and refinish the original floors. Repaint the walls and add wainscoting. Replace the heavy curtains with white shades. Make it her safe, happy, forever home.

Exhaustion settled over her like a weighted blanket, and she decided a 10:00 bedtime was perfectly reasonable for a newly minted country girl. She locked up and carefully checked every window, then turned off the lights before trudging upstairs toward the small bedroom she'd always slept in.

But when she passed her grandmother's room, the sight of the bare floor stopped her. Only one chest of drawers remained, and the once-crowded room now lurked as a sad expanse of shadows. It felt so odd to think she would move into her grandmother's sanctuary herself soon. Weird, but also meaningful. Another Abrams keeping the history of this place alive.

How many other Americans still lived this kind of life, mapping out a continuity of blood and family with their bodies? People roamed and moved and resettled where the jobs were. But she was returning home to her roots.

What a blessing, and it had come right out of the blue.

Lauren settled into bed, enveloped in peace. She breathed in, let the familiar scent of cedar-lined closets and flowering vines into her lungs. She held each breath there for a moment before slowly letting it out. Her body relaxed. Her mind floated.

For a few minutes. Then she heard a noise. The house creaked and popped as it settled into the cool dark of autumn. It always did, but tonight it sounded almost like it was shifting, crouching, bracing itself for something. An animal yipped far away, then howled. Closer to Lauren, there was a scratching sound. Close enough that the sound must be in the house. Or on it. Was that an animal? A mouse? A rat?

A *serial killer*?

Ridiculous. She'd already had her encounter with a serial killer, and surely there was some lifetime limit.

She kept scowling at the ceiling, ears aching with strain. The scratching continued.

Bobby Edward Kepnick knew this place. He knew *her*. Should she be nervous?

Kepnick had raped and murdered nine women in the Sacramento Valley during the '80s, and his reign of terror had not only intersected with Lauren's life, it had practically *started* it. She'd been born the week after her father's false conviction for one of those murders.

Her mom's bulging, round presence must have cemented her credibility in the courtroom. Donna Hempstead had been a desperate, scared woman perched on the stand, deep into her ninth month of pregnancy, and when she'd raised a hand and sworn that the father of her unborn child had confessed to murder, who could counter that? Why would she put this man in jail where he could never give any kind of financial support? Why would she lie?

Scorned woman, the defense had claimed, but there'd been no evidence of rejection. He'd wanted the child and had even moved her up to Sacramento to be with his family.

Scorned woman. Turned out they'd been right.

Lauren had only occasionally thought of Kepnick in the years since her father's acquittal, but something about being back here, plunged into this place . . . "Come on, girl," she huffed out into the dark, blank space above her bed. "Get a grip."

She tossed aside the blanket and jumped from her bed to shove open the curtains and glare outside.

A half moon shone between racing clouds, and she could clearly see the yard. Sure enough a steady breeze rocked the branches of the huge old tulip tree outside, swaying the branches in wild arcs. None of the ends touched her windows, but she could see the way the fingers of the tree stretched toward her dad's old room. The rhythm of their movement matched up perfectly with the scritch, scritch that had plucked her nerves like bowstrings.

"Maybe I should get a security system," she murmured, fogging the pane of glass. She would feel better, and if anything did happen out here, there were zero people within shouting distance. The roof of one barn was visible a quarter mile away, but the rest of that property was hidden by copses of trees and shrubs separating the two hills. Unless things had changed in the past few years, that neighbor was a reclusive man just as old as Lauren's grandmother. He might have a shotgun, but there wouldn't be any racing over to rescue Lauren in the middle of the night.

She returned to her bed and unfolded the quilt at the bottom of the mattress to build a cozier nest for herself before climbing back in. Then she unlocked her phone and took comfort in the cool blue light.

The lives of her—or Bastian's—friends were still going on in LA, dancing past her on Instagram. She hadn't commented lately. Hadn't even hit LIKE.

She'd never needed a lot of friends. She'd kept her world small, and maybe it wasn't only her mom who'd shown her how to do that. Her grandma and dad hadn't exactly been welcomed back into this community with open arms.

As different as they'd been, both sides of her family had taught her to keep herself contained and to dole out her trust with cautious hands.

Plus what if she interacted with her old friends and they didn't respond? What if she hit LIKE on one of Bastian's posts and he ignored hers? It was a sticky, tarry pit of self-consciousness and hurt that she knew she'd get sucked into if she touched.

Luckily he wasn't overly active on Instagram or any other social media, for that matter. He was too busy running or doing yoga or working sixty-hour weeks at the City Builders Foundation, his life overflowing with real people and meaningful interactions. In other words he was the exact opposite of Lauren.

Though he hadn't posted his own pictures often, he'd enjoyed her taking photos of him. He'd always posed happily for sexy postworkout shots. Good Lord, he looked like a wiry god with sweat glowing on his warm, brown skin. His lack of online posts was a goddamn blessing now. She did not want to see pictures of him dressed up and out at a bar, putting off charisma and friendliness in pheromone-scented waves, just like he had been at the work party where she'd met him. He'd received an award for volunteering the architectural plans for a series of community centers throughout the state. She had done the graphics for one of the signs. An unequal partnership from the beginning.

Was he dating?

He hadn't been cheating, as far as she knew, hadn't left her for a lover. He was more likely to miss sexual signals than to pick up on them. The demise of their relationship had just been a slow deterioration of their bonds. Or his bonds, at least.

She'd always made things too easy for him. Even as she'd acted out her love, she'd known she was being a pushover. She'd dedicated everything to his happiness. She'd melted herself into his town, his home, his friends. And in doing that she'd known that if she lost him, she'd lose it all, so she'd accommodated and nurtured until she'd smothered him half to death.

But the truth was that she'd been lonely for a long time, even with Bastian. Or especially with Bastian.

Something had to change. She needed friends and she needed distraction. Badly. And maybe she wanted Bastian's attention, if only to make him regret losing her.

And she knew exactly how to get it.

CHAPTER 4

DONNA

"You know you don't have to go," Tomás insisted. "You can just stay here, and we'll figure it out."

"I want to go."

He threw his arms up in disgust. "But it's Sacramento! Jesus Christ. I mean, seriously, girl. *Sacramento?*"

"I can always come back. I'm not going to disappear. Sacramento isn't another planet."

"Are you sure about that?"

Donna rolled her eyes and snorted, but Tomás kept frowning. "I don't trust that man."

"Calm down. I don't trust him either. I'm not stupid. But . . ."

"But what?"

She closed and latched the door of her tiny U-Haul trailer. "I didn't expect him to be so damn happy, Tom. I thought he was going to scream that I was ruining his life. At the very least I figured he'd insist on paying for an abortion. Instead he was . . . Jesus, he was over the moon. What am I supposed to do with that kind of response?"

Oh God, she was crying again. It kept happening all the time, and she hated it so much. She'd spent her whole life feeling like she had utter control of her emotions. She wasn't weak or sappy. She didn't give an inch to anyone, and she damn sure wasn't needy or demanding with men. *She* was the one who demanded. That was what men liked about her. She kicked ass and took names and always kept shit cool, and she never needed anything from anyone.

Now she was tearing up over Hallmark greeting card commercials. Pitiful. "These goddamn hormones!" she yelled, swiping at her cheeks. "This is complete bullshit."

"I think it's cute," Tomás crooned before dodging her fist. "Look at you, all emotional!"

The second time she threw a punch, it landed on his slim stomach. He ignored it.

"Listen," he ventured when she stopped growling. "You need to do what's good for you, and I'm not pushing you to try to make you cry. I just want to be very clear that you don't have to run off and marry the guy who knocked you up. This isn't the '50s and you're not Catholic like Tommy. We're your family, Donna. We'll help. We can do this together."

"I know. I really do. But he wants to be involved, and if I'm going to have a kid, I think I have to give that my best shot."

"And you're sure about the kid?"

Was she? No. She couldn't pretend she was sure. If she hadn't turned up pregnant, she'd have happily maintained her child-free status for the rest of her life. But she'd lived without family for so long, and she'd never had the family she wanted. The acceptance and warmth that others took for granted . . . she suddenly found herself craving it, a dry sponge in search of water.

"I'm not *sure* about this, but I'm willing to give it a shot. Not marriage, though. I don't think I want that. But Michael wants to be a father, and if he wants to help with this baby, why not let him?"

"Can't he help from *there*?"

She laughed. "Everywhere I go these days, I imagine hauling around a stroller and a diaper bag. What would I do with a kid here? You think they want a screaming infant on our favorite restaurant patios? Am I going to breastfeed while I have a Bloody Mary over Sunday brunch? Nap with the kiddo so I can hit the clubs after ten? It would just be weird trying to fit a baby into my current life. It would be *sad*. And I'm definitely not putting a crib in my tiny bedroom."

Tomás grimaced in sympathy.

"I'd rather start over somewhere else so all the changes won't be so in my face. Plus at least if Michael is around, I know I'll be having sex for the foreseeable future. Are you going to help me pick up men while I'm waddling around in a maternity dress?"

Tomás's booming laugh made Donna laugh too, and she felt relief that she finally wasn't crying. "At least I can wear my Doc Martens all through pregnancy. Heels already feel out of the question, and I'm not even three months along. I'll be a Weeble wobble in no time."

"Aw. *Mamacita*," he crooned, cupping a warm hand over her already growing stomach.

"All right. Enough of that. I need to hit the road if I want to get there before dark."

"Are you moving in with him?"

"Definitely not. I'll find a place of my own. At least until he brings me those final divorce papers."

"Settle somewhere safe, okay? Please be careful. And please call and let me know you made it. Don't leave us hanging."

"I'll spring for long distance when I arrive, but only because I love you."

She kissed Tomás and his mother goodbye, gratefully accepting the paper bag full of cookies his mom had baked the night before. Tommy was already at work, but she'd shed some tears during their goodbye an hour before. Of course she had.

When she finally pulled away from that last, long hug, she swallowed more tears and hurried to her car. To put a stop to her crazy emotions, she popped a cassette into the player to start the long drive off right. Convertible top down, Patti Smith blaring, this was going to be an epic road trip!

Donna merged onto the freeway, pulled a cookie from the bag, and cackled before she popped half of it into her mouth as she pictured her route like an animated map on a movie screen, with a dotted line tracing her path.

Michael had no idea she was coming.

Oh, he'd been all breathless claims of support and happiness, but that was much easier to pull off over the phone than it was in real life. She wanted to put herself right in front of him, nose to nose, and push until she knew she was getting a genuine response.

He wasn't a man built for action. She knew that. She loved pressing him until he cracked, until he exploded into anger or passion or laughter. And he *needed* that from her. He liked being stirred up and agitated out of the cozy little life he'd created for himself in Sacramento. But even she hadn't managed to shake him free from his dead marriage. Probably because it had been safer for Donna to let him lie there in his separate bedroom in that unseen, sterile home, wishing for her, ever unattainable. She liked knowing he was miserable without her.

"Shit," she hissed into the hot wind blowing over her head. That fantasy was gone now, snatched away by the greedy little alien growing in her womb. It would eventually emerge a baby, and even Donna wasn't selfish enough to deny a baby the love it deserved. If there was a chance Michael would cherish this child of theirs, Donna had to make that opportunity available.

That was the main reason she'd decided on this move. She was a restless soul, anyway, and she'd lived in LA for so many years now. Time to try out somewhere new. In the darkest parts of the night, she could also admit to herself that she was hoping for something so far off and sweet that she hated to name it.

Her own father had been distant, as so many fathers of his generation were. Well, for the first twelve years of her life he'd been distant. He'd worked long hours, brought home the bacon, expected dinner on the table at 6:30 every night, and Donna and her brother had been taught to change into pajamas at 8:00 p.m. and stay out of his hair, goddamn it. *Kids! Your father has to be up before dawn! Leave him alone and let him read his paper in peace!*

He'd been a vaguely menacing figure, but sometimes funny on the weekends once he was a few glasses into the Scotch. Then when Donna's body had created breasts and hormones, he'd been disgusted with her. She'd just been so *present*. So *flagrant* with her crop tops and tight jeans and loud mouth, no longer easily ignorable. She'd been a problem. And he was a man who fixed problems.

Her mouth twisted at the memory, so she shook it off as she left behind the city and headed into the dry hills. She'd walked away from that asshole and never looked back. If there was going to be a man taking a belt to her ass, it would be at her request, not because he was drunk and afraid that the neighbors would call his daughter a slut.

Michael wouldn't be that kind of father. He delighted in the way Donna acted out. He laughed at her filthy jokes. He lit up when she gave him all her attention. Wasn't that all a child needed from a dad? Happy attention?

But she needed to know once and for all if he could really, truly do this. She couldn't hover in a solitary space four hundred miles away, wondering if his promises were empty trash bags floating on the wind. When they'd met the year before while he was holding meetings with her PR firm, he told her he was separated and the divorce would be final soon. He'd yet to pull that rabbit out of his hat, not that she'd pressed.

She'd enjoyed their arrangement, after all. Their near-daily phone calls, their hot-as-the-fires-of-hell monthly assignations. Sometimes he'd managed a whole week with her in LA. Sometimes he'd paid for her to meet him in some hole-in-the-wall motel perched on a gorgeous cliff on the coast. It had been exactly the right amount of attention to reel in Donna, and she damn sure hadn't been fantasizing that he would wrap up his legal fight and christen her his new maiden of laundry and home-cooked meals. She'd thrived in the role of exciting girlfriend.

But now she was on the line for cleaning and meal preparation with or without him. She may as well get the bonus of hot sex along with the drudgery. If he'd actually meant all his promises.

A baby, he'd gushed. *Donna, my God, I've dreamed of this for years. Being a dad. Having a little boy—*

Or a girl, she'd insisted.

Yes, or a beautiful little girl just like you. We tried for years, but my wife can't . . . well, she's not capable, and we didn't find out until it was too late. Jesus, I can't believe this is real. You're really, absolutely sure?

Yes, she'd waited until she was absolutely sure. Sure she was pregnant and pretty sure that she meant to stay pregnant.

And now she was moving to Sacra-fucking-mento. The idea made her laugh into the warm sky.

She'd never even been to Sacramento, but relocation was the only option for giving this kid a shot at a full-time dad. Donna had a low-level job she didn't care about that barely covered her bills even without a baby. Michael, on the other hand, was a VP at a huge produce distribution company. He couldn't leave his job, and Donna was frankly relieved to leave hers.

She'd find something else up north. Maybe get a cushy position with the state. They were always producing brochures and public relations campaigns, looking to keep kids off drugs and workers productive. She'd sold out to the Man years ago and found it paid a lot better than being a rebel artist. She was happy to rebel on her own time after clocking out.

She'd figure out something no matter what happened. She always did.

When the first burst of travel adrenaline wore off, she popped out the Patti Smith cassette and slid in her favorite X album to keep her bright eyed and bushy tailed for the rest of the drive. A fitting send-off from her favorite LA band.

Once she got to Sacramento, she'd find a cheap hotel room for the night, and then she'd surprise her boyfriend and find out what kind of future he really had in store for her and their kid.

After subleasing her apartment, she had enough money to get her through a few weeks before she would need to make a more permanent decision about whether Michael would be a real father or just a child-support check. A few weeks to reassure herself about him. Throw herself headfirst into love or leave him in the rearview mirror.

Love him or leave him. A simple, logical decision.

But in her deepest, most secret soul, she had her heart set on something sweet and good for this kid. And maybe even, finally, for her.

CHAPTER 5

LAUREN

"This is it!" Lauren cried. "I'm almost done!"

She gave a mighty tug at the last giant square of rose-colored carpeting that had lived in the dining room for far too long. When the nails resisted, she growled loudly and tried one more time. "I can do this!" she yelled, and after a few strained seconds, the carpet finally tore free with a satisfying rip.

"Yes!" She dragged the huge piece of carpet across the room, then returned to the camera to offer a victory dance. "It's done. And the wood in this room looks great." Swiping an arm across her head to wipe off any shine, Lauren beamed at the lens. "Hold on one second and I'll show you."

She grabbed her phone from a shelf to sweep it in an arc. "You can still see some of the original color in here. And no water stains at all. Just some worn areas from constant foot traffic. Wow. It's overwhelming to think that people in my family walked across this floor a hundred and thirty years ago. My great-great-grandmother stood right here on this wood."

She turned the camera around. "Okay, enough talk about feelings. Time to earn your keep. I have a poll."

She'd aired her first livestream two weeks earlier, the initial episode just a test, but at this point she was starting to get the hang of it, saving each video to post to Instagram and Facebook.

"This breeze feels amazing," she exclaimed when she opened the door. "I needed the fresh air." She let the lens focus on the wide expanse of old trees that protected the front of the house from the California sun. The wind kicked up and freed a few of the rust-colored leaves that clung to the branches. She followed their fluttering journey with the camera for a moment. "Look at that," she murmured. "I feel so blessed in this place. I wish you could all be here with me."

The strangest part was that she meant that. It seemed easier to interact with people this way, without that immediate fear of getting too close. Plus she got to show Bastian that she did know how to take risks and have fun.

She turned the focus to the porch. "Now for the poll! I've narrowed the floor stain down to two choices. Weathered oak." She zoomed in on the first chunk of wood she'd stained yesterday, then panned to the right. "And driftwood. It's all up to you, friends! Remember, my finished wall colors will be grays and slate blues and moss greens. Like this."

Pulling back, she framed up the two pieces of wood nestled against a big rock she'd pulled from the garden. It was rough stone, peppered with lichen and moss, and it perfectly captured the cool tones she wanted in the home.

"I want the house to reflect everything I love about this place. I think both of these colors are perfect. Not quite gray, but still a nice cool brown. So I need your help. Weathered oak or driftwood. I'll have the poll up in ten seconds. You've got twenty-three hours to choose! Thanks again for all the supportive comments. This is more fun with friends."

After clicking the RECORD button off, she rushed to her laptop and made the vote live. Not that it would be much of a poll. She'd had only forty views of yesterday's video. Still, it gave her something to do to distract from the quiet.

Twelve people had already voted, splitting the poll evenly between the two colors.

She'd carefully done her makeup and hair to look like she'd started streaming without thinking twice about her appearance. Her old T-shirt was paint splattered and faded, but it was also tight in just the right places.

Because Bastian was watching. He had to be. She'd posted about her projects every day online, complete with step-by-step pictures, and all their *formerly* mutual friends had chimed in with encouraging comments. Some of them had even seemed genuine. *Lauren, omg, that place is gorgeous!* Jill had written. *You're so brave! I love it!* ♥ ♥ ♥ *Lucky girl!*

Lucky I'm not waiting for you to text back anymore, Lauren had muttered as she hit the heart icon next to Jill's comment.

While she was carefully checking to see if Bastian had given any hint of his presence, she got a notification that someone had tagged her on a post, and it wasn't someone she knew. In fact, it was a stranger with ten thousand followers, saying, *I love this old house so much! I can't wait to see the floors all polished and shiny! This is my new favorite renovation porn!*

As Lauren watched, her Instagram got five more followers, and she followed them right back. "Putting myself out there," she said with a smirk.

She might have started this with a few dodgy intentions, but making the videos had honestly cheered her up and absolutely distracted her from her solitude. In fact, she felt more plugged in by herself in this farmhouse than she had in LA, surrounded by people. How funny was that?

Screw Bastian and his giant network of real-world friends. Maybe that had never been the life for her.

Still, despite her defiant words, she refreshed her Instagram one more time to see if he'd liked the post. Not yet, but he'd liked some of the others.

After stretching hard, she put her hands on her hips and looked around. She needed to clean up today's mess, have lunch, and take a quick shower before starting on a project that actually paid: designing a new logo for a pet-grooming shop.

"Maybe I should get a dog," she muttered. But not while she was refinishing the wood floors. She could just picture the prints in the stain, and hair embedded in the new trim paint. "Okay, maybe not until the whole first floor is ready." After that a dog would be really, really nice. A big dog. Or maybe a scrappy, protective terrier. Or just any dog who would bark if there was actual danger nearby.

She was still having trouble sleeping at night, waking up with every random creak and thump. This place was packed full of good memories for her, but there were bad thoughts lurking too.

Her mother had passed on some of those dark tales, but Lauren had manufactured many of them on her own. That first visit to her grandmother's had been so strange that she'd barely slept at all.

When she shook her head to dissipate the darkness, dust flew, and Lauren sneezed. A shower *before* lunch, then.

She tugged her phone from her pocket and sent a text to her dad with the video link. The carpet is gone! Her grandmother didn't have a smartphone, so Lauren had to show her clips of the videos herself when she visited. She'd been there a few times already, and she hoped to bring Grandma out to see the finished floors once she got the okay from the physical therapist.

Lauren suspected her father didn't watch the videos at all, but he wrote back with encouraging comments to each of her texts. Eventually. This time he was quick. Hi, pumpkin! Let me know what else you're planning! I'm proud of you.

He clearly hadn't had time to watch it yet, but she still glowed. Thanks! Love you, Daddy!

Stomach growling, she hurried into the back parlor to drag the last scraps of carpet out of the house to the dumpster she'd rented. It would be a quick shower today, but she'd have plenty of time to soak her sore muscles tonight. Her schedule was pretty open after the sun went down at 7:00.

She'd just hauled the carpet and padding down the porch stairs when her phone buzzed. Hoping it was her dad—or maybe even Bastian—she dropped her hold on the trash and reached for her pocket before remembering the heavy work gloves. The buzzing stopped before she'd freed one hand.

"Damn it!" The most coverage she ever got here was two bars, and those connections were as fleeting as shooting stars. The norm was one bar fading into none, unless she raced out to the south side of the yard.

After tossing both of the gloves to the ground, Lauren pulled her phone free and was just able to glimpse the missed-call alert when her phone rang again. She slid open the ANSWER button at the exact moment the caller ID flashed onto the screen.

Oh no.

Oh no.

Her mother.

Shit, shit, shit, she silently mouthed, shaking her head in denial. She hadn't spoken to her mom in nearly two years, and the calls had been few and far between in the decade before that. But as much as she didn't want to speak to her mother, she couldn't just hang up in the woman's face. Could she?

She pressed her fist to her mouth for a moment. No. No, she couldn't just hang up.

"Hello?" she finally offered.

"Lauren? Is that you?"

"Yes. Hi, Mom. How are you?"

Her mom responded with a long, loud sigh that hovered some-where in a mysterious land between exasperation and relief. "Lauren, what have you *done*?"

Oh boy. She'd known this would come up at some point, but she'd hoped it would be a conversation in the hazy, very distant future. Five years from now, maybe. Ten, even. After emotions had time to settle. "What do you mean?" she asked.

"Lauren, you bought *that house*."

"I . . . Yes, I did. Grandma sold it to me at quite a bargain. I'm very lucky. Everything is great."

"Everything is not great!"

"No, you're wrong. I love it here, and things are going really well. How did you even find out about this?"

"Facebook! This is awful!"

"It's not awful. I'm very happy."

"That's it, then. I won't ever come there, you know. You're officially part of a cult."

Lauren lost her grip on her temper. "It's not a cult!" she yelled, feeling exactly like the thirteen-year-old girl she'd been the first time she'd screamed it. "It's my family! She's my grandmother, not some weird stranger!"

"Lauren, please," her mom pleaded instead of shouting back. "I love you. I've tried to give you space, but I thought when you got older you'd see through their games and wise up. I thought you'd come back to me if I just gave you time. I tried. I honestly tried!"

Lauren took a deep breath and pushed it out through her clenched teeth before speaking. "Do you have any idea how hurtful it is when you tell me their love and affection is fake? I love them, Mom. I've loved them since the first time I came here. How should I feel when you say they don't love me back?"

"I'm not saying they don't love you. I'm saying they are dangerous. They're *dangerous*, Lauren!"

"Oh my God, Mom." She dropped her head and let her fury drain out of her until all that filled her chest was the dull burn of weariness. "Mom, you're the one who's dangerous. How can you not see that? All those things you put in my head . . . Are you just so far gone that you can't understand? You're the danger here."

"I've never hurt anyone in my life."

"For God's sake, how can you say that? You lied! You lied and you sent my father to prison for something he didn't do! And you know what? You spent years brainwashing me. You always called them a cult, but you're the one who . . . God, how could you possibly think you've never hurt anyone?"

"I didn't lie. I never lied."

"He didn't do it, Mom! He couldn't have confessed anything to you because *he didn't do it!*"

"You're wrong."

Lauren flung both hands high in the air and growled like a frustrated animal, holding the phone high above her head. "Mom!" she yelled at it. "Stop it! Just stop! *Stop, stop, stop!*"

If her mom said anything in response, Lauren couldn't hear her, and that was exactly the way she liked it. She loved her mother. She'd always loved her, but for decades each word out of her mouth had been another drop of acid on raw skin. Withdrawal was Lauren's only path to relief.

She slowly put the phone back to her ear. "I am not having this argument with you again. This has gone on far too long. Bobby Edward Kepnick killed that woman. He confessed to it. He pointed the police to where he'd buried her things, which was *proof* he did it. Case closed. That's why Dad has been a free man for twenty-five years!"

She heard her mother take a deep breath and rushed to cut off whatever she meant to say. "Listen to me, Mom. I will never explain this to you again. I don't need to. I'm done with this conversation and I'm hanging up on you now. Goodbye. Please don't call again."

Lauren ended the call and stared at the screen for a long time, half expecting the phone to ring in her hand but knowing it wouldn't. Her mom was obsessive about this one thing and always had been, but she really had given Lauren space. That much was true. Too much space, maybe, but that was what Lauren had begged for.

A tear plopped onto her phone. She tried to sniff the rest of them back as she opened the contact screen and stared at the last option listed: BLOCK THIS CALLER.

She'd thought about it many times. Just cutting her mom off like a dying limb. But it didn't feel right. Her mother was good at keeping her distance. She wasn't clingy. In fact, she had the opposite problem, retreating resentfully when rejected.

And what if there was an emergency? What if something happened? It wasn't as if the woman had led a healthy, stable life. She'd been living in run-down apartments, working nights, barely scraping by for decades, and she'd smoothed over all that stress with drinks and cigarettes.

Lauren stared for a long while. She stared until the words blurred and waved. Then she closed the screen. It just wasn't in her nature. She'd hurt her mom badly enough over the years, and even though that had been necessary self-defense, it still didn't make Lauren feel good to know she'd walked away from her own mother.

Her dad had been released from prison when Lauren was ten, and he'd won the right to visitation within a few months. After all, he'd been considered an upstanding citizen after his conviction was wiped.

Lauren remembered the whole drama in painfully vivid detail because her mom had panicked for weeks, sure he'd try to get full custody, and Lauren had been terrified she would be sent to live with a killer. Would he have prison tattoos? Wild eyes? A dark, irresistible craving for vengeance on Lauren's bloodline?

She and her mother had hit the road, trying to outrun the court system, but it had found them in a shitty apartment on the Strip because her mom had finally collapsed in exhaustion and filed for food stamps.

When the court order for visitation came down, her mother had drilled instructions into Lauren for too many days to count. What to do if he touched her inappropriately. What to do if she were kidnapped and hidden. How to find help if she needed it. *Write down everything that happens while you're there, even the smallest detail. I will fight this, Lauren. I'll fight with everything I have, and I'll use every detail you record.*

But in the end, her mom's standing in the eyes of the court had been trash. After all, she'd lied under oath and sent an innocent man to jail. The fight hadn't lasted long. She'd run out of money, and then she'd been completely disarmed and defeated. By her own daughter.

Lauren could remember only her mother's reactions and not her own. She could only watch those days like a film that led up to her first meeting with her father. He'd sported a huge smile and grand gestures as someone from the county had dropped her off at this very front door.

This beautiful, picturesque, fantasy front door and the fantasy family who had lived behind it.

That first night, lying in bed, scared to death of this father who was a stranger and definitely a killer . . . that night had soon dissolved and re-formed into a week of her lying in bed, worrying about returning home to her mother. Five more days. Then four. Three. Two. Then one painfully quick day before she had to head back to her mattress on the floor under that rattling window in downtown Las Vegas.

Lights flashing every minute of every night. People shouting. Hot rods revving. Walking to school on sidewalks papered with flyers of nude girls, their red lips glinting out endless promises, their printed faces scraped and torn by the broken glass littering the pavement. Men catcalling her, asking when she'd be old enough to party. And her mom always working, working, working every night.

Every visit to her grandmother's made it harder to say goodbye, no matter where she and her mother were living at the time. Reno. Tahoe. Bakersfield. Every moment away from her mom was another countdown toward the reunion, each trip more painful than the month before.

Three years of being pulled in two, until Lauren had finally been old enough to voice her opinion to the court. "I would like to live with my father now, as I feel my life and schooling would be much safer and more stable with him than with my mother."

It had been the right choice, but her gut still clenched with pain at the sight of her mom's pale, stricken face in that judge's office. Her shaking hands. Darting eyes. Clammy skin. She'd looked like a woman wishing for death. A woman betrayed in the worst possible way by her own child.

Thirteen-year-old Lauren had put her head down and waited for it to be over, and then it had been. She'd hugged her motionless mom goodbye, and she'd gone home with her dad. The end.

He'd had his own place by then. Nothing as idyllic as the ranch, but still a loving and supportive environment. The trip to buy new clothes before the school year had felt like winning the lottery. Lauren had been starting at her sixth school in three years, but for the first time she'd felt like a normal kid.

Which was quite a funny feeling for a girl living with a father who'd gone to prison for murder, but she'd thought less about that and more about the superficial clues that would show up on the radar of middle-school girls.

Her clothes were new and nice. She hadn't cut her own bangs with a shaky hand and dull scissors. She didn't reek of cigarette smoke. And she wasn't transferring in two weeks before the end of the semester like some sacrificial lamb tossed into a lion's den.

She'd made friends and found classes she loved. She hadn't walked to school past still-drunk partiers, then come home to fend for herself in a hot apartment until 3:00 a.m. Her dad had paid for her school lunches, and she'd had money left over for a quick soda or snack after class. And she'd joined band because her dad could afford to rent a flute.

She'd been average and unremarkable, and she'd loved every moment of blending in.

The few episodes of visitation with her mom after that had been painful. Her mother had overflowed with warnings and weeping and way too many beers, her anger and paranoia foaming up uncontrollably.

Lauren wondered if she'd gotten better since then. If things had stayed the same, surely she wouldn't still be alive. Her mother had turned seventy this year. She must have cleaned up. She couldn't still be working the bar all night at honkytonks and nightclubs.

Her phone hadn't rung again, so Lauren tucked it into her pocket with a little more confidence that she'd made the right choice. Her mom had called only once in two years. There was no reason to take such a drastic step and cut her off entirely. It didn't feel fair, and Lauren had spent her whole life trying to be fair.

She gave people the benefit of the doubt. How could she not? It was a lesson she'd learned hard and early. Things weren't always what they seemed. You couldn't believe the worst of people.

She tugged the gloves on and bent to her task, the muscles of her back stretching. These were muscles she'd seemingly never used before, judging by the way they protested after every day of work. If she kept this up, she'd have awesomely defined shoulders in no time. She could practically feel them growing more muscle.

The dumpster was a little too far from the front door, but she hadn't wanted it mucking up her view during the months of work, so she dragged the remnants an extra forty feet around a curve in the drive and hoisted them over the low lip. Next time she visited her grandmother, she had to ask about the key to the ancient work shed. No way there wasn't a wheelbarrow in there somewhere.

Taking a moment to lean against the dumpster and catch her breath, Lauren realized she could see the neighbor's house from here. More than that, she could see the actual neighbor.

He stood halfway between his house and a clothesline, a basket clutched in his hands as he stared at her. When Lauren waved a hand in greeting, he startled and turned quickly to hobble toward the line, giving her a view of his tanned neck and snow-white hair.

"Jeez," she muttered. "So much for country kindness." Over the years, she'd glimpsed him only from afar, usually as he was leaving in the morning or returning at night. She hadn't expected a home-baked cake or anything, but a hello would have been nice.

The man dropped his basket of laundry near one of the clothesline poles and kept walking. For a moment she had a strange thought that he was going to the barn for a shotgun, probably because of the way he glanced over his shoulder to place her location before he disappeared around the corner.

People in the country had shotguns, after all. There was probably one somewhere in her own house. She'd have to ask.

Lauren pushed off the dumpster and was stepping onto the gravel drive when he suddenly reappeared, white hair easing around the edge of the barn, followed by a bit of his face and just one eye. He watched her. She watched him. And he stayed there, his eye right on her while she began to walk in reverse, reluctant to turn her back on the creepy behavior until she rounded the curve of the drive and safely left him behind.

"Well, Jesus, that's not weird at all," she said just to break the silence.

Had he watched her before? Did he know she was living in the big house alone?

"He's probably just a prepper," she reassured herself. Her grandmother had often referred to him as a loon, but she'd never called him a creep.

Another thing to ask her about on their next call. Is the crazy man next door dangerous to solitary women or just generally odd? Is there a gun in the house, and do I need it?

What an adventure.

CHAPTER 6

DONNA

"That lying, worthless asswipe," Donna snarled, hunched down in her car and squeezing her blue steering wheel in murderous fists. Despite her best efforts she didn't put a dent in the hard plastic, though the bumps of texture definitely bruised her palms. "You goddamn *asshole!*" she yelled.

The convertible top was up against the damp morning, so hopefully the sound stayed muffled. Donna didn't want to be seen on this tree-shaded lane lined with beautiful old houses, and she was safely hidden beneath a weeping willow. But did it even matter? Wasn't she going to confront him eventually? Scream at him? Beat his chest and roar out her fury? Maybe punch his stupid straight nose and give it a little character to warn people off?

Michael had been lying to her the whole time.

Donna had accepted long ago that maybe he hadn't been entirely truthful about his separation. Not when they'd first met, at least. But since then? He'd told so many stories of his ice-cold, dried-up wife and their utterly fractured relationship. Separate rooms, weeks-long silences, wrangling over the terms of the divorce until some glorious day when one of them might finally give up and cede possession of the house. He'd painted the very picture of lonely, hellish isolation.

But this morning's scene outside his home had played out like the opening credits of a cozy 1940s movie.

Michael stepped out the side door of a Tudor bungalow that looked plucked from the English countryside, all angled rooflines and timbered stucco. He started down the steps, then paused, his head turning attentively toward the still-open door. A blond woman peeked out, a legal envelope in hand to offer him.

Divorce papers, maybe, but only in the fraught fantasy that Michael had sketched for her. He smiled up at the woman, and she smiled back; then she granted a kiss when he stretched himself up in a clear request, not a hint of tension between them.

He took the envelope with another smile, then hopped jauntily down the steps toward the pretty little detached garage, which was nearly hidden behind layers of deep green ivy and flowering bushes.

The woman paused to watch, a faint smile still on her lips as the garage door rose and he disappeared.

She wasn't ice cold or dried up. She looked practically fucking dewy from this distance.

Michael had explained that she was five years older than he was, and her advanced age—forty-one now—had likely contributed to her infertility. But whatever age she was, she looked elegantly beautiful when she stepped out to watch her husband leave, her frosted blond hair feathered back and falling in curls around her shoulders. Even at this early hour, she wore slim khaki pants and a loose yellow blouse that emphasized her skinniness. Pink lipstick brightened the mouth that had kissed him. Michael. Her husband. The man she supposedly hadn't touched in three years.

A car backed out of the garage, and it was a car Donna had been in. She'd sat in that front seat on that beige leather, and she'd made out with that man driving away from that picture-perfect home. More than made out, actually. Much more.

His tan sedan backed toward her and swung so wide into the street that he was only twenty feet from Donna when he changed gears. She watched his window roll down, and she could even hear him singing along to Steely Dan.

"You stupid easy-listening asshole," she growled.

She put the car in gear and pulled out soon after he cruised away, intending to follow him to work, but when the front door of his house opened, Donna hit the brakes.

The woman walked down the quaint stone steps with a bouncing little Yorkie on a leash. His wife—Did Donna even know her name? Karen? Carol?—had plopped an adorable sun hat on her head and slipped on delicate white sandals. Every step down her narrow front walk brought her prettiness closer into focus. Donna watched in open-mouthed shock until Michael's wife looked up and met her gaze.

She appeared startled for a moment, jumping a little and pressing a hand to her chest, but then she laughed and called out, "Oh, sorry! Can I help you?"

Donna snapped her mouth shut and hit the gas.

She knew where Michael's office was on the map, so it wasn't hard to anticipate a right turn out of his neighborhood and catch up with him despite her momentary pause. She cursed him as she drove, calling him every name in the book and making up a few more that fit. He wasn't weeks away from finalizing a divorce. He never had been. He didn't even look like he was stressfully separated. He looked like a man with a loving wife and a beautiful home and a slutty, stupid mistress on the side.

Or more than one. Was there any reason to believe she wasn't part of some unwitting harem?

"I'll kill him," she promised herself. "I'll kill him, and then I'll give birth in jail and give this baby up for adoption to some reasonable family." Maybe Tom and Tom would decide they were ready for a child. She knew a woman who'd been a surrogate for her gay friends. The Toms would be far better parents than Donna and her cheating, asshole boyfriend.

When she realized she'd placed a protective hand over her belly, she grimaced and forced her hand back to the wheel, but then her eyes got blurry with tears. Cursing, she wiped the tears away and shook her head. Fine, she wouldn't murder him and put the baby up for adoption. But she was going to kick his skinny white ass up and down the parking lot of his office, giving everyone he worked with a prime view of his punishment.

Had the man who'd sublet her apartment moved in yet, or could she swoop right back home and block his arrival? She could be back in six hours if she tried hard.

"I can't believe I moved to fucking Sacramento!" she yelled. Her throat ached from holding in too much fury. She had to let it out.

She was going back. There was no way she could stay here. Michael could send child-support checks and explain it to his wife however he cared to. Or maybe Donna would tell the woman everything.

After a ten-mile drive on the highway, she followed Michael down an exit and onto a road that serviced business parks and warehouses. Train tracks paralleled the street, with little spurs leading to the largest hulking buildings. Almonds and apples and grapes and oranges stacked up inside in crates to be shipped all over the country. She'd heard all about the fucking fruit from Michael because he loved to talk. Didn't they all love to talk so damn much?

Michael turned into a big office complex that backed up to one of these warehouses. Donna turned too.

He pulled his ugly tan sedan into a space marked with his name, only one slot away from the front door. Donna glided to a stop right behind his bumper and hopped out of her car before his door opened.

He emerged and looked even more startled than his wife had when his gaze caught her there, waiting, arms akimbo, feet planted wide. "Hello, *Michael*," she sneered.

"Donna! What are you doing here? I didn't know you were coming!" To her utter surprise, he sounded a bit happy, especially when his eyes slid down to her belly. "Is everything okay with . . . ?"

"No, everything is not okay, you asshole. I saw you and your gorgeous little wife this morning, playing kissy face next to the garage."

"Oh," he said, and that was it. Just *oh*, and then his eyes slid past her to scan the parking lot for witnesses.

"You fucking liar," she spat.

"Donna, listen—"

"No, you listen, you goddamn asshole. I can't believe I actually bought your shit. That you loved me. That you were happy about this . . ." She stabbed a finger toward her stomach. "That you wanted to be a family."

"I do! You don't understand! Please just—"

"No, I sure as hell don't understand. You're nothing but a nasty, humping dog, and you were never planning to leave her, were you?"

"That's not true! It's just that things . . . are complicated. My wife and I—" He closed his teeth with a click, gaze darting to the left, and Donna swung around to see a guy in dusty overalls approaching. The man's eyes widened when she glared at him.

"Getting all this down?" she snapped. He looked away from her and hurried past so quickly he was almost running.

"I will ruin you," she snarled as she swung her head back toward Michael. Her neck strained. She felt like a bull aiming all her weight at him. "You can kiss your wife goodbye. And you can say goodbye to this bastard family you pretended to want."

He held up both hands. "I can see why you'd be mad, but please just listen, Donna. Please. It's not what it looks like, I swear."

"Swear on what? Your lying ass?"

He glanced around again, then moved forward, one hand out, palm up. "Let's go get some coffee and talk. Have you had breakfast?"

No, she hadn't had breakfast, just one sour cup of motel coffee, and her stomach stirred to angry life at his words. *Yes*, it growled, *let's go eat breakfast*. Shit.

"I'm sorry," he murmured. His fingers curved around her elbow. He touched her gently, and his fingertips slid up and down the sensitive skin of the crook of her arm in careful millimeters. "Ever since you called, my mind has been racing, trying to figure all this out. It's just . . . it's more complicated than I've told you, and that's my fault. I know that. But I'm doing everything I can to make sure that you and I *will* have this family. Together. That's all I want, Donna. You and me and this baby."

Shit, shit, shit. She was melting, her fury burning itself out. She could feel it dying and leaving aching hurt behind.

She jerked her arm away, but her skin felt too cold without him. Why was her body so stupid for this man?

"Let's go grab a quick breakfast," he said. "It's not good for you to skip meals."

This was why she loved him. *When* she loved him. He wasn't afraid to say kind things. To be considerate. He bent when he needed to bend, and he let her see him do it. He was good and he was bad and she loved the strange pull between the two.

"I hate you," she murmured, sighing the words like they were tender tokens of love.

"I know," he whispered back. "I'm sorry."

"Whatever. I'm hungry. If you're going to feed me, let's go. But one meal doesn't mean I believe you. Got it?"

"There's a truck stop diner half a mile back, just before the highway. Meet me there?"

Without answering, Donna stepped around him and got in her car. It was still running, so she threw it in drive and headed toward the diner. She hoped he wondered if she was simply driving away from him forever. But despite all her big words, she knew the truth: she didn't want this to be hopeless. She wanted to be hopeful for once in her long, strange life.

She'd left home at fifteen, running away after one last beating from her father. He'd called her an embarrassment, a slut, a piece of trash, all because she'd stayed out past curfew. He'd thrown her across her bed and put his knee on her back to hold her down as he spanked her over and over again for the second time that month. The first time had been because she'd called him an asshole under her breath during an argument. That beating had started with him punching her in the stomach. At least this time she'd only been bruised on the backside of her body.

Her mother had been as useless as ever, standing in the doorway with tears in her eyes. *You knew what would happen if you broke the rules. Why can't you just be a good girl, Donna?*

Because she wasn't a good girl and she wasn't interested in kissing the ass of a man who had violent tantrums. Her parents had tried to force her to show respect, but instead they made very clear that they weren't worthy of it. So she'd left, and she'd never spoken to them again. Let them parent their golden son, he of many baseball trophies and hot girlfriends, who got to stay out as late as he wanted.

So Donna had joined the ranks of the kids who clogged the streets of San Francisco, fleeing bad situations in order to suffer on their own terms.

Were her parents still alive? She hadn't thought about them in so long, but now she was going to be a mother. Her own mom's face came to her, thin and a little drawn, already showing wrinkles around the mouth from smoking. She had seemed just another cog in a problematic machine back then, but Donna could imagine now that she had been wildly unhappy too. Married to an unforgiving man who sucked all the joy from the house when he arrived home from work.

He was probably dead. Cold men with anger issues and a smoking habit didn't often see seventy. But what about her mother?

Donna glanced into the rearview mirror to see Michael's car catching up to hers, and she realized she was thinking of her parents only to avoid thinking of Michael.

Was she actually going to believe whatever bullshit he was about to spout? Surely she wasn't so stupid. Hadn't she made fun of all the other women who accepted crap from their faithless boyfriends?

Then again, weren't they all faithless? Isn't that why she'd hesitated to keep one around for any length of time? *Break up with them before they can break up with you.* That motto had served her very well. *Leave them before they hurt you. Never let your guard down. Never give an inch. Don't be like all the other girls they've known.*

And now here she was, waiting to hear his fake explanations. The man was married, and solidly so. What excuses were going to explain that away?

Hating herself, Donna turned into the huge lot of the truck stop diner and parked her car. It wouldn't hurt anything to hear him out before she told him to piss off. She might as well get a free breakfast out of it.

She'd found a booth in a back corner before Michael entered the place, and she didn't look up from perusing the sticky menu when he sat down.

"Donna—"

"I want my food first," she interrupted just before the waitress trudged over to fill their coffee cups. "Steak and eggs, both medium," Donna said, ordering the priciest thing on the menu. "And orange juice. And a short stack of pancakes. Thanks."

"I'll just have coffee," Michael added.

"I'm not sharing my pancakes."

"I already ate."

"Oh yeah? Did your wife make you an omelet this morning? French toast? She looks like an early riser. Does she cook a hot breakfast for her man every day?"

Michael cleared his throat and offered a bright smile to the staring waitress. "Thank you."

After she walked away, he tried to take Donna's hand, but she pulled back, glaring at the wedding band she'd never seen him wearing before. "My wife isn't stable."

"She looks pretty stable. She also looks beautiful and happy. Isn't that strange, Michael? Your ugly, frigid wife looking downright gorgeous as she gave you a kiss goodbye this morning? *Does that strike you as odd, Michael?*"

"Please don't make a scene," he said so calmly that she felt a little ashamed of herself. "I'm trying to explain."

She clenched her jaw and jerked her chin at him to continue.

"When I tried to leave the marriage, she attempted suicide."

Donna frowned. "How? When?"

"Almost a year ago. A month after I met you. I'd been making plans for the split for a long time. We hadn't been happy for years, but I was finally getting up the courage to end it once and for all. Then I met you and I was sure."

"You told me you were already separated."

"For all intents and purposes, we were."

"What the hell does that mean?"

The waitress brought the orange juice, her eyes darting between the two of them when they went silent. When she finally withdrew, she lingered at the next table to clear the dishes.

Michael leaned toward Donna and lowered his voice. "She was depressed about the infertility. She kept going to see her mother and staying longer and longer. Two weeks. Three weeks. We stopped having sex. We didn't talk. That went on for almost two years. I just didn't know how to end it without hurting her. After I met you I realized I needed to leave her regardless. There was no good way around it. But then . . ."

"Then what?"

"I told her I wanted a divorce. That day while I was at work, she took a bunch of pills. I came home just in time to save her. Her stomach was pumped. Her parents blamed me. They made me promise to stay until she was better."

"She looks pretty good now."

"How someone looks doesn't define this problem. She might be fine today, and then she might not get out of bed for a month. I've been struggling this whole time, trying to figure out how to make myself happy and keep her safe. And now . . ." He waved a weary hand.

"Now what?"

"Now if I leave her and she finds out we're having a baby? I'm terrified of what she'll do, Donna."

Donna sighed and shook her head. Did she actually believe this? Did she actually feel bad about it?

She did.

She'd lost a good friend to suicide ten years before. She knew how terrifying it was. How hopeless everyone felt watching someone struggle. How much she'd blamed herself after. "You can't stay with her forever. You have to get her help."

"I know. Maybe if I can convince her to stay with her parents for a little while. I can tell her while she's there and has support. They'll be with her. Maybe that will help."

Donna shook her head again. "I don't know. I just . . . Are you telling me the truth? Because you two looked very happy this morning. I felt like I was watching an adorable old movie of the good old days."

"That's part of why I've been so damn lonely. Everyone thinks I have the perfect life, the perfect wife, and then I go home every night and I'm walking on eggshells, trying to keep all these broken pieces from hitting the floor. It's exhausting and heartbreaking." His eyes filled with tears. "Jesus, I'm sorry," he muttered as he rubbed his face. "I feel like everything I want is right here and I can't get to it. I want a life with you. My sexy, prickly, magic girl. I'm just trying to find a way."

"Shit," she cursed, rubbing her own face. She wasn't crying this time, at least, but she was softening. Softening into an idiot pile of goo. "You've been lying to me this whole time. That's the real story here. What am I even supposed to do with that, Michael?"

"I haven't been lying. I'm just trying to survive in that house. I love my wife, I admit that, but I love her like a sister. I don't want her to hurt herself. We don't have sex. We don't have fun. We're roommates, Donna. We're only married on paper."

"She thinks you're married, though, doesn't she? You're not a roommate to her. I saw the way she looked at you. She still loves you."

"Yes. I think that's true."

The food arrived. Plates and plates of it. And as upset as she was, her stomach didn't turn at the sight. It growled. She poured syrup over the pancakes and sighed. "What am I supposed to say, Michael? That it's okay? It's not okay. You've betrayed her *and* me."

"I know that. I'm trying to fix it."

"How?"

"I'm making plans. And don't look at me that way. Yes, I've been dragging my feet, but now I have a deadline, don't I? You're having a baby. No more excuses. I'm going to make this happen."

"We'll see," she said archly, then popped a piece of steak into her mouth, trying to ignore the way her heart pattered with hope. Maybe it wasn't all over. Maybe there was still a chance for this to work out.

"Now, tell me what you're doing in Sacramento! Did you decide to ditch work and come see me?"

"No. I decided to quit work and move here."

"Oh."

"Yes. *Oh.*" She watched him carefully to see if the blood drained from his face, or the whites of his eyes showed in terror. But he only looked puzzled.

"You're moving here?"

"I *moved* here. And if that bothers you, then you're still lying, aren't you? You can't quit your job, so how are we supposed to be a family if I'm not in Sacramento?"

"No, I'm not upset. I'm just surprised. I wasn't expecting to show up to the office and find my girlfriend waiting for me. That's all."

"Yeah, right."

"We're going to make this work, babe. You'll see. You're giving me the family I've always wanted. I'll help you find a place and a job. Maybe you could even work for my company."

"Really?" She perked up a little at that.

"There's always secretarial work to be had."

"Jesus, I'm not a secretary! I'm an artist. I make things happen. I don't answer phones. You're such a goddamn idiot sometimes."

"Right. Sorry. We'll figure this out. I know a lot of people in this town. This is all going to work out. You just have to trust me, Donna."

Trust him. It was the dumbest idea in the world. But she felt more tired than she ever had in her life. Exhausted. Weak. Things had been hard for her years ago, but she'd been young and blinded by boundless energy. She'd taken action just for action's sake and assumed that the ripples she smashed into the world would carry her along until she reached safety. She'd punched and thrashed and drifted, and sure enough she washed up on the beaches of Los Angeles and made a home.

But now all she wanted to do was sleep and cry. She wasn't a kid anymore, and for once in her life she just wanted . . . well, she wanted someone to take care of her. Was that so wrong? Was it pitiful? Was it immoral to ask this of a married man, even if he had been lying to her the whole time?

Still, if he'd truly been working toward leaving his wife . . .

"I want to make this work," she finally dared to say, and it was the most she could admit to him. She could never, ever say the rest. *Please love me. Please keep me safe. Please, please, please don't hurt me like my family did.*

But it was all she needed to say. Just like that, Michael lit up. His face softened into a smile that made his blue eyes shine as if she were the only person in his world and she was all he needed.

She wouldn't have fallen for him in her twenties. He wasn't edgy. He wasn't dangerous. But maybe she'd matured.

Or maybe now that she was older, she was tired of trying to keep up with wild boys. These days they just left her exhausted. Michael was steady, and he had his own money, no hitting her up for her pot or a place to stay. He was stable enough to make her feel safe, but he loved egging on her wild side and watching it burn. He was desperate and then removed, and she needed both to stay interested.

"I want you here with me," he leaned close to say. "We'll make it work. Leave it all up to me, sweetie."

For once in her life, maybe she would.

CHAPTER 7

LAUREN

"No."

Lauren stared at the white paper she'd dropped to the dirt of the narrow shoulder. It looked like nothing there, a harmless white rectangle shaking slightly in the breeze, just a few inches from the toes of her stain-spattered Keds. A piece of litter that might blow away and eventually disintegrate into nothing after a few good rainstorms.

It had to go away. It had to be nothing.

Hoping if she watched long enough the words would disappear and cease to exist, Lauren waited. The printing remained.

A little birdie told me you're back. Welcome home, Lauren. Let's reconnect.

Not explicitly threatening. Not dangerous at all, really. Until the next paragraph wormed its way through eyes and nerve bundles to the brain cells beyond. *We have something to discuss, and you really won't want to involve the authorities in this, I promise. Text me. We'll talk.* A phone number was listed in bold digits, and after it, the letter was signed simply *BEK.*

Bobby Edward Kepnick.

"Shit," she whispered, nudging the letter a little with her shoe. It didn't wriggle and spring to life. It couldn't hurt her.

But of course it could. There was no address on the envelope. No stamp. No postmark. This letter had been left in her mailbox by a person, stuffed in by some cruel hand. A hand that could deliver more than a letter, surely.

An accomplice? Or just a random person paid to deliver a note?

She tried to hold as still as she could, a prey animal making herself small, but a car zoomed past and scared the hell out of her. Lauren yelped, and the car drove on. But was it possible someone was watching her?

She turned in a circle, checking for spies. When she saw none, she snatched the letter from the dirt and jogged back up the hill toward home, her neck on fire with prickling awareness. Who had left this? Was it a cruel prank or something more sinister?

When Lauren reached the front yard, she sprinted up the porch stairs and locked the door behind her. She'd been lulled into a false sense of security by the peace of this place, leaving the door ajar whenever she went out to work in the yard or get the mail. She held her panting breath for a moment, straining her ears to listen.

Nothing crept or creaked except the ticking of the clock and the soft hum of a fan she'd set up in the dining room window. The final coat of satin varnish was dry. It looked beautiful. And now it was all ruined.

When Lauren inhaled, her head filled with the sharp ache of the drying varnish, and that calmed her. This was her home. Kepnick was in prison. This was some kind of awful prank played by a resentful neighbor or a bored teenage kid.

There was no threat here. No crime. The cheap white paper wasn't scrawled with mad, slanted rantings or threats. It wasn't even filled with a single-spaced monologue of inkjet perversions.

Let's reconnect.

Anxiety prickled over her skin like spider's legs.

What did that mean? He had no right to say such a thing. They'd never been connected. Never.

But that wasn't quite right, was it?

She bit her lip hard, hoping the pain would distract from the memory. The memory of the letter she'd written at fifteen.

Blood rushed to her face as the old shame glowed through her. She'd been a confused young girl, wrestling with the weirdness of her life. She hadn't thought much about Kepnick in the first years after he'd confessed, but at fifteen she'd seen a news special about another serial killer, and her interest in Bobby Kepnick had been sparked.

She'd gone to the library over and over again, looking up information on Kepnick and what he'd done. Lauren had seen a couple of scowling, scary images of him in the news during her father's exoneration, but her teenage research had turned up kinder pictures. At the time of his first trial for three of the murders, he'd been a thirty-three-year-old man with bright-green eyes and a charming smile. Not movie-star handsome but not ugly. Not at all.

As an elementary school student, she'd had a bad habit of developing secret, childish crushes on male teachers, and he'd looked like that kind of harmless man. Accessible and almost fatherly. Kepnick was a monster, but he'd also been the man who'd saved her father's life, in a way, and for that he'd been a warped kind of hero in Lauren's teenage mind.

She could feel only hot shame now because that was why she'd written to him at fifteen. To *thank* him. To string some faint connection between her bright future and her strange past.

Lauren blinked and realized she'd slid down the wall and was sitting on the newly finished floor of the entry, the paper now a crumpled mess in her hand.

Let's reconnect.

Lauren scrambled up from the floor, hands nearly sliding out from under her as she twisted herself up too quickly. She hurried over to the table.

"Come on, come on," she urged as her laptop slowly blinked from sleep.

She typed in Kepnick's name and hit the NEWS tab. The screen filled with articles immediately, but a quick scan made it clear they were all years old.

When she followed a link to Wikipedia, she found even more reassurance waiting. There hadn't been any parole or pardon. He was serving five life sentences in maximum security.

It could be a prankster. There were thousands around here who must remember her father's trial and conviction and then ultimate release. Her grandmother had once implied that her neighbors had been thrilled to witness a true scandal. *A fall from grace is very exciting for the onlookers,* she'd muttered. Still, none of those people could know that Kepnick had any personal connection with Lauren.

Had Grandma known?

She'd been staying with her grandmother for five weeks that summer while her dad did some traveling up and down the state in hopes of raising his sales and earning a promotion. It had worked. They'd moved out of their apartment and into a gorgeous townhouse the next year.

But without cable Lauren had been left with too much time on her hands in those hot summer weeks, and her teenage imagination had scrambled frantically into strange corners to fill her days. Puzzling over Bobby Edward Kepnick had been one misbegotten hobby. She'd also developed a brief habit of using binoculars to spy on the men who worked horses at a boarding facility a half mile away.

Puberty was a strange beast.

At the end of her stay, she'd suffered a sudden fear that Kepnick might write back to her after she'd gone, and she'd felt sick that her grandmother would find out what she'd done.

And Lauren had so wanted her grandmother to love her and forgive her and never regret that they'd taken her in. Her stomach had been sour for two full weeks after her stay, but then her mind had turned to anxiety about the coming start of her first year of high school.

Lauren had always assumed there'd never been a return letter, but was that true? What if he'd written back and then written again and again, a terrible stream of letters that had terrified her grandma with his continued presence?

No. Elizabeth Abrams spoke her mind unreservedly even if the truth hurt feelings. If he'd written, Lauren would have heard about it and been thoroughly scolded at the least.

"There was never a connection," she said aloud, and the sound of her own words gave her a little bravery.

She wasn't fifteen anymore. Kepnick had given her father back to her, yes, but he'd taken him first. He'd stolen her childhood, and he'd killed that woman and murdered at least eight others. He wasn't a monster hero; he was just a monster. And he was toying with her now. If he knew anyone on the outside, he could've sent that note with a twenty-dollar bill and requested a special delivery. It wasn't that scary.

Was it?

No, she just felt vulnerable being alone. That was all.

Lauren jogged over to get her phone, opened the app, and started streaming.

"Hey, everyone! I know I already posted today, but I wanted to show you another quick glimpse now that the sun is coming through the west windows. Can you believe the depth of this finish?" She moved slowly toward the slanted rays of light glowing through the kitchen. "You did such a good job picking the color! I love it so much there might be another poll coming soon . . ."

She swooped the camera around to the wall she'd marred with four huge swatches of different paint; then she twisted quickly away again. "I'll tell you the names tomorrow. Paint names are ridiculous and amazing, and I can't get enough of them. I'm going to be sad when I have to leave the swatch books behind. Anyway, thanks again, friends. I feel like you're all here with me, cheering me on, and I can't tell you how much that fills me up with love."

She ended the video and scrolled through the latest comments, pretending she wasn't checking for a message from one specific person. But she was. And it wasn't there.

Could she tell Bastian about the letter? Would he be worried?

Her eyebrows rose as she considered it. He knew about her history, and he wouldn't judge her for what she'd done at fifteen. He was a reasonable man.

Ugh. Too goddamn reasonable. So reasonable she'd felt like maybe he didn't give a shit about her half the time.

She should have listened to those instincts. That was the prevailing wisdom, wasn't it? Trust your instincts? Well, right now her instincts were screaming that she should reach out to Bastian.

So she did.

Hey, she texted. Things just got really weird around here. Can I call?

As soon as she hit SEND, adrenaline flooded her with heat and anxiety, ratcheting her heart rate nearly as high as it had soared when she'd glimpsed that letter. *Re-ply, re-ply, re-ply*, it begged in its thumping beat.

And its prayers were miraculously answered. In a meeting . . . so I can only text. ☺

An invitation to respond.

"Nice," she muttered as her thumbs began picking out just the right words. A serial killer just sent me a letter. THE serial killer. It was left in my mailbox, Bastian. I'm freaked out.

Dots of response appeared almost immediately; then they faded away while she watched. If he didn't answer, she'd take that as a sign. She'd walk away and give up. And this time she'd mean it.

When her phone vibrated, the screen announced an incoming call. From Bastian.

"Hey." Her voice was too high and hoarse.

"What the hell, Lauren?"

"I thought you were in a meeting."

"I excused myself. Are you kidding me? He *wrote* to you?"

"Yes. I just got the note. I don't know why he wrote. I don't know who left it there."

"What did he say?" he asked.

She hadn't spoken to him in weeks, and she thought it would be shocking to hear his voice again, but it was too familiar to shock. It didn't feel strange at all. It felt normal and right, his words a soothing balm. She'd always loved his voice. He could've made a killing as a therapist just on his voice alone, but he didn't have patience for bullshit and drama. That was one of his favorite lines, usually used to imply that she was creating it.

She took a deep breath and read him the whole thing.

"Wow."

"Yeah. Wow."

"Are you sure it's from him?" he asked.

"It's got to be from him or some fan, at least."

"Shit, that's creepy."

"Yes!" She laughed in relief. "Yes, it's extremely creepy!"

"What the hell does that even mean? *Reconnect?* That's a threat, right? It has to be. He's threatening you."

"I don't . . ." She hesitated. "I . . . I'm not sure if it's a threat."

"He's a killer, Lauren, and his only connection to you is a murder. It sure sounds like a threat to me, and you need to get in contact with the police, no matter what that letter says."

This was the moment. The secret she'd never told anyone and had never planned to tell.

But there was comfort in having a cool and logical boyfriend who floated above the mess of mere mortals. He had no patience for drama, after all.

"There's a possibility," she said carefully, "that he's referring to something else."

"Something like what?"

"Please don't think I'm a terrible person, Bastian. But . . . when I was fifteen, I wrote to him."

"To *Kepnick*?" He sounded shocked, so she responded quickly, trying to smooth it over.

"Yes. It was a few years after my dad was exonerated, and I suddenly wanted to know more. About everything. And about *him*. I just . . . I sent him a letter. I have no idea why. It seems insane now. It seemed insane right afterward, in fact."

"I'm not sure about that. Wanting to know more seems like a pretty normal reaction to a fucked-up situation."

"I guess, but not by reaching out to him. That wasn't right. I just . . . I got caught up in finding out what had really happened and who this man was. His motivation. What made him tick. And the pinnacle of that brief obsession was sending him a letter to ask why he finally told the truth about the murder. But I also . . . Jesus, I *thanked* him. For saving my dad. I know it was wrong. He killed all those women, and I said thank you . . ."

"Lauren, it's okay."

"I've never told anyone. I was embarrassed, and as soon as I mailed it, I was so afraid my dad or my grandma would find out. I don't know why I took that kind of chance."

"You did it because you were a teenage girl who'd been through hell, that's why. Maybe it was irrational, but you weren't exactly in a rational situation, were you?"

Relief swamped her so quickly she felt untethered and dizzy, swept away on the wave of it. Bastian's kindness had been an overwhelming gift to someone with a needy heart like Lauren. She'd mistaken it for love even after his infatuation with her had faded. "I guess I wasn't. But I was old enough to know right from wrong."

"What you did hurt no one. All you did was express yourself. Teenagers lash out in way more damaging ways than that."

"I suppose."

"So how did he respond?"

Lauren sighed. "He didn't. Not while I was staying with my grandmother, anyway. I volunteered to walk to the mailbox every day for three weeks, and I never got an answer. He could have written back afterward, I guess, but I think my grandma would have read me the riot act if he had."

"Yeah, she's pretty blunt."

Her grandmother had never liked Bastian. Lauren hated to think it was because he was biracial, but she couldn't help but suspect. Then again, her grandmother always had a good reason ready for her dislike. *That man thinks he's more charming than he actually is,* she'd said of Bastian. *He treats you like an accessory lucky to have a place in his wardrobe.*

That one had stung because Lauren had *felt* lucky to have a spot in Bastian's life. He was cool and successful and steady. She'd worked hard to fit in. To set him off. Just like the perfect accessory would.

"Do you think he has someone watching me?" she asked. "That's what he's implying, right?"

"Maybe someone saw your videos and told him."

Lauren blinked. "Oh. Maybe. He obviously has access to a phone. And an accomplice nearby who's watching me and doing his bidding."

"Um . . . Okay, popping a note into a mailbox isn't exactly 'doing his bidding.' But I still think you should call the cops."

"I'll think about it," she said, but she couldn't forget the warning about involving the authorities. Her dad hadn't exactly had the best experience with the justice system. Lauren couldn't just choose to throw his name back into the mix again, not if Kepnick had mischief in mind. What if he recanted and stirred up all those old stories?

"Do you have a security system?" Bastian asked.

"No, but as soon as I get off the phone, I'm going to look up my options."

"Good. I'm worried about you."

His warm, soft voice twisted through her and tied her heart into a knotted rag. The words *I miss you* pushed hard for escape, but she closed her throat against them.

"Will you be okay?" he asked.

Maybe. Regardless, she couldn't be clingy, not the way she had been. The whole point of her little home improvement show was to let him know she was strong and capable and maybe even bold. "I think I'll ignore it and hope that's the end of it. I'm not exactly sure what I could report him for anyway. One letter isn't harassment even if it's from a prisoner."

"Okay, but let me know if you get another, all right?"

Her body prickled with an uncomfortable mix of pleasure at that invitation and fear over the words. "I will. Thank you."

"I'd better get back. Be safe. Bye, Lauren."

She hung up and tried to ignore that he'd ended the call with *bye* instead of something less final.

CHAPTER 8

DONNA

"Okay. Good." The doctor snapped off the latex gloves and gestured that Donna could close her legs. "That's about it."

She jerked her feet from the stirrups and clapped her knees together, grimacing at the slide of the jelly between her thighs. At least it wasn't cold anymore.

The doctor—Vanderbeck or Vanderbeek, she couldn't remember—frowned at her chart. "You don't have a more precise date for the start of your last period?"

"No, I don't keep a period diary, Doc."

"Well, based on the week you said you had sex with the . . . *father* . . ."

The personnel in this office seemed very taken aback by the fact that she was pregnant and unmarried. Or else they were taken aback that Donna treated the circumstances as if they were normal and not worthy of apology. Come on, folks, it was 1985 already. Welcome to the future.

"I'd say you're about nine weeks along. I'll estimate your due date at May 13."

"May. Wow. Okay. At least I won't be nine months pregnant in the summer. That's something."

"Yes. And there's more than enough time for a wedding if you're so inclined."

"Oh, I think I'll be okay."

"*Ms.* Hempstead," he said dryly, emphasizing the Ms., "at your advanced age, this is considered a high-risk pregnancy, especially as it's the first child you'll carry to term."

"Advanced age!" she sputtered. "I'm only thirty-five!"

"Yes, thirty-five is considered an advanced maternal age. Most women have children in their twenties. Even age thirty or thirty-one raises the risk of severe birth defect and complication. Thirty-five and up is hard on both baby and mother."

Mother. What a strange word to hear directed at herself. Her thighs slid against each other when she stiffened and shook her head. "Thanks. I'll be fine." But would she? She wasn't going to win any mother-of-the-year awards raising any child. What if the baby wasn't healthy?

"Be that as it may, I'm going to refer you to an obstetrician who specializes in women your age—"

"Oh, for fuck's sake," she huffed, not quite realizing she'd said it out loud until the doctor's face turned red.

"Ms. Hempstead," he scolded.

"You're an obstetrician, and I'm an unmarried woman carrying a bastard child; I think we both know what the *F* word means, Doc."

"Regardless," he continued valiantly, the red climbing up to his receding hairline, clashing with the strawberry-red strands still desperately clinging to his scalp, "Dr. Appleton will recommend all of the needed testing to ensure everything is proceeding apace."

Apace. Jesus Christ.

The one good thing about needing some so-called specialist for old wombs was that she'd never have to see this guy again. Michael had helped her find this office, calling around to see who could fit her in for an appointment this week. Now she understood why the doctor wasn't flush with patients. His bedside manner was complete crap.

She walked out of the office with a slippery crotch; about twenty brochures, each more frightening than the last; and one business card for the special obstetrician she was supposed to see. There was also a big, flashing neon sign in her head that read MAY 13! in red letters. She had a due date.

A due date.

"This is crazy," she wheezed to herself as she slid behind the wheel of her car, the sun beating down on her head like a jackhammer. Her due date to be a mother. Then again, she might not make it to motherhood if her old body didn't survive this.

Snorting, Donna threw all the brochures into the back seat and hoped some of them would blow out when she hit the freeway. *Warning Signs of Preeclampsia. Thriving during an Unplanned Pregnancy. Your Healthy Diet. The Dangers of Cigarettes during This Important Time. Being Ready for Baby!*

Screw it all. She drove to Mervyn's instead.

Not that she had enough savings to fund a big shopping trip, but she did have a credit card she hadn't maxed out and a boyfriend who'd sworn to support her.

Michael had been everything he'd promised since she'd arrived in town the week before. He stopped by to see her after work. He'd spent nearly all of Sunday with her. He'd helped her find a thirty-day rental *just until we figure things out.* And he'd shown up with a shopping bag full of veggies and fresh fruits and insisted she visit a doctor immediately.

"I'm going to take good care of this baby," he'd said. "And you. I can't risk anything happening. We'll find you a good doctor and a good place to live. I love you, Donna."

Did he?

She pushed the thought away and pulled into the parking lot of the shopping center. She didn't need maternity clothes yet, but her flat stomach definitely wasn't flat anymore. She could no longer zip up even her baggiest pair of old jeans.

Muzak hovered over her head like a cloud of diseased mosquitos as she took a tiny cart and headed into the store. Her gaze swept over the misses department and landed right on juniors, and she marched straight toward it, hoping she could get by with some stirrup pants and a big sweater. All the sweaters were oversized, but when she picked up the first one, it was too short to cover any belly bulge.

"Ugh." She put it back and kept browsing, forgoing anything with lace or artfully placed zippers. She did pick up a couple of purposefully ripped sweatshirts and stared at them wistfully before putting them back. She was not going to be a sad woman of *advanced maternal age* trying to dress like a teenager . . . even if she would've been able to pull off the look three weeks earlier.

At long last, she made it into some racks with shirts that looked suitable, if uninspiring.

"This is cute," she murmured, picking up a blue long-sleeved tunic. She held it up, loving the slight A-line that would hide all her sins. Or just one sin, really. Fornication. And the price was only $12.99. "Jackpot," she said with a laugh. Then her eyes registered the word *maternity* just above the price on the tag.

Donna yelped and dropped the shirt to the ground, her eyes flashing up and around until they landed on the sign notifying her that she'd wandered out of juniors and misses and straight into the maternity section. The baby clothes started ten feet away.

Abandoning the cart where it sat, Donna spun and rushed through the racks of clothes, pushing past puffy down jackets as if she were clawing her way out of a jungle. Sweat prickled her brow as she finally spotted the doors and rushed into the shimmering air of the parking lot.

Why the hell was it so hot today? It was October. And why had her body been drawn to the damn maternity section like an animal to water? She didn't wear frocks and muumuus! She was young and hip.

Clutching her purse, she panted until she'd gotten enough oxygen, and then she was just standing there sweating and feeling sorry for herself. Another thing she hated. Not the sweating; she'd lived in LA for too many years to take that seriously. But feeling sorry for herself. Her favorite hobby lately, but she'd always thought she was too cool for that crap.

"Grow up, Donna," she said weakly. "Just fucking grow up already." Her pants didn't fit, and she was going to get bigger and bigger, because that was how pregnancy worked. She could squeeze herself into a new pair of bleached jeans this month, but no matter what she wore, she'd be huge in the end. There was no winning this fight, so she could go down struggling or she could surrender gracefully.

"Oh, fuck that," she muttered, but she turned and walked into the store. She marched right back to that blue tunic still lying on the ground, and she put it in the cart before wheeling around toward the shoe section. She desperately needed some comfortable flats. But on the way toward the shoes, she stopped in the accessories area and picked out a sheer scarlet-red scarf to tie around her neck. It perfectly matched her favorite lipstick and would hopefully add a Parisian vibe to her new look.

She'd make this work. She'd rock it.

After making peace with that battle, Donna felt nearly giddy on the way out of the store. Things were honestly going *well*. Was that possible? That hope she'd wanted to let herself sink into . . . it was getting deeper and more welcoming. Softer. She almost felt ready.

Realizing Michael would be off work in half an hour, Donna decided to head toward his office in hopes of snagging him on his way to his car. They could have dinner, maybe. She'd tell him all about the doctor, though she'd definitely leave out the details about her shriveled and ancient womb. That was not an image she wanted to plant in her boyfriend's head.

Donna tossed her new purchases into the back, popped in a cassette, and let the air slap and swirl its way over her as she drove, drying her sweat and making the warm October afternoon the perfect temperature. It wasn't LA, but Sacramento was starting to grow on her. There was no smog, little traffic, and it was still warm enough to enjoy her convertible.

The music scene was atrocious, of course, but that was hardly her biggest concern these days.

Donna turned into the vast parking lot of Michael's workplace and chose a spot toward the back that still offered a sight line of his reserved space. It was just before 5:00, so she settled in to wait for a while, slipping on her sunglasses and relaxing back in the soft leather of the wide bench seat.

After stretching hard, she idly fished the old pack of cigarettes from her purse and tapped one out, if only to hold it wistfully between her fingers. She let her head fall back and closed her eyes before raising the cig to her nose and breathing gently in. The spicy brown scent of tobacco filled her, raising goose bumps on her skin. There was nothing sweet about the smell of it burning, but dried and delicate like this, it made her mouth water.

One wouldn't hurt, surely, but it seemed she was already cursed with too many dangers and drawbacks at thirty-five, so she tried to content herself with just the delicious aroma of it. But God she wanted a drag. One deep, perfect drag to get her through. That and a shot of tequila would do wonders for her stress levels.

She slipped it between her lips, held it there, fantasizing. Lucky for her, she hadn't had a steady habit and usually only lit up when she was drinking. Or after sex. Or, of course, when she discovered her period was late. That was a real killer of a trigger.

Donna let her eyes drift open to the afternoon light, aware that she'd fall asleep if she didn't. She'd been so tired lately, falling asleep at 9:00 p.m. while the television droned on through her ten hours of solid slumber. But it felt so peaceful out here in the warm day, just the right amount of breeze touching her scalp.

It took a moment to register that Michael's parking space was empty. *Empty.* She frowned, cocked her head, then sat up straight with a gasp. The movement brought her vision in line with the parking lot entrance to her left, and there he was, pulling out.

Donna cursed, the cigarette falling from her lips as she started her car, freaked out that she might lose him. Maybe he'd decided to stop by her place today and find out what the doctor had said. She'd really wanted to surprise him and be whisked off to dinner—he loved surprises—and now she'd screwed it up. She couldn't call him at home. Couldn't talk to him at all if she didn't catch him now.

His car had vanished by the time she pulled out of her space. Donna cursed more loudly and sped down the row until she could take the same turn he had. She thought she caught a glimpse of his tan car ahead, already disappearing, and she stepped on the gas.

When she drew a little closer, she realized he was heading toward the freeway entrance, and she expected he'd turn south toward her new apartment. She'd missed the chance to surprise him at work, but she'd easily catch him on the freeway with the V-8 rumbling under her hood. She could pull up next to him and wave. Not what she'd planned, but it would still make him laugh. Now she was regretting that she hadn't put on her new red scarf.

Donna was just starting to relax when he passed the on-ramp and kept driving.

So he wasn't going to see her. Fine.

Now she was just following him like a crazy woman, but it couldn't be helped, and when he hit his turn signal, she felt a surge of validation. Because Michael wasn't turning onto the opposite on-ramp or even another street. His car slowed, and he bounced into the rough, potholed parking lot of a bar. She followed thirty seconds later and watched him park in a space near the door.

Donna took a hard right into the row of cars closer to the street, hoping he wouldn't spot her distinctive convertible, because now she definitely didn't want to stop and wave at him. Instead she watched as Michael locked his car door and headed inside. When he opened the blacked-out glass, she caught a glimpse of pool tables and a television playing a football game, and then the door closed slowly behind him.

Well.

He was allowed to go out and have a beer with his friends. He'd probably ducked out early to meet some guys from work. But she sat and waited, and no other cars arrived in the next five minutes.

The place was called Lucky's, and there wasn't much more to see besides that. Neon beer signs blazed in the high windows, but the lower windows had been blacked out just like the door. No one wanted the 6:00 p.m. sun blazing in when they were trying to get blasted. The place looked like an average joint that catered to locals and maybe a few truckers passing by. Pickups and beat-up sedans lined the lot. All the lights in the big green Lucky's sign were functional, but that was the only indication of exceptionalism.

When a vehicle finally pulled into the lot behind her, Donna parked in a space with a view of the door but left her car running. There was nothing for her to do here unless she meant to go inside, and that wasn't quite the fun surprise she'd wanted.

Let down, Donna reached toward the gearshift, but as her fingers touched it, the door of the bar opened and a woman came out. She was a waitress, if her extremely tight Lucky's T-shirt was any indication. It was thin, worn, and cinched up in a little knot to show off her flat stomach. Just below the bare strip of skin, tight cut-off jeans started and then abruptly ended a centimeter below her crotch, strands of faded denim brushing against her tan thighs.

Donna growled. Now she knew why Lucky's was so popular even in the late afternoon. A man in cowboy boots and a hat approached the door, and the woman smiled and opened it for him before she lit a cigarette and took a deep drag, her huge breasts rising up to make room for her expanding lungs.

Was that what Michael wanted? Some bimbo with big tits and a flat stomach? Because Donna might be able to accommodate the first as her body expanded, but the second was already a memory.

"Screw him," she growled, throwing the car in reverse. He could drink beer and ogle waitresses all night if that was what he wanted. Donna wouldn't answer her phone or her door. Let him go home to his frigid wife.

She banged the steering wheel and cursed him all the way home, ignoring the alarmed glances the other drivers threw her way. She was pissed off and pregnant, and they could deal.

She yelled all her thoughts into the exhaust-laden wind and called him every name in the book, and by the time she got back to her ugly rental, she felt a little better. After a Hungry-Man TV dinner, she felt almost calm.

Maybe she'd just been hungry.

When the phone rang, she nearly gave in and picked up, but she clenched her fists and let her answering machine tape run. Smirking, she listened to her slightly tipsy voice from two years before declare that she was "out on the town, having fun!" But the smirk died as soon as she realized it wasn't him. Instead, the woman from the leasing office droned out instructions for how to drop off the weekly rent check after hours.

Donna curled up on the couch and glared at an ancient episode of *All in the Family* that played silently on the TV.

Had this all been one giant mistake? Was Michael really going to upend his life to take care of her and this baby? It had been a fling. A wild ride with weekend-only rules. How was that supposed to transition into a family?

No, not just a family. A *happy* family. That was what she was looking for, wasn't it? A chance to prove that she could finally be a part of something supportive and good? That she wasn't too much to love?

She tentatively slid a hand over her belly and held it there for just a moment before moving it away. Did she really think she was cut out for this? She'd dropped everything to run here in the hopes of something impossible, when she should have been sitting tight and saving up her money for this kid.

"I'm so stupid," she whispered, letting her face crumple into tears. "What am I doing here?"

Grabbing a throw pillow, she pressed the rough fabric to her face to try to keep everything in. The tears, the words, the rioting thoughts. She'd fucked up before. She would figure this out. She would.

Tomorrow she'd work on her résumé. She needed to find a good job before her belly started showing. And an apartment in a quiet part of town. The one thing she wouldn't do was limp back to Los Angeles with her tail between her legs after a couple of weeks of half-assed effort on her part.

Her original plan still stood: move closer, get support, and demand that Michael do his part. Between the lower rents here and child support from Michael, she'd be fine. She could grow the hell up and make this work even if her kid's dad wanted to spend his evenings drinking beer and looking at tits.

If she'd let herself fall in love with him, that was her own dumb problem to figure out. For once she wouldn't respond to a breakup by slashing tires and throwing drinks.

"I'm a mature and capable adult," she said aloud to herself before bursting into watery laughter. Maybe she wasn't, but she could be if she tried.

Just when she'd reached the height of her internal independent-woman speech, the metal slide of a key in a lock pricked her ears. She was sure it was the apartment next door, but then the knob turned and the door swung in.

"Hello, darling," Michael said, and her angry strength crumbled into dust.

"Michael? I thought . . ."

"Thought what?" he asked distractedly before holding out a big plastic bag. "I stopped and got chicken wings for you. You said you were craving something spicy."

That was why he'd been at the bar? Donna jumped to her feet and raced over to throw her arms around his neck.

"Hey!" he laughed, but his free arm wrapped around her waist. "You must be hungry?"

For once she wasn't, so she pulled his head down and kissed him hard and deep until she heard the plastic bag drop to the floor and Michael was backing her toward the couch. He smelled of beer and cigarettes, and she closed her eyes and lost herself like she had so many times after a long night out partying, tearing at his clothes until he was panting and hard and rough with her.

"God, I love you," he rasped as she bit his neck and groaned.

And finally she decided for once in her life to just let go and fall.

CHAPTER 9

LAUREN

She hadn't slept well since she'd received that letter, tossing and turning and sitting up straight in bed at every stupid sound. During the day she pushed the worst thoughts away, but at night the worries squirmed under her skull like worms, waking her up and taking over. Did Kepnick have someone watching her?

When dawn broke over the tops of the mountains on the third day, Lauren grumbled and decided she might as well get up and surprise her grandmother with a morning call. Grandma woke at 6:00 every day, a late start compared to her ranching days, she said.

Lauren smiled as the phone rang, planning to explain the poll to her grandma and describe the winning paint color: a gray that edged toward sage green in sunlight. It would set off the white of the cabinets when she finally got around to painting them.

But a hurried male voice answered when the line finally opened.

Lauren's heart skipped a terrified beat as she imagined the worst. "Hello?"

"Yes, ma'am?"

"I'm looking for Elizabeth Abrams?"

"Oh, she's in the shower and then off to breakfast. Can I take a message?"

Lauren slumped with relief. "Please let her know Lauren said to have a good morning and I'll call back later."

At least the momentary burst of fear had woken her up, so she headed downstairs to start coffee. Maybe once her grandmother felt up for it, Lauren could bring her out for a nice homemade breakfast on the garden patio she loved so much.

The farmhouse sink made Lauren smile as she drew water. The kitchen truly only needed new appliances and a tile backsplash to perk things up after she painted.

While the coffee brewed, she sat down with her master list. "Forgot about the lighting," she murmured. She couldn't manage a rewire and installation of can lights, but she did plan to convert the drop light above the sink into a strip of fancy LEDs that would provide six times the light with the same amount of power.

She was kind of good at this. It may have started out as a ploy for attention, but she felt damn proud of what she was doing.

She poured herself a cup and walked to the bathroom to stand in the doorway and sip her coffee. It wasn't a terrible space as it was. Her grandmother had kept it spick and span, until this past year of pain. The clawfoot tub was beautiful, and the floor was still nice, though a couple of the terracotta tiles had cracked. The Western-themed wallpaper definitely had to go, but there really wasn't a need to truly renovate this room, especially when she'd be adding a more modern bath upstairs.

Dragging from the lack of sleep, she gulped down half the coffee and fired up the shower to let it warm. Every time she climbed into the tub to shower under the attached nozzle, she was shocked that her grandmother had done this for years. The lip was high and made higher by the lion's feet of the tub. It was more beautiful to look at than it was to use.

Twenty minutes later the hot water ran out, and she reluctantly climbed back out onto the cold tile. She shivered in the cool fall morning air, but she did feel better. Bright and awake and ready to work. But not at the computer. And not inside.

She'd had a fun idea under the shower spray.

Lauren styled her hair into a messy bun; took fifteen minutes to apply a natural, sun-kissed makeup look; then dressed in jeans and a cute sweater.

"Good morning, everyone! It's a tiny bit crisp here today, which reminds me that I want to head up to Apple Hill. Cider doughnuts are pure deep-fried joy. Unfortunately I don't have doughnuts for you, and now that's probably all you want. But I do have a surprise. Today I'm going to bust the lock on the ancient storage shed and find out what's in there once and for all! Nobody knows where the key is, so we're going to have to find another way in. And I already bought a sledgehammer. Isn't a sledgehammer more exciting than doughnuts?"

The screen door squeaked when she walked out the back of the house. She'd briefly considered oiling it, but she loved the noise. It sounded like home.

"I can see my breath!" she exclaimed, then immediately shook her finger at the camera. "Do not make fun of me, non-Californians! Sweater weather is exciting stuff!"

Laughing, she set her phone on its little stand on top of a peeling picnic table and aimed the camera at the shed before bouncing out to stand in front of it.

"I haven't yet bothered breaking open the shed, because there were plenty of tools around, but now it's time. Mama needs a wheelbarrow! Keep your fingers crossed! Ready?"

Lauren raised her arms in a fake cheer before picking up the sledgehammer. She slipped on sunglasses as a token nod toward eye protection, then hefted the sledgehammer high above her head before bringing it down on the lock. It grazed the metal with a loud ping, then breezed past it and hit the ground with a thud that vibrated all her joints.

"Oof. One more time. Maybe two. I'm new to this violent destruction thing."

She lifted it and swung again, and this time she was rewarded with a crack along with the slap of metal. Lauren dropped the head of the hammer to the ground and cheered. "Yes! It's off!" The metal plate hung at a ninety-degree angle, the lock still tight and dangling off it. She pulled until the whole thing twisted off.

"This is it! Let's see what's inside. Hopefully not *too* many family skeletons."

Yikes, she thought to herself. Not the right joke for her family.

After retrieving the phone, she tugged at the door, then pulled harder when it resisted. Tufts of grass had grown up in the path of the bottom edge, and in the end she had to give up on subtlety and yank as hard as she could to drag it open six inches, then a foot. Once she could wedge her shoulder in, she was able to leverage her body weight and swing it wider to let in the light.

"It's a wheelbarrow!" she shouted, aiming the phone at the first thing she spotted. "We hit the jackpot!" Then she shifted the angle of the view. "A jackpot with a flat tire. But I can fix that, no problem. Google exists for a reason."

An old gas can sat in the well of the wheelbarrow, and she was thankful to find it was empty when she picked it up. "I'm not sure what you're supposed to do with ancient, unknown flammables. Bonfire, maybe?"

She swept the camera over the space. "Boy, there are a lot of spiderwebs in here. No spiders, though, right, guys? Ha ha."

At first all she saw was junk filling the rest of the shed. A pile of rotting two-by-fours; an ancient, rusted bike.

"If any of you spot anything valuable, shout it out in the comments." She moved the wheelbarrow outside so she could step farther in. "That looks like some kind of old dirt bike. And that . . ." She aimed the camera at a leather bag perched on a sawhorse. "Is probably a duffel bag full of money. What else could it be? Let's check."

She angled her body so that the light from the open door was hitting the crumpled brown leather. It looked like some kind of heist bag from the 1950s, something a bank robber would thrust at a teller with a demand for all the cash.

Holding her phone as steady as she could, Lauren reached for the big metal buckle and worked the stiff strap out of it. "This better not be full of bugs," she murmured as she tugged the strap free, wishing she'd left her gloves on.

"All right. Concentrate on thoughts of treasure!" Pretending it was someone else's hand, she shoved her fingers into the seam of the bag and worked it open.

"This doesn't look like money," she said for the camera, tugging out a faded old crewneck. The elastic at the neck crinkled when she pulled. "It's just clothes." She pulled out a pair of burgundy corduroy pants. "I think these are bell-bottoms! I see some old sandals. Wow. We've entered a time warp. The '60s or '70s? Regardless, it doesn't look like anyone robbed a train or anything. Let's move on."

She picked her way through the rest of the shed, exclaiming over an old cast-iron sewing machine and a pair of spurs hanging on the wall above it. Then she spotted a ridge of wood under a cardboard box and stopped.

"What's this?" she asked as she nudged the box aside with her foot. "Is that . . . ?" She moved another box and stepped back. "Is that some kind of *door*? A secret door? Hold on."

She jogged outside to grab her phone stand and set it on the sawhorse. "I'll be covered with dust, but let's find out what this is." Cringing, she picked up the boxes and set them outside, then worked at moving a stack of pitchforks and rakes aside. Once she slid the wheel of the old dirt bike off, it was clear what she was looking at. "It's a door to a cellar!" she exclaimed.

The wooden plank door, which still looked sturdy, was locked to a frame set in the floor of the shed. She'd assumed it was solid ground beneath her, but now that she'd scuffed it up, she realized there was wood beneath her feet.

Lauren turned slowly to the camera, eyebrows raised. "Well, folks. It looks like we have another secret on our hands. I need to find a flashlight and maybe a ladder. Meet me here in one hour for a spooky October adventure!"

CHAPTER 10

DONNA

Now that she'd decided to let herself fall, Donna felt awash with terror. Happy and hopeful, yes, but terribly, terribly afraid.

She wanted this all so much that it ached in her chest, a shallow pain just an inch beneath the skin, scraping against the underside of her breastbone.

She could touch the fantasy now, a passionate family wrapped up tight together, laughing and fighting and loving. Michael would never be cold with their child. He hadn't even met it yet, and his eyes already shimmered with love.

"Stupid alien," Donna muttered, cupping a hand over her newly hardening belly as she shrugged down lower in the seat of her car.

What if she lost it all now? What if she was a fool?

He'd left her the night before, as she'd known he would. She'd woken up alone and utterly out of sorts. She wasn't used to patience or trust, and she burned with the need to do something, anything, so she'd paced her apartment for hours, puzzling out a way to just be *sure*.

Everything felt out of her control, just beyond her reach. She wanted to grasp it and hang on tight.

So here she was, parked deep in the shade of the weeping willow two doors down from Michael's home.

Michael was still at work, she knew that. He'd explained his plans for the day already. His wife had volunteered them for a neighborhood barbecue, so he'd leave work at 5:00 to play reluctant host, and he wouldn't have time to stop by the apartment.

So why was she sitting on his street at 4:30? Was she really going to tell his wife?

She tapped the steering wheel and scowled at her indecision. She always took action in life. She made choices on the fly and rarely second-guessed them, and frankly, she'd found that any problem could be resolved if you poked at it hard enough.

Do something. Say something. Make waves and then ride them out. That was how she got through life.

With Michael, there was one easy way to create a tidal wave: walk across the lawn. Knock on the door. Let the truth free like a thrashing giant whale. Things would happen. Lives would change.

But she was still slumped in her seat when the front door of Michael's house opened and his wife walked out, her yippy little dog on a leash.

His wife—Carol?—said something to the dog and then laughed, that wide smile lighting up her face before she donned the straw sun hat and set off down the sidewalk away from Donna's car.

Donna got out.

Hands shaking, she moved quickly to catch up with the woman. It wasn't difficult—his wife ambled along, allowing her dog to stop and sniff half a dozen things before lifting his leg on each one. By the time they reached the end of the block, Donna was only steps behind her. And the woman was singing.

She paused for another potty break before glancing over her shoulder. "Oh, hello!" she said brightly.

Donna stopped dead and blinked, her lips parting.

"I'm Carol. Are you new in the neighborhood? Oh, you must have bought that little bungalow around the corner! I saw that it sold last month!"

"Uh, yes," Donna said, stunned. She'd chased this woman down, and now what? Was she ready for this?

"I love that house. I didn't really know the owners, but I walked through it during the open house. So lovely and bright. You and your husband are very lucky."

"Thanks."

Her eyes darted down. "Are you pregnant?" she asked, the words rushing together into one long string of letters.

Donna realized she'd cupped a hand over her belly in a way that women did for only one reason. She jerked her traitorous hand up to hold it hostage with the other.

Carol's face tightened for one quick moment before she smiled again. "I'm sorry. I shouldn't have asked. I'm just . . . oh, I'm hyperaware, I guess. I've never—well!" She waved a hand to brush her own words away. "Never mind about that. I'm so glad I got to meet you. What did you say your name was?"

"Donna," she said immediately, watching for the smallest change in her expression. Had Michael ever called her a friend or a colleague? Had he ever whispered her name at night? But no. There was nothing. Not even a twitch of the eyelids.

Instead Carol reached for her hand and shook it gently. "I'd better get going or Twinkle will rebel. Unless you'd like to walk with us?" She glanced doubtfully down at Donna's Doc Martens.

"No. But thanks."

"Bye then!" Carol bounced happily off, her dog pulling her around the corner, no sign of depression or instability in her smile or walk. She seemed . . . just *nice*.

Donna turned on her heel, sand grinding between her boot and the cement, the sound of her own crushing guilt. If that woman had mental problems, it wasn't her fault any more than it was Michael's. Donna couldn't spit in her face and hurt her so ruthlessly.

Was that how Michael felt too?

Or was he even telling the truth? She just needed him to be telling the *truth*. "Please," she whispered to herself.

Maybe the key to making good things happen in life wasn't blind, reckless action. Maybe what she needed to do was talk to him. She could calmly explain that she still needed reassurance, and if he gave it, she'd let herself feel better. She'd trust him. Trust herself. She was strong enough to do that, surely.

She didn't like it, though. It didn't feel natural at all. It felt . . . scary.

"You're a brave, ass-kicking bitch," she muttered to herself as she slipped back into her car, purposefully ignoring the soft jelly of her insides vibrating with anxiety. "You don't have to like it, girl, you just have to do it."

Strange that this felt far more frightening than any other risk she'd taken.

She wanted to talk to him. Tell him the truth. That she could picture her life with him now. All the evenings together, talking about news or books or movies. The little chores around the house. They'd get to know each other in ways she hadn't quite managed with other men. The quiet ways that had always felt too gentle to share.

Did she dare try to catch him as he pulled up? Or should she sneak into the barbecue and steal him away for a moment?

She snorted at the naughty idea. She was a new neighbor, after all. Someone who was supposed to be in his space. She wouldn't be out of place at the party at all.

She tried to swallow back her surge of excitement at the idea. She knew damn well her biggest problem in life was that she didn't mind causing trouble. In fact, she really *liked* it. Liked to stir things up, to yell and scream and knock over furniture. She'd always been good at getting attention, and she'd discovered over the decades that attention was thrilling no matter what kind it was.

Was that what she'd chased with men since childhood? Anything to get her ice-cold dad to notice she was in the room?

While a surprise appearance in his backyard would certainly get Michael's attention, she decided to be more mature. No blowing things up. No waltzing into his party to shock him.

But damn, it would've been fun.

A glance at her watch showed that it was already 5:15. Michael would be home in minutes. She could watch him, at least. Get a naughty glimpse of him as he pulled up, completely unaware that she was hiding. That would be wicked enough to tide her over, surely. And if he walked down to the mailbox before he went inside, she'd wave him over. A tiny reminder to this man that she could be bad if she wanted but she'd be good because she loved him.

Chuckling, she dug a nail file from her purse and shaped her nails. Then she read through a gold-panning adventure brochure she'd picked up somewhere along the way. She ignored the last of the pregnancy pamphlets in the back seat. When the small of her back began to ache from sitting so long, she leaned her seat back a little and tried to relax.

The clock ticked past 5:20. Then 5:30.

By the time it was 5:45, Donna felt fury start to build.

The street ahead of her was as quiet as it had been before. No cars parked at the curb, no pedestrians carried covered dishes, no music or chatter cut through the silence.

There was no barbecue, and there was no Michael. That bastard.

Heart aching, Donna started the car and took off toward Lucky's, aware that she knew so little about this man that she had only one clue to follow.

By the time she arrived, the lot was overflowing, but she persisted and eventually found Michael's car parked in a dirt square behind the back doors.

Angry tears burned her eyes. She should just leave. Drive away and keep driving, never even give him an explanation.

But hadn't she just decided to be brave and honest? To risk her heart and speak the truth and live with whatever happened?

Donna parked her car in the fire lane directly in front of his sedan and got out.

As she rounded the building to get to the front, broken glass glinted far too brightly in the dimming evening sun. She was warm and thirsty, and her head seemed too light on her neck. When she made it to the front, she had to blink the disorienting rays of sun out of her dry eyes. Maybe that doctor had been right. Maybe she was too old for this baby.

Of course, she'd been a high-risk girl her whole life. It made sense that her pregnancy would be the same.

She opened the door and walked into the blessedly cool dimness, but the smell of old beer turned her stomach, forcing her to swallow down acid. By the time that had passed, her eyes had adjusted, and she blinked around at the crowded tables, assuming she'd spot Michael right away. There was no sign of him.

Turning left, then right, she eyed each table to be sure she hadn't missed him. Once she'd finished screening everyone in sight, she had the strength to move toward the bar that squatted in the middle of the huge square space.

Two male bartenders worked the drinks, but all the servers she spotted were women in tiny shorts and tight shirts, and ninety percent of the patrons were male. It wasn't a strip club but seemed only one step removed. Even as Donna watched, someone at a table slapped a server on her ass. The woman winced, but she pasted on a smile as she scolded him. His friends hooted like approving monkeys excited by his display of aggression. None of them were Michael, thank God.

Donna glided forward, feet numb as if she were walking through cold water. No Michael at the bar. But there were tables on the far side of the barstools, so she pushed through.

"Hey, sweet cheeks!" a man called as she passed. She ignored him, not even bothering to give him the finger, which was a real sign of just how weary she was.

And then she saw him. Michael was seated at a small table next to the swinging kitchen door, and he wasn't alone. One of the servers sat next to him, perched at the very edge of the chair as if she meant to hop up at any moment. Their heads were close together, his dark blond, hers glossy brunette with thick waves adding inches to her height, which looked to be somewhere around five feet.

As Donna watched, the girl—who must have been twenty-one but didn't look it—threw her head back with a laugh and then hopped up to her feet, grabbing a tray she'd set down on the table. Michael grinned up at her, all easy charm. Just flirting. Wasn't he always flirting? He was a naughty boy, and he liked to be teased for it. Liked her to call him an asshole. Liked to know he was treading the line but would still be forgiven.

But it wasn't just flirting when he reached out for the hand of the girl. She was turning away, stepping toward the kitchen, but at his touch she paused and swung back with a glowing smile. It wasn't flirting when he tugged her back down and planted a kiss on her cheek only a hairsbreadth away from the corner of her lips. She playfully swatted his arm, laughing again, laughing because he was so funny and cute and attractive. Laughing like he was *hers*. Then she returned the kiss, her mouth touching his this time for a moment that stretched on far too long.

Her heart split and her mind twisted in broken fury. Donna had let herself fall, and this bastard wasn't going to catch her.

She lost it.

Charging across the room, she reached Michael just as the waitress disappeared through the kitchen door, safely beyond Donna's grasp. But Michael wasn't, and she hit his shoulder at full speed with both open palms.

"Hey!" he yelled as his beer flew across the table and into the wall. "What the—?" But then his gaze rose and his eyes went wide. "Donna!"

"Yes, it's Donna, your pregnant girlfriend. Remember me, Michael? Or are you too busy with your face buried in some other chick's tits to recall who I am?"

"Hey, calm down. What's up with you?"

"What's up with me? I just watched you kiss another woman. That's what's up with me. A wife and one whore not enough for you, Michael? You need more than that?"

His eyes darted past her, looking quickly to her right and left.

She glanced wildly around at the nearby tables, finding all eyes on her. "Are you worried that I'm causing a scene? Because if you're not *sure* I'm causing a scene, I'm obviously not doing enough. So to be clear . . ." She raised her voice. *"Fuck you, you cheater!"*

The door to the kitchen swung open, and there she was, the girl he'd kissed. Her dark clouds of shining hair. Her tiny, tan waist exposed beneath the frayed edge of the shirt that hugged perfectly round breasts.

"I'm pregnant, bitch," Donna snapped. "So enjoy the ride until he loses everything to a divorce *and* child-support payments, because they're both coming down the line at full speed."

She swung back to Michael and shouted, "It's over!" right into his face, watching her spittle land on his cheek from her screaming.

And then she spun. Or the world spun. Neon flew by in beautiful streaks. A glass smashed. Someone shouted, "Hey!" And then the floor floated high and turned fuzzy gray, and she felt numb relief.

CHAPTER 11

LAUREN

Her grandmother hadn't said a word about a cellar, and Lauren wondered if it had been here so long everyone had forgotten about it. Even her mom had never mentioned it in her wild ravings about the house or the cabin or the spooky hills. Lauren carried junk out of the shed, clearing a path to the door in the ground, excited that she might find family heirlooms.

"I might need a lantern," she murmured to herself, adding another mental note to the list. She'd need a big flashlight too.

She knew it was likely just a filthy square of dirt where her great-grandparents had once stored canned goods, but what if it was an actual cellar with artifacts and keepsakes? Maybe there was even old furniture down there from the original homesteaders. Or a hundred-year-old wedding dress!

A stupid fantasy, as those things were all likely to be stored in the house instead. Still, she was having fun.

She'd checked her comments to look for that one special name, and for the first time she saw it in real time. Bastian was watching and had chimed in. *I think you should stay aboveground, Lauren!*

She laughed with giddy delight and made a mental note to touch up her lip gloss before restarting.

Her phone buzzed as she left the shed. Be careful down there! Bastian had texted. Grinning, Lauren put her phone away. Bastian could sit tight and watch with everyone else as she played sexy adventurer.

After gathering supplies, she ditched her sweater for a cute T-shirt, and she wrapped a bandana around her head to keep out any cobwebs . . . and whatever might have made them.

"All right, friends, who's ready to explore?" she asked when she fired up the feed. "I've been reading your comments, and I don't think there's an old mine down there, and probably not D. B. Cooper's skeleton either, but you never know."

She picked up the sledgehammer and sent a wild grin toward her viewers. "I am really starting to love this thing. Everyone should get one! I feel so badass." With one last nod for the camera, she took a step back and made a mighty swing.

The lock flew right off the door along with a few pieces of wood that clattered into the boxes she'd shoved against a wall. "That'll probably be okay," she said as she awkwardly picked up the phone in her gloved hand and aimed it down.

"This is it. Big reveal number two of the day! I already scored a wheelbarrow, so I'm holding out for a treasure chest this time."

Lauren took a deep breath, reached down for the edge of the door, and flung it wide open. It crashed into the wooden crate next to it so hard that she jumped. No bats flew out, thank God.

Laughing, she grabbed the flashlight and clicked it on. "Whoa." A set of stairs descended into blackness, so steep they were more like a ladder. "I guess this is our invitation to come on in. The wood looks solid."

Still, she didn't have a death wish, so she leaned farther down and swept the light in a wider arc before inserting her feet into the dark maw. She could see the bottom of the stairs, a dirt floor, and then the first surprise: an old wooden chair. "What's that?" she whispered.

Her throat went a little dry with nervousness. "Uh." She needed water, but that was the one supply she'd neglected to bring, and now she was choking on dust and the dead air floating up from this room.

She leaned farther forward, toward the hole, and those few inches of movement revealed more. The stark wooden chair looked like the kind you'd steal from a kitchen set, but next to it sat a folding lawn chair, a couple of the woven plastic straps broken and hanging limply from the frame.

"Just some old furniture, so far," she managed to say, blinking back her strange anxiety as her mother's old paranoia crept up like a ghost. "And is that a smashed beer can? Hold on one second. Bear with me," she murmured as she twisted to put her knees to the ground; then she dipped her toe down, searching for a solid place beneath her.

It was simple once she got going. One foot after the other, firm wood beneath her toes. Nine steps and her foot touched solid dirt, the sound scraping through the dark space around her.

As soon as both feet were planted, she whirled, light high and phone up. All her breath left her in a whoosh of shock, relief, laughter. "What the hell?" she yelled as soon as she'd gasped in another breath. "Look at that!"

The entire wall in front of her was lined with stacked beer cans, silvery and glinting in the beam of the flashlight. Lauren giggled. Then she laughed so hard she snorted. "You guys! I think I found my dad's teenage beer stash!"

She took a step toward the wall and accidentally kicked a free can with her shoe. It skittered away with a ping. "If I find old porn magazines down here, I'm going to lose it."

Turning slowly, she highlighted the rest of the space with her flashlight. The room was small, only about eight by eight. An old kerosene lamp hung from a rafter, and a large black radio sat on an upturned milk crate. The wall behind her was lined with shelves instead of beer cans, a few jars of old canned beans still perched there, along with some yellowed paperbacks. She wanted to go closer to see the books, but she feared if she touched them they would dissolve into piles of dust and silverfish.

No stacks of nudie mags appeared in the beam of her flashlight, but there was a poster tacked to one side of the shelf. It was a girl with huge feathered hair wearing nothing but skimpy bikini bottoms, white heels, and ice-blue eye shadow. Her hands clasped her naked breasts, covering them from view.

"Oh boy," she breathed, shaking her head. "I really do hope that's as risqué as it gets down here."

The only other thing worth noting in the whole space was a cooler, no big surprise there. The top was missing, revealing nothing but a white rectangle littered with dead bugs.

"Well, for anyone who guessed secret beer bash clubhouse, you're the big winner today. I don't think I'm going to find any antiques down here, unless someone really adventurous wants to try forty-year-old pickled green beans. But maybe I could make some Botox out of the juice."

She laughed at her own joke, but she was really laughing with relieved joy that she'd dodged the ghost of her mother once again. Those seeds of doubt had been planted deep, in the rich soil of her growing brain, and no matter how many times she pulled the weeds, they reappeared. Stubby and parched, but still alive and waiting to be revived.

"I'll try to catch up on the comments this afternoon. Right now I really need a shower. Thank you so much for keeping me company in the haunted cellar, everyone. Share your own creepy house stories in the comments. I'd love to read them."

Lauren signed off, then approached the wooden chair and lowered herself gingerly into it. "Jesus," she muttered, wiping a hand over her sweating brow. She picked up the beer can she'd kicked to check for a date somewhere in the type.

"Busch beer," she murmured. If she remembered correctly, it had been a favorite among frat boys on a budget when she was in college. She could vividly imagine her dad down here as a teenager, listening to a baseball game and sneaking beers with his friends, completely out of sight and sound of his mother, nestled in a cool, hidden cave in the heat of the summer.

The space was grim and desperate, dirt floor and rock walls, and a ceiling that stood barely more than six feet tall, but boys weren't very discerning at that age. Especially if there was beer involved.

Lauren tipped her head back and caught sight of something pale on one of the ceiling beams. She squinted and stood, aiming the light higher. It was a white oval sticker sealed to the dark piece of wood. It read, *Property of,* and the name MaryEllen was printed carefully in a child's hand. An old girlfriend?

A sweep of the light revealed two more stickers, one a pink heart and the other a blue cupcake. They were obviously very old, the colors faded to dull pastel, even here away from the sun.

Lauren climbed halfway up the stairs to grab the lantern from the edge of the doorway; then she hopped down and turned it on high to get a better view of the room. The space was mostly bare aside from a wooden beam in the middle that helped hold up the ceiling.

She circled the room, eyeing the walls, the ceiling, the shelves. It looked like something out of a horror movie, sure, but not because of the contents.

Lauren was turning back toward the stairs when the lantern light caught the center beam and dragged a shadow across something gouged into the wood. She moved closer and held the light as close to the beam as she could. There in the wood she saw the rough scratches form into something almost legible. Squinting, she tilted her head up a little and saw it.

ME WAS HERE
NO BOYS ALLOWED
4-25-61

The inscription was followed by a crooked little heart. ME? MaryEllen?

Her dad had only been twelve in 1961, but he must have known who would've been down here before he'd used the space to party in his teens.

She couldn't wait to tease him about his beer-can collection. And to ask him about MaryEllen.

Lauren took a picture of the wall of cans before packing up and climbing out of the cellar. She wanted to text her dad right away, but in the interest of safety, she first carefully closed the access door and tested to be sure it was still sound. The wood seemed hard and solid, but she still piled a few boxes on the door to keep herself from walking on it. Just in case.

After removing the dusty bandana and swiping at her clothes, she sat down at the rickety picnic table and sent the picture to her father. Dad, what the heck???

She barely had time to remember how thirsty she was before he wrote back with a laughing face. I totally forgot about that! Now you know all my secrets, pumpkin!

I am not going to ask how old you were when you started that wall.

Please don't.

The original man cave, she texted back, and got another laughing emoji in return. Lauren smiled so hard her cheeks hurt. Just a heads-up, your secrets are now immortalized on my social media.

Thanks for the warning. Glad my kids are under parental block on our home internet. I wouldn't want them to see that.

She cringed a little. Sorry, Daddy. Do you want me to take it down?

No, it's fine. Maybe once they get to be teenagers, though. We'll see.

Her smile faded. Oops. She hadn't thought about that at all. Maybe she'd take down the video in a few days. She didn't want him upset.

At least Grandma doesn't watch! she texted back. A few minutes later she received only a thumbs-up in response and deflated a little. She recognized the way he drifted away from their text conversations.

Hey, one more thing, she responded, hoping to draw him back in. Who's MaryEllen? After a few minutes passed, she tried again. I saw her name down there. Was she a neighbor or something? Maybe even a CRUSH???

Her screen finally lit up with a response. Ha. Sorry, pumpkin, gotta go. Text later.

She sighed, defeated. It wasn't that she was jealous of her half siblings. They were good kids, if a bit spoiled. She just wanted a little piece of his delight too. But his attention was divided in so many ways now. And even if the physical distance wasn't a thousand miles, it was enough that when her brother and sister had been small, Lauren had visited only once a month. She felt more like an aunt than anything, and not even a favorite aunt. Suki's sister played that role. Now they mostly treated Lauren like an obligation, calling to offer polite thank-yous for her gifts.

But that was on her. She was the adult, and she couldn't figure out how to wedge her strange square into the circle of his new world.

Finally, feeling guilty about her own neediness, she wrote, Love you, Dad.

After five minutes of waiting for a response, Lauren gave up and trudged inside for water.

CHAPTER 12

DONNA

"Baby. Wake up."

Donna waved an irritated hand and turned her face into the warmth she rested against. "Mm," she hummed. The warmth smelled like Michael, the clean, spicy scent of him snuggled right against her.

"Donna? Are you all right, sweetheart?"

It *was* Michael. She so rarely got to spend a night with him, so she grinned into his shirt and smooshed her nose against him. "I'm fine," she murmured, luxuriating in the way his body supported her. The couch was uncomfortable, and her back ached from sleeping on it, but what fun they'd had before they'd dozed off.

She shifted around, her hand brushing leather, and she realized she wasn't on her couch. She wasn't in her apartment.

Nausea rolled up her gut, pressing against her throat, and she sat up in sudden alarm that it might escape. She threw out a desperate hand to grab on to anything solid as the world slid under her body. Her head spun a little, but mostly it hurt, pounding in time to her pulse. When her hand caught leather again, she frowned. "What happened?"

"You fainted. Are you sick? Is the baby okay? Should I take you to the hospital?"

Frowning, she looked around her. They were in the back seat of her car, the door still open, a Styrofoam cup in Michael's hand.

"The bartender gave me water. Do you—?"

Mouth dry as an LA sidewalk, she snatched the cup from him and downed the whole thing in four long swallows. "More," she demanded, thrusting the cup back at him, pressing it to his chest.

"Okay," he agreed, but his face twisted with concerned doubt. "But maybe the hospital first?"

"I don't need a hospital."

"But the baby . . ."

"It's fine or it's not fine. It's a little early for me to give birth to a preemie, Michael. I just got dehydrated or exhausted or fucking overwrought. Get me—" But then she looked toward the ugly concrete wall of the bar and the one dim lightbulb over the metal door of the employee entrance, and she remembered everything.

She took the cheap cup from his hand, and this time she threw it hard at his chest. Regrettably it was far too light to hurt him. The white Styrofoam bounced off his body and ricocheted off the seat in front of him to roll out the door and onto the gravel.

"Where's your little girlfriend, Michael? Didn't you bring her out here to help *manage* me?"

He sighed. Sighed as if he were the one who was weary and put upon. As if *she'd* done something wrong instead of him, him, him. "She's not my girlfriend, Donna. I barely know her."

"I saw you kiss her, so save your asshole excuses, you lying piece of shit. I've given you every benefit of the doubt, and this—" She tossed a hand toward the back of the bar. "This!"

"Donna . . . ," he started, but then his face crumpled, and he shook his head, and she realized he was crying. Real tears welled in his eyes and spilled down his cheeks as his nose and eyes went red. "I'm sorry. I screwed up. I know I did. I've just really been struggling. I didn't want to tell you. I was scared, and . . ."

"Tell me what?" she spit out.

"My wife is . . ." His hand floated up, turning, gesturing toward the whole world before he scrubbed it through his hair. "I don't know."

"Your *wife*," Donna said, stretching out the word, "seemed really nice when I talked to her."

"What?" His head snapped up. "What are you saying? You *talked* to her?"

"Yes."

"What did you tell her?"

"Not much. I introduced myself. She thinks I'm your new neighbor, so she's happy to chat with me anytime I drop by for a cup of sugar."

"Why the hell would you do that?" he shouted. "Why would you risk everything?"

"Because I don't know what to believe anymore, Michael! I feel like I'm going crazy! Why are you still there? And why . . . ?" Her throat closed on sorrow as she gestured helplessly toward the bar.

He stared at her for a long moment, eyes wide with shock. She studied him right back and waited to see what kind of fairy tale fiction he'd spin.

But then Michael finally looked away and shook his head, and his shoulders slumped. "I've been coming here after work. Drinking too much. I admit that. I don't want to go home, and I don't want to lie to you, so . . . I'm sorry. I hate going home, so I was coming here to get drunk, and when I get drunk I flirt, and I'm really sorry about that. It won't happen again."

"You don't want to lie to me about what?" she pressed.

"What?"

"You said you don't want to go home and you don't want to lie to me. What are you saying?"

"Shit." He scrubbed a hand through his hair and drew in a long, hissing breath through his teeth. "I don't know how to do this. That's what I'm saying. I want to be with you. It's all I want. But I can't figure out how to do it."

"It's really not complicated. You go to your wife, tell her you're leaving, and then you leave. The end."

"It's not that simple."

"You're not God's gift to women, Michael. She'll survive. There's not even custody to arrange. Stop jerking her around. Stop jerking *me* around!"

"I don't have any money," he blurted out, the words tumbling over themselves to fall at her feet with a thud. "We're in debt up to our eyeballs. If we divorce, I'll still be in debt plus I'll have to pay for a second home and pay her alimony too."

Oh no. Donna shook her head. "It can't be that bad. You have a great job. You're a VP."

"I have a good job, but I don't work for Wall Street or a petroleum company. It's agriculture. I make a decent living, but we have a nice house, two cars, a time share. There were fertility treatments. So many fertility treatments. Do you know how expensive those are? And when the treatments didn't take, we tried to distract ourselves with travel. We went to Europe and Mexico. We—"

"That's why you haven't left her? Because of money?"

"No! What I told you is true. She's fragile. She had a breakdown. She's been seeing a psychiatrist for years, and believe me, that isn't cheap either."

"And your solution to all this is to hang out at bars and screw around with cocktail waitresses?" she screamed.

Michael held up both hands. "No. Of course not. I just didn't know what to do, and I was stressed. I started drinking. I behaved badly, I'm sorry. I didn't know how to tell you about any of this. I wanted to develop a solution first and then present it to you. I'm sorry, Donna. I love you. I love this baby. I will figure this out."

She didn't know what to say. Her head pounded. Her tongue grew thick with thirst again. "Please just . . . get me another glass of water."

He bolted from the car as soon as he was given release to flee, and Donna watched him go with tears in her eyes. What the hell was she going to do?

He might break her heart, she could feel the bruises on it already, but she'd thought the one thing she could count on from him was financial stability for their child. He'd seemed to have it all, the nice, dependable father figure she would have chosen for herself if she could have.

She looked up to see him returning, a tentative smile stealing over his handsome face. "I should have told you before," he said as he handed her the cup. "I feel so much better being honest with you. Getting it off my chest."

"Yeah well, I don't feel better, Michael. I quit my job. I left my place. And now I need to find an expensive doctor who specializes in ancient births, apparently."

"What does that mean?" His eyes flew wide with alarm as hers filled with ridiculous tears.

"It means I'm considered a high-risk pregnancy because I'm not as young as your girlfriend in there, that's what."

"Let me take you to the hospital just in case."

"I'm fine," she said, sipping the water so her leaking eyes wouldn't progress to full-on sobbing. "I was running around all day, that's all. God." She swiped at a tear and turned her glare on him. "I thought I could believe in you. In us. I'm so fucking stupid. What the hell am I even doing here?"

He clasped her hands and pressed his forehead to hers. "Please don't say that. I screwed up. I know I did. But when I saw you faint, when I carried you out here and held you, wondering if I should call an ambulance or take you to the ER or just let you rest . . . Christ, Donna."

"I'm fine," she snapped.

"I'm glad. But that moment I thought I might lose you, lose our baby . . . That was it. It's all so crystal clear." His fingers eased down to curve over her belly. "I don't give a damn about the house or the cars. This is my family. And I need to do whatever it takes to make this happen. I *will* do whatever it takes. Just give me a few more days. I have an idea."

"What does that even mean? The only idea you need is to find the balls to get a divorce."

"Trust me?" he asked.

"Oh, fuck no," she muttered, hating that she wanted to.

He had the nerve to laugh. "All right. Then don't trust me, but give me a few days to prove myself."

"Why?" she asked.

"Because if it works out, we'll be together forever."

Damn him. Damn him straight to hell, because her stupid little bruised heart thumped hard in response. Together forever. A family. A place. A home.

She thought she'd left all that behind long ago, and good riddance to it. But it seemed there'd been a home-shaped gash in her chest for all these years. A terrible yearning for the family she could vaguely pull from her earliest memories. Before her mother was so tired and her dad so quick to explode. Before they'd both lost all their hopes and dreams.

"One more chance," she whispered. "One more, and then I'm out of here, and I'll let you know where to send the checks, but that will be the extent of your involvement in this child's life. Got it?"

"You won't regret this," he whispered back, his lips against her hair.

But she knew she would, and she told herself she was ready for the pain.

CHAPTER 13

LAUREN

Lauren had gotten another call from her mom while she was in the shower. When she glimpsed the missed-call alert, she groaned.

She couldn't hate her mother, despite everything. She knew she'd lived a tough life. She'd run away because of an abusive dad, and she'd had to make her own way in the world. It had always seemed to Lauren that her mom had just . . . *lost* herself somewhere on her journey. She'd been empty somehow. Aimless. Hollowed out. Tired and overworked and worried.

If she'd ever been someone else, Lauren had never known that woman. She'd made occasional mention of the paintings she'd created before. Before Lauren, before her father. But Lauren had seen no sign of artistry growing up. There'd been no space to store canvases in their tiny apartments, no square footage for art. No room in their shitty cars for transporting painting supplies during their frequent moves. And definitely no money for something so impractical as acrylics or watercolors.

And what would Donna have painted, anyway? Scene after scene of smoky bars and drunks hunched over their beers? Views from a tiny window of a dumpster or the backs of other apartments? Maybe a still life of slot machines?

Her mom's life had been working every night, getting Lauren off to school in the morning, then starting the whole cycle over again after waking up around 2:00 p.m. to head back to work. She'd kept the house clean and brought home groceries. She'd bought Lauren a new pair of jeans and cheap sneakers once a year and taken her to Goodwill to shop for the rest. She had *provided*. She had. Lauren knew that alone made her luckier than some.

But there'd been no vibrancy, barring the occasional night off when her mom might invite a couple of friends over to drink and smoke and laugh uproariously at jokes Lauren had been too young to understand.

She'd never abused Lauren. Her mother had kept her safe and alive, and Lauren had been fine. It was just that her childhood had been mostly . . . gray. One struggle after another. The only sparkle in her world had been that broken glass on every street outside every apartment they'd lived in.

The grayness was a hanging shroud because her mother had honestly been haunted. In the early years, Lauren had known why. Her father had been a monster, and Donna had saved Lauren from a life with him.

She'd turned him in to the police for murder, and she'd run from that awful past so that she could keep herself and her baby safe. Who wouldn't be tormented by the terror she'd fled?

I never thought I'd have to do this alone, she'd repeated so many times. A mantra. Michael had been a wolf in sheep's clothing. A murderer disguised as a loving boyfriend.

He'd also been a married man, and even as a young kid, Lauren had wondered how anyone could think a married man was a good boyfriend. Those two things didn't go together. Shouldn't her streetwise mother have known better? Been on guard?

After age ten she'd realized that her mother had been haunted by something very different from what she'd always claimed. She'd been haunted by the truth of what she'd done. Her own lies. The lies that had started as an explosion, with blows that rippled out, on and on, disturbing Lauren's world with every passing wave. The ramifications gentled as time went on, like all ripples do, but they still affected the whole family to this day. Nothing would ever be normal between mother and daughter. It couldn't be.

Her phone chimed, and Lauren saw there was a voicemail that had probably been delayed by the poor connection. She put her wet hair up in a towel and slumped onto the couch, still cozy in her thick terrycloth robe.

"Lauren," her mom's voice said, "I'm sorry."

Lauren blinked hard. She hadn't heard that from her mother very often in her life. One of the layers of her defenses had been to employ aggression in the face of doubt.

"I really am sorry. I shouldn't have argued with you. Please call me. I had some good news to share, and I wanted to reach out with something happy and . . . well, I obviously got off track, and I apologize for that."

Wow. An apology *and* the promise of good news? That was a rare offer, indeed. Unheard of, really. Her mom had actually sounded normal for once. Not agitated and not drunk. Just . . . calm. A little tired, sure, but calm and maybe contrite.

Certain that she would regret it, Lauren decided to take a leap of faith. She pulled in a deep breath, nodded to herself, and returned the call. "Hi, Mom," she said simply.

"Lauren! Thank you for calling me back, honey. I shouldn't have . . . well, I shouldn't have gotten so upset. I shouldn't have said those things. I let my temper get the better of me."

"Wow. I guess . . . thank you for apologizing?"

"Are you okay?" There was a little worry in her voice now, a hint of panic even, but Lauren tried to let it go as her mother continued. "I just want to know that you're okay. That's all."

"I am."

"Good. Good. I'm, um . . . I'm actually not too far away from you now. Just in case you need me, you know? I'm in Tahoe. A quick drive from where you are."

Tahoe. Lots of casinos there. Lots of work. They'd lived there for nine months once. But her mom was seventy now. She had arthritis. She coughed. Sadness seeped through Lauren at the thought of her still working long hours serving drinks. "It's beautiful there," she finally said. "Where are you working?"

"Oh, I retired! Got my full Social Security benefit, and I decided that was good enough for me. All those years of paying taxes finally paid off, and my feet hurt too damn much to keep working, anyway."

Relief rushed through Lauren on a sharp breath. "That's wonderful, Mom! I'm so happy for you! You honestly sound great. It seems like retirement has been awesome for you."

"It is. I feel good. That was why I was calling, actually. Well, I was meaning to call, and then when I heard . . . I guess we won't talk about that. Things have been pretty nice, otherwise."

"You have a place?"

"Oh sure. I'm living in a small house outside town. Gorgeous view of the mountains, if you lean far enough."

She really did sound good. Clear and settled. "Did you stop drinking?" she asked, and that was a mistake. She could practically hear her mother stiffen through the phone.

"No, Lauren, I didn't stop drinking. The drinking wasn't ever the problem. It was my work and my hours and my whole damn life after—" She cut herself off with a curse, which in itself was an improvement. In the past she'd never bothered reining herself in when she got riled up. This was progress, Lauren told herself.

"Anyway," she started again. "Whatever. I did drink too much once you left. I was terrified. I'd failed you. I just . . . Anyway, I've tried to give up so much worrying, so now I don't need to drink to get to sleep at night. I learned a little meditation."

"Meditation?"

"It's something that Oscar is into. Oscar is . . . Well, Lauren, the truth is that I went and got married."

Lauren's jaw dropped. Married? Her mom sounded almost embarrassed when she said it, which made it seem real. During her childhood, she'd never even known her mom to date. And she'd always spoken of marriage as something only idiots would do. *If you want to fool yourself into thinking love lasts more than a year, much less forever, please be my guest. I guess you'd just better hope he's not a goddamn murderer, and best of luck to you, you optimistic asshole.*

And now she was *married*? "Mom. Wow. Congratulations?" That came out as a question, which she hadn't meant.

"It was no big deal. We went to the courthouse. Better tax rate and all that. Plus we have to think about Social Security death benefits. We're both old as hell. May as well pass our benefits to each other." She laughed. "Whoever goes first, anyway. You know what I mean."

"His name is Oscar? What's he like?"

"Nice. He's real nice, actually."

Tears pricked her eyes at the softness in her mom's words. She'd always been such a hard shell, hollow and knocking around, all her softness dried out long before Lauren had known her. Maybe she was gentling again. Letting that shell crack. Maybe she could find some peace for herself after all. "That's great, Mom."

"He was a trucker. I worked at a diner a few years ago, and that's how we met. He's quiet and steady. Easy to get along with. Plus he puts up with me, and he likes dogs. Likes to fish too."

Dogs. They'd never had a pet. Pets cost too much to care for, and landlords didn't like them. After Lauren had moved in with her dad, she'd never even asked him about a pet. He hadn't been a dog person, and he curled his lip at cats, and she had done her very best to fit silent and seamless into his life. Asking for a pet would have made him frown, and she hated to make him frown.

But now her mom had dogs and a husband and a little house in the mountains. How strange life could be. All Lauren's childhood dreams come true at long last. But Lauren wasn't part of them. "Do you fish?" she asked in surprise.

"I do now," her mom said. "It's quiet out there. I like that."

Lauren couldn't imagine her mom sitting quietly in nature, but everyone changed with time.

"I was thinking . . . ," her mom started before fading into a questioning silence.

"Yes?"

"Since you're back up north and I'm only two hours away . . . maybe we could meet in the middle somewhere. Get a cup of coffee. Or lunch. There's that place with the wooden bear on top just off the highway, do you know it?"

"No," she said, though it sparked a vague memory.

"Well, I just thought . . . it'd be good to see you. It's been three years."

More like four, actually, since they'd seen each other in person. "Things are pretty busy here . . ." She stared hard at the dead rectangle of the television. Stared until she realized she was looking at her own reflection. Then she closed her eyes.

"I . . . Look, Lauren. I didn't lie. I didn't. I have no idea what happened, but I didn't lie about him."

"Mom—"

"But maybe I was wrong. I don't know. Maybe I mixed something up or I was so scared that my memory betrayed me. I can't say. I really can't. I've thought about it so many times that maybe I don't have any real memories left. It's been thirty-five years . . ."

Lauren was always clear on exactly how long it had been because she could never forget her own age. Thirty-five years since her mother had sat on that stand and testified that he'd confessed to the murder. *He told me he did it,* she'd said to the jury. *He said it was an accident. That things got out of control. He thought he could tell me and I'd help him. Maybe because of this.*

She could picture perfectly her mother gesturing at the huge, taut mound of the baby beneath her voluminous, flowered maternity dress. She could picture it because she had seen photos. Her mother younger and round-faced in a way Lauren had never seen her. Her cheeks full and flushed. She'd looked like an angel. Younger than thirty-five. More like a twenty-year-old still softened with baby fat.

But the baby fat had been Lauren's, not her mother's, and Donna's face had drained into a long, lean mask after that, hardened with wariness.

"Maybe the pregnancy," her mother said into her ear. "They say you get forgetful and scatterbrained, and I was high risk. Advanced maternal age! Can you believe that? Advanced maternal age at thirty-five. I'll never forget them telling me that."

Lauren winced. She still wanted kids. Was thirty-five considered old these days? It didn't seem like it. Women had careers. They had whole lives before they settled down. But she had been very aware of forty looming for a while now.

"Maybe I was wrong," her mother said again, each word quieter than the last. "I don't see how I was, but maybe." She'd never even approached the idea of fault before. Not once. Not to Lauren, at least.

Lauren's eyes burned, then her throat. "Okay, Mom," she managed to choke out. "Okay. Coffee sometime. Or lunch. That would be nice."

The tiniest gasp traveled through the phone. One soft inhalation. "All right," her mom said. "Lunch. Let me talk to Oscar. See when he needs the car."

"Great. I've got a couple of deadlines this week, so maybe next week?"

"That sounds great," her mom answered.

And it was done. After she hung up, Lauren dried her hair and got dressed, feeling strangely buoyant. She floated through the next hour, doing a few chores. Then she caught up on her online comments.

People seemed to find her funny, and that felt unexpected. She'd always been self-conscious in groups and mostly stayed quiet at parties. She did best one-on-one, losing herself in conversation, and maybe that was the benefit of these videos. She wasn't talking to a crowd. She was having a conversation with an individual. With that one person sitting at home watching her.

She signed off with a grin, though exhaustion was beginning to drag her down. It had been quite an eventful day, but she felt *good*. Really good. Now she needed to put in some hours on an actual paying job.

She stood and stretched, then slid on flip-flops to walk down to the mailbox to wake herself up.

For the first time since it had happened, she didn't think about that letter. She didn't walk down the hill with tension, didn't narrow her eyes when she reached for the crooked metal door, which made the blow that much more brutal when she pulled the pile of mail free and saw the white envelope on top of the stack, the blank paper glaring its threat.

"No," she whispered, but the envelope stayed solid and real in her hand, waiting patiently for her to open it if she dared.

CHAPTER 14

DONNA

Donna wiped her forehead with a shaky hand and stepped back to get a wider view of her work in progress. She hadn't meant to start this painting. Hadn't intended to capture this woman's pain, but maybe it was easier to put the pain on Carol's face than on her own.

Michael's wife glared at her from the canvas, mouth stretched wide, throat straining, her skin mottled with blues and whites and blacks. The brushstrokes were wide and wild enough that even Michael wouldn't recognize this twisted face, but Donna knew who it was. And it was vibrant and bitter enough that she might even be able to sell it for a decent amount.

Her work had gotten tamer in recent years, the anger from her earlier life squeezed out to a trickle. But this. This was alive and real.

If only she had contacts here. Perhaps she could start making the rounds, meeting dealers. But then she had a better idea. She still knew artists in San Francisco. One of her young street friends had even grown up to own a successful gallery near Union Square. He'd always been a hustler, so she wasn't surprised.

When her phone rang, she picked it up idly, still staring at her work.

"Have you been calling my house?" Michael demanded when she said hello.

"What? Why would I?"

"For the same reason you talked to my wife yesterday."

Donna waved a hand even though he couldn't see it. "She's not my enemy, Michael. You are. You asked for one more chance, and I'm giving it to you."

He sighed into the phone, and she heard a soft shush as if he were rubbing a hand over his face. "I'm sorry. Carol says someone called the house three times today and hung up."

"Probably just kids. It wasn't me. Are you coming over tonight?"

"I have to drive out to my mother's."

"Your mother's? I thought she lived here in Sacramento."

"She's a ways out of town. I told you I grew up on a ranch."

Donna laughed. "Right. For some reason I can't picture you on a horse."

"Shows what you know," he said, a smile in his voice. "My sister and I could ride before we could walk."

"I'd honestly pay a lot of money to see that. I bet you look cute as hell as a cowboy."

"You will see it," he promised.

She let herself smile for one wistful moment, hoping it was true.

"I need to make a few phone calls," he said, the words trailing off into a distracted goodbye. "I'll see you tomorrow, okay?"

"Going to visit his mother?" she muttered as soon as she got off the phone. Should she trust him? Maybe. But not yet. Love was enough for now. He'd need to build the trust with his own two hands, brick by brick.

There was no question he'd still been at work despite that it was after five. She'd heard the familiar background noise of distant ringing phones and clacking typewriters past his closed office door. But something in his tone had been off. Too tense over a few hang-up calls.

She stood and paced, telling herself to let it go. He was at work and stressed, and to be fair his mistress *had* introduced herself to his wife the day before. She barked out a laugh at that, half proud and half embarrassed.

Should she trust him? Was that so dangerous?

It felt dangerous. It felt like risking her whole life, plus another. And what could it hurt to check up on him? She wouldn't let him know.

Something bright came alive inside her, urging her on. Yes, she could double-check one last time, and if he seemed to be telling the truth, that would be her proof. It would be her point of finding faith and accepting this love he claimed.

There wasn't really a downside. Either she'd discover something and protect herself or she'd find nothing and she could embrace him and their future together.

Buoyed by her own reasoning, she grabbed an orange soda and headed for the car. When she put on some music, it felt almost like a celebration, one last taste of a bad habit before she settled down into contentment.

~

Twenty minutes later, she was parked in the shade and watching Michael emerge from the office, his face drawn into an irritated twist and his eyes cast down. He threw his briefcase into the back seat of his car as if the case had pissed him off; then he slammed the door so hard the crack of it echoed against the building.

She grinned at his bad mood because it was a good sign, wasn't it? This wasn't a man on his way to flirt and party. Maybe he'd had a big argument with his wife. Or maybe he was planning a tough conversation with her.

Donna almost let him go. Almost. But as soon as he turned out of the lot, she changed her mind. She'd hang back and follow him for a few exits to reassure herself he was heading out of town. Then she'd return home and start thinking about baby plans. She'd need things. A stroller and . . . a playpen probably? A crib? Or did she need a cradle? She had no idea. Staying far back to avoid being seen, she followed him toward the freeway.

When he crossed beneath the overpass and kept driving, Donna frowned. By the time he turned into Lucky's bar, she felt numb with confusion. This wasn't right.

It wasn't *right*.

Because despite all her grand protests, she actually had trusted him. She'd only followed him for the proof. The happy, bubbling relief that she'd done something right for once in her life.

Michael pulled around to the back, hiding his car from Donna or his wife or his employees. How could she know how his mind worked? Donna stayed in front, car idling, too dulled to even decide what to do. Follow him in and make another scene? Crouch by his car and slash his tires?

She hadn't done that in quite a while, and the idea of being bad appealed to her. One last go-round before she was sleep deprived and covered in spit-up and utterly on her own. In the olden days, she would have started a vicious fistfight with the girlfriend too, but she'd grown enough to know it wasn't worth it. There was no blame on the girl's head.

Donna parked and grabbed her purse. She'd carried at least a small pocketknife her whole life, unwilling to give up the sense of safety it had granted her on the streets. She also had a Swiss Army thing, gifted to her by a friend, and that had a little knife on it too.

But when she rounded the corner, she pulled up sharply and hustled back behind the wall.

Michael's car wasn't parked. It was idling right next to the employee entrance, the passenger door ajar just a couple of inches. As she peeked around the corner, a hand flashed out from the car and pulled the door closed completely. Then Michael pulled away into the alley, his passenger hidden from view by the high seat back.

But Donna didn't need to see the person riding beside Michael. There was no question who it was.

It didn't hurt yet, but it would. Worse, she couldn't even feel sorry for herself. Of course he was cheating on her. He'd cheated on his wife, and Donna had felt nothing but scorn for that sad woman. She had no right to be surprised now, much less self-pitying. You reap what you sow, and all that bullshit.

There was only one thing to do now. Donna got back in her car and drove straight to Michael's home.

She parked right in his driveway and marched up to ring the doorbell. There was no answer, so she tried again, knocking hard this time.

Nothing.

Fine. She had all the patience in the world tonight.

It was just her now. Her and her baby. Somewhere deep inside, she'd always known it would be.

A half hour later, as numb as she felt, she registered that she was hungry and thirsty. She couldn't wait for someone to take care of her. That wouldn't happen anymore, so she drove away for a brief retreat.

At a gas station, she used the restroom and bought a *Rolling Stone*; then she got herself Jack in the Box tacos and a large 7UP. Once she returned she had a picnic in her lover's driveway, savoring the tacos before she read her magazine. She stayed and she waited.

When they'd started the affair, Michael's wife had been nothing to her, not even a person. That woman had been his past. A blip in history. Since then the image of her had slowly evolved, but it had still been blurry and transparent, a shadow of a woman. After all, he'd explained Carol away as a hated enemy, and he was the one who knew her best.

But Carol wasn't an enemy. She wasn't even the past. And now Donna wondered how Michael was describing his pregnant girlfriend to this new girl. He must've explained away the outburst. *She's crazy. She's obsessed with me. I broke up with her months ago, and now she's deranged and trying to blame her pregnancy on me when I can't possibly be the father.*

And what would happen if he tried to deny it in court? She could get a blood-typing test to show possible paternity, but did she have any other proof at all?

She shook her head at the thought. If he denied paternity, he'd never get to see his child, and she did believe he wanted to be a father. No one was that good a liar.

The sun set, so Donna put her magazine away and got out of the car to stretch her legs. The house stayed dark and silent, and when she checked the garage, both cars were gone. Of course today was the day his wife had decided to leave the house and stay away. Today, when Donna was finally determined to tell her.

Restless now, Donna pulled on a sweater and strolled down the block. It was so quiet here, nothing like any neighborhood she'd ever lived in. Not even a car had passed since nightfall. No corner stores or busy streets nearby offered background noise.

Donna shivered. There were probably foxes and coyotes everywhere here. Maybe bats. Or maybe she was the only predator here, lurking outside a house in the dark, stalking people in the night.

She spun and paced back to his house, and this time she marched right up the front lawn. With a glance over her shoulder to make sure the street was still empty, she eased past a row of bushes and pushed onto her tiptoes for her first glimpse into the life Michael had hidden from her.

The curtains were open, letting in moonlight and strange gazes, as if they had no fear inside these walls. As if nothing bad had ever happened here.

A long couch sat next to a cozy chair and ottoman angled near it. The upholstery colors were lost to gray in the dimness, but Donna imagined something treacly like dusty rose with slate-blue accent pillows.

Magazines had been spread in an artful fan across a coffee table. The only cover she could make out was *Better Homes and Gardens*.

"Jesus Christ," she muttered.

Still, the space wasn't as perfectly neat as she might have imagined. It wasn't a showroom, but a true family space. A worn pair of slippers lay in front of the couch. A book was spread open on the arm of the chair, the clasped lovers giving it away as a romance novel. A glass was abandoned on a side table, and next to it sat something that made Donna frown and tilt her head.

Roses. A vase full of roses. There were at least a dozen, and they seemed to be red, from the dark look of them in the moonlight. Red roses. A thoughtful offering to a wife from her devoted husband.

There was no other explanation for cut red roses in a crystal vase. Michael had brought them to his wife. Perhaps as an apology for all those late nights the past two weeks. The late nights he'd spent with Donna.

He hadn't ever brought her any flowers.

She stared at the night-black roses for a long time before she turned to slide free of the bushes and sit on the front step, too heartbroken to even cry.

She sat on that step until her ass went numb and her back ached. She sat there until she felt she'd go mad. Past 9:00 p.m. Then 10:00. Finally, desperate to warm up her limbs, she stood and hopped in place for a moment.

She wouldn't leave. She was strong enough to finish what she'd started. She'd tell his wife, and that would be the end of this. No more listening to his stupid promises, craving a happy ending like a little girl who'd never finished growing up.

That wasn't who she was, was it? She'd had to grow up quick and early. She'd faced the world down.

Christ, she was no longer sure she even wanted his money, much less his involvement. He didn't deserve this child. He didn't deserve to play happy daddy and generous father.

And she knew he would play that part magnificently. If she let him in at all, he'd swan in once a month or twice a year, dripping gifts and sweets and extravagant affection. He'd play the hero father, long-suffering and shut out by his cruel ex, unable to participate the way he would if she weren't so evil. Donna had seen it over and over again among her divorced friends. Dads playing Santa Claus during every summer break.

She could just leave him in the dust and do her best on her own, whatever her shitty best turned out to be. She felt a frightening tug inside her chest, something important pulling apart, and she pressed a shaking hand there to protect it.

"I can't," she groaned. "I can't, I can't." She wasn't a mother. She was a stray cat. A party girl. A mad artist. The cool friend. She'd always taken pride in exactly who she was. Even if she wanted to do this on her own, she didn't think she could.

Or maybe something magical would wash over her during the birth. She'd hold her wet, wrinkled newborn and be born anew herself, filled with natural instincts and a deep well of maternal nurturing . . . not to mention some mysterious windfall of a few hundred extra bucks a month to cover the new expenses.

"I can't do this," she whispered.

Her numbing fury was finally wearing off. She felt exhausted and overwhelmed with a kind of sadness she hadn't felt since those first days after she'd run away. This was *loss*. She wanted to go home and sleep or paint or cry. Home. Not *here*. Home to her little LA apartment or maybe even home to her squeaky twin bed in her childhood room, knowing that her mom was downstairs warming up Campbell's tomato soup to help her feel better. She'd bring crackers too, and ginger ale. She'd putter around the room, humming peacefully until she heard the family car pull up.

Donna's mom had been a decent mother as long as her husband wasn't home, and wasn't that instructive? Wouldn't Donna have been better off without a father around? She must have learned something about caretaking from her meek, quiet mother. She could just imitate what she remembered of her own childhood. *Fake it until you make it.*

Donna had just decided to throw in the towel and disappear when a yellow light began to glow from far down the road. When the light brightened and focused into the clear beams of headlights, her heart leapt into a rapid beat of panic.

No, she'd changed her mind. She didn't want to confront this woman with the truth. She didn't want to watch pain bloom in her eyes. His wife deserved none of this.

Panicked, she jumped into her car and reached for the ignition, but she'd taken the keys out at some point. She patted her hands along the passenger seat, sliding them over the leather and around her purse. When she slapped the magazine aside, her fingertips finally touched the cold, pointed metal of a key, and she grabbed it tight.

Too late.

The car slowed, then stopped. A moment passed. A dozen heartbeats. Then it carefully pulled in behind her. Donna squeezed the keys until they bit her hand, pricking her with an aching pain.

She'd made a mistake.

But she'd been wheeling and dealing her way out of bad situations her whole life. She'd lived through far worse than this. Adrenaline brightened her up, and she lurched into an idea, tossing open the door of her car.

Donna threw a leg out and surged to her feet, letting herself sway with the motion. She raised a hand into the glare of the headlights and waved her keys. "Hey!" she shouted as the door of the other car opened. "Hey there!" She grinned wildly and stumbled forward, playing drunk and friendly.

She'd had a few too many and gotten confused in this new neighborhood. She'd pulled into the wrong house, and now she just needed a gentle nudge from her neighbor to send her on her way.

The headlights cut off.

"What the hell are you doing?" Michael demanded, his door opening, the interior lights revealing no one else in the car.

Donna let the grin drop, and she snapped as straight as she could, planting her feet wide. "You!" she growled, the fibers pulling again, gaping open to reveal her raw heart. "You worthless piece of shit."

"What are you doing here?" he asked again; then he looked wildly around as if making sure there wasn't a crowd. "Jesus, get inside."

"Inside?" she wondered aloud, but his hand was already on her arm, guiding her toward the door. Or dragging her maybe. She was so confused at being ordered into his house that she let herself be swept up the driveway toward the side door.

"How long have you been here?" he asked. "Who saw you?"

"No one saw me. Where's your wife?"

"She's at her parents' place in Napa." He unlocked the door and pushed her in. "Jesus Christ, you were waiting for *her*? That's why you're here?"

"No, Michael. I'm camped out on your wife's doorstep because I missed you, you lying bastard. *Of course* I'm here to see your wife! How would I know she's away? *You* certainly didn't tell me, did you?"

"I don't fucking need this tonight," he snarled as he shut the door with a crack and snapped on a light. "I don't fucking need this. Do you think I don't have enough going on?"

"*You?*" she screeched. "You think *you* have a lot going on? I'm *pregnant*. At *thirty-five*. With a *married man*. I need to find work. A place to live. A way to support this baby without you, because you're a lying sack of wet shit, Michael. Does that sound like *a lot?*"

Michael threw his hands in the air with a violent groan. "We already talked about this! What the hell are you excited about tonight? Your hormones are out of control here."

Donna saw red. Her head filled with it. Red, pulsing blood screaming for vengeance. She reached for something, anything, and found a hard, cold weight she could heft in her hand. She reared back, watching first disbelief cross his face, then shock, then sweet, sliding fear.

When she whipped her arm forward, Michael ducked, and the vase full of roses shattered against the wall behind him like a bomb. Glass, water, leaves, petals—it exploded into a cloud for a moment; then gravity sucked it all back down in a cascade that crashed to the floor next to Michael's dirt-flecked shoes.

"What the *hell*, Donna?" he screamed.

"I saw you at Lucky's tonight. I saw you pick her up. So don't you ever, *ever* mention my hormones again or I will gut you like a fish and plead momentary insanity in court, you lying monster."

His arrogant sneer disappeared like she'd wiped it clean. For a moment his face became a pale blank. Nothing there. No thought or emotion. Then it melted, sagging down into dismay, his lips pulled at the edges by incredible weight. She was the one sneering now. She was pure, righteous arrogance in the face of his stupid guilt.

"I . . . uh, I did go to Lucky's. You saw me there, yes, but it wasn't what you think."

"Sure it wasn't, Michael."

"Really. I mean it. After that incident—"

"Incident?" she snapped back.

"After you confronted me there, I just needed to wrap it up. To explain, you know? I figured she was the one calling my house, that she'd found me in the phone book. I wanted to tell her I shouldn't have been flirting. I wanted to apologize and let her know you were okay and I was wrong and I wouldn't be coming around anymore. I promised that, remember? I told you I wouldn't go there anymore, and I was worried it would escalate if I just stopped showing up."

"All of that because you flirted? Give me a break, Michael. You were sleeping with that girl, just admit it!"

"I wasn't! She just took it all too seriously! You know some girls are crazy and clingy. I flirted with her, and yes, okay. Yes, I asked her out once, but that was before you got here, and it never even happened! She was pissed because I told her I wasn't married. That's all. We talked it out. It's over. Everything is fine."

Donna couldn't believe she'd let herself feel something for this man. How could she have been so stupid and soft? "Everything is fine?" she bit out, trying to hold back tears. "You're out there telling every woman you meet that you're not married? You're asking them out, cheating on your wife *and me*, and everything is *fine?*"

"You and I were not exclusive before this, and you know that. We never decided that."

Shit. She wouldn't admit it, but he was right. For a while, Michael had just been a fun way to pass the time. She'd certainly never wanted to settle down with him. Not until this ridiculous slipup. He'd been good sex and great companionship.

Donna scrubbed a hand over her forehead, squeezing her eyes closed. "Michael . . ."

"Come on, sweetheart. I know I haven't given you much reason to trust me, but can't you give me the benefit of the doubt here? I was going to shower and change and come by your place because I have news. Good news."

The water drip-dripped behind him. One petal stuck to the wall just beyond his head. Red, just as she'd suspected. Red for love and devotion. "What news?" she heard herself ask, despising her mouth for forming the words.

He gestured toward the back of the house. "Can I just . . . ? I've been running around like crazy. Let me jump in the shower and change.

You sit down and have a glass of water so you don't pass out again. How long have you been here?"

He sounded worried. Concerned about her. And Donna was so exhausted she suddenly felt like wilting onto the couch and crashing into sleep.

"Come on, babe. Don't step on the glass. I'll clean it up later."

She could hardly believe it when she followed him. He took her hand and guided her around the mess she'd made, pulling her down a hallway toward a kitchen she could just make out past the light.

"Are you hungry?"

"No," she murmured.

"I'll get you some water." He led her to a kitchen chair, one of those wooden chairs with a tufted cushion tied in place, and Donna collapsed willingly, the bones of her anger turned liquid.

"What news?" she pressed as he cracked ice into a glass.

He glanced yearningly toward another hallway behind her, but then she saw his shoulders slump in defeat. He filled the glass with water, then joined her at the table.

"I talked to my mom tonight."

"Okay."

"She's so excited about our baby."

Donna jerked back, water sloshing over the rim and onto her hand, the cold a shock against the heated room. "You told her?"

"Of course I did. You're having her grandchild. How in the world would I keep it from her? *Why* would I keep it from her?"

All her dreams and ridiculous, impossible hopes surged inside her as if angry she'd defied them. This was what she'd wanted, why she'd come to Sacramento. A family. "Michael, I'm . . . I didn't think . . ."

He wrapped his fingers into her wet hand and squeezed tight. "It's up to you, of course, but . . . You need a place to stay. My mom has a small house on her property. Used to be for the ranch manager. It's not much, more of a cabin, really, and it needs fixing up, but she wants you to have it. Will you come out and look at it with me? I think you'll love the place. The light is amazing out there. You're always talking about light."

Donna blinked and blinked, unable to process this sudden spin in thinking. "You're serious?" she asked.

"I'm serious. She's excited for you. For *us*. She wants to get to know you, and we're going to need help after the baby comes. I wouldn't even have to worry about money for a while. This could be perfect, Donna. A real life for us."

He wasn't wrong. It could be perfect. And the idea of it tore through her heart like a spinning blade, opening up the damaged flesh again. A place in the hills in golden sunlight. She and her baby and her man, all together, happy and peaceful. A kindly grandmother, even, thrilled at the chance to help out with a little one.

And this was real. Meeting his mother was something bigger than she'd even considered. It was a promise. A pact.

"I can't think," she whispered.

"I understand. Relax for a minute. Rest. I'll clean up the roses and take a quick shower, and then we'll talk. We could drive out there tomorrow, if you like. See what you think."

She squeezed his hand, her gaze drifting over the kitchen and over his rumpled dress shirt and down to the fingers laced in hers. "What happened?" she asked, seeing an angry scratch on the back of his hand. It wasn't bleeding. It wasn't from the vase she'd shattered.

"Oh." He pulled his hand away and tucked it into his lap. "It's nothing."

She glanced toward the empty rooms around them. "Did you fight with your wife? Is that why she left?"

"Yes," he answered, his voice cracking a little. "We got in a big fight."

"You told her too?"

"Not about you. But I broached the divorce again. I'm trying, Donna. I swear I'm trying. Please just give me a chance to make this right."

Her throat thickened and burned with all the grief that had fueled her reckless anger. "Michael," she croaked, but then she couldn't speak at all. It was too much. Tears welled and poured from her eyes. She laid her forehead on her crossed arms and rocked her head back and forth in denial.

She heard him scoot his chair close, then his arms were around her, his face pressed to her hair. "I'm sorry. I really am trying. I promise. I was so excited to tell you . . ."

She'd meant to end it all tonight. To burn down this world that was tumbling around her. But now he was holding her, asking for yet more trust. Did she have it in her? One last, best shot at making this wrong into something right? "I'm so tired," she rasped.

"I know. Take a moment. Rest. We have our whole lives to figure this out."

Jesus. Did they? An hour ago they'd had only a few more seconds together. A few ugly words left to fling. But now a whole new life had opened up before her if she was brave enough to claim it.

She had no idea if she was.

CHAPTER 15

LAUREN

You ignored my first letter. That wasn't very nice. I just want to talk. You sure wanted to talk all those years ago, little Lauren, and I finally have something to say.

I heard your grandma stroked out. You wouldn't want her getting upset about a new story in the news, would you? High blood pressure and all.

A threat. That was definitely some kind of threat.

Send me your number and we don't have to involve anyone else in this conversation. Unless you want to.

What the hell did that mean? And how did he know she was here? How did he know about her grandmother?

An hour after reading the note, Lauren's fingers were still trembling. Her heartbeat had finally slowed a little, which was a good thing, since she wasn't sure how long it could race without failing entirely.

Was it someone she knew? She glanced toward the window that faced the neighbor's property. God, this was ridiculous. She should just go to the police. Kepnick was stalking her, taunting her, and threatening . . . something. A news story?

It was hardly an empty threat, despite the exoneration. Troubled waters could suck you under and drown you before popping you back up to the surface like discarded trash. Whatever lies he wanted to tell would be disproven, but that didn't mean they wouldn't stress her grandmother to death in the meantime. And scar her father's life again.

And yours, a tiny voice chimed in. She was trying to build a future here. She was just starting to settle into her new hopes and dreams. And still, all these decades later, this false accusation hung over her family like a shroud. Her mother's touch still a contamination.

Lauren checked both doors again, then walked from window to window, testing every lock. The afternoon air felt still and thick, but she couldn't risk opening even a crack to the outside. Someone was watching her. Someone wanted her scared. Kepnick might be locked safely behind bars, but whoever left the notes was free as a bird.

She grabbed her phone and typed out a message to Bastian. I got another letter. I'm scared. This time there was no ulterior motive at all. No need for attention. Her nerves vibrated with fear.

He wrote back almost immediately. Hold on. Pulling over.

She paced across her shiny, perfect floor. She had work to do. Two paying projects she needed to finish by morning. She couldn't freak out all evening. And she couldn't shut her whole life down. That wasn't right. It wasn't brave.

Her phone buzzed in her hand, flooding her with relief.

"What's going on?" Bastian shot out as soon as she answered.

Lauren took a deep breath and then read the letter to him before throwing it on the table. The paper wafted disappointingly to a gentle stop. "What the hell does that mean? 'We don't have to involve anyone else'?"

"That's not okay. Call the police."

"You don't understand. Even a hint of anything will get the media involved again. The press is obsessed with serial killers. Hell, the entire world is. If he pops up with some crazed new story, people will go wild. Someone will probably make a goddamn podcast! And my poor grandma . . ."

"So you're just going to let him do what he wants?"

"All he wants is to *talk*."

"It's a game, though, isn't it? He's using you as some sick entertainment."

"Maybe. And maybe I can handle that if it means protecting my family. He can't hurt me."

"What about this friend he's involved?"

Lauren nodded, pressing her hand to her heart. It was thudding with fear, but it was also full to the point of soreness from the worry in Bastian's voice. "Not that I've been checking the tracking number obsessively, but the security system kit is supposed to be here in three hours."

"That's good," Bastian muttered. "This is insane. How are you feeling, babe?"

Babe. He hadn't called her that in a long time. Pleasure snaked through her, responding to the phantom brush of his affection. "Afraid," she answered, then laughed in exasperation. "I feel afraid. And stupid. And really pissed off."

"Listen . . . I'm heading up to San Francisco for a couple of meetings on Monday. What if I drove up a day early and stopped in? I could help you install the security stuff and put in an appearance in case someone is watching. That might help you feel a bit better."

Lauren held her breath for a moment, dizzy with this sudden shift. She'd wanted just a scrap for so long. Any tiny crumb of reassurance that he still cared. This was more like a full-fledged meal. "That would be great, Bastian. Really great."

"I'll be there by five tomorrow, probably. Sound good?"

"Yes."

"Keep me up to date in the meantime. And keep everything locked down. Promise?"

"I promise."

She hung up and stared blankly for a few moments. He'd be here tomorrow. In her house. "I need to shave my legs," she muttered before her brain scolded her for her softness. "He's just coming to help out," she insisted to herself in as firm a voice as she could muster. He hadn't even made it clear if he'd spend the night or not.

But he might.

She hurried upstairs to take a look at her bedroom options. Unfortunately, they were exactly the same as they'd been before his call. Her room offered two ancient twin beds on ugly oak bedframes. "Ugh," she groaned.

Her father's room was better equipped, with a queen bed for when he and his wife visited. But it was her father's room; his pictures from high school were still tacked to the wall next to the dresser. He grinned out at her, arms around his buddies' shoulders.

There was still her grandmother's room, though.

Frowning, Lauren walked down the hall to check it out. The bed and most other furniture had been cleared out. More important, all the pictures and knickknacks had been transported to her new place. There was no faded, youthful face of her father staring down at her. A little dusting and sweeping and Lauren could move the queen bed in here and be done. It would give Bastian a comfortable place to crash for the evening.

Sure. That was her exact wish. To tuck him safely in for a good night's rest.

She shook off any thoughts of her real desires and got to work on cleaning. Thoughts of Kepnick coiled through her brain like snakes. The back of her neck tingled anytime she got near a window, and she found herself inching the curtains apart to peek outside. She caught glimpses of the neighbor's barn and the trees between them, and her gut tightened.

Hadn't he been strange from the very start? Hadn't she heard her grandmother spit his name out like a curse the few times she'd mentioned him? Carter, maybe. Or Carver. Something like that.

Whoever he was, there'd been no warm relationship between the neighbors. He'd definitely be privy to all the news about Lauren and her grandmother, and his mailbox was only thirty feet past hers. He could sneak notes to her without blinking an eye.

Lauren had popped in to visit her grandma already that week, but she'd have to stop by again and gently probe for more information. Was he an asshole, or was he a dangerous creep? Her only consolation was that he must be nearly as old as her grandmother, with that shock of white hair and the slightly hunched back. Surely he wouldn't be crawling through windows or setting up traps.

By the time she'd examined each of her worries, the whole room was clean, though she'd need another shower to wash off the dust. But first she'd move the bed.

She piled the bedding in the hallway to take down to the washer. The mattress was big and unwieldy, but she managed to wedge it up on its side and slide it into the hallway too. From there it was an easy trip to her grandmother's old room.

The box spring was lighter, at least. She tipped it up and pushed it out with no trouble. But then she was left with the mess on the floor.

There was no headboard, just a modern wheeled bed frame that had covered a couple of old boxes and quite a few dust bunnies.

A little wary, Lauren braved a peek into one of the boxes and discovered piles of baseball cards rubber-banded together. When she tried to pull a card out, the band dissolved into several stiff pieces. She'd have to let her dad know that she'd found them. He'd taken her to a game in Oakland once. The lights and colors had dazzled her eyes, and she'd leaned happily against his arm the whole time, intoxicated with delight.

She realized now how much her dad adored attention, but back then all she'd known was that he adored *her*. She'd worshipped him as everything a girl could want in a father, and he'd basked in that warm glow. Those years of being a daddy's girl had felt magical. Just the two of them. Oh, she'd had friends, and he'd dated, but they'd been mostly on their own.

She'd learned to cook so she could have dinner ready every night. He'd brought her by his office constantly so the clerks and administrative assistants could coo over how adorable they were together. She'd become an expert in copying and filing, proud to show off how helpful she was.

It hadn't been until she'd left for college that he'd grown too busy for her. He needed taking care of, so Lauren needed replacing.

She shook her head and set the box aside. No, that wasn't fair. He'd been dealing with an empty nest. Of course he'd started dating. Of course he'd had pretty women in and out of his place constantly. If a man lost ten years of his life, he deserved a little midlife crisis. He'd settled down eventually.

She opened the second box and was greeted by an old Polaroid of her dad on top of a jumble of papers and scraps. He looked unbelievably young, handsome and tanned in a pair of orange swim trunks, his bare arm draped around a woman who was not Lauren's mom. Which made sense, of course. She doubted any pictures had ever been taken of them together. Her mom had been the secret other woman.

Was this smiling, cheerful blonde his first wife? They both looked like college kids, and her hair was long and wavy, parted in the middle as if it were still the 1970s. Lauren stared at their happy faces for a long moment, trying to glean something of the story she'd never been told. His wife must have been so broken after everything, and it made Lauren's stomach ache to think of her. So she never had. Never even let herself wonder.

"Oh, Dad," she sighed, old enough now to accept that he hadn't been perfect. "You idiot."

She set the picture aside and found a clipped newspaper article about his exoneration lying beneath it. Lauren still remembered the exact text of it. It was one of the articles she'd read while haunting the library in her teen years.

She leafed through a few other papers. His selective service information. His prison release documents. The final divorce papers stapled to his original marriage certificate. Carol Wilkinson. That had been her maiden name, and Lauren had never heard it before.

Wilkinson.

What had become of her? According to the paperwork, the divorce had become final a few months after his conviction. She'd gotten everything in the dissolution. The house. The cars. The bank accounts, though she'd agreed to transfer $5,000 into his name, "in a voluntary spirit of generosity," whatever that meant.

What had happened to her after that? Lauren hoped she'd been able to move on and find happiness. What a nightmare this all must have been for her. Not only had she believed her husband had been a murderer, but the investigation had exposed his cheating and the existence of a pregnant girlfriend.

Lauren pulled a few documents out before shutting up the box. When she opened the closet door, she caught a glimpse of hanging clothes before she was suddenly assaulted by a crazed, flickering onslaught.

Screaming, she threw her hands up to shield her face and scrambled back so quickly she tripped over the boxes and tumbled straight onto her ass. The flickering dissipated, and when one dark demon came to rest on the wall, she realized she'd just been defeated by a moth. Well, a lot of moths. At least six of them.

"Shit!" she cursed, then whined as sensation flooded into her bruised behind.

When she stood, her embarrassment that her legs were still trembling morphed quickly into disgust at the idea of more moths in the closet. Worse than that was the idea of *larvae*. Worms! Hidden inside all those clothes.

"No, no, no," she muttered as she rushed downstairs for the huge yard-waste garbage bags she'd used for renovation trash. She also grabbed rubber gloves and the vacuum. This day was going downhill fast. She'd have to buy mothballs to protect her own clothes for a little while, but not until after Bastian's visit. Bad enough that she was living in her grandmother's old house; she refused to smell like she was ninety.

If any of the clothes in her dad's closet were treasures, then they were just going to have to be sacrificed. She opened the garbage bag wide, slipped on the gloves, and started pulling stuff off hangers. Luckily, it all looked like trash. Ancient cardigan sweaters. Old T-shirts. A plaid sports coat that had several moth-eaten holes in it already. As soon as every bit of fabric was in the bag, she tied it tight, her face screwed into a grimace the whole time.

All that remained in the closet were a few games and puzzles. She vacuumed every bit of space that she could, paying careful attention to the corners of the floor. The back wall of the closet was patched with plaster, and Lauren laughed at the idea that her grandmother might have discovered a stash of pot or cigarettes and furiously sealed up a hidey-hole. Her dad had been wily, for sure.

She marched the trash straight out the front door and down toward the dumpster. After tossing the bag high over the side, she shook off her gloves and spun around to return to the house, already planning her second shower of the day.

It wasn't until she'd taken a few steps toward home that she registered the wild barking next door, staccato bursts of sound interspersed with quieter moments of whining she could barely hear. Lauren froze and cocked her head. It didn't sound angry. In fact, it sounded more hurt than anything.

She looked around as if some other neighbor might be lurking near the road, eager to step in and investigate. But it was only her. When the dog went quiet, she waited a few moments before deciding the creepy owner had probably figured out the problem. But after she took five more steps, the dog began barking again, the agitated sound trailing off into a brief howl.

That sounded bad.

"Hello?" she called out far too faintly for anyone to hear. Anyone but the dog, because it stopped the noise for a moment. Eyes still on the fence line, she dared to take a few slow steps toward her house.

The barking immediately started again, of course.

"Crap." She tossed the gloves toward the front porch, missed by twenty feet, and turned to pick her way through the brush toward the fence.

Yes, the neighbor was weird, but that probably didn't apply to his dog. If it was injured or sick, she had to help, didn't she? Even if that meant risking a strange encounter?

The dog's barking pitched higher. "What is it, Lassie?" she muttered under her breath, hurrying up a small hill. She slowed when she got near the fence. The trees looked much taller now that she was near, and the house was farther away than she'd thought. Only the barn came close to being on the property line.

Lauren called out a soft "Hello?" The only response she heard was louder barking. Louder because a German shepherd was now racing toward her at a full-throttle run.

Lauren took three rapid paces back and raised her arms as if the dog might leap over the fence and pounce right on her. But the dog pulled up short ten feet away and raced back in the other direction, still barking.

"Well, shit," she said. Resigned to the idea that she was really going to do this, she climbed the wooden slats and perched uncertainly on the top for a few frenzied beats of her pulse before dropping down.

"Hello?" she called again, more loudly this time. "I'm on your property to see if someone needs help!" Craning her neck forward, hoping for a view, she inched along the path the animal had taken. "Your dog is barking!" she added unnecessarily.

When she didn't hear the cock of a gun and the dog didn't race back to bite her, Lauren moved a little more quickly, grimacing at taking this stupid risk. But her fears were just that: fears. As far as she actually knew, a normal grumpy old man lived here. "Hello?" she called one more time.

Then she heard a soft moan. At the low sound she came to such a sudden stop that her shoes slid in the gravel and she nearly fell. She pressed a hand to her mouth to stop her breath and waited, muscles burning with adrenaline. Was it the old man? Or could she have stumbled into something sinister?

Lauren got her phone out of her pocket and opened the keypad. She dialed a nine and a one, then waited another few seconds before inching forward.

Jaw locked tight against the uncertain whimper she wanted to add to the dog's, she followed a bare path in the scrub around a copse of olive trees. She held her finger directly above her phone's keypad before forcing herself to stick her head out past the last branch.

She spotted him immediately. An elderly man in jeans and a plaid shirt, laid out on the ground near a ladder. The dog perked up from his spot next to the man's leg and barked in Lauren's direction when she hesitated.

She didn't hesitate long. Her fear fell away and she sprang into a run toward him. "Sir?" she yelled as she tried to cover the last thirty feet at a sprint. "Are you hurt?"

He stirred, thank God, putting a hand to his head as he began to push up on one arm.

"Sir, don't move!"

"I'm fine," he moaned as she dropped to her knees at his side.

"What happened? Are you okay?"

"I fell," he rasped.

She glanced toward the ladder.

"Not off the ladder. I was coming down and I felt dizzy. Made it all the way off, though."

"That's good. Can I . . . ?" She reached slowly to touch his head, then ran her hands over the loose white curls to check for any lumps. "I don't feel any swelling."

"I didn't hit my head. I don't think."

"Hold on." She dialed 911 and started explaining as soon as the dispatcher answered.

"I'm fine!" the man protested, but she ignored him and asked for an ambulance. "What's the street address, sir? Nine fifteen?"

He reluctantly corrected her to 917, but insisted he didn't need help. She ignored him.

He stared at her for a moment before his eyes narrowed. "Oh. It's you."

"Hi," she said, her smile tightening a bit. "You know who I am?"

"You're that lady next door."

She cleared her throat, deciding not to interrogate him while he was vulnerable. And he did look vulnerable, frail and bony in the dirt. She had trouble imagining he could have anything to do with Kepnick. "I'm Lauren. Lauren Abrams."

"I know who you are," he finally said, as if he didn't like it. Then he muttered his own name. "Carver Calhoun. And I'm fine. I just need a drink of water."

"We'll see what the paramedics say." The dog whined and wiggled into the space between them, nuzzling its nose to Carver's face. "Your dog has been so upset. He barked until I finally came over to check on you."

"She," he said. "Brenda."

"Your dog's name is Brenda?"

"Yes, it is," he snapped, as if she were rude to question it.

She couldn't take any offense. He'd named his dog Brenda, and he looked so vulnerable that she itched to reach forward and pluck each piece of dry grass that had lodged in his hair. "Can I go get you some water?"

Carver shook his head and darted an alarmed look toward his house. "Just help me get up."

"I don't think that's a good—"

But he was already rolling to his hands and knees.

"Oh," she yelped, then scrambled to her feet to help when he got a foot under him and started to rise. He was stronger than he looked, and he got up fairly quickly, though she noticed the way he closed his eyes and steadied himself after. He let Lauren keep a steady grip under his elbow and didn't shake her off.

Eventually he moved toward his back steps and sat down there. Before she could offer to get water again, she heard the faint whine of sirens. "Sounds like they're almost here."

"That means you can go, then."

She should go. Get out before he got his senses back and became even more stern. Standing, she watched the red and blue lights climb up from the shallow valley below. When the ambulance finally pulled up the long drive, Lauren felt some of the steel tension in her muscles relax. The dog, however, vibrated against Carver's leg until the paramedics turned off the wailing siren.

She explained to them what she'd seen and what Carver had said, then backed off to let them work. They were a whirlwind of activity, checking pulse and blood pressure, pupil response and temperature. They left an oxygen sensor on his finger for a long time before seeming satisfied with the reading.

Fifteen minutes later, he shot her a triumphant look when they said he seemed okay. "We highly recommend that you let us take you to the hospital for a full workup, sir," the female paramedic insisted, but he waved her off.

"I'm just old," he said.

And he was old. From a distance, she hadn't realized he was African American. His skin was only a touch darker than hers, but up close she could see his features amid the deep wrinkles on his face. So deep she imagined he must have spent a lot of time outside in his youth. As frail as he'd looked at first, now she could see the wiry strength in his forearms. An old cowboy maybe.

There was another fifteen minutes of packing up and signing things and several more refusals to go to the hospital. He finished the bottle of water they'd given him, then sighed deeply. "I guess I should offer you a cup of coffee?"

Her eyes darted toward the screen door. She still didn't know him, and she had no idea why he seemed to dislike her.

But a quick visit might kill her suspicions. If he didn't have a telescope set up to spy on her property, she would feel okay about checking him off her list. Though the list consisted entirely of him since she didn't know any other neighbors.

She waved for him to go first and followed him up the steps, anticipating a room packed full of clutter and madness, but when she paused at the doorway, she found herself looking at a very tidy kitchen. Old-fashioned, yes. She thought his golden-yellow fridge might be an actual antique. But the only clutter on the kitchen counter was a set of white containers that were labeled FLOUR, SUGAR, COFFEE and one sleeve of chocolate chip cookies. The rest of the counter was clear and the kitchen table bare of anything at all. No binoculars, no telescope, no inkjet printer churning out threats.

He moved to an electric coffeepot plugged into the wall and pulled a mug from a cabinet. "Here," he grunted, holding it toward her. He didn't offer milk or sugar, and she didn't ask. She didn't really want coffee at all.

"How long have you lived here?" she asked.

"Since '75."

Since 1975. That meant he knew her family's entire history.

She felt his eyes on her as she sipped the strong coffee, and she squirmed a bit as she tried to steal glances into the living room. As far as she could tell, it was just as tidy as the kitchen. She moved to the kitchen sink to look out the window. There was no hint of her house here. Just trees and hills.

"So you know everyone around here?" she suddenly blurted out.

He raised both eyebrows. "I've lived here more than half my life."

"Have you seen anyone unfamiliar lately?"

"Besides you?"

Lauren cleared her throat and decided to be blunt. "Someone has been leaving notes in my mailbox."

"Huh."

That was all he said, offering no alarm or assistance.

"Have you spotted anyone hanging around down there?"

"Nope."

That seemed to be the end of that discussion. Knowing how long he'd been here, she thought of a thousand other questions, but they felt like a betrayal to ask. Her grandmother was still alive, and she'd believed firmly in keeping family issues in the family. But he must have known her dad and her grandmother. Was it possible he'd even met her mom?

She opened her mouth to ask, but Carver slapped a pad of paper on the counter, startling her.

"You got a number I can call if I see anything?"

That was what Kepnick wanted too. Her number. A way to contact her. She shook off the thought and rattled off the numbers as he jotted them down.

"Here's mine," he said, tearing off the bottom of the sheet to hand it over. "You'd better get going," he said as she took the paper from his hand. "I still have work to do."

"Oh. Right. Thank you." She dumped the coffee in the sink and rinsed out the cup. "You should probably take it easy, though."

When she turned back to him, he was exactly where he had been, head cocked, eyes narrowed. He didn't seem angry, but he watched her for a long enough moment that she squirmed.

"Your grandma's gone?" he finally asked.

"Yes. I mean, she didn't pass or anything. She's fine. She's staying at an assisted-living place for a while." She didn't want to imply that she'd be alone in the house forever.

He nodded, then busied himself with putting away the paper and wiping down the already clean counter. "Well, thanks for checking on me."

Lauren cleared her throat. "I'm glad you're feeling better."

He tipped his head in a nod and then gave Brenda a little scratch, obviously waiting for Lauren to leave.

"You must know my grandmother," she finally dared to say. "And my dad?"

He snorted. "I said I've got things to do around here."

"Right. Okay." Strangely she almost felt relieved, though she wasn't sure why. She said goodbye and made a quick escape to hurry back toward the fence line. What exactly had she been looking to hear from him, anyway?

Her grandma had told her dozens of family stories about what the ranch had been like in the good old days, so he couldn't add much to that. And she knew more of the truth about the murder and trial and exoneration than any neighbor could have gleaned from old gossip.

End of story.

On her way home Lauren missed whatever game trail the dog had taken her on and ended up climbing over her fence at a different spot. A deep ditch had been washed out here, and she hiked up a bit to get around it. The knee-high grass swished against her legs, and grasshoppers jumped in wild alarm. She finally reached the ruts of an old ranch road and headed down toward the house.

But when she glanced to her right, she spotted one of the collapsed outbuildings and hitched to a stop. It was the old ranch manager's cabin.

She glared for a moment, angry at the way her mom's lies could still buzz to life around her like swarming insects.

The rotting wood lay tangled on a cement slab, cheap particleboard and plywood looking like a PSA about hazards during fire season. If it weren't so dry and windy in these hills, she'd burn it herself. A fun autumn bonfire to rid this place of its ghosts once and for all.

She wished she could reduce it to ash, but she couldn't, so Lauren turned on her heel and left her mother's memories behind.

CHAPTER 16

DONNA

"This is crazy," Donna said for the fourth time as they bounced over a pothole in the rural road. The surface was paved, at least, but anytime another car approached, both vehicles had to slow in order to inch by each other on the narrow lane.

"She's going to love you," Michael assured her.

"You're married to another woman! Carol is her *daughter-in-law!*"

"My mother is very clear on what a nightmare the last few years have been for me. She wants me to be happy."

"Did she *say* that, though? Or are you just hoping? Because that seems like an awful lot to expect from her."

"She said it. She wants you and our baby in her life because she wants me to be happy."

Donna nodded vaguely. She seemed to be doing everything vaguely these days. Reality felt just slightly out of reach to her.

Or maybe this was what it was like when life wasn't hard and everything fell into place. Maybe she was inside the cushion that happy people seemed to curl up in, safe and shielded from the sharpest blows of life.

None of this felt *real*, though. How could she have gone from being the most dangerous secret in his life to being escorted to Michael's family home? How could he have told his mother the actual truth? And how could the woman accept it? This just wasn't something that happened.

Yes, Donna had imagined she might raise this child with him, but she assumed she'd be shunned by the people in his world. Hell, she'd thought of that as a bonus. She didn't want to be a suburban corporate spouse enveloped in his suburban corporate world. The idea repulsed her.

She'd wanted to be a scandal and an artist. Always out of reach. Always a mystery. Maybe she would've eventually had a nice home, but she'd stand apart from the other moms in the neighborhood. She'd kind of hoped they would all be intimidated and a little afraid of her. That sounded like fun.

And Michael? Sure, he'd be a good father, but they'd be pushed away by the rest of his family, forced into beautiful, reckless isolation.

And now? She'd be a guest of honor at the family reunion and the company picnic?

This is crazy, she said to herself one more time as Michael slowed and turned onto a gravel driveway. "Oh God, are we here?"

He chuckled. "Calm down. This will be great."

They drove under the shade of a huge, ancient tree, then uphill and around a curve. The hills undulated around them, broken only by fences that seemed to go on and on for miles. Michael rolled down the window, and she heard the distant lowing of cattle that were too far away to smell, thankfully. All she smelled was dust and grass. She had the strange feeling of being on a road trip, moving between destinations.

Far too quickly for her taste, a house appeared ahead. A beautiful house like something out of a picture book, the porch dotted with the reds and pinks of potted flowers. A dinner bell rocked slightly in the wind just above the steps. An honest-to-God wooden rocking chair waited next to the door for someone to rock it.

It was a movie. The opening scene of a wholesome Western. A pleasant setting she'd wandered into while looking for the lot next door.

In the far distance a pickup truck lurched up a dirt road, two workers bouncing along in the bed. She watched them for a long moment before movement drew her eye back to the house. The screen door had opened. A woman stepped out.

The first thing Donna noticed was the wide, welcoming smile. She blinked rapidly in response to that happy sign and realized her eyes were wet.

"Shit," Donna hissed.

"Watch your language while we're here, okay? My mom isn't used to that kind of thing."

Donna shook her head, not even sure what she was answering. At any other moment in her life, such a request would lead to much louder cursing on her part, but today she sat dumbly as Michael pulled close to the lawn and parked.

He got out of the car and shut the door, hurrying toward his mother with a nervous smile. "Mom!" she heard him say past the glass. He didn't look back to the car; he just threw his arms around his mother and squeezed. Donna opened her door and forced herself to step out, her knees trembling a little as she stood.

"There she is," the woman said, sounding pleased as punch. "Donna!" Her voice was closer now. When Donna straightened and looked up, Michael's mother was heading right for her, arms outstretched. "Welcome! It's so good to meet you!"

She was enveloped in a hug before the car door finished swinging closed. "Oh! Thank you."

"How are you feeling, my dear? Are you having any morning sickness?"

"Not much," she said, still midsqueeze. She patted the woman's back nervously.

"That's good. I had such awful illness with Michael, but he was worth it, of course."

"Of course."

She drew back to smile into Donna's face. "So pretty."

"Thank you. It's really nice to meet you, Mrs. Abrams." His mother looked to be in her fifties, a little lined from the sun, but her plump cheeks helped her hold on to youth. The waves of her hair were likely dyed blond to hide the gray, but the color suited her slate-blue eyes. It made the world swing a little around Donna to see Michael's eyes in his mother's face.

"I want to show you the foreman's cabin, but maybe you need a break first. How about some of my famous lemonade for the walk? Or do you need to sit down? Put your feet up for a spell? This must all be so stressful for you."

"No, I'm good. I'd like to walk. It was a long drive."

"Michael, get her a glass of lemonade! You can catch up."

"Yes, ma'am," he said before trotting toward the house.

His mother looped her arm through Donna's and turned her toward the yard. "The cabin is just far enough away that you won't have to feel like you're living under my nose. You can have your own space. Your privacy."

"Oh, I'm not absolutely sure about this yet, Mrs. Abrams. I've never lived outside the city before, and I have no idea how I'll feel about being so isolated out here." She hadn't been sure, but she was feeling more and more safe.

"Nonsense. I'll be five minutes away, and there are workers here all the time. Look, there's Joe. Hi, Joe!" She waved toward a Hispanic man nearly a hundred feet away who looked to be rolling a spindle of wire up a trail. He paused and raised his hand uncertainly in response.

"There's good, clean air. Lots of space for walking and staying strong. You might like the quiet if you give it a try. City folk pay lots of money to come to places like this."

Donna laughed. "That's true."

"And Michael says you're a painter. Think of all the beautiful sights to paint out here."

Donna imagined Mrs. Abrams was picturing serene watercolor landscapes, and Donna had no interest in gauzy scenes of nature, but she kept her mouth shut until she was pulled to a stop and eased around to face Michael's mother again. "I know this must seem strange, but, Donna . . . you're family now. You *and* this precious little baby are both family now. And we take care of family here. I'm the fourth generation to live on this land. This child will be the *sixth*. Imagine that. Imagine all that love and protection and history waiting here for your little boy or girl. Can't you just picture little chubby legs racing along this path? We can teach my grandchild how to pick apples, bake pies, ride horses, work the land. Right here!"

Definitely a wholesome Western. Or maybe a fairy tale? A warmth glowed beneath Donna's skin as if she were embarrassed, but that wasn't it. It was too happy for that, but still filled with self-consciousness.

Mrs. Abrams raised a hand toward the hills ahead before sweeping it in a slow circle. Donna's eyes couldn't help but follow the gesture to the huge trees and those golden hills and then the perfect blue sky, dotted with white puffs of clouds. "It's so beautiful," she said.

"And it will all belong to your child one day. I don't have any other heirs, you know."

That warmth swelled inside her chest at those words. It pulled at her lungs and her heart. The security of that for her child. Just *imagine*.

His mother was right about that part. Donna could barely wrap her head around what it might be like to grow up as a child with a charming, happy father and a loving grandmother and acres and acres of land, knowing that it was all permanent. All promised. How would that feel?

Even though her father had worked a good job and owned a house, every day had been a litany of complaints and paranoid fears that he'd be laid off or demoted. An entire long life of resentment and suspicion that had fed on itself until he seemed almost a caricature of the stern father he'd been years before.

Donna cupped a hand over her belly and imagined something better.

Mrs. Abrams watched her and smiled. "Let's go see the cabin. It's in rough shape right now, but that means you can turn it into whatever you want. Make it yours."

Michael caught up just as they crested a rise, and when his hand touched her back, Donna glimpsed the cabin for the first time. It wasn't much. It wasn't cozy. Just a wooden square in the dirt, like a house a child might draw in crayon with a triangle top, the front broken up with a door in the middle and twin windows on either side. But Michael's hand flattened on the small of her back, and they looked together, all three of them, pausing to gaze at it like it might be something.

A tree stood next to the cabin, not as large as the trees near the main house, but large enough to cast a bit of dappled shade on the roof. There wasn't a porch or even a walkway, but she could imagine setting chairs in that shaded patch of grass beneath the tree. She could lay a quilted blanket on the ground and let her baby stretch out in the fresh air, little eyes marveling at the play of light and shadow above.

Michael handed her the icy glass. "Let's go inside and look," he whispered, and Donna nodded, unable to speak. It was a beautiful spot, and it felt private, tucked back from the other house. There was even a little dry wash a ways past the house, and she imagined it as a trickling creek in the springtime. A place a child could splash and chase toads.

She'd seen that kind of thing in movies, so she could picture it with no problem. She'd even chased toads herself in grade school, though that had been in a drainage pond behind a grocery store. It had held no fish but had offered up treasures like old glass bottles and the threatening edges of aluminum pull tabs. They'd caught turtles there too. It had felt like a country adventure.

Michael took her hand, and they walked into the cabin. The front was just one big room and felt quite large, though the tiny galley kitchen to the side looked as if it had been installed as an afterthought. A small wood-burning stove promised cozy winter nights on a sofa, though the only pieces of furniture present were a folding chair and one canted brown recliner with the stuffing coming out in patches on the arms. In the city those would be put out on the curb. Here, she had no idea what people did with trash.

Surprisingly, the place reeked of cigarette smoke and cooking grease. She'd assumed the cabin had been vacant for years, but it didn't look disused, exactly. It just looked filthy in a way that implied several men had been residing there on their own.

"Is someone living here?" she asked. "Would I be kicking them out if I moved in?"

Michael's mother waved a dismissive hand. "They're already gone. Don't worry about it."

Donna drained the delicious lemonade and sighed with contentment.

Michael put his arm around her shoulders. "We'd clean it top to bottom, of course. Paint the walls. Get nice furniture. There's a bedroom too. We could keep the crib in there for a few months."

He took the glass and let her wander to the bedroom door. Right now two bare mattresses lay on the floor, but she could picture a nice bed under the big window, the sunlight warming them beneath their blankets every morning.

We, he'd said. We *could keep the crib in there.*

And they could. The room wasn't huge, but there was space. For all three of them. A family.

"You'd live here too?" she asked to be sure. "It's far from work."

"I could manage it. It's forty-five minutes. As soon as everything is settled. We'll figure it out. I had a good childhood here. It's exactly the right place for our baby to grow up."

She cast an eye toward the kitchen, where his mother was fussing over one of the cabinets. "I'm not sure. What if it's weird? Your mom would be around all the time."

"She's pretty busy running the ranch. I'm not sure she'd have time to be constantly bothering you even if she wanted to be."

That was true. Michael had said she owned cattle as well as almond orchards and orange trees. She had a business to run and land to manage.

"What would she charge for rent?"

Michael laughed. "Nothing! I'm her son, are you kidding? That's the best part. I could support you! You could just relax. Make plans. Paint pictures. Imagine that. Heck, maybe you could restart a career in art. This would give you a little time to get that going."

Oh God, it would. She could spend the next few months getting back in touch with herself, stretching out her style, weaving an actual connection with the place that surrounded her. No job, no partying, no chaos to stop her from concentrating on what she loved most.

"Is this what you really want?" she asked. "Tell me the truth, for the love of all that's good in this damn world. Are you really in this with me, Michael? *Really?*"

"Yes. I'm here. With you. Maybe I haven't handled it well. I know I haven't. But I want this more than I've ever wanted anything. *This.*" He stretched out his arms, eyes locked on hers and glowing with hope. "I love you, Donna. I love you and I love this child."

That vicious strength clawed inside her again, turning and turning, scratching for a way to grow even bigger. It was hope. Love. Yearning. And it was this pregnancy, filling her up with a dream for more.

"Yes," she said as softly as she could, but Michael heard her.

His face lit up. "Yes?"

"Yes. We'll try. But it might not work out. Don't—"

But whatever she'd been about to say was cut off by the press of his lips against hers and the warm grip of his arms around her.

"I guess I've got myself a new neighbor," his mom drawled behind them.

Donna laughed and actually felt herself blushing at being caught as if she were that wild, bubbling teenager she'd once been. "If you'll have me," she said.

"We'll start cleaning today."

And they did. His mother brought buckets and mops and a huge, ancient vacuum she made Michael carry up from the house. Donna explained that she didn't have much, but she certainly had enough furniture and kitchenware to make this place into a home with hardly any spending at all. She could probably start moving in the next day if she continued the cleaning herself in the morning.

"There's no phone line," his mom explained, "but we hooked up the electric years ago, and you can come on down and use my phone anytime. And heck, we can even hang a cowbell up here to ring in case of emergency if you tend to get nervous by yourself."

Donna laughed. "I honestly have no idea if I'll get nervous! I've never lived anywhere like this. I was raised in Seattle, then San Francisco, then LA. This will be a whole new experience for me."

"I'll tell you right now not to mind the foxes. They make a terrible racket. Sound like a woman screaming, but they won't hurt you."

Prickles shot over her arms. "Yikes. I might need that bell after all."

By the end of the day, they were all grimy with dirt and sweat, but they washed their hands and faces and sat down to a fine dinner that waited in the oven when they returned to the main house. "I have a girl" was all Michael's mother said in explanation. "She cooks for me a few days a week. Makes a great roast chicken."

Donna fell quiet as they ate, too exhausted to say much. The food was as wonderful as promised. Chicken and green bean casserole and baked potatoes. The dining room clock tick-ticked in the silence. She heard a couple of truck doors slam before the workers drove away; then it was just crickets chirping and the breeze through an open window.

Would she like this quiet? Would it frighten her? She was willing to find out.

Michael stared pointedly at her empty plate when she finished. She wasn't sure what he was trying to convey until he stood and picked up his plate and glass. Donna pushed to her feet and gathered her dishes.

When his mother didn't rise, Donna cleared her dishes too and followed him into the kitchen.

"Michael can show you where the dish towels are, dear!"

When he put his dishes in the sink and began to walk away, Donna hissed at him. "Stop right there. I'm not your wife. You wash. I'll dry."

He grinned like a little boy who'd been caught being naughty, but he took a towel from a drawer, handed it to her, and grabbed a sponge for himself. It still felt too traditional for her, but it didn't feel bad, exactly. Just an odd fit. She might be able to settle into it.

By the time they walked out of his mother's home, the world was full dark and almost chilly. When she shivered, Michael pulled her close, arm warm and comforting around her shoulder.

Halfway to the car, Donna stopped in her tracks. "Wow. I can see everything out here!" she exclaimed, looking around at the blue landscape.

"It's the full moon."

He raised his head, and she followed his gaze straight up to the huge white moon setting everything aglow, before looking around in wonder again. All the outbuildings were visible, yes, but she could see into the distance for a mile, maybe more. Pale hills of dry grass were turned light blue. Dark splotches of trees arrowed against the land. The rolling earth loomed against the black sky in rounded peaks.

"This is amazing," she breathed.

"What do you think?" he asked. "Is this the most beautiful place you've ever been?"

Maybe. It was very close, at least. Perfect and peaceful. A safe oasis for her and her child where nothing bad could happen. "Yes. I love it here. I honestly really love it here, Michael."

Why not let her guard down for once in her life and just enjoy the fall? Why not just let go? She laughed and took his hand, and the world felt exactly right.

CHAPTER 17

LAUREN

Lauren's feelings about Carver Calhoun only grew more tangled as she cleaned her house on Sunday morning. He'd asked to exchange numbers as if he were inching toward neighborly goodwill. He could call if he saw something strange. She could call to check on him after a hot day.

She felt hopeful about that, but another feeling squirmed inside her, and she couldn't quite puzzle it out. The confusion in her head buzzed like static as she puttered around the house with a steady frown. But as she carried the clean bedding upstairs, she nearly tripped when the static inside her went crystal clear for one brief moment.

What she felt was . . . *disappointment*. Disappointment that Carver had her number and Kepnick didn't.

She wanted to talk to that monster.

That couldn't be right. It *couldn't*. Because this time around, she'd hardly be able to brush off the desire as some fickle teenage impulse. What could she possibly want to hear from him? He was a rapist and a killer, a man who had deceived and betrayed his community with every fiber of his being. Whatever he was cooking up, it wasn't the truth. It was a sickness. A game.

In fact, with at least two of his victims, he'd admitted to toying with them, saying he'd let them go if they convinced him they'd fallen in love with him. They'd tried, even as he'd strangled them.

Lauren shuddered at the way he'd matter-of-factly repeated their hopeless pleas to detectives.

Maybe her compulsion had more to do with her own silence than anything else. Even before her grandmother's stroke, Lauren would never have asked her about that time. The same went for her father. Years ago she'd asked him a single question about the murder, but he'd shrugged and snapped, *I wasn't involved. How would I know?*

Her dad was funny and charming, and he gave her a place in this world, but he wasn't a person who invited deep conversations. Issues and doubts were made to be glossed over. If a problem could be left behind, he left it behind. That was what made him such a great cornerstone for happy thoughts and normalcy and the stability Lauren had desperately needed. She worried too much about everything. Her father worried not at all.

She truly didn't have the right to dredge up what was likely more cruel gossip about a family who'd suffered enough.

But Kepnick . . . No one would know she'd spoken to him. And she had to find out what he was planning, didn't she? Any kind of new drama might kill her grandma.

Elizabeth Abrams had lost so much over that poor girl's murder; she'd sold nearly everything valuable to her to cover ten years of legal fees, and the only thing she'd managed to hold on to was her family. Her wealth, her land, her standing in the community, the worth of the Abrams name, nearly all of it had vanished in one endless tumble, and it would never return.

After getting herself a drink of water Lauren moved restlessly around the house, pacing from space to space, too out of sorts to be productive. Was she really so curious about an outside perspective that she might contact *Kepnick*?

She paced to the front parlor and picked up the papers she'd brought down from her dad's room, the past drawing her deeper into its sticky embrace. What the hell kind of restless curiosity had that monster stirred up in her?

When she picked through the pages, her attention caught on the marriage certificate and the maiden name of her dad's first wife.

Carol Wilkinson.

She hadn't testified in the trial. She'd never even done one interview about Michael or his family. She'd never revealed what she knew about her husband and his mistress and the mother-in-law who'd betrayed her.

Lauren sighed. Hadn't that whole episode revealed cruelty on the part of her grandma and dad? They'd colluded to keep his wife in the dark, colluded to cover up his worst deeds. Didn't that alone make them a terrible, untrustworthy team? Still, her mom had been a member of that team too. They were all untrustworthy to some extent.

Her mom had refused to ever admit any fault, and Lauren hadn't been able to forgive her for that, but the harsh truth was that she'd never demanded the same of the other side of her family. She'd never asked them to confess to the lies they'd told at the time.

There'd been few innocents in the story, but one of them had been her father's first wife.

That lingering sense of familial guilt must have pushed Lauren to avoid any curiosity about Carol. She'd decided to love her dad. She'd chosen him over everything she'd known before him.

In the early days of their reunion, it had felt sticky and gross to even touch the idea of his wrongdoings. Lauren had swung toward the safety of hero worship instead, grasping on to his love and charming attention and holding tight.

No, not just in the early days. That was a lie. She'd clung to hero worship for years. More years than not. She still touched it occasionally, like a favorite old talisman.

But the truth was that he had been married to Carol, and he had cheated, and he had been planning some sort of double life for his girlfriend and bastard child.

Her mom had claimed he'd promised a divorce, and he'd admitted in interviews that he had indeed mentioned divorce to his girlfriend. He also said he'd never meant it. He'd loved Carol, and when he finally came clean and told Donna he didn't plan to leave his marriage, she'd lost it completely and manufactured a false confession to ruin his life.

Her mother's plan had worked beautifully. She'd done the cops' work for them, and they'd closed the book on a case with no other leads.

Lauren wondered still if her mom had spun that whole dangerous web out of pure spite or if somewhere inside she'd believed it. Her dad had admitted to a brief sexual relationship with Tori Bagot. Two people from her work had testified to seeing him with her. One had claimed that Tori had called him her boyfriend.

I wasn't a choirboy, Michael had confirmed. No. Not a choirboy. Not even close. But Lauren had needed him to be an angel so badly.

Because a deep chasm had opened inside her soul when she'd finally processed her mother's lies. Those tales had been the framework of Lauren's whole life. Things had been tough for them, and life had been uncertain, but her mother had been a *hero.*

When the truth had finally soaked in, Lauren had realized that everything shitty in her life had been forced on her by her mom. The isolation, the poverty, the terror, and the constant dark knowledge of the tainted blood that flowed through her veins. Her mother hadn't saved her. She'd *ruined* her.

Frustration warmed Lauren's face, then her throat; then it burned its way into her chest and caught at some dried and cracked kindling there. Why was she still tiptoeing around as if *she* had done something wrong? Why couldn't she ask any questions she wanted?

She sat down at her laptop and opened a browser window to search for Carol Abrams. So many hits. So many mentions. But all of them were decades-old articles she'd read before.

She scrolled through a dozen pages before giving up and typed in Carol's maiden name instead. That search brought up all the typical background-check websites—*Find out more about your neighbor!*—but she found a couple of Facebook links as well.

Eyes narrowed with doubt, she clicked on the first one. The account was semiprivate, but Lauren could see a tiny photo of this Carol Wilkinson, and she looked to be the right age, race, and face shape.

"Hmm." She logged in to her own Facebook account, hoping to see more. This Carol could definitely be an older version of the woman Lauren had seen in that picture. And Facebook said she was seventy-six years old, which was about right.

She lived less than thirty minutes away, which wasn't exactly surprising. She'd probably lived in this area her whole life. She owned a little storefront in the tourist town of Placerville, selling tea and books. The name of the place made Lauren's mouth quirk in a hesitant smile: Loose Leaf.

Carol Wilkinson's personal page was pretty spare, so Lauren clicked over to the Loose Leaf page and found it full of photos of old books and peppered with pictures of people sipping tea around small wooden tables. She scrolled through dozens of those photos before finding a shot of the owner. This candid photo looked even more like the woman she'd glimpsed in her dad's keepsakes. She was tall and thin, and though her hair had gone silver, it still fell in a wave past her shoulders.

Loose Leaf sold games and used books and was open only five days a week, but one of those days was Sunday. Today.

Lauren didn't know if that was a sign or not, but the frustration was pushing up again, sizzling through her as a restless urge to do something. To ask, to push, to stop sitting here like a victim, hoping she could stay small enough to escape notice. She'd kept her hands over her ears for decades, sure that if she let one doubt inside, she'd explode like an overfilled balloon.

She just wanted to be happy. How many goddamn years had she spent desperately ensuring that everything was *fine*? That everyone was fine? That she'd pleased and patted and relaxed and satisfied? Who the hell ever worried about *her* peace? Who made sure that *she* was fine?

Lauren looked at her car keys, glanced at the clock. It was still early. Was she going to sit here all day by herself, worrying about her father's past and her own future?

She jumped to her feet and grabbed her keys and purse, then hurried toward the door before she could change her mind.

Something felt off, an undercurrent flowing, parting around her like a stream. She could feel the pull of it tugging at her, trying to draw her deeper. For the first time in her life, Lauren wanted to jump into the current and find out more.

Maybe it was the quiet here. She'd been distracting herself from negative feelings her whole life by staying busy and taking care of others. First her mom, then her dad, then each boyfriend she'd latched on to along the way.

Latched. That was the right word exactly. Latched like a barnacle clinging for sustenance and praying not to get scraped off and left behind.

But there was nothing to latch on to here. No one to take care of except herself, and that felt like a strange, foreign task. Still, if she didn't take care of her own needs, she'd start grasping at Bastian again and lose herself in anticipating what his visit might lead to. Sex? Resolution? Reconciliation?

She couldn't get lost in him again.

Lauren grabbed her purse and keys and raced outside. She practically threw herself in her car and backed up so quickly that gravel pinged the undercarriage.

Anxiety rode her hard as she drove the narrow curves higher into the hills. She kept easing off the gas and making herself go slow; then she'd glance down and find she was speeding again. Her fingers strangled the steering wheel, and she couldn't seem to make them stop.

She had to get this all over with at once, get it out in the open. She'd face Carol, and if it felt right, she'd ask questions.

But how could it feel right? Lauren herself—her existence, her presence on this earth—would be the worst possible reminder of a time in Carol's life she must hate with every fiber of her being. The woman might break into a rage. Scream obscenities. Throw teacups. But that would be better than the most dreadful response of all: heartbroken tears that a physical reminder of her pain had shown up to taunt her.

"You're okay," Lauren reminded herself after unclenching her jaw. "You're just walking into a shop. Anyone can go in."

And that was all she'd likely do. Walk in. Prove that daring to explore her own past wasn't scary. She didn't have to stay closed off and careful for the rest of her life. After all, she couldn't face Kepnick's lies with her head buried in the ground.

"You're okay," she said again. And maybe she was. Or maybe not.

A laugh hiccupped out of her at that, but her smile died when she saw the sign for Placerville.

The town seemed dead quiet. The summer rush had faded, and winter travel to Tahoe hadn't yet begun. Lauren didn't pass any other cars as she followed GPS instructions to the narrow main street. Lined with two-story wooden storefronts, it looked like a postcard for a gentrified Old West town. She drove slowly past Loose Leaf, the sign painted in pretty gold script, and easily found a parking place just a few doors down.

She wanted to sit in her car and gather her thoughts, practice a few casual lines, convince herself to be brave. But she couldn't take the chance that she wasn't brave at all, so she forced herself out of the car and walked quickly toward the tea shop.

She saw only her own reflection in the glass windows, a frowning, dark-haired woman in jeans and a shapeless blue sweater. A metal bell jingled when she opened the door. The silver-haired person behind the counter looked up . . . and it was her.

The tables between them were empty. Lauren was alone with the woman her father and mother had so callously betrayed.

"Beautiful day!" Carol called out. "Welcome!"

Oh God, she looked as pleasant and lovely as a person could appear at first glance. The wrinkles around her eyes folded into deep creases when she smiled. Her cheeks were pink as if she'd been bustling around the store.

Lauren smiled back, a strange twitch of her lips that probably looked even more unnatural than it felt. "Yes. It's nice. Outside, I mean. Really nice. A little chilly."

"Our tea menu is on every table if you're thirsty."

"Thank you!" Lauren said far too loudly before dropping into a chair near the door. She snatched up the menu and stared daggers at it, her face beginning to heat.

"I'll be right back," Carol said before moving into the book area of the store, perhaps sensing that her customer needed a moment to compose herself.

"Jesus," Lauren whispered, wiping a shaky hand over her brow.

Her mouth had gone so dry she had to peel her tongue off the back of her teeth. She ran her gaze over the menu in a panic, trying to focus on one thing, *anything*, that she could manage to push out of her mouth as an order.

Or she could simply walk out.

Her stomach rolled. She set the menu down, placed her hands on the table, and was just about to stand up when Carol returned. "Did you find something that sounds good?" she asked.

Lauren managed to snatch one trailing thread of thought and hang on tight. "The relaxation blend," she blurted.

"Sure. Milk with that?"

Lauren nodded and clutched her hands tight together to stop their trembling as Carol rounded the counter. Maybe the tea would help her come to a decision, though unless it was brewed with actual opium seeds, it probably wouldn't succeed in calming her down. The only ingredient she could remember was chamomile, and that sounded as effective as spitting into a bonfire.

She didn't need to bother this woman with questions. Just daring to look the past in the face felt like a breakthrough. Her father had wronged Carol deeply. So had Lauren's beloved grandmother. And that was okay. She could still love them. Her world remained intact. Now she only had to pay for her tea and she could leave.

Carol set a beautiful porcelain cup on the table along with a matching teapot and small milk pitcher. Her hands were slim and spotted with age, adorned with only one simple platinum band where Lauren had expected several clunky flower-child rings. It was a tea shop, after all.

"Would you like some ice water? Or maybe a cinnamon scone? You look a little pale."

"This is good, thanks so much."

"All right." Carol displayed a tablet with the total. "That's five eighty-seven, but you can pay later if you'd like to look around. Please take all the time you need."

Lauren shook her head and raced to get out her credit card to pay. She handed the card over and watched as Carol swiped it through the attached reader.

It was only as the seconds ticked by and Carol read the screen for confirmation that Lauren realized her awful mistake. Her name was on there. On the card. On the screen. *Lauren Abrams* seemed to glow and pulse within the white square of details.

Oh no. Her heartbeat drummed in her ears as she watched Carol watch the screen. But then the woman smiled and angled the tablet

Victoria Helen Stone

toward her for a tip and signature, and Lauren gladly hit the thirty
percent button and scrawled a crooked line. "Thanks," she croaked.

"You're welcome. I'll be in earshot if you need anything else."

Lauren poured tea into the cup with a clumsy hand, then followed
it with too much milk. Tea spilled over the side and pooled in the
saucer. She ignored the sugar cubes on the table and sipped it without sweetener. She didn't have time to wait for the sugar to dissolve.
Thankfully the milk had cooled the brew enough that she didn't burn
her tongue.

Her eyes shifted, taking in the shop, the little wooden tables that
matched in size though each was a different color and style. The tables
had obviously been carefully collected. A small rainbow flag hung above
a stand of greeting cards next to the register. A shelf of ancient-looking
paperback books lurked next to that with a handwritten sign that read,
We're Free to a Good Home!

Every adorable detail made Lauren sink deeper into her chair. She
took another gulp, hoping to get this all over with quickly. Almost
done.

"You have his eyes," Carol said as she swiped a towel over the top
of the counter.

Lauren gasped, an intake of breath so sharp there was no way to
pretend the other woman hadn't heard it. She exhaled just as hard.
"Wh-what?" she stammered.

"You're his daughter, right? Michael's?"

"I'm sorry," she said immediately, already reaching for her purse.
"I'm so sorry. I'll go."

"It's fine. You're here. I assume you must have come for a reason."

A reason. Was there a reason? Because she'd thought she was prov-
ing something to herself, but now she couldn't figure out what it was.

"I'm sorry," she repeated, but Carol stayed calm, face unflushed, as
if she'd dealt with far worse in this life. And of course she had.

"I don't know what I was thinking," Lauren said in a rush. "I found some papers in his old room, and . . . I guess I . . ."

"Oh. I see. Did he pass?"

"No! It's nothing like that! I bought my grandmother's house. My grandmother is okay," she babbled. "I mean, she had a stroke, so she moved. She's out of rehab and in a senior apartment now. She's doing better."

"Oh," Carol answered. "That's good."

"I think I should leave."

"Please don't. I'd like to know why you came here. You don't seem to have wandered in unawares."

The uncommon word struck her as funny, and Lauren barked out a laugh without meaning to, then shook her head frantically. "No. Sorry. I found some documents, and I looked you up. You were so close, and . . . I'm not sure what I came to ask. It's just that everything has always been so . . . *skewed*. You know? First one side, then the other. I feel like I've been in the middle of a tug-of-war my whole life, and maybe I'm finally cracking." Mortified at her babbling, she reached for her purse again, but Carol dropped into the chair across from her, freezing Lauren's movements.

"It's okay," she said, covering Lauren's clenched hand with her own. "I don't mind talking, if you want to."

"Really?" The woman's warmth seeped into her icy skin. No one had ever offered that before, not about this. Just to *talk*. Something desperate opened inside her, craving more.

Carol looked a little paler than when Lauren had first walked in, her smile tipped with more doubt, but her eyes still looked kind. "I really don't mind. It was a long time ago, and I was a very different woman then. If you'd reached out ten years after, I might have slammed the door in your face, but now . . . I'm not the woman who was married to Michael Abrams anymore. I can barely remember who that woman was."

"I'm sorry," Lauren said again. "I didn't even know him until I was ten. That was after he was released from . . ."

"Prison. Yes, I know. I'm sorry you had to go through all that."

"You went through worse, I think."

Her shoulders lifted. She cocked her head. "Maybe. But you were a child who never had any choice at all. I had inklings that Michael wasn't a good husband, and I ignored them for years. Then again, I never suspected he'd be going to prison for murder. That was quite a blindside! When he was exonerated, I think I was finally able to take a deep breath and move on. And I'm good now. Happier than I dreamed I could be when I was that woman. True to myself. Strong."

Lauren brushed off her brief burst of envy and nodded. "That's really good. I'm glad."

"So was there something you wanted to ask me?"

"Maybe?" She couldn't quite remember her questions. "I honestly just wanted to see you. That probably sounds strange."

"Only a little. We are creatures of curiosity, after all. I've certainly wondered about you, and now here you are. I hope life has treated you kindly."

"I think it has, actually. I mean, the first part took some twists and turns."

Carol laughed, a surprisingly husky sound that made Lauren smile.

"But I guess . . . everyone in my life has their own agenda. I always felt like I needed to take a side and plant my feet firmly, with no doubts, no wavering. Now maybe I'm finally growing up. I hope? That feels stupid to even say aloud, because I'm a thirty-five-year-old woman. I've been an adult for a long time."

"I didn't grow up until I was nearly fifty. I was always either someone's dependent or someone's victim. So you're not the latest bloomer at this table." When she started to draw her hand away, Lauren reached for it and squeezed, craving the anchor of her warm fingers.

And for the first time in decades, she asked the real question. "Will you tell me what really happened?"

Carol squeezed back and offered a sad, crooked smile. "To me? I was cheated on and betrayed, and I got a divorce. I guess that's my story of that time. But if you're asking if your father murdered that girl, the evidence is clear that he didn't."

Lauren nodded, overwhelmed with a relief she couldn't explain. She'd known that truth already, so why did the words make her feel so light?

"As for everything else, you know as much as I do. I had no idea he had one girlfriend, much less another with a baby on the way. So I can't help you as far as insight and revelation. I certainly had none." She laughed again. "None at all."

When she drew her hand back, Lauren let her go.

"I didn't have to testify since we were married," she continued, "but I couldn't have answered anyone's questions regardless. I was visiting my parents when she was killed. Michael practically pushed me out the door, insisting I needed a break. But that was because he wanted to spend time with your mother, and it had nothing to do with Tori Bagot."

"And my grandmother?"

Carol's smile faded. "What about her?"

Lauren's stomach turned again. "We've always been so close, but my mother hates her. It makes me crazy."

"Your grandmother was kind to me." She stopped there until Lauren raised her eyebrows. After a long pause, Carol sighed. "Until the end, obviously. That was a terrible blow."

"Because she took my mom in?" Lauren asked.

Carol clasped her hands together and leaned back in her seat.

"Things had gotten a bit tense between us those last few years. I couldn't conceive a child." She shook her head. "It was bad luck, and I was heartbroken. But I reconciled myself, and I wanted to adopt. Michael wasn't enthusiastic, but I tried to convince him. I think his mother really encouraged him not to consider it."

"I'm sorry."

"He really, really wanted children, but for years he wouldn't even discuss adoption. At my lowest points, I thought about leaving and letting him move on with his life."

"You must have felt so alone."

"Yes. For a few months his mother seemed angry with me. Michael said I was imagining it, that nothing had changed. I felt like I was going crazy, to be honest. He always told me I was too sensitive. And maybe I was." She shrugged. "Then one day everything was fine. Michael invited his mother over for dinner, and she was in a great mood. I was relieved. That was when they proposed the adoption."

"What adoption?"

"*Your* adoption."

"Mine?" Lauren drew back. "That doesn't make any sense. You didn't know about me."

"I didn't, but in a roundabout way, I suppose I did. Not in the way you mean. I can assure you I had no idea you were Michael's actual daughter! But adopting you seemed like the perfect solution. I was thrilled."

What the hell was this woman saying? Lauren shook her head and tried to smooth the incredulity on her face to mere doubt. "Adopting *me*? How was that supposed to work?"

"They told me Michael's sister was pregnant and didn't want the child. It was that simple. We'd be adopting, but this way we'd be taking in his niece, his bloodline, and that seemed to please him. I was over the moon."

Lauren felt her face slide from skepticism to slack disbelief. Her lips parted as the breath leaked from her tightening throat. Before she could force her voice to work, Carol smiled and spoke again.

"Honestly, that was one of the happiest moments of my life. I thought I could give this baby—*you*, I mean—a wonderful home. It was all I'd dreamed about for years. I was ecstatic."

"Carol," Lauren croaked, "I'm sorry, but I have no idea what you're talking about. I wasn't up for adoption. And you must know my dad doesn't have a sister."

Carol straightened, and the nostalgic smile faded to a straight line. "Oh, that's not true. He does. She ran away years before I met him."

Lauren's mind spun, overwhelmed and cringing away from ideas she could hardly process. Thoughts flitted by like sparks from a wildfire, each one a tiny danger to everything around it. Finally, one landed and burned through her. "I have an aunt?" she whispered.

Carol's brows drew down in a deep, sudden frown. "Oh my. Wait a minute. I can't believe it's never occurred to me, but what if they were lying about the sister too? But no. That doesn't make sense. I knew about her from before we were even married."

"But . . . I've never heard a thing about any of this! What adoption? What sister?"

"She left when she was a teenager and never came back. She didn't get along with her mother at all. 'Like oil and vinegar,' Mrs. Abrams said. She was a daddy's girl, and after her father died, she became a very defiant teen, from what I gather. She ran off at seventeen, and they never heard from her again. God bless her for having the courage to do it."

Lauren had been hoping to alleviate some of her confusion with this visit, but now she was spinning with a hundred more questions. A thousand. *My mother didn't want me? She meant to give me away? She'd lied about that too?*

And yet her father had planned to be in her life from the start. That was a good thing Lauren could grasp and hold. A good thought. And she had an aunt. That might be good too.

"You know," Carol's voice came from far away, "you might be able to find her now. Everyone is online these days."

"I don't even know her name," Lauren whispered past the tumbling shock in her head.

"Oh, that I can help you with," Carol said. "Her name is MaryEllen."

CHAPTER 18

DONNA

Donna stretched hard, sore from too much time standing in front of the easel. The slightly open window let in puffs of cool breeze and a bit of dust, but the fine grit sparkled in rays of light, making it seem more magical than disruptive. When the wind picked up, she could smell the gorgeous fragrance that lifted on the air from the flower garden in back of the main house. Donna didn't know anything about flowers, but these smelled sweet with a touch of green that cut any hint of cloying from the scent, and she loved it.

She would ask his mother about it when she stopped by in the morning. Mrs. Abrams always came by early before starting her day, and it would give them something to talk about and make their minutes together less awkward.

As promised, she had mostly kept out of Donna's hair, briefly visiting only once or twice a day. Unfortunately, her one guaranteed daily visit occurred at 7:00 a.m., and Donna was decidedly not a morning person. Regardless, as much as she didn't want to roll out of bed at the ass crack of dawn to get dressed and start coffee, it certainly felt easier now than it ever had in LA.

After dark, the whole world went still here. Not quiet. There were coyotes howling and wind rustling and crickets chirping. She tried to let the charm of that sink in, but it only ever held her attention for a few minutes, and then she needed to move on to something busier. She'd made a lot of progress on cleaning and painting because she could get only two channels on her television. Cable was definitely not hooked up, even at the main house.

God, she wanted a drink. Though if she were wishing for impossible things, she'd order up a wild night out with dancing and frozen margaritas and stumbling back to her apartment at dawn with a big group of friends. But the truth was, she'd take just an evening on the couch with Tom and Tom at this point. She was lonely here, waiting for Michael to join her.

She eyed the purse sitting on her chipped dining table and clenched her teeth. She still had a few cigarettes in there, toting them around like life jackets in case of emergency. Was loneliness an emergency?

Michael had left three days before, after spending several days helping her get settled. She knew the separation was only temporary, but it still felt strange, living out here by herself on his mother's land.

The knock startled her just as she was edging toward the table. Donna jumped in sudden guilt, a yelp flying from her throat.

"Donna?" Michael's mother called through the door just before it opened.

"Oh!" she said in response, surprised by the sudden invasion. That was new.

"You left this at the house." She held up a Tupperware container of leftovers she'd packed up after their tuna casserole dinner. Donna hadn't eaten tuna casserole since she was a teenager at home, and she'd eaten three servings and purposefully set the leftovers aside on the counter so she wouldn't cradle the bowl like something precious. Then she'd promptly forgotten it while doing dishes, apparently.

Her irritation temporarily vanished beneath her gratitude for the food. "Thank you."

"I thought you might need a snack later. I noticed you stay up awfully late."

She'd gone to bed at 11:30 the night before, which didn't feel late. Was his mother watching for the glow of her lights from down the hill? She settled for thanking her again before she took the container and popped it in the fridge. His mom was well meaning and kind, and it wasn't her fault that Donna was still adjusting to having a mother figure around. In the city she could move anonymously through her days. All this space in the country should be freeing, but it felt stifling instead.

"The place is shaping up a bit," Mrs. Abrams said.

Donna glanced around. She considered it pretty much done at this point. "It's really working out great."

"Are you settling in?" she asked, sweeping her eyes over every surface of the living room and kitchen as she left Donna behind and moved toward the bedroom. "Everything good?"

"Absolutely," Donna answered, biting back a protest as Michael's mother turned on the light in the bedroom and peered in.

"Well, it certainly looks as if you two are cozy up here."

"When he's here, yes."

"He called to tell me he'd try to stop by tomorrow."

Donna's head snapped up in surprise. "Oh. Michael called?"

"Yes, just after you left."

A bolt of irritation hit her, but she wasn't sure why. She had no phone up here, and Elizabeth Abrams couldn't exactly come racing up the hill each time he phoned. "Well," Donna drawled, "I hope he can make it up to see me for a few seconds tomorrow."

"He's doing the best he can," she said, the words faintly sharp at the edges.

Donna still wasn't entirely sure about that. But even she, as sarcastic and hard-nosed as she was, couldn't bring herself to be rude to this woman who had every reason to hate her, yet had given her a home on her own land.

"Would you like a cup of decaf?" she asked instead, hoping to smooth things over and hoping even more that the gesture would be enough and Mrs. Abrams would decline.

She did. "No, I need to check the water pump and make sure the last repair we made is holding. Then I'm off to bed." She started to bustle toward the door, but she changed her trajectory at the last moment and headed toward Donna with a smile instead.

"I've really enjoyed our time together, Donna. I'm looking forward to this little one, of course. And it's been nice having Michael around more often. But I truly enjoy our meals together. And I love seeing a friendly face each morning when I start my work."

"Oh, thanks. This has been really nice for me too. I'm painting more than I have in years."

Michael's mother glanced toward the wild, dark colors of the large canvas on the easel, but her eyes darted quickly away, as if the strokes and lines disturbed her. It *was* disturbing, Donna supposed, just as she wanted it to be. A woman thrashing violently in a dark pool of water.

"Yes, well . . . I'm so pleased this is working out for you. And for our little one."

Before she could react, his mother had reached out and spread her fingers over the small swell of Donna's belly. Donna's whole body jerked in surprise, but she suppressed the urge to push the other woman away. Just because she wasn't used to that kind of intimacy didn't mean it was wrong. It *felt* wrong only because she'd been on guard her whole life. She squirmed as subtly as she could.

"You've made this old woman so happy," Mrs. Abrams whispered, though Donna had no idea if she should respond. Was she speaking to Donna or to the baby? Cringing, she held her breath, waiting for the touch to lift. When it didn't, she finally shifted away, forcing the hand to slide awkwardly off.

"Just a few more months!" Donna said with forced cheer.

"Donna . . ."

She nodded at the long pause, trying to hurry her up, but Mrs. Abrams reached out to cup her shoulders.

"This has been a light in my life." She moved in close for a hug, her arms wrapping tight and holding on. And holding on some more. *Squeezing.* Donna offered a quick hug in return, then held herself stiff, waiting in vain to be released. Her family had not been affectionate. Not in that way. Her mother had sometimes made cookies when one of her children had been sad, but aside from the occasional awkward back pats offered in comfort, that had been the extent of it.

"You're like the daughter I never had," his mother said, giving Donna one more tight squeeze before releasing her at long last.

"But you—" she started, thinking of the childhood stories Michael had told her, but when she saw the tears in the woman's eyes, she cut herself off. "It's okay," she said instead. "I'm really happy to be here."

"Oh, look at me!" Mrs. Abrams swiped at her eyes with a laugh. "I must be tired to be carrying on like this. Don't pay any attention to me. I'll see you in the morning, my dear."

"Absolutely. And I'll come by tomorrow to use the phone, if that's all right. I need to check in with my friends in Los Angeles. I haven't talked to them in two weeks, and they'll worry."

"Of course. Anytime."

She left after one last shoulder pat. Donna made sure she was out of sight of the window when she slumped in relief. She needed to put curtains on her list of essential items for her next trip into town.

Into town. Like she was Laura Ingalls Wilder. Donna snorted at her melodrama and glanced around for the phone before remembering that she didn't have one. Maybe she was more like Laura Ingalls Wilder than she thought. If something happened out here . . .

But nothing would happen out here. That was the point of this place. She was cozy and protected, removed from the stress of the outside world. Hadn't she felt relaxed as hell for the past couple of days? Wasn't she painting again?

Still, she wished she could speak to Michael. She missed him, and she was lonely. She found herself craving gossip about anything, even people she didn't know, although she would have guessed she was above gossip before all this. Now she realized the truth. She hadn't needed to gossip herself before because her friends had provided all the dirt she needed on a daily basis.

But more than that, she was dying to get a little gossip from Michael. Because . . . hadn't he mentioned a sister?

CHAPTER 19

LAUREN

Were you going to give me away?

Lauren couldn't force the words out, despite the way they swelled inside, filling her up and pressing hard against her bones as her mom spoke about her new life in Tahoe. The words were a nearly unbearable pressure in her chest.

She'd been leaving Placerville, reeling from this new information, when she'd spotted the highway sign. To the left was home. To the right was South Lake Tahoe and Carson City beyond it. Her mom was an hour away. Her mom who hadn't meant to keep her.

Burning with something bigger than anger, she'd pulled over and grabbed her phone to text her mother. Let's meet.

She'd sent one more short text too, before her mother had even responded. After opening the photo she'd taken of Kepnick's first note, she'd tapped the number in. Her churning fury suffused her with courage, so she'd gathered Kepnick under the umbrella of her rage and texted, WHAT DO YOU WANT?

Kepnick hadn't responded, but her mother had.

Now they were seated across from each other at a sticky table in a diner, eating overpriced club sandwiches meant for tourists. Her mother was talking about her house and her husband, but Lauren only heard her voice from deep underwater.

Were you going to give me away?

Still, she held the words tight because the answer might be too much to bear.

Throughout Lauren's childhood, her mother had cast herself as the sacrificial hero of their story. She had saved Lauren, saved the case, saved the day. Hell, she'd saved the whole world from the violent evil of Michael Abrams. Only she had been strong enough to step forward and be brave.

Everyone thought he was so perfect. But I knew the truth, and now he'll never set foot out of prison. I won't let them have you, and I won't let them hurt you.

All that big talk and the whole time her mom had been planning to hand Lauren over to the Abrams family from the start?

It made sense, though, didn't it? It made *much* more sense than a married man's family embracing his pregnant mistress and giving her a place to shelter. Why would her oh-so-proper grandmother have volunteered to usurp her son's nuclear family and celebrate his mistress and bastard?

Lauren had accepted this tale because that was the deal she'd made in her most secret heart. Her loyalty and love would make her worthy despite her mother's transgressions. Still, the story had always tugged, like an insect vibrating alerts along a spider's web.

She and Bastian had once visited her grandmother's home for a weekend, and they had slept in separate rooms despite the fact that they lived together in Los Angeles. Lauren hadn't even asked, because her grandmother wouldn't have allowed them to share a room without being married. But this same woman had somehow volunteered a love shack and an utterly scandalous arrangement for her married son back in 1985?

No. There was another explanation, and Lauren had just discovered it. Her mother had been an unexpected surrogate. The silver lining to a destructive, raging storm cloud of an affair.

His wife had been infertile, and he hadn't wanted to adopt a stranger's baby. His pregnant mistress had never, ever planned to have kids. It had been the perfect solution to a bad situation.

So what had gone wrong?

Her mom had always claimed that when she heard about Tori Bagot's death, she'd wanted to do the right thing and tell the truth. But her truth was impossible, of course. Bobby Edward Kepnick had been the real killer.

The defense team had called her mom a spurned woman, jealous of the marriage and enraged that he wouldn't leave it. That was why she'd thrown a bomb into his life and exploded it into little bits.

That felt more like truth. Maybe, despite her plans, Donna had grown more attached during the pregnancy. More attached to the baby and more attached to Michael.

Hadn't her mom lived her entire life in reckless, impulsive bursts, swinging wildly from one plan to the next? That was how Lauren had found herself starting a new school every six months or so. Her mom would work her ass off at a job for weeks, then storm home, complaining that the boss was a bastard and this apartment was a shithole and they were moving on.

Always moving on.

Sometimes on those nights, she'd drink too much and offer a different truth to her daughter. She was scared. Scared of things that made no sense. That Michael would find them. That his mother would hunt them down. That they'd take Lauren away.

And her terrors had come true, though not in the way she'd feared. Instead, they'd stolen Lauren's love, and her mom had lost her child after all. A loss was a loss. Perhaps she'd had a premonition that it would happen one day. More likely it had just been guilt nipping her heels all those years, driving her to run.

"Lauren?" her mom said, popping the cloud of writhing memories around Lauren's head.

"What?" she asked automatically before glancing down to see the picture her mom had open on her phone. Two big dogs and one little one, all staring eagerly at the photographer. All three looked like mutts, and her heart would have been warmed by that if she'd been anything but pure ice in that moment. "Nice," she muttered, still too afraid to ask for devastating truths.

Life was so much easier when you didn't have to question anything. When you didn't have to question *everything*.

She could just let it go. Leave it buried beneath the decades of silt that had already smoothed it over. Everyone was different now.

Her mother looked good. She'd gained a little weight, and her cheeks had lost the hollows she'd always carried, as if she'd deflated somewhere along the way. Her face was so lined, though. So much older than it had been the last time Lauren had seen her. And her hands looked like a ninety-year-old's, all bone and liver spots.

But she smiled when she talked. If Lauren had seen that before, she couldn't remember it.

"Will you *ever* admit it?" The words were out of her mouth and asked before she even heard them. She'd been holding so tight to that other question that this one had flitted by and escaped.

Whatever her mom had been saying, she fell silent. Her eyes narrowed into a glare that soon dropped to the half-eaten sandwich on her plate. Her hand reached for her purse, no doubt seeking the comforting touch of the pack of Marlboro Lights she always kept on her.

"Lauren—"

"I'm happy for you, Mom. Happy you've found someone and you're doing well. You look really good. You sound good. But if you truly want to have a relationship with me, you have to tell the truth. I can't walk around with all these lies in my head anymore. They're killing me. I feel . . . stuck. I feel crazy, Mom. Do you understand that?"

This was the point where her mom's mouth would tighten into a flat line that made her lips vanish. She'd snap her purse closed and lurch to her feet and stalk away without a backward glance. They'd had this conversation before.

If they were in private, Donna would rage and yell and defend herself with every breath. But not here. Here she'd just walk away, and that was what Lauren wanted. She couldn't do this. She was too old or reeling or just plain tired. She couldn't do this anymore.

But her mom didn't rise. Instead she took a deep breath and reached for Lauren's wrist. Her fingers stayed loose, almost floating above Lauren's skin. "I love you," she said, gaze rising up to meet hers. Her lips disappeared in that tight line for a moment, but then they twisted into a wobbly sort of smile. "I love you so much, and I didn't want to admit it to myself, much less you."

Lauren's skin buzzed until she could no longer feel her mom's hand. She couldn't even feel her own breath passing her lips, though the sound roared in her ears with each quick intake. "Admit what?" she whispered.

"You think this was all some vicious scheme. That's what he's always said, right? That I was a crazy woman out to destroy him? That's not true. That was *never* true. What I wanted was a good life for you, whether that was with him or not. Yes, at some point I wanted a family with your father. I thought we might be able to make it work." She laughed at that, and her hand slid away, back to rest on her purse.

"Tale as old as time. I thought I was above that kind of bullshit, but I sure as hell wasn't. And I can't even blame my youth. I was a grown-ass woman."

"What are you *saying*?" Lauren asked, though she wasn't whispering anymore. In fact, the words were too loud and her mother winced, but her sad smile never disappeared.

"Here's the truth, baby. Here's what you always wanted. I saw your father that night. The night Tori went missing. He was with her. He'd promised to never see her again, but I assumed he was lying because he's a man and he's Michael, so I followed him one night. *That* night. He drove there, and he picked somebody up."

"Somebody?" Lauren interrupted.

"Yes. He went to the bar where his girlfriend worked, and then she went missing. I saw a hand close his passenger door. I'm so *sure* I saw that. I didn't see her face, but I knew Tori had been calling his house and hanging up. She could have told his wife everything she knew about me. About *you*. What do you *think* happened, Lauren? She was a threat!"

"He didn't confess to you, did he?" It didn't sound like a question when Lauren asked it, because she meant it as a statement. And finally, for the first time in her life, she heard the truth.

"No. He didn't confess. We all know damn well Michael Abrams would never confess something like that to anyone."

Strange, but Lauren didn't feel anything. Her mother's words entered her ears and wiggled along the bones and nerves into her brain, and she heard them and took them in and felt *nothing*. She'd always known it, after all. Everything else had been a confusing mess, but this had been a rock in a sea of mud. She wasn't sure why. Maybe her mom just wasn't a good liar. Maybe because it had been the one thing she'd leaned so heavily on when she was panicked or drunk or angry.

He told me he did it, Lauren. He told me!

But he hadn't.

"You have to understand," her mom said, voice pleading as the strange, crooked smile finally faded. "I only said it because I knew he'd done it. I saw him there that night, and she was never heard from again. Of course he did it! He needed her gone."

"To what end? *You* were still there, weren't you? I was going to be born a few months later, and then what?"

They were finally to the crux of it. Because her dad wouldn't have needed to silence that girl if he and Donna had truly meant to raise Lauren together. That made no sense.

But if her mom had handed over her baby and taken off, then he could have gone back to his beautiful house with his wife, and Donna could have gone back to her imperfect party life in Los Angeles. The end. Everyone would have been the winner.

Even Lauren.

And wasn't that the real source of all this anger? Not that her mom would have given her up, but that she *should* have. All of them could have been perfectly happy and content if Donna Hempstead hadn't decided to destroy everything. Lauren's world could have been completely different.

"He didn't do it," she said past numb lips. "And you know that."

Her mom's jaw set for a long, strangling moment before she finally sighed, letting her shoulders slump. "Maybe you're right. Maybe I did something awful. I don't honestly believe that, but I have to concede that I could have been wrong. I'll take responsibility for that because I want you back in my life, Lauren."

Lauren felt like she was watching from above. An out-of-body experience. Her mom was finally saying the words Lauren had waited twenty-five years to hear, but she didn't feel anything. Not even anger.

In fact, it felt almost good to know about the original plan. Her dad had wanted her desperately from day one. He'd meant to keep her. Even though her arrival had meant nothing but complications for his life, he'd *wanted* her.

"It wasn't malice," her mom continued. "I wasn't a spurned woman looking for revenge. I thought I was doing right. I swear to God, Lauren. I blew up my world too, but I thought it was for a good reason." A hard laugh barked from her throat. "For the first time in my life, I thought I was doing the right thing. But I guess it's possible I

192

panicked and misread the whole situation. I thought I was going to be next. I thought . . ."

Lauren hovered above, watching impassively as she inhaled the smell of cooling oil and potatoes. She'd heard that story before too. Her mom out on the big, dark ranch, isolated and afraid, sure she'd be killed too. A stuck door that she'd decided must have been barricaded against her. No way off the ranch. More ravings.

"Can you forgive me?" her mother asked.

Could she?

She'd waited for this for decades. Asked for it. But now that it was here, she didn't feel forgiveness blooming anywhere. Not in her heart or head or left pinkie toe. She could think only about those wasted years. First while her dad was in prison, then when she'd felt so guilty about leaving her mom behind. All those years for what?

"I forgive you," she said because it made no difference at all. Easier to say she forgave her so she could get the hell out of there and go home. She could always block her number later when she had the breath and energy to move on with her life.

"Thank you." Her hands were on Lauren again, clutching both her wrists tightly, like a woman hanging over the edge of a cliff, pleading for rescue. "Thank you. I'm sorry I lied. I'm so sorry. That night when I told the police . . . I felt like I was in a horror movie. It was like a bad dream."

Just like that, Lauren was back in her body again, her skin too hot under her mother's grip. She'd spoken words of forgiveness, and now she wanted to leave. She wanted to get away from her mom and back to the life she was building.

And now she knew. It had been a lie, but these doubts her mother had planted were seeds that had sprouted. Now that Lauren knew, she could tear them up by the roots, confident her worries about her father were nothing but toxic weeds, twining around her, clinging with poisonous thorns.

"I need to get going," she said, pulling her arms back to cradle them against her body. "I'm expecting a guest tonight."

"Oh, that sounds fun," her mom said.

Lauren slid out of the booth. "Yeah. Fun."

"I'll keep watching your videos!"

"Thanks."

When Lauren scooped up her purse and turned away, her mom tried to slide free of the booth too. "Lauren, wait—"

"I've got to go," she muttered without turning back. She couldn't stay there. Grief was welling in her eyes, and she didn't want to deal with emotions right now, she just wanted to be *gone*.

A moment later, she was. Tears streaming down her face, she was dodging tourists and truckers, weaving her way out of the big parking lot to the freedom beyond.

She was going home.

CHAPTER 20

DONNA

"So your mom just completely cut your sister out of your life?" Donna asked, pressing harder for answers to these strange questions.

"She ran away. That broke Mom's heart. She's been gone more than twenty years now. What were we supposed to do, Donna? I don't have a sister anymore, and I haven't since I was sixteen. That's the truth."

Everything inside her tightened in stunned alarm at the verbal slap, and she knew exactly why. She'd left home twenty years ago too. Did her parents tell people she was dead? Worse, that she'd never existed? Did her brother claim to be an only child?

Jimmy was a grown man now and had likely gotten married and had kids. Hell, he'd probably divorced and remarried twice over. Did Donna's mom consider his wives the daughters she'd never had?

She trembled at the thought. Shivered as if someone had walked over her grave.

Most people were truly and irreversibly fucked up, and she was apparently no different. Had she moved here just to re-create the family she'd once had? She'd slipped into her place on the Abrams ranch like the long-dead sister coming home, filling the exact space she'd created in her own family when she'd run away so long ago.

"Good Lord," she muttered, pacing back and forth along the foot of the bed while Michael watched her, his gaze on her bare breasts. They'd finally put together her headboard, and the place looked almost normal now, aside from the old sheet she'd tacked over the window in place of blinds.

"Don't you think that's weird?" she asked again.

Michael stretched hard and threw the covers off. "I don't know. I'm going to hit the shower."

"You're *leaving*?" she screeched.

"Of course I'm leaving. It's the middle of the workweek. I told her I was having dinner with my mom and then I'd be home."

"Jesus, Michael. I'm trying to be patient, but you know goddamn well that's not in my nature. When is this going to be over? Are you doing *anything* to hurry it along?"

"I told you I've made an appointment with the divorce attorney I saw last time. I can't rush this and mess it all up. Be reasonable!"

She paced faster, nibbling at her thumbnail. *Be reasonable.* Wasn't she the most reasonable fucking woman in the world, waiting out here like a cloistered nun while he led a picture-perfect life with his beautiful wife? Well, maybe not exactly like a cloistered nun. She swept an angry gaze over his nude body as he headed for the bathroom. Not one of the obedient nuns, anyway.

"I'm going crazy out here," she growled. "There's not even a phone. Can't we get a phone? I went to use your mom's this morning, and she stayed right there the whole time, wiping down counters and pretending not to listen. I didn't have any privacy at all."

"Are you seriously complaining? You don't have to worry about anything here, you've already finished three paintings, and she feeds you home-cooked meals every damn day. Is that so terrible? So awful that you've decided to freak out about my mom being in her own home while you're on the phone? Really nice, Donna."

"I've lived alone my whole life! I hate depending on people. This is kind of an adjustment for me, you know!"

"Then *adjust!*" he snapped before he turned on the shower and shut the door.

"Asshole!" she screamed, hoping he heard her loud and clear over the spray. She tugged on a robe and stomped the twenty feet it took to get from her bed to the kitchen.

Michael had grilled steaks tonight for all three of them, and it had been a lovely, peaceful evening. Afterward, he'd taken her to bed and devoured her until she'd practically begged him to stop. He'd been her old Michael, mischievous and arrogant, as if he had everything he wanted right there in his arms. That was the Michael she'd fallen for before she'd realized she should take a closer look at the stories he told about his separation.

She'd been so happy a few moments ago, but now her skin itched with discontent. She couldn't even blame it on pregnancy hormones. She'd always been this way. Restless and unhappy as soon as her attention shifted away from a moment's pleasure.

Still, she was determined to make this work. This was the life she wanted for her kid. Maybe even herself. It was an adjustment, to be sure, but it was a far better situation than raising a baby alone in a tiny apartment with thin walls and no yard. She loved Michael, his mother was kind, and she had to learn how to slow down her brain and relax into this. In a year or so, they could move someplace else. An old neighborhood with a bohemian feel. But for now they would need this support.

Maybe she could think of this place as an artsy commune. Too many people around, not enough privacy, but all working together toward a common goal: raising this child.

Her little internal pep talk did nothing for her restlessness, so she wandered into the kitchen. Reaching for the freezer door, she frowned at the business card attached to the front with a magnet. She needed to make an appointment with that doctor. Michael had told her he'd call and take care of it since he had access to a phone all day, but he hadn't mentioned it since. She pulled out the carton of rocky road ice cream and closed the door again. The fluorescent-pink smiley face of the magnet annoyed her too. She couldn't wait for the fluorescent trend to die. The smiley face trend too.

She popped open the ice cream and grabbed a spoon before dropping onto the couch to eat from the carton. She was the only one who lived here, after all.

Michael was right about one thing, though she wouldn't admit it. She had gotten a lot of painting done since she'd moved in.

The light was perfect, just as promised, bright and warm, with enough haze to give everything a golden glow. Hell, she might even try her hand at a landscape one of these days. She loved taking her easel outside to work beneath the shade of the tree. The distance inspired her, letting her eyes relax enough to see shapes she wanted to draw from.

She understood it could be blazing hot here in the summer, but the fall weather was ideal, and her growing size would keep her warm through winter and early spring, so the climate felt perfect for now.

As chocolate melted on her tongue, her ears strained for every noise coming from the bathroom. She couldn't quite tell if he'd finished washing the smell of her from his body until the water finally stopped and silence boomed through the tiny house.

"Asshole," she said again, more quietly this time because everything hit her at once, and she felt tired. Good riddance to him, anyway. He tended to steal the covers in the night because he was a selfish asshole even while he slept.

The bathroom door opened, but his feet padded into the bedroom instead of finding her. Michael was ready to go. He hated confrontation and blame. A few minutes later he emerged from the room, fully dressed and tucking his shirt into wrinkled slacks, his hair still dry. He'd washed only the parts of himself that she'd soiled. He couldn't go home smelling like fresh shampoo. Donna didn't have the right brand.

"Thanks for your patronage, sir," she said. "We hope you found everything you were looking for."

"Donna," he whined on a weary sigh. "Come on."

"I'm tired. Good night."

He sighed again, a great gust of breath that shouted a hundred things about how irrational she was. But how could she be the irrational one when he was sucking up the love and support of a wife, a mistress, and a mother all at the same time and still feeling exasperated that Donna got upset? What a greedy shit.

He retreated to the bedroom for the last of his things, then walked past her without a word. Before he could scoot out the door, though, he paused for a dramatic moment, head hung low and heavy. "I love you, sweetie. You know that."

"Tell your wife I said hi," she responded, then smirked when he slammed the door. Her self-satisfaction quickly dissolved, though, and her mouth fell from a sneer of triumph into a pout.

Was she being unreasonable, or was he an asshole? "Both, probably," she muttered.

Donna got up to drop the empty ice cream carton into the trash. She opened the freezer again, but aside from two TV dinners, only a yawning white space greeted her. Not a drop of ice cream to be found. She opened the fridge and stared at the half gallon of milk and a bowl of leftovers. She didn't even have condiments in this place yet.

Now desperate, she tried the freezer one more time and glared at the turkey dinner, wondering if she could pop out the dessert square to heat it in a pan on the stove.

"Oh, screw this," she muttered. She slammed the door and grabbed her purse, then stuffed her feet into her boots. She was going shopping.

It was only 8:00. There was more than enough time to drive to town and hit the supermarket before it closed. And her mood shifted just that quickly, excitement thrumming through her at the idea of a full grocery bag of snacks to choose from.

"Hell yeah," she murmured as she practically jogged to her car. She eased her car past the bright lights of the main house, and then she was free, off to load up her trunk with every impulse she could possibly indulge.

"I'll rent a movie!" she yelped, even as she wiped a tear off her face. How in the world could her eyes be leaking when she was no longer thinking about her stupid, impossible situation? "Stop it, hormones," she demanded. Then she wiped at more tears and squealed onto the county road, determined to throw herself the best pity party ever.

An hour later she had two movies, three bags of groceries, and a whole stack of magazines and newspapers to read. She'd stay up all night, maybe, and sleep all day. She could tape a note to her door that she'd had insomnia and needed a very long nap. She might even be able to buy herself a whole twenty-four hours of solitude with this scheme, time to take a hot shower, paint her nails, eat cake for breakfast.

This long stretch of uncertainty would be over soon, and she did need to learn a little patience. Things would settle down. Michael would file for divorce, he'd work out the details with his wife, and Donna could concentrate on the future, whatever that might be.

She knew she would never be some fantasy version of a Suzy Homemaker. She wouldn't magically transform into a perfect mom just because she'd given birth. There were plenty of terrible mothers out there to prove that not everyone was a great parent. She'd need help. Even those natural mothers needed a break from caring for an infant. It truly was a miracle that his mom had thrown herself into the idea of the grandchild and held out open arms to Donna.

Thank God Donna had lost her shit with Michael and not his mom. She needed that woman on her side. Maybe she'd go over and spend a nice evening with her in a few days. Offer to try her hand at dinner. Ask for more stories about this place.

After her twenty-four hours of solitude.

Donna pulled up to her little cabin and quietly shut the car door as she got out. Yes, she just needed one day alone, and then she'd put her heart and soul into making this work.

Smiling, she hauled the bags inside, trying to decide which of the movies she'd watch. Happy hormones flooded her body, and she practically floated as she opened a can of bean dip and some Fritos.

"Oh God," she whispered around her first chip. "Amazing."

Maybe this wasn't good for her and her "advanced maternal age," but stress wasn't good either, right? And she felt like melting butter now, smooth and warm and perfect. That had to be good for the little fetus.

After firing up her stereo, she popped in a Pretenders cassette and set it to a reasonable volume.

Perfect.

She sank onto the couch with a soda, curving into the cushions for one heartbeat of absolute comfort. Then the music hit her the way it did sometimes.

A year ago at a dingy little club, that was the last time she'd heard this song. It had been late, 3:00 a.m. maybe, and she'd been drunk in that end-of-the-night way, flirting with a guy who was way too young for her, because the only other alternative was paying the tab and heading home. He'd been twenty-three at most. Trainable, maybe, but nothing to get excited about the first time. Eagerness in a man was something, but it didn't win the big awards.

In her twenties, she would have taken him home just to avoid silence, but that night she'd been as mellow as this song, enjoying the moment for what it was, a caress of connection before the long night turned to morning.

She'd gone home alone, and she'd stood on her patio in the pre-dawn quiet and smoked a cigarette while looking out at the whispering palms, and life had been so sweet.

The craving came back just that quickly, building to a quick crescendo that prickled sweat under her arms. Just one cigarette. One couldn't hurt.

She took a swig from her soda and grimaced as it went down. Okay, not even a *whole* cigarette. Half a smoke. Maybe just a few puffs! She needed that pure happiness back that she'd had a few minutes ago.

A few puffs of a cigarette, then some dessert and a movie. She'd put up her homemade sign pleading for a late morning, and then she'd pop up some Jiffy Pop on the stove and drag a whole pile of blankets to the sofa for a wonderful night.

Grinning with the high of being naughty—God, hadn't she always loved that?—Donna danced over to the table and grabbed the crumpled pack from her purse. She stopped for a moment to crack the small kitchen window so she could hear the music outside, then she slipped out her door and around to the big tree.

It was her favorite spot, and there was enough moon to look out over the vista as she tapped a smoke free and fired up her lighter.

The first draw sizzled, and the taste hit her tongue as she drew it in. Heaven. "Oh my God," she groaned, smoke curling from her mouth and around her head as the words sighed out of her. It had been a hell of a long time since one breath of nicotine had gotten her high, but she felt it immediately, a light-headed buzz.

Yeah, definitely just a few puffs. Instead of being a habit, it felt like an actual drug now, and you weren't supposed to give kids drugs.

Her head fell back, and she stared up at the dark claws of the tree above, scratching restlessly at the navy sky. The music trickled out, weaving around her. She shivered with pleasure.

"What do you think you're doing?"

Despite the warning of the hard words, Donna wasn't prepared for the slap that stung her wrist, and she dropped the cigarette to the grass with a shocked grunt.

"What the fuck?" she barked, jumping away and twisting to see what crazy monster had swooped out of the night to strike her from behind. Fear flooded her veins, easily chasing away the nicotine.

It was pitch dark beneath the tree, but the small window traced the faintest light over a silhouette, and Donna immediately identified her attacker. Elizabeth Abrams lurked two feet away, arms lifted from her body, fingers curled as if she meant to strike again, more forcefully this time.

Donna stretched tall, and she felt her chin edging forward as she inflated herself for a brawl. "What the hell do you think *you're* doing?" she shouted at the woman.

"I think I'm protecting a tiny baby that can't protect itself! What right do you have to puff on some cancer stick and poison my defense-less grandchild?"

Donna darted her gaze to either side of her, hoping another person was somehow close enough to confirm the insanity she was hearing. But she was alone out here, so there was no way to snap herself out of the sudden madness. "Jesus Christ, are you spying on me, you fucking psycho?"

"Watch your foul tongue!"

"Are you insane? You just *hit* me, and now you're worried about my language?"

"You're the one who's crazy," the woman spit out. "Poisoning a baby? Are you trying to get rid of it?"

"It was *one puff.*"

"As if I'm supposed to believe that. That was probably a beer I saw you sucking down in there too!"

Donna whipped her head toward the open window. Had she been lurking out here? Skulking against the side of the house and watching Donna through the window? The bedroom window was covered with a sheet, but she realized now that there was a line of sight from here to the living room, and it even caught the edge of her bed past the open bedroom door.

"You've been watching me," she breathed, a statement instead of a question.

"Oh, don't be so full of yourself. I heard a car drive up, and I came to check on you. It's late. Irony of ironies, I was worried. I obviously had the wrong dangers in mind."

Mrs. Abrams suddenly lunged, and Donna threw up her hands and pushed outward, but she only caught the side of the woman's arm as she shoved Donna out of the way. "Now you're trying to burn us down!" Michael's mother screeched as she stomped and patted the ground with her work boots.

A trail of smoke drifted up from the grass, twining around itself in the moonlight.

Donna watched dumbly, lips parted in shock, hands still tightly fisted. Another stomp caught more sparks, and she realized this wasn't manufactured drama, but she still couldn't move. "I'm sorry," she whispered.

"You should be!" The stomping seemed done now.

Donna's head buzzed. She shook it and tried to draw herself up again. "It was just one puff," she repeated. "I'm having cravings, and I thought one little taste would let me move on."

"You sound like a drug addict," his mother snapped.

"I'm not."

She muttered something under her breath as she whipped away. Donna thought it sounded like "Pure trash," but she wasn't sure. Her heart was beating too loudly in her own ears.

Just like that, Donna was alone in the dark again. Or was she?

She'd taken comfort in the fact that there was no sight of the main house from her cabin, but that comfort had been as false as the slow affection building between the two of them.

Had his mother been spying the whole time?

Eyes still darting down the path, she leaned over and snatched up the lighter she'd dropped. A glance at the ground didn't yield her cigarette pack. She really didn't want to look away from the danger of the darkness in front of her, but she finally ducked her head and ran her gaze over the grass. She turned in a circle until she finally spotted it. Mrs. Abrams had stomped the cigarettes into smithereens.

"That fucking bitch," Donna snarled before retreating to the cabin and slamming the door as hard as she could. She shot the lock, then rushed to close the window as well.

That was no protection from prying eyes, though. She dug through a few boxes until she came up with two bath towels and another sheet. Unfortunately it was a fitted sheet, but she'd take anything at this point. She covered up all three small windows, nailing the fabric into place. She'd worry about letting light in tomorrow.

She wanted to call Michael right now and tell him what his mother had done, but she had no phone. She considered tearing the hell out of there and driving to the nearest gas station to use a pay phone, but what would that solve? She'd have to call his home, wake up his wife, and say what? *This is an emergency, your mother slapped my wrist!*

She laughed at the imagined conversation, and a few breaths later, she felt slightly better.

That bitch had been completely out of control, and Donna would never forgive her, but . . . she hadn't been wrong, exactly. Donna shouldn't have been smoking, and she knew that, but she wasn't a child either. Her body was hers, and this pregnancy was hers, and this baby was hers. No one had a right to put hands on her.

"I should've punched her right in the throat," Donna said. Even as the words left her mouth, she knew she didn't mean them, but damn, it still felt good to say.

She checked the lock again, then got her pack of Twinkies and a bag of chips and loaded the VCR. She felt too drained to make popcorn tonight. She felt too drained to do anything now, and she felt herself nodding off before she'd even made it past the movie previews that preceded the film.

Crap. She wrapped her blankets around her, trundled into the bedroom, and snapped off the light.

She dreamed about a missing baby and tossed and turned in sweaty sheets the whole night, her hands reaching out to slide over and under the damp fabric. But she never found her child.

CHAPTER 21

LAUREN

"Dad!" Lauren yelped, throwing the car into park before it had even rolled to a stop.

She threw her door open and leapt out as her dad stepped off her front porch.

"Hey, pumpkin!" he called as she raced toward him, relief and love fizzing in her veins like bubbles.

She jumped into his arms and held tight as he swung her around like she was still a little girl. "I thought I'd missed you!" she squealed. "I stopped by to see Grandma, and she was napping. The staff said you'd been visiting."

"I guess all that fun wore her out. Figured I'd stop by to see you too. I was just about to text and track you down."

"I was out for a while . . . running errands." If he noticed her hesitation, he didn't give any sign. He just kissed the top of her head and let her go.

"I assumed you were out on a lunch date or something. You know, you have to get back on the horse and get out there."

"I know." She didn't mention that Bastian was arriving in a couple of hours. Not because her dad would object. He and Bastian got along fine. But because she felt self-conscious about inviting her ex to visit.

Everyone kept telling her to get back out there, but she couldn't stop interacting with the same old guy.

At thirty-three, she'd started talking about kids. Bastian had agreed in principle, but he'd rejected the immediacy of it. Home prices in the city were insane and only getting crazier. You couldn't raise a kid in a one-bedroom condo. Children needed space and nature! They'd agreed that they would get around to it when they were more settled. Those discussions had lasted two years until she'd finally exploded and asked when they'd be settled enough for children.

His response had been a reminder of something she'd known her whole life: don't ask a question if you might not like the answer.

"The floors look great, pumpkin," her dad said.

She'd locked all her doors, but he'd had a key for fifty years, of course. "Thank you. Did you have lunch?"

"I ate with Mom in her room. I was hoping for a grand tour of all the changes you've made, though."

She pulled him into the house and opened the curtains to show off the floor, though he'd already seen it. Grinning proudly, she watched the light glow off the stain. "I bet you never knew there was so much wood under there!"

"Definitely not. I would have loved racing trucks through the house if it had looked like this."

"Grandma would've killed you."

"Without a doubt. But I still would've tried it. I had two huge Tonka trucks that I loved with all my heart. They're probably buried under the mess of one of the collapsed outbuildings now."

"If I find any, I'll let you know."

She led him to the kitchen to point out the changes she would make, then held her breath as she fired up the planning software to give him a preview.

He glanced at the screen but only nodded. The air slowly deflated from her lungs. She thought the changes looked gorgeous on the computer, and could only hope they looked half as good once she was done. "You don't like it?"

"No, it's really great."

"I'm going to keep Grandma's sink, obviously. People pay thousands to get their hands on a sink like that. And I'll just refurbish the butcher block. All that history! You must have so many memories of her working there."

"Sure," he responded, offering a distracted smile. "What about upstairs? Big plans?"

She put her best effort into answering his smile, but she felt it wobble at the edges. "Eventually. No time soon, though."

"Why don't you show me what you have planned?"

"Oh, I haven't even—" But he was already bounding up the stairs, all long and lanky energy despite his age.

Lauren followed.

"You're not getting rid of my room, are you?" he shouted over his shoulder as he moved down the hall. "Hey, where's my bed?"

Blood rushed to Lauren's face until her skin felt on fire. What a silly reaction. Her dad knew full well that she and Bastian had been intimate. They'd lived together. Still, she went ahead and lied. "Grandma took her bed to her new place. I needed something bigger than a twin in there." She let the implication that she was staying in her grandmother's room hover so it wasn't quite a lie.

Her dad shrugged. "All right. Looks like you haven't changed much up here, anyway."

"No. Nothing yet. I can't do plumbing or major construction myself. I assume I'll eventually put the bathroom over the kitchen since everything is already wired and plumbed right under it, but who knows? I need to get someone out here to talk logistics before I make any plans."

"So you'll finish downstairs first?"

"Yes. I have no choice! I need the practice before I work up to anything else. I can probably do the design for this bathroom on my own.

And I should be able to figure out laying tile after I do the backsplash in the kitchen. I think I could install a bathroom sink?"

He nodded, his eyes moving over his old room, touching each wall and corner. "Well, let me know if you plan to destroy the rest of my childhood. I might want to say goodbye first. Or take a few posters." He caught Lauren's grimace and winked. "You're doing great, pumpkin."

Well, it wasn't much, but it appeared to be all she'd get, so she took the compliment and grinned. "Why don't I make some coffee? It's been so long since we had time together."

She'd stopped by her grandmother's on impulse to ask about MaryEllen in the gentlest way possible, but found her deeply asleep. When she leaned in to press a gentle kiss to her grandmother's head, she felt like she'd been granted a reprieve. A dreaded task she'd been able to avoid.

Now she could ask her father, but . . . why? Couldn't she just relish this huge boulder she'd finally rolled off her shoulders? After thirty-five years, her mom had admitted to the one big lie. The lie that had ruined *everything*. Hadn't Lauren told herself for years that getting that answer would bring her some peace?

She had her truth now, and her dad was the only parent she wanted in her life for the moment. He was the one who'd wanted her from the start. Why the hell would she make herself a nuisance now?

I've missed you hovered on her lips, another clinging plea for reassurance. But she wasn't a little girl anymore. Her dad loved her. He always had. Why couldn't she hold that close and accept it?

He put his hands on his hips and took one last look at the room. "I guess I'd better not stay for coffee. Cody has a soccer match this evening."

Another soccer game.

But only an immature child would see her dad's busy life as a rejection. "Sure," she said, trying for a casual note of cheer. "Another time. Maybe I'll come watch a game soon."

"You should! They're having a great season. But I'd better get going. Suki is probably already pissed I'm not there helping load the truck."

Lauren couldn't honestly complain, even if everything in her chest felt tightly coiled. His other kids were young, and they deserved the same amount of attention she'd received from him at that age.

Plus it was getting late, and she had things to do. She needed to shower and do her hair and makeup before Bastian arrived, so he could regret his decisions.

She smiled. "Have you talked to Suki about Thanksgiving? I'll have the kitchen done by then, and it would be amazing to have everyone home. Here, I mean. *Your* home."

"Maybe. We're looking at a place on the beach in Mexico. The kids are off all week."

"Oh. Well, we'll see, then."

"Have Grandma out, at least," he said as he brushed past her and headed toward the stairs. She frowned as she followed, her fantasies of everyone gathered in the dining room together now dashed. He and Suki loved to travel, and if they were thinking about Mexico, they were going to Mexico. His life with Suki was a new kind of adventure with more money and freedom.

Their house wasn't huge, but it sat on a hill overlooking Menlo Park, its modern walls of windows offering views and no privacy. She'd rather have her little house in the country.

Frankly, she should be thankful instead of asking for more. She'd had her dad all to herself until she'd gone off to college. His younger kids were blindly living the suburban dream, with parents who worked long hours and a nanny who had half raised them. But Lauren and her dad had been a team. They'd built a whole new life together.

Maybe that was why she didn't know how to fit in with his new family. When she was a teenager, it had been her and Dad against the world, fighting for happiness after all that injustice. But then the world had joined them.

She needed to work on finding a place in his new family. Try harder.

By the time she walked out to the porch, she'd made a conscious decision to feel better, and she accepted his hug with all the warmth in her heart. "Let me know about Thanksgiving," she said, just in case. "And I'll get in touch about coming out to see a game. I'm so glad you came today, Daddy. It was exactly the surprise I needed."

"Love you, pumpkin," he said, and then he was gone, just a trail of dust rising from the drive.

She watched for only a moment before she hurried back inside. Bastian would be here in a few hours, and she had to be ready to face him.

~

Three hours later, a chicken was in the oven and she was at the front window, watching for a faint cloud to signal another visitor. Thank God she'd gotten all the throwing-herself-into-male-arms impulse out of the way with her dad, because when she spotted the dust of an approaching car, Lauren actually had to blink tears from her eyes.

When Bastian had broken things off, she'd still loved him, still wanted him. The house and the renovation had proved to be admirable distractions, but that was all they had been. Tonight, after all the upheaval of the day, the echoing hole inside her felt bottomless.

It wasn't only about love, though. She'd had that her whole life in some tattered form or another. What she craved down to her bones was the certainty of knowing she *belonged*. She wanted love that could not be withdrawn. Something she wouldn't have to cling to or appease.

Jesus. What she needed more than anything was a therapist. After everything was settled and life had calmed down, she'd find one. And she wouldn't chicken out like she had a few years before.

His car pulled into view, a sleek black hybrid hatchback with one politically progressive sticker placed discreetly on the lower windshield. She edged back from her window so she wouldn't look like she was desperately awaiting him. She wasn't, really. Everything had just gotten so weird, and Bastian was so familiar.

She spied on him as he pulled to a stop beside her car and got out, all smooth movement and cool shades. He slipped the sunglasses off and looked around, his sharply defined jaw rising a little to take in the sky and the trees.

Jesus, he looked good. He always looked good, and not in a self-conscious way. His jeans were ancient and snug, his button-down shirt worn soft by a thousand washings. Only his perfectly groomed work boots gave away any sign of vanity, the laces pristine and bright red.

He smiled as he gave the landscape one last, satisfied look, and Lauren made an involuntary, yearning sound at the sight of it. When he faced the front porch, she ducked safely away.

How long since she'd seen him? Six weeks?

Holding her breath, she waited. His boot hit the first step, and by the time he knocked, she had ordered herself to calm down. She'd lived with this man for three years and knew everything about him she could know. He was no cipher to make her hands shake. She'd cleaned the toilet after he'd had stomach flu.

She waited a few more moments before she walked over to answer the door.

"Lauren!" he exclaimed, his smile wide and white and easy, the kind of smile that drew strangers into his circle.

"Hey, Bastian," she said, trying to play it cool and sounding irritated instead. She pitched her voice higher. "How was the drive?"

"Great. Look at this place!" He moved back toward the steps, and Lauren followed so they could gaze out at the view together. "This is amazing!"

"Can you believe I actually own this?"

"No, but only because a place like this in LA would cost four million. You're living like a damn CEO up here, babe."

Her laugh was too loud and too long, but there was only so much coolness she could fake.

"You look great," he said. She kept her eyes straight ahead when he turned toward her. "You've never had that dark a tan in LA."

"It's a farmer's tan," she warned. "I've been weeding the gardens."

"Well, give me the whole tour! I want to see it with new eyes now that it's yours. The porch is gorgeous, and you know I love that original woodwork around the windows."

By the time they finished the tour, she'd relaxed back into her old groove with him. Bastian had lost the stiffness he'd shown in their last few weeks together. He was back to his former, charming self. He was a fantastic listener when he wanted to be, which made it that much more painful to lose his attention.

"So nothing else has happened?" he asked as he started unscrewing the ancient doorbell to rewire it for the new video bell.

"Absolutely nothing," she answered, deliberately leaving out her text to Kepnick. She didn't want to talk about it. There'd been no response, and now she regretted her angry impulse. It hung over her like a trap about to drop, and she was thinking of blocking the number so she could stop waiting for the snap.

"I brought you a surprise," Bastian said with a wide grin.

"What is it?"

"I brought my GoPro and the extra battery pack for you to use. If you have any idea when the letters are being left, we could set it up to take time-lapse photos. It will go for about six hours at one frame every thirty seconds. It's not a live feed, but it's something, and I figured your mailbox was too far from the house to wire a video camera."

"Wow!" She glanced guiltily toward the driveway. It was a great idea, but she doubted she'd need it now. "Thank you so much."

"I was worried you'd want to stake it out yourself or something, so this seemed like a better option."

"Absolutely."

By the time the chicken was ready, a motion sensor had been installed to cover the parlor and the end of the stairway, and entry sensors had been placed on both doors.

"Is it working?" she asked as she took the corn bread and the roast chicken from the oven.

Bastian looked up from her laptop and gave her a thumbs-up. "Cozy as Fort Knox! I set up the GoPro to run tonight, so we'll see how that goes too."

She buttered the squash and carved the chicken while he pointed out all the features on the app. She could've done all of it on her own, but his offer had meant he'd wanted to see her. And she'd wanted to see him.

She opened a bottle of wine without asking, and as they sat down to eat, it felt so sweet and natural, just like the old days, back when they'd been content to stay home with just each other. There had been more and more socializing in the end, Bastian craving time with other people. But not tonight. Tonight his eyes stayed locked on her face as they talked.

When dinner was finished, she tipped the wine bottle for one last glass, but only a few drops slid out. "Uh-oh," she said with a grin.

"Whoops," Bastian responded with his own smile.

"I'd open another, but I think I should get your renovation advice before we get drunk." Not that she wasn't already tipsy. "Can we talk about the bathroom I want to add? I don't know where to put it, who to call first, what to look out for . . ."

"Absolutely. Let me check out the layout down here one more time. Get a feel for where the old plumbing is."

She made sure she didn't sway when she stood to follow him. She liked watching him move through this space. This space belonged to *her*, and she felt suddenly powerful and bold, the person who held all the cards. This was her beautiful house, in her hometown, and she was the one who didn't need him for once.

Her lips curved into a secret smile as he took a few pictures on his phone. She knew he'd stay the night. He hadn't mentioned anything about driving, hadn't refused a second glass of wine. And Bastian was nothing if not responsible. He wouldn't drive into San Francisco half-drunk. No, he meant to stay. And she meant to have him.

"Shall we?" he said with a wink as he led the way upstairs.

"Absolutely," she purred. *Purred.* Lauren Abrams purring! She floated up after him and followed him into the main bedroom.

"The kitchen is right below that corner," she said. "And the downstairs bathroom is there. This bedroom is good-sized, but it's not that huge, so if I put it here, I'd need to keep the bathroom space small. A shower and a pedestal sink and a toilet. But I'm still afraid the sleeping area will get too confined. Maybe one of those barn-style doors on rails would help."

"That's a good idea in a small space."

"But the other choice is to turn a spare bedroom into a bathroom. I'd really hate to lose a bedroom, but there are four. And the laundry room is right beneath this one." He followed her into her dad's room.

"That's a good idea if there's plumbing right below. You could just knock out this wall," he said, gesturing toward her dad's closet. "You can turn this into a bathroom *and* add a small walk-in closet. You could keep the existing doorway here for access from the hallway for guests, but you'd still have private access from your room too."

"And," she said, waggling her eyebrows, "I'd get to knock out a wall, which would be a blast."

"I could come back and help," he said with a roguish smile. "Spend a little time . . ."

Just like that, tension snapped into existence in the air between them, and Lauren was powerful again, shoulders back, head cocked, eyelids heavy with arousal.

He stepped forward. So did she. Except then she changed her mind. She was always the eager one, and this time she meant to be cool. She *was* cool.

Lauren moved back. His eyebrows dipped a little until his gaze dropped and he saw her smirk. One side of his mouth tipped up in answer. He stepped forward again. She stepped back. And then she had nowhere to go. The wall at her back. Bastian stalking forward. She parted her lips to let out her quickened breath, and then he was on her, mouth at her neck, hands on her hips, and Lauren groaned.

Sensations shook through her, bouncing along her nerves, and it felt as if her pores opened up to soak in his familiar scent.

He reached for the button of her jeans, and she managed to rasp, "Not in my dad's room."

Bastian chuckled and turned her body, easing her into the hallway and backward toward the main bedroom. Lauren tried to forget that it was still her grandma's room and found it was a little easier with Bastian's hands pushing up her shirt and his teeth scraping along her skin. God, his body was so warm beneath her grasping hands.

When he got her shirt off, he kissed her, deep and long, and then she was falling back into the bed. The late-evening sun gilded his skin in gold and orange, and Bastian looked like a dream above her. *Her* dream.

He stripped while she watched, his face serious now, not a hint of laughter.

The power inside her swelled like an aura, and she felt it touch him, felt him respond in kind, until they were desperate with it. He entered her almost immediately, but the sex wasn't quick and rough. Not at all. It was intense and building, their bodies sliding with sweat, mouths forming guttural, gasping sounds as they kissed and panted and fucked.

Lauren came hard, once, then again, until Bastian finally collapsed on top of her.

That was when he laughed. She laughed too, a shocked burst of pleasure that pealed from her mouth until tears leaked from her eyes. "I guess I missed you," she said, and he chuckled as he kissed her before twisting away to collapse on the sheets. They lay in comfortable silence as the sunset darkened to dusk around them.

"You really need an upstairs bath," he said finally, and they laughed again, their hands curling together in the purple light.

"Hey, if you need to go downstairs, grab more wine when you come back up."

"So . . . ," he drawled, "does that mean I can stay the night?"

"I suppose." Her tone tried at coy, and she might have pulled it off out of sheer lethargy. "If you don't have anywhere else to sleep."

He leaned over to kiss her again before he got up to tug on his pants. "I'll go grab my bag and be right back."

When she heard the front door close, Lauren shook off her relaxation and hurried downstairs to use the bathroom herself. When she finished, she found him waiting outside the door. He cast an appreciative eye down her naked body. "Don't worry," she said as she planted a quick kiss to his mouth. "I'll get the wine."

He returned eventually, and they picnicked nude on the bed, sipping wine and brushing cookie crumbs off each other, and they talked. They talked for hours, because Lauren had been so damn lonely here, and being with him still felt like the most natural thing in the world. Later they made love again, and for a few blissful moments, something felt possible. Something sweet and serious and bigger than they'd had before.

She'd taken a chance here. She'd grown more confident and larger, away from the city where she'd fit herself into his life like a puzzle piece jammed in too tightly. Maybe he'd be willing to fit himself here, where there was all this space to build new things.

Lauren felt him kiss her head just before she fell asleep.

When she woke up to morning light, he was gone, his empty wineglass and the soreness between her thighs the only two signs he'd been there.

CHAPTER 22

DONNA

She woke to a knock on the front door and sat up with a gasp. Confused and sticky with sweat, she looked frantically around the room, unsure where she was at first.

The cabin. Michael's family ranch.

It wasn't early, it couldn't be, judging by the slant of light through her makeshift curtain, so this wasn't the daily 7:00 a.m. visit.

Had his mother called Michael this morning and confessed to her violence? Had he come by to check on her?

She swiped damp hair off her forehead and got up, tugging her pajamas back into place while silently cursing that she was a person who wore pajamas now. "Knocked up," she muttered, "living in the country, and wearing a matching pajama set like your mother used to own."

Good God.

She opened the bedroom door and tiptoed toward the front. If his mom was there, that woman could just keep knocking. Donna wasn't interested in a friendly little chat quite yet.

She crossed to the window instead of the door and carefully eased up one corner of the towel. Michael wasn't waiting. Neither was his mom. Donna didn't see anyone. She pulled the towel higher and craned her neck. No one there at all, though she saw the shadow of an object in front of the door.

"Hmm." She stepped over to unfasten the bolt lock and carefully pushed the door open. A wooden tray sat to the side, a red thermos and a Tupperware container on top of it, and she saw a note taped to a small glass bottle.

Donna glared suspiciously around the yard, but when she didn't catch anyone spying, she picked up the tray and hurried back inside, letting the door swing shut behind her.

It hadn't occurred to her that the note could be anything but an apology, but her imagination had been far too limited. There was no *I'm sorry.* The neat handwriting simply said, *You missed breakfast.* It had been taped to a bottle of prenatal vitamins. *Now with more folic acid!* the label read cheerfully. Donna recognized that term from one of the pamphlets, but it still meant nothing to her.

She popped open the Tupperware to find a piece of coffee cake. The thermos held coffee—decaf, no doubt—and Donna eyed that more warily. It probably wasn't poisoned, even if that was only out of concern for the unborn grandchild.

The cake was still warm, and the scent of cinnamon and brown sugar finally overwhelmed her suspicions. "No one is trying to kill you, you self-centered asshole," she said to herself as she retrieved a fork. And if they were, death by warm cake was probably the way to go.

By the time she finished, she felt ninety percent better, and she even considered walking down to hash it out with Mrs. Abrams. It wasn't as if her wrist were bruised or permanently damaged. Even her ego would recover in time.

She wished she could just call Michael and talk it over, but she'd have to drive into town to get any privacy, and mornings were his busiest time. The few occasions she'd tried to reach him before noon, he'd always been away from his desk, organizing . . . whatever it was he organized. Shipments? Distribution? It was none of her business. He hadn't asked about her job either.

She felt a surprising wave of yearning at the thought of her job. She'd held no deep love for the idea of working for the Man, but now she missed the camaraderie of it. She missed the murmur of voices, the unexpected interruptions, the reliability of every weekday showing up right on schedule, bright and early.

Now she had nowhere to go, nothing to do. A month ago she would've said this was living the dream, but now she knew why rich people were all crazy. She felt unbound and aimless and likely to take up some strange hobby like shooting helpless exotic animals or taking over a small, underdeveloped island nation.

Her own thoughts made her laugh at least, but she wasn't sure that was a good sign.

Finally she got herself a yogurt, gathered up her big stack of new reading material, and headed back to bed. Her plan had been to hide inside, and she couldn't see any reason a surprise attack should make her throw open her doors and take on the day.

She thumbed through an entertainment magazine, but the pictures of beautiful people having glamorous fun only made her sneer with jealousy. She glared at the slim waists and glowing skin before tossing it on the floor.

The Sacramento newspaper caught her eye, and she unfolded it with raised eyebrows. There couldn't be much going on in this town, but she should probably make an effort to get to know her new city.

The front page was all about some basketball team, the Sacramento Kings, and Donna rolled her eyes. Sports belonged on the sports pages, not spread across the first page with multiple exclamation points.

She passed over a few more boring sheets, flapping them in her rush, but when something caught her eye, she stopped so quickly that the paper snapped in her hands and dipped in on itself, covering the picture that had frozen her muscles.

The paper refused to cooperate when she tried to straighten it, but she finally slapped it into submission and stared at the photograph. The young woman's wide smile and dark hair looked familiar, which made no sense. Donna didn't know anyone here.

The headline turned her insides to stone, but she wasn't sure why: "Nearly Two Weeks Since Local Woman Seen."

Brow drawn into a tight frown of confusion, Donna tried her best to read the story, but her eyes kept skipping ahead. *Missing. Cocktail waitress. No word.* And then she saw it. The connection that triggered a spotlight focused bright and ruthless on a gut-wrenching picture—*not seen since her afternoon shift at Lucky's.*

"Holy shit," she whispered, fingers rising to cover her lips in horror. It was her. The cocktail waitress Michael had been flirting with. The one she'd seen him pick up at Lucky's.

Donna sprang up on the bed, the weight of her body carelessly crushing the paper, her heel tearing part of it when she twisted. She leapt toward the doorway, moving with more speed than she'd managed in weeks as she raced to the front room.

Her purse sat on the small table, and she flipped it over, disgorging the contents onto the scarred wood. A lipstick rolled off. Her keys clanked onto the linoleum. But her checkbook dropped right into the middle of the pile, and Donna snatched it up.

She knew it was Wednesday, so she trailed her finger over the tiny digits of the calendar printed on the check pad. How long had she been here? It felt like six weeks already, but no. She'd been here for one full weekend, and she'd moved in the previous weekend. So . . . ten days? Eleven maybe? And she'd seen Michael with that girl a day before.

"Almost two weeks," she said aloud, her voice scratchy and hoarse.

She stared at the tiny numbers until they blurred; then she shook her head hard. No. She had to be mistaken. She squeezed her eyes shut to clear them, then tried again, tracing the days, the weeks, racking her brain for the exact day she'd seen him at Lucky's.

Almost two weeks.

A Friday evening.

"What the hell?" she barked. "What the *hell?*"

She meant to race to the bedroom, to get dressed, to act quickly, do *something*. But she stood there, dumb. Dumb and bubbling over with more curses, more questions.

It didn't mean anything, surely. So what if Michael had seen that girl just before she'd gone missing? Everyone in the bar had seen her. Before she disappeared. This girl. This young woman. Before she vanished from the earth and everyone who knew her.

"No," Donna said aloud. That was part of the story too. She—Tori Bagot, the paper said—had come here from somewhere else the year before. Ottawa. She was a stranger in this place just like Donna. She had no family here and so far no family had been located in Canada either. She'd only been working at Lucky's for six months, and she'd rented her apartment around that time too.

So maybe Tori Bagot had simply left. Disappeared, yes, but only because she'd stepped back into whatever life she'd had before Sacramento. She'd fallen off the radar because the radar wasn't strong or steady enough to pick her up. She was happy and laughing somewhere, that beautiful smile inspiring jealousy in some other middle-aged woman in some other place.

Donna didn't race to her bedroom to get dressed, but she didn't climb back into bed either. Instead she very calmly brushed her teeth and showered. By the time she walked out of the cabin, it was 11:00, and Mrs. Abrams's shiny white pickup was gone from beside her house.

Donna knocked on the door before letting herself in. "Hi!" she called. "I just need to use the phone!" No one answered. Donna had privacy at long last.

She called Michael's work and crossed her fingers that he was done with his busy morning and back at his desk. Her pagan prayers must have worked, because his secretary put the call through.

"Abrams," he answered.

"Michael!" she said. "Oh my God, Michael, have you seen the paper?"

"Donna? What paper? What are you talking about?"

"That girl. Tori. That girl you were seeing, she's missing!"

She heard his chair squeak and the door close, shutting out the loudest background noise. "Come on, Donna. I wasn't seeing her. I was just flirting. It's no big deal."

"Who the hell cares about that now? Did you hear what I said? She's *missing*."

He sighed long and low, so weary, so put upon. "Missing how, exactly?"

"What do you mean, 'missing how'? She's gone. No one has seen her in almost two weeks."

"Does that mean she's missing? She was a cocktail waitress at a roadside bar. Did she have kids or something? A husband?"

"No. Actually, no. She doesn't have any family here. That's what the paper said. But she didn't show up to work the next day. Her friend called the police."

"Okay. So why are you calling me?"

"Because you know her. You might have information. Hell, you might have been the last person to see her."

"I find that pretty hard to believe. Look . . ." He cleared his throat. "I was just a customer. She brought me beers. That was it. I hardly knew her."

Donna hesitated at his rote words, though she had no idea why. She opened her mouth, glanced around at the empty room, closed her mouth, and looked again. Finally she turned toward the corner and hunched over the mouthpiece. "You took her somewhere."

"What?" he snapped. "What the hell are you talking about? I didn't take her anywhere, and you'd better not be telling people that!"

"Who would I tell, Michael? I'm living on the goddamn Abrams ranch in the middle of nowhere with your psychotic mother!"

"My psychotic mother? Good God, Donna, you're a real special piece of work. It's not enough to be crazy about one thing at a time, you need to throw a little more raving into the mix?"

"I'm not crazy, you asshole. Your insane mother slapped me last night! How's that for crazy?"

He paused for a long time, and Donna knew, she *knew*, that he must be heartbroken and confused. But she was wrong.

"Mom already told me what happened. She slapped a cigarette out of your hand. Is that right?"

"She—"

"A cigarette being smoked by a pregnant woman who's already old enough to be at high risk for miscarriage and birth defects. And she's the crazy one here? *She* is? What the hell is wrong with you? That's my kid too, Donna. I thank God she was there to stop whatever little drug party you'd decided to throw yourself."

"I wasn't . . . Jesus!" She threw her hands up and growled in fury. "I was drinking soda. I wanted one drag of a cigarette. That's it. And she hit me."

"An old lady slapped your hand. Do you think you're going to be okay? Do you need me to take you to a shelter? Or maybe straight to the emergency room?"

She hated him with every fiber of her being then, mostly because she'd settled on the same reaction this morning and recognized the logic, but she wanted him to be upset first. To show rage or concern or anything other than scorn.

She wanted—*needed*—someone on her side for once in her life. "Michael . . ."

Another gust of air, but this time the sigh seemed to temper his mood. "I'm sorry she did that. I am. You freaked her out. You must be able to understand that. And if it helps at all, she was a big believer in corporal punishment when I was a kid. This just means you're truly part of the family now."

Donna laughed, and then she kept laughing, descending into slightly hysterical giggles that brought tears to her eyes. "The daughter she never had," she managed to choke out.

"Exactly. Did she bring you some food afterward?"

"She did, actually."

"That's her way of apologizing for losing her temper. She did it every time I got a spanking."

Donna couldn't believe she felt herself thawing at that, but there was a distinctly warm feeling in her chest. And she could respect a bout of out-of-control temper every once in a while. Hadn't she thrown a vase at Michael's head just two weeks earlier?

"She brought over pregnancy vitamins," she said.

"There you go. She's worried about you. That's all."

Donna very clearly remembered the only time she'd ever been afraid of her own meek mother. Donna had borrowed a pair of those metal wheels that strapped onto tennis shoes to turn them into roller skates, and she'd devised a fun game of crouching low and rolling straight down the driveway into the street. When her mother had witnessed it, she'd yanked Donna hard by the arm and whipped her butt about fifteen times in a row, screaming about cars and death and danger. So she wasn't unfamiliar with fear making moms lash out. It happened.

"I thought you two were getting along," he finally said.

She waved an impatient hand, already tired of the appeasement. "I called about that Tori girl, anyway. You don't even care that she's gone missing?"

"I mean, I guess I care." The creak of his chair cut through the quiet. "She's a person. But she didn't mean anything to me. We didn't have a relationship. All I ever did was flirt with her. I made that clear to you at the time, didn't I?"

Donna slumped against the wall, the cool of the plaster soaking into her shoulder. "I don't know. Where did you take her that night?"

His voice rose. "I didn't take her anywhere."

"I thought . . . No, I *know* she was in your car."

"She wasn't. You know, now that I think about it . . ." Movement ruffled the sound. She pictured him changing the receiver from one ear to another. "Hell, maybe she had more of a crush on me than I realized. I went in and I apologized and made it clear I had a girlfriend and there was nothing between us. That's what happened. So maybe she freaked out and left. Maybe she took off her apron and got out of town."

"Because you told her you had a girlfriend? Come on, Michael."

"I don't know! You know how sensitive some women can be. I didn't say it was rational, I just said it was possible."

Donna didn't concede the point, but she had to admit to herself that she hadn't actually seen that girl. She'd seen her hand. Hadn't she? Could Michael have been reaching across to pull his own door closed?

But what did it matter if that girl might have only left town?

"Even if you just saw her that night, you should still tell the police. They're asking for any help they can get. Literally no one has heard from her since she left work."

"I'm not volunteering my name for no reason! That's insane. I didn't do anything, so why would I get involved? What clue could I give? 'Yeah, I saw her, she was carrying a bottle of Budweiser to a table.' You think that would help?"

She shrugged to herself. "I don't know."

"I think you and I have enough going on already without having the police knocking on doors to ask for alibis. You were at my house that night, remember?"

Right. She'd lost her shit and gone to his home to confess everything to his wife.

"I was there with you," he pointed out.

"Fine," she finally allowed. "I get it."

"Try to keep things cool with Mom, all right? I'll have things settled soon."

"I guess."

After hanging up, she scrubbed both hands over her face, feeling more than a little frazzled. All she'd wanted was one quiet day. Instead she'd dealt with a sneak attack and a missing persons case.

"Well, fuck me," she murmured, tired of it all. She'd lost her chance for a relaxing day, but she'd done her shopping, and she still had movies.

Turning away from the phone, Donna caught sight of a shadowy figure a few feet away and shrieked in terror. It was only after she'd managed to clamp her mouth shut that she recognized the wavy curls and set mouth of Michael's mother.

"Good afternoon," the woman said while Donna was still wheezing air past her tight throat.

"I . . . Yes. Hi. I was just . . ." She gestured toward the phone. "Talking to Michael."

"Interesting. How is Michael?"

"You spoke to him this morning, didn't you?"

It didn't seem as if the woman could've pulled herself straighter, but she somehow did. "He called to see how we were doing, yes."

We. As if they were a package now. A team. Were they?

"Great," Donna said, the word twisting somewhere between dry and cordial. "Thanks for the phone. I guess I'll get back to my painting."

"I hope you'll be joining us for dinner?" Was that the royal *we*, or was Michael coming? Maybe she was just referring to her housekeeper's work.

"Sure. Thanks."

That seemed to be all the apology she would get, so Donna hurried out, vaguely wondering how much his mother had overheard. But Donna wasn't an introspective type, so she put the question aside before she even reached the front step of her cabin. The woman had heard whatever she'd heard.

Another Tupperware container sat in front of her door. This one held a ham sandwich and potato chips. Donna tried not to let the gesture warm her heart, but it did. If this was the way that woman showed love, then maybe Donna needed to learn to relax and accept it.

Families forgave each other, didn't they? She'd been too young to see that when she'd fled her home so many years ago. Maybe she needed to accept imperfection and embrace the family that was right in front of her.

"Maybe," she said as she brought the sandwich inside and put it safely in the fridge for later.

She pulled her easel out to the tree and stared over the hills toward the play of light and cloud over the land.

For the first time in her life, Donna started painting a landscape. If it turned out well, she'd take it down to the main house as her own gesture. If they were going to make this work, even just for a little while, she'd learn to make peace.

Maybe she was maturing after all.

CHAPTER 23

LAUREN

Lauren stared in wide-eyed shock at the empty sheets beside her. The morning sun threw everything into cool, stark light, every wrinkle in the cotton, the dip in the pillow, the triangle of blanket thrown cruelly back as he'd left her there, sleeping.

But then she heard a clink downstairs and the familiar thud of a cabinet closing.

"Oh," she sighed, her whole body deflating from tension into relief. Bastian hadn't left without a word. He was making breakfast.

Her wistful thoughts the night before may have been tinged with impractical lust—he couldn't pick up and move to Sacramento with no planning—but that didn't mean there couldn't be something between them. Maybe, with time, they could work on a healthier relationship together. He obviously still had feelings for her, and she still loved him. If they could negotiate a new path with more respect from him and more strength from her . . .

She could dare to give it another chance.

Hope floated gently inside her as Lauren watched the dust motes dance in sunbeams above the bed. This really was a lovely room, so much brighter and airier than the tiny room she had at the other end of the house. It was time to move in, make it hers, draw up plans.

She pulled on skimpy panties and a worn, oversized T-shirt and sauntered downstairs, looking as sexily disheveled as she could. She felt a little too satiated to pull off powerful this morning, but surely she could manage a little sleepy hotness.

"Can I make you some—?" Her question fell off a cliff when she turned the corner and spotted Bastian in the kitchen. Yes, he was still there, but not quite. He was already laced into his boots and pushing a top onto his favorite travel mug.

The guilty way he tipped his face only halfway up confirmed her first impression. "Morning."

"You're leaving?"

"Gotta hit the road." He tried to strike a cheerful note and raised his cup. "I made coffee!"

"Thanks."

"I was just about to come up and say goodbye." He closed the space between them and pulled her into his arms.

Let it go, she ordered herself as Bastian gave her a quick kiss.

"I have to get to that meeting. The app says I should already be gone."

"Aw. Well, maybe you can stop by on your way back. Dinner was nice."

He laughed when she winked. "I wish I could, but I need to drive straight back, so I'll be jumping on the 5 way south of here."

"Oh. I see." Did she see? She wasn't sure, but she was determined not to leap right back into clinginess with him. She tried out a smile. "But you will have to retrieve your camera at some point, so . . ."

He kissed her again, then let her go. "That would be a bad idea."

"Picking up your camera?"

"No, I mean . . . you know. Seeing each other again. We shouldn't confuse the issue."

Lauren snapped straight, her attempts at a loose and easy mood vanishing with a nearly audible pop. "Confuse which issue, exactly?"

Bastian's lips tightened. He turned his back to her to retrieve his coffee. *Her* coffee. "It was nice to see you," he said to the counter. "Really nice. And I'm glad you're doing so well here, Lauren."

She stared dumbly, shocked to be so casually dismissed when she'd felt so much more powerful than before. She hadn't been clingy. *He'd* been the one reaching out. He'd volunteered to visit, brought a little gift, asked if he could stay.

"You just . . . you just dropped by for a booty call? That's what this was?"

"I wouldn't say that. I told you when you left that I still wanted to be friends."

"Friends?" she shouted.

"Lauren." That was it. Just her name. Like he shouldn't even have to say the rest, it was all so embarrassingly obvious.

"No," she insisted. "What? *Lauren*, what?"

He held up his free hand in surrender. "I wanted to see how you were doing, and you wanted some help. I was already coming up here, and we're still friends, so . . ."

"So you decided you'd get in a little drive-by fuck on your way to the city?"

"I don't understand. We had that long talk before you left, and things were cool between us. And things have been cool since. We text. We talk. We're friends. And I want to be friends."

"Friends," she repeated, images of sex flashing through her mind, his mouth at her neck, his body inside hers, sinking in, filling her up, over and over.

"I'm sorry," he said, voice dark and deep with sincerity. "We didn't talk about it last night, and maybe we should have. Jill and I have started seeing each other, so this can't happen again."

For a moment she felt only confusion, like the painless first tug of paper slicing through a fingertip. The stinging pain beneath it came two heartbeats later as the edges of the wound parted. Jill? "Excuse me?"

"It's nothing official, but I should have been upfront." He glanced at his phone. "I'm sorry," he repeated. "I'll call you, and we'll talk and figure all this out. I hate to walk away in the middle of this, but I really have to go. Traffic is picking up."

"Right," she whispered, desperate to remain calm, to hold on until he left. She couldn't let him see. Couldn't let him know how much it hurt. He didn't *deserve* her pain.

He edged past, brushing a brief kiss on her jaw as he moved. "I'll call," he said again. "Just mail the camera when you're done with it. And let me know if anything else happens, of course."

She stared at the counter where he'd left a faint ring of moisture. Probably just plain coffee, because she didn't have that expensive oat milk he insisted on. The front door closed softly, as if he were afraid a loud noise would break the lull and awaken her anger.

But she just stood there. If his car started, she couldn't hear the soft turn of the electric engine, but she finally heard the crunch of gravel when he pulled away. She rooted her feet to the ground, determined not to look, not to fly out, not to rage or even breathe.

Rage. That was it. Pain, yes, but the rage was rising mercifully fast.

Why so much anger? They'd both wanted to have sex, and they had. She'd been the one to let her guard down in the end and imagine it might mean something more than a wet spot on her clean sheets.

But what had she even been picturing? That they could get back together and . . . have a long-distance relationship that would somehow work better than their living-together relationship? Or had she thought he might leave his friends and home and job behind, the way she had three years earlier? That he might do that for *her*?

"I don't know," she whispered to her own question.

Had she thought in the deepest, most secret places of her heart that he'd see her new home and love it so much he'd wonder if this was where they could be *more settled*? A place with bedrooms for children and room for that huge garden he'd always wanted?

She shook her head at her own secret wants.

She just . . . still loved him. She wanted this place, and she wanted him too. Wanted him to see that she was better and brighter now. But it didn't matter. He was dating Jill. He'd moved on. This had been some sort of twisted goodbye.

She finally moved, taking a towel from a drawer to wipe up the coffee ring. She poured herself a cup, then set it down without drinking it. After all the wine, her stomach was tumbling in sour waves. Instead, she put water in the microwave for oatmeal, then stood at the butcher block island, hands flat, lips parted.

She should do some work today, catch up on her paying projects. She could also take another look at the plumbing and figure out some plans. Or . . . or she could explode into violence.

Her gaze rose to the ceiling.

The microwave dinged, but she wandered away from the kitchen to stare into the laundry room, where the pipes were directly beneath her father's bedroom. He'd told her that when he was young one of his chores had been hanging the laundry to dry. There had been no clothes dryer then, just a motorized wringer. He'd been terrified his fingers would get pulled through.

Would he be angry if she turned his old bedroom into a bathroom? Did she care?

No. Fuck him too. Fuck all of them.

She grabbed her phone and raced up the stairs. She opened all the curtains in the bedroom, cackling at the way light spilled across her sex-rumpled sheets and dented pillows and the two wineglasses on the bedside table.

Perfect.

It took an hour to gather the tools, to measure and scan, to double-check. Not a load-bearing wall. No electrical lines. No hidden metal pipes.

She washed her face and pulled on yoga pants, but she kept her hair loose and rumpled and even left on the worn T-shirt that slid off her shoulder to reveal a little skin. She looked like a woman who had just risen from bed, and that was exactly the way she wanted it.

When she was ready, she went live, straight to all her friends.

"Good morning, everyone! Big progress here in the house. I've been mulling over the largest project, one I haven't been brave enough to even plan yet, much less tackle. The upstairs bathroom. Ooooo! Fun stuff. I've been wishy-washy about where to put it, how big it should be, whether I want to sacrifice a bedroom or just make this one smaller."

She scanned the room slowly with her camera, pausing on the bed and the wineglasses still pink with the dregs of merlot. "Luckily my ex-boyfriend Bastian stopped by last night. He was *so* helpful and hands-on." She finally shifted the view off the bed to the wall. "He suggested I knock out this wall and expand into the next room, and I've decided that's the best idea. He had to leave early this morning, so he won't be able to help, but I don't need him, do I? Who's ready to knock out a wall on this fine morning?"

A glance at the comments coming through on her phone made her smile, though none were from Jill. Yet. "I think a few of you have some anger issues, and it turns out, so do I!" She tipped the view down to her assembled tools before she set her phone on a stand. "I should probably cover the bed with plastic, but I need to wash those sheets, anyway."

She smiled and winked for the camera. "I've spent my whole life thinking I couldn't do things on my own. That I needed someone to prop me up and give me a boost at every step. And honestly, I never expected enough in return. I didn't even ask for it. And you know what? You teach people how to treat you. So I'm ready to learn a whole new path and start kicking ass and taking names. And this? This I can absolutely do by myself. So let's destroy something, friends!"

She slipped on safety glasses for this, unwilling to lose an eye to a flying piece of lath, pulled on gloves, then hefted the sledgehammer onto her shoulder before pausing to grin at the camera with all the bright anger coursing through her. "Here we go," she promised, then Lauren raised her sledgehammer and swung hard at the wall. It only cracked a little. "Shit," she gasped before collapsing into laughter. "Okay, let's give this another try. Girl power."

She notched the hammer onto her shoulder. She thought about her mom and Kepnick and her father and Bastian and every man she'd given everything to while expecting the absolute minimum in return, and then she swung the sledgehammer again with a roar.

"Yes!" She'd broken right through this time. Plaster crumbled and collapsed as the laths buckled inward. "Look at that! Oh God, there's no turning back now, folks. I've really done it."

Once trepidation over that first good whack lifted, Lauren's blood bubbled with exhilaration. And something else. Something that burned in her muscles and made the sledgehammer feel light.

Righteous, simmering fury.

She threw the hammer over and over, gasping in delight as the wall fell before her. She exposed one stud, then a second and third, then worked her way lower, clearing out the old plaster and wood. "This is as much fun as they say it is!" she yelled for the camera. "But I must look like I fought a losing battle against the Pillsbury Doughboy."

Once she'd broken through to the other side, she paused, panting. "I am going to be so sore tonight. Thank God I have that big clawfoot tub downstairs."

She clapped her gloved hands, then sputtered at the blast of dust that hit her face. "Oops. Okay, I won't make you all watch this entire process. I imagine this will take a couple of days. Then I'll need to think about framing, I guess. This is kind of a passion project, and I haven't thought it all the way through. Demolition is first, right? Then planning?"

She laughed and tugged the gloves off, feeling better already. "I guess what I really meant to say is . . . fuck you, Bastian. I've got this."

Hardly believing her own words, she stopped the stream and slapped a hand over her dusty mouth. A startled laugh leaked past the barrier. Then another. Until tears were streaming from her eyes with the giggles.

Had she just done something *bad*? She never did anything bad. She was *nice*. And considerate. And always, *always* accommodating.

But in one fell swoop she'd publicly given a giant finger to Bastian, to Jill, and to her father, just for the hell of it.

After all, what the hell had she ever done to anyone? Hadn't she kept her head down her whole life and just *tried*? Tried to be a perfect daughter, tried to be a decent person, tried, tried, *tried* to be the partner every man claimed to want.

And what was she left with after all that eager, demeaning work? An ex who used her as a roadside fuck, a friend who'd been waiting to move into her bed, a father who couldn't be bothered to give her one holiday, and a mother who'd lied to her for decades.

And a fucking serial killer stalking her!

How the hell had this become her life? "No more," she growled. "No goddamn more." People could learn to accommodate her for once.

Her phone buzzed with a text. WTF LAUREN

Lauren smiled as she muted Jill's texts. Let that woman rage into the void.

She saved the video to her phone, then sent it to Facebook as well, smiling the whole time at every comment she glimpsed.

Ooooo. Get it, girl.

OMG! This is crazy!

Yes, Lauren! Let it all out! You got this!

Maybe she did have some real friends after all. She'd make note of which of her online acquaintances might be people she'd be able to build a real connection with. Not because they liked Bastian, but because they liked *her*.

Thirsty and feeling more than a little drained, she trotted downstairs to grab an iced tea and hit the shower.

The hot water felt glorious. She washed her hair and let the warm flow cascade over her like a waterfall, a baptism. She scrubbed her skin and soaped all the dust away until she felt clean and new.

This was her home and her new beginning, and she had to stop looking back. Her dad had been the hero she'd needed as a teenage girl, but she wasn't a child anymore and he wasn't a lonely guy starting over. He'd moved on, and she wouldn't find what she needed with him or any other man she met along the way. She had to accept that and make what she wanted for herself.

A life, friends, maybe even kids. She'd do it here on her own two feet.

When her phone trilled, Lauren ignored it with a smile, imagining Bastian calling to scold her. She finished her shower and towel dried her hair, then pulled on her warmest robe to counter the icy tiles beneath her feet.

It was only when the phone rang again and she glimpsed the unfamiliar number on the screen that she remembered.

Kepnick.

She stared at the ten meaningless numbers that might be anyone, anywhere. It could be a junk call. It could be a client. It could be him.

Her new bravery vanished like dissipating smoke, but she managed to touch the ANSWER button and slowly, slowly raise the phone to her ear.

"Hello?" a man said softly.

Oh God. What had she done?

"Is this Lauren Abrams?" he asked. No, it wasn't a soft voice. Not exactly. It was low. Hushed.

She recognized it from interviews he'd done. A slight country twang, nothing Southern about it, just rural. It was him.

Water dripped from her hair and traced fingers down the nape of her neck. Shivering, she managed to push a sound from her dry, clicking throat. "I . . ."

"I can't talk long. If a guard sees this phone, I'm fucked. I need more money ASAP."

"What?" she croaked.

"My bitch of a wife finally took off, so whatever your dad sent her over the years, it disappeared with that slut when she sold my house and left town. Forgot to leave me a fucking forwarding address, if you can believe it."

"I . . ." Lauren blinked frantically. "I have no idea what you're talking about."

"It's Kepnick," he said, as if that explained anything.

Her forehead ached with a frown so tight she felt like she would never smooth it out. "I know who you are. I just have no idea what you're saying."

"The money. It's gone, and I need some goddamn cash in my account right now. Not to mention my boy. She left his ass high and dry too."

She shook her head as if she could somehow make him stop, but he kept talking.

"Had a hell of a time trying to figure out the logistics. The wife took care of that shit for twenty-five years. Kept most of it for herself too. But I still had your address, and my boy headed out there and found your grandma. Apparently she didn't appreciate his visit, since her brain popped off!" He laughed. Laughed about her grandmother's stroke. Lauren felt her mind fracturing, one side trying to process Kepnick's strange request, the other side picturing the horror of her grandmother's fall.

Kepnick's son had been there?

"No," Lauren said, but he made no response at all. Just chuckled a while longer, and in that moment she knew what he must have sounded like when he'd tortured those women. The squirming horror of that rough laugh. "Stop it. Stop."

"What's wrong?" he asked.

What was wrong? She was talking to a murderer, and his son had been in this house with a helpless old woman. Lauren snapped. "Did you scare her? Is that what caused her stroke? Did you and your son terrorize my grandmother?"

"Now come on. My boy says she got real pissed and had a fit. He didn't scare her. But I decided to handle it myself this time. I've got a more delicate touch."

This was a nightmare. "You did this. You sent your son to her with this stupid lie, and he—"

"Shut the fuck up," Kepnick suddenly growled, and Lauren's teeth snapped shut at the ice in that voice. "You listen to me. I'm gonna need a raise. If your dad was willing to pay ten K a year to get out back then, I bet he'll pay more to stay out now. Hell, he's older than me! Fucking senior citizen by now!"

"Ten K?" she whispered, completely lost in a swirl of nonsensical words. Was he trying to extort her family?

"Don't go thinking I'm a cheap date. There was more up front, but ten K a year kept me invested in his freedom, you understand? And I am invested. I really am. But I find myself needing to accommodate an increase in the cost of living."

She should hang up. He was obviously lying. Using her grandmother's illness to try some extortion scheme with the threat of tearing their world apart one more time. She couldn't let that happen. So instead of hanging up, she strained her ears for every word he dangled. "You're trying to blackmail me."

"Blackmail? This is a goddamn aboveboard business deal. Your dad paid me to take credit for that murder, fair and—"

"You're a liar!" she spat out, the words flying from her mouth before he'd even finished talking, a shield to stop his disgusting attack.

"A liar?" he drawled. "I suppose you can think what you want, honey, but I bet the news reporters would love to hear my story." He laughed again. "Don't you think?"

This was madness. A cruel, evil game. She'd only just got her feet solidly beneath her, and now the floor felt like a rolling sea, threatening to toss her into impossibly deep water. She'd sink beneath it. She'd thrash and drown and never get back to the surface.

"You're a murderer," she rasped. "Whatever story you come up with, no one will believe you, because you're a disgusting monster and a killer, and my dad did nothing wrong!"

His low chuckle scraped her frayed nerves like sandpaper. "Why would he pay me, then, do you think? If I did kill her?"

"He didn't pay you!" she screamed.

"Listen, little girl." His voice had gone cold again, his patience with her at an end. "Money leaves a trail. What happens when I tell my story and the detectives find hundreds of thousands missing from your dad's accounts, starting with a big ol' lump sum just a month before I confessed? Huh? Then who will they believe?"

Her mind jagged, dodging this way and that. *No.* None of this was true. There was no money and no trail. But if there was . . .

What if there was? Anguish tore through her. Was this what her grandmother had felt? Was this what pushed her blood so hard that it ripped open the vessels of her brain?

Lauren swallowed the impossible lump in her throat and tried to make herself feel courage instead of fear. "Even if my dad paid you, it's only because he was framed. He . . . he had to find a way out of prison because he didn't do it. You knew where her shoes and purse were buried. You said . . ." She pressed a shaking hand to her sweat-slick forehead. "You buried them so she'd be unidentifiable. *You* said that!"

"Oh, a little birdie told me about that part."

"That's not true!" she screeched, voice cracking with desperation. "You're lying! You're just lying!"

"Why would I bother lying? I confessed because I had a wife and a little one then. I needed the money. I was already in for life, so no skin off my back. Easy cash for my family. But that bitch is gone, and I got nothing to lose and a whole fuck ton of time to kill. Recanting won't get me free, so what exactly would be my motive for telling you this, Miss Lauren Abrams?"

Her skin exploded with gooseflesh at the way he said her name. Like he knew her. Like they were old friends. It was all warm, secret familiarity creeping into her ear.

"This is a joke to you!" she yelled. "That's your motive! Time on your hands and a sick sense of humor."

"It's no joke." The phone clinked, and the line went dull and muffled for a moment. "Listen, missy, I've gotta go, but I'll call back soon, so you work it out before then. Fifty thousand a year. No negotiation."

"No—" she started, but the screen lit up and the line went dead.

Her fingers ached from squeezing too hard, but when she tried to loosen them, the phone slipped from her sweating hands and dropped to the floor, grazing the side of her foot. She barely felt the pain.

This couldn't be happening.

How could Kepnick have known about her doubts and deepest fears? How had he known he could pry open those cracks and whisper in his disgusting taunts?

He was lying. He had to be. He'd killed Tori Bagot.

She was shivering in the cool bathroom now, her feet ice against the tile. Her fingers shook so hard she needed three tries to pick up her phone. Teeth chattering, she forced her stiff legs to lift her up each step toward her bedroom. She had to get dressed. She couldn't stay vulnerable like this.

The second floor was warmer, but she still shivered all the way to her room, where she pulled on her warmest sweatpants and a long-sleeved

T-shirt, then topped it with a hoodie that she tugged up over her damp hair.

Her body kept trembling.

Why? Why was this happening?

A whine leaked from her throat. A whine like a cowering animal. But it built, fueled by her anguish, until she parted her lips to let free a straining, breaking cry. She curled into herself, collapsing to her bed as the sound grew and twisted until she was finally screaming.

"Why?" she shrieked, drool sliding over her cheek and into the dull green of her childhood blanket. *"Why?"*

She'd lived with this since the womb, the unbearable weight of who she was, who'd created her, what her very existence had set in motion. She'd lived with the tight ropes of having a murderer for a father, but even when those ropes had been cut, the marks had remained. The ghost of that old knowledge had stayed, yes, but also the doubts she'd stuffed so deep inside her that they'd turned to dark, deadly ice. That was the space inside her she could never fill. The space that swallowed everything.

She wanted free of it. Free of them all.

"I hate you," she cried past tears and snot, unsure who she even meant. "I hate you," she said again.

She hated herself. Hated her mother. Hated Kepnick. Hated her father and Bastian and every other greedy man in between. She sobbed it over and over until she wasn't sobbing anymore, she was snarling it out past spit and clenched teeth.

"Ihateyoulhateyoulhateyou."

She didn't need them. She didn't need any of them. Whatever Kepnick was saying, it didn't matter. Either it was true or it wasn't, and she'd tell her father to deal with his own fucking devils.

Yes.

Her heartbeat slowed. She wiped the wet from her face and sat up.

They were her father's devils. She wasn't responsible for them. She'd tell him what Kepnick had said, and her dad would tell her it wasn't true, and that would be the end of it. She'd give him Kepnick's number. Let him take the reins.

Lauren blew her nose, picked up her phone in shaking hands, and called her dad.

"Lauren!" he snapped when he answered, making her jump in surprise.

"Daddy?"

A static hum of sound made her think he was outside in the wind. On his sailboat maybe.

Or driving.

"Just stay put," he said, his voice loud over the noise.

"What?" She screwed up her forehead as if that could help her brain think. "What are you talking about?"

"Don't do anything," he said; then his voice rose. "And don't touch anything!"

"Dad, what are you saying? I just need to talk to you because someone called me. And, Dad, it's really—"

"Great. Good. I'm on my way. Just . . . Never mind. Christ. We'll talk when I get there." He bit out some curse that was cut off by the call ending. Lauren blinked hard several times.

Had Kepnick called him too? She'd never heard her father so distressed before, so he obviously knew something was deeply wrong. He was coming to talk to her. To explain. And for a moment she felt nothing but sheer, utter relief. She could let him take care of it, and everything would go back to normal.

Wouldn't it? She'd still have her beloved grandmother. Still have this wonderful home and this new, growing strength.

Except . . . She looked around her room, her mind dazed and spinning. He'd told her not to touch anything. What would she touch? Receipts? Notes? Canceled checks?

If he was worried about evidence, that meant Kepnick's story was true. Her father had paid him off. But no. Lauren couldn't let it be true.

How could she have her peace and strength and happiness with extortion hanging over their heads?

Her phone flashed a low-battery signal, so Lauren made herself get up on shaking legs. Her dad might call back, so she needed her phone. She shuffled down the hall, aware of the way her muscles already ached and trembled. From anxiety, yes, but when she walked into her grandmother's bedroom, she was greeted by the destroyed wall and remembered all the rage she'd thrown at it.

That felt like a lifetime ago, but it had been an hour? Maybe two?

She stared at the jagged hole in the plaster, at the sunlight shining through from her father's room. A moth suddenly fluttered up and out to flap uselessly at the wall before settling again and folding its wings.

A moth.

Don't touch anything.

Oh God.

Hands limp at her sides, eyelids heavy with despair, Lauren picked her way through the debris. The hard bits of white dug into the bottoms of her feet. She felt the sharp sting of a splinter but didn't care enough to react.

When she stopped she could see through to her father's room and the edge of his closet wall. The wall she'd broken through at the corner. Where the moths had been.

Lauren looked down into the space she'd created and saw only blackness. "Please, please, please," she murmured, praying to some unknown god of innocence.

Her heart thundered so hard it was all she could hear as she turned on the flashlight of her phone and held it out a foot above the jagged edges of the debris. Something dark rested at the bottom of the narrow void between the walls. A bit of metal glinted.

Lauren pulled more lath away. When another moth flew free, she barely noticed. She just put her hand down into the space and reached her arm as far as she could. Her fingers touched something cool. Leather. She gripped it and pulled it free.

It was a woman's wallet, burgundy leather with an old-fashioned gold clasp that snapped it closed.

"Oh, Dad," she breathed as she brushed the dust away, because she knew. She knew in that one moment whose it must be, even before she pried the clasp apart and let the wallet fall open. A penny dropped to the floor and bounced once before making a quiet landing in a pile of plaster. An accordion set of plastic sleeves half unfolded and hung against her hand. The first pocket displayed a California driver's license.

Tori Renee Bagot.

But even after seeing that name, what struck Lauren like an ax was the tiny square of Tori's face, still young and smiling and *alive*.

Kepnick had been telling the truth. He hadn't killed Tori. Because her dad had her wallet. Because he'd been with her that night.

Because he'd done it.

Lauren pressed a hand to her throat, trying to hold down the sickness that lurched up.

Her daddy. Her hero. Her safety and one true love. The man she'd chosen over her own mother and held as a burning, righteous wedge between them for all these years.

Now that wedge had cut through to the bone. But the edge of it was jagged, not sharp, and she couldn't imagine the pain would ever stop. Everything she'd ever believed in was open to the world, a torn gash that spread wider with each breath.

Her mom had been right all those years ago. She'd lied for a good cause, and she'd lied to save Lauren. And Lauren had chosen *him*.

She stared at the picture, at Tori's smile so wide and bright, even for a license photo. The air felt too hot as she dragged it in on rough breaths. The photo seemed to shimmer, dancing before her eyes, like Tori was shaking, trembling.

She'd been found naked in a ravine, covered by leaves and rocks. He'd ditched the purse and clothes separately, he'd said—Kepnick had said—burying them in a narrow hole, far easier to dig than a deep grave to hold a woman's whole body. He'd told the detectives he figured her skeleton might be found in a year or two, but they wouldn't know who she was without her things.

That poor, broken girl, her cold skin barely covered by a layer of dirt and leaves and crawling bugs . . . She'd been found by a hiker just three weeks later.

But her wallet had never been recovered. Kept as a souvenir? Lost somewhere along the way? Tossed back into his car for the cash? He'd never said.

But here it was in Lauren's hands. The first hands to touch it since her father's. She groaned past teeth still clenched tight to keep her bile down. Her blood drummed so hard in her ears she thought it could be a truck engine and cocked her head in alarm.

Her father was coming. He'd said he was. Coming to Lauren's house. Why? To set things right?

Or . . .

Her breath rushed out of her with a hard cough. What was there to set right at this point, except Lauren herself?

Oh God.

She could put it back. Return it to the wall. Play dumb. She could let him retrieve it and destroy it, and no one would ever know. Just her. Just him.

She could tell her dad that Kepnick had been harassing her and let him deal with the price: $50,000 a year. He could manage that for a while, surely. It had nothing to do with her.

Lauren would smooth things over with her mom, quietly withdraw from her dad, and live a normal life. A totally normal life with no upheaval, no murder, no trial, no reporters, no consequences.

She could. But tears began to run down her face, and her chest seized with a tortured sob.

Her father. Her own beloved daddy.

Just a few hours ago, she would have bounced with excitement that he was coming to see her. Now . . . now her neck prickled at the idea of how close he might be.

She needed to move. Needed to decide. She couldn't sit around crying.

Lauren shook off her horror and heartbreak. She had to. Before she tucked the wallet under her arm, she snapped a picture of the license inside it, then emailed it to herself. Just in case.

As she started to move out of the room, she paused for one long breath, then swallowed hard and reopened her email to type out a quick note to her mother. **I'm so sorry I didn't listen to you. Forgive me. I love you, Mom.**

It sailed into the ether with a whoosh, and then Lauren was racing down the stairs.

Her panting breath scraped through the silence of her home. *Her* home. The one thing she'd finally accomplished in life.

She'd been fixing things, hadn't she? Working toward some realization that she could be alone and be okay? That on her own, as she was, she was just . . . enough?

And now she was utterly broken. She could feel the different parts of her scraping against themselves, barely holding together, connected only by thin, stretching skin. Her legs wobbled as she grabbed her keys and purse before she stuffed her feet into a pair of tennis shoes and stumbled toward the front door.

Once she was in the car, she turned the wheel hard and hit the gas, bouncing over grass and flowers as she spun the car around and headed out.

When her phone rang, she glanced down to see *Mom* on the screen. No. No, she couldn't do that. She couldn't process all the unforgivable words between them right now, the distance and hurt, all because Lauren had believed her father. Because she'd turned her back and walked away and broken her mom into dry pieces like—

"No," she snapped, ordering her own thoughts away before they could break her too.

Lauren muted the phone and tossed it facedown next to the wallet. She skidded around the wide curve of the drive, and she was already to the road when she registered that Carver was at his mailbox, hand on the latch, lips parted as he stared in surprise at the dust rising around her car.

"Sorry," she murmured past her tears. To him. To everyone.

She turned left and tore down the road, too terrified to head toward the highway in case she'd spot her dad coming toward her. Scared of her own dad or just scared of what she knew about him now? God, she didn't know, she just drove.

To where, though? "I can't," she rasped, unsure what she even meant. *I can't do this. I can't think. I can't survive knowing it.*

She drove blindly until she dead-ended at a county road, then stopped and stared at the sign in front of her. A right turn would eventually take her back toward the highway. But a left would take her toward a series of tiny towns, one of which she recognized. She'd found it on a map years ago. She'd peered at the spidery roads as if she could see the land they cut through. She'd wanted to see it all those years ago, and now she could.

Lauren turned left. She curved herself over the wheel, jaw tight, teeth grinding. Her body was trying to keep the truth contained, maybe, trying to keep everything inside, bury it deep and dark and unknowable.

Despite that darkness, or maybe because of it, she suddenly felt horribly aware of how beautiful the day was. A small creek she passed over sparkled with the sunlight, and the dry yellow grasses bloomed into green as they curved down the bank toward cool water.

As her car floated down a gentle hill, Lauren rolled down the window and gasped at the sweet, crisp air as if she'd been locked away for years. Her cheeks were still wet with tears, and they went numb in the wind, but she left the window open as she slowed around a curve. Her car came so close to a roadside garden she could actually see fat bumblebees fumbling around a late-blooming bush.

How had she been unhappy yesterday? Last week? Last month? How could she have craved anything more than the peace of a normal, boring day all on her own, with no one else there to tear the fabric of her life apart?

She finally hit a straight stretch of road and sped up, letting the wind whip her hair. Ten minutes later she'd reached the exact spot, and she pulled over onto a state park access road that had been chained off so long ago that grass had overtaken the rest of it.

Lauren eased out of the car, every joint tight, and she carried Tori's wallet with her. Her pace felt strange and jerky, like her limbs moved on puppet strings, but she kept stepping, kept walking until she made it. Her feet stopped at the edge of a crumbling cliff, and Lauren stared down into the creek bed where Tori Bagot's body had been found.

Lauren had never been here before, not in person. She'd seen pictures and maps and read the descriptions, but she'd never come. It wasn't her connection, she'd told herself. It never had been. Just a tragedy that had accidentally collided with her real life all those years ago. This place had had nothing to do with her.

But it had. "I'm sorry," she said aloud to that poor discarded girl. "If I had never . . ." She shook her head, unable to speak the truth about the havoc her life had wreaked before she'd even been born. Because if Lauren hadn't existed, her mother never would have come here, and Tori never would have threatened to tell the truth, and she . . .

"I'm just sorry," she gasped. "I'm so, so sorry."

CHAPTER 24

DONNA

Amazingly she and Mrs. Abrams had been getting along well for a week. Donna had volunteered to make a stir-fry one night, and Mrs. Abrams had been wary but pleasantly surprised. She'd stopped coming by every morning, which had left Donna feeling friendlier in the evenings after the silence of the day.

It had all started to feel almost cozy, so she had no idea why the woman was so tense over dinner tonight.

Granted, Michael had reneged on his promise to join them for a big ham dinner, and that had irritated Donna too, but his mom was strung wretchedly tight, setting her cup down too hard, glaring at her plate. Her mood was starting to piss off Donna too.

"Is everything all right?" she asked for the third time, her voice pulling the other woman from her own thoughts with a visible jerk.

"I'm fine," she said curtly. "I have a headache."

"Oh. I'm sorry. I'll clean up and go, then."

"That's probably for the best. I'm out of sorts."

"Is it all right if I come back to get my things out of the dryer later?"

She was answered with a dismissive wave. "Do whatever you like. I'll lock up after."

"Thanks for dinner. Those were the best au gratin potatoes I've ever had."

"I add cream cheese."

"Great idea!" Donna replied as if she had any idea what went into the dish.

She cleared the table in a hurry, then put her clothes in the dryer and rushed through the dishes. Not an easy task, considering that everything had been put onto serving dishes after cooking and then had to be transferred to Tupperware before she could hand wash the whole load.

Maybe she'd drop a hint about those nice high-powered dishwashers you could get these days. She snorted at the idea that her advice might be welcome, then started the drying.

Michael had dropped by three days earlier to show her a surprise. A copy of the divorce papers his attorney had drawn up. He still had to present them to his wife, but at least things were in motion now. The sight of the papers had loosened some tight bind that had squeezed Donna's heart into a strange, distorted lump. It hadn't released completely, but it had eased somewhat, and she no longer felt wildly restless.

Instead of snapping at Michael the way she normally did lately, she'd thrown herself into his arms and kissed him. *This is really happening?* she'd asked against his mouth.

Yes. He emphasized the yes with a hard kiss.

Your commute will be so long.

It will be worth it.

She let him go and hugged herself to try to keep her hope contained. *When? Soon?*

I'm still working out the details. I have to get all the finance questions resolved, figure out every number. I don't want any surprises. As soon as that's done, we'll arrange a trip to visit her family. She can't be alone when I tell her.

Next month? she pressed.

Maybe. I'll need to sit tight and play nice until it's all finalized, though. If she finds out about you . . . We can't afford that, Donna.

She'd decided not to push him that night. He'd finally taken a big step, and she wanted to embrace that for the moment. *I made your mom something.*

Like a cake?

Sure, you idiot. That seems likely. No, I'm working on a painting.

His eyebrows rose. *Will she like it?*

Does she like violent female nudes?

Um . . .

Oh, close your mouth. I obviously didn't paint a nude for your mother. She picked up the canvas from the floor and turned it to face him. *My first landscape. What do you think?*

Wow. Great color. It's really nice. I think she'll actually approve.

She turned it back toward herself and held it out. It was a bit more realistic than most of her work. She'd tried to tame her wildest brushstrokes. *It doesn't look smarmy?*

It doesn't look like a Ramada Inn special, if that's what you're asking. I like it a lot. Maybe my favorite of yours. It's more refined or something.

Oh. Great. He hadn't picked up on her irritation, and she'd been surprisingly grateful for his blank nod. She hadn't wanted to ruin the mood, and Michael's bad taste in art wasn't worth the fight.

Maybe she'd work on the painting a little by lamplight tonight.

"Finally," Donna muttered as she put away the last dish. She hung up the towel and moved quietly toward the front room.

Mrs. Abrams was sitting rigid in a chair, hands clasped hard around a folded newspaper as she stared out the window into the dark.

"I'll leave you alone now. Thanks again for dinner."

She nodded and didn't respond. She hadn't offered dessert or left-overs tonight, which was highly unusual. She must be feeling awful.

"Can I get you anything?" Donna asked as she slipped on her shoes. "Water? Aspirin?"

"I'm fine!" she barked before repeating it even more loudly. *"I'm fine!"*

"Whoa." Donna recoiled from the outburst.

"Just go," Mrs. Abrams said, her neck pulled into twin cords of anger as she strangled the paper in her hands. "Go!"

"Jesus. Fine. I'm going." Reeling from the sudden anger, Donna watched over her shoulder as she headed out the door. When she made it down the steps, she peeked toward the front window before leaving. His mom was still sitting there, fingers clawed around the paper, her chest heaving.

"What in the wild fuck?" Donna whispered. This woman had some serious issues. Was she having a breakdown? Or was there something in that paper that had her freaked out?

Maybe she'd seen an obituary for a friend. Maybe she'd kept a secret lover for decades and he'd suddenly died and no one had bothered to tell her. As dramatic as the idea was, it was none of Donna's business.

She walked away shaking her head at that lie. She was going to get straight into that woman's business as soon as she went back for her laundry. She needed to know if Michael's mother was stable. All her visions of a steady, loving grandmother teaching a tiny kid to bake cookies and set the table would be meaningless if that grandma might snap and beat the kid with a spoon at any given moment.

This place was an idyllic paradise with a strange river flowing beneath it, the water tugging at earth she couldn't see. But maybe that was every family's truth. Maybe maturity meant accepting the good with the bad.

Because some of it was really, really good. If her fifteen-year-old self would've been starry-eyed at a tiny apartment in Hollywood, what would she think of this? A little cottage on a California ranch? Days filled with painting in the shade as distant horses grazed? She'd been a bit of a wild child, sure, but even she had nurtured the standard teen fantasies of somehow acquiring a horse and becoming a beautiful rider. She could learn to ride here. A stable still stood on the other side of this hill, though there were no horses now.

She'd talk to Mrs. Abrams about it; maybe that would soften her up. She'd spoken once of the riding she'd done when she was younger.

~

Donna tidied up her own place for the next hour and felt supremely grown up for instantly forgiving the woman's bad mood and tantrum. Forgiving, but not forgetting.

Her back protested when she moved down the hill too quickly. She pressed a hand above her hip and slowed her pace. Her belly wasn't that big yet, but it was already pulling things out of place. Things like Donna's whole damn life.

She needed to break free from her long days here and start making connections with some galleries in town. Maybe she'd even take a day to drive into the city and stop by her friend's gallery. She'd need a career. She would never be content to be Suzy Homemaker, and she'd have a whole collection of paintings to offer within a couple of months.

Almost giddy at the idea, she tiptoed to the front window of the main house and peeked in, though it was too dim to see much. This was the kind of adventure she loved. Something just on the edge of right and wrong.

She opened the front door quietly and discovered an empty parlor. His mother was gone, and the paper was gone too.

"Damn," she whispered as she stopped to listen. She could hear a clock ticking somewhere, but the dryer had stopped. Nothing moved.

Now she'd never find out what had caused that eruption. Maybe it really was a dead lover, and she'd taken the obituary upstairs to gaze at the picture. Or what if . . .

"Oh," Donna said aloud, suddenly imagining that it could have been news about Michael's long-vanished sister. What if it was her face Mrs. Abrams had seen in those pages? Maybe that shocked look had been the first stage of grief. Shock, and then that anger when she'd lashed out. Those were the first steps of loss, weren't they?

Unsure where else to look, she checked the little rack in the bathroom, but it only held a few copies of *Ladies' Home Journal*. Her last choice was the kitchen, but it was as spick and span as normal; no newspaper spread out across the counter.

She glanced in the trash as she completed her circle of the kitchen, and there it was. The paper, rolled up tight and shoved into a corner of the garbage. "Bingo," she breathed before glancing anxiously at the ceiling.

Unfortunately the paper was pushed in deep along with the food Donna had scraped into the can earlier. She pinched an edge of it between her thumb and forefinger and tugged. It shed a few pieces of ham as it emerged, and a big glob of cheesy potato stuck to one of the pages.

"Ew." She shook the paper, then unrolled it with careful moves until she could hold it gingerly in front of her. Not as much basketball on the front page this time, but nothing that caught her eye either. After giving the paper another small shake, she peeled it open.

At the top of the third page, she saw it: "Body Found; Believed to Be Local Missing Woman."

No.

"What are you *doing*?" someone screamed behind her.

Donna whipped around, snapping the paper into a crumpled mess as her rolling eyes sought out Michael's mother. She stood in the back door, hand still on the knob, one foot across the threshold.

"I was just—"

"Digging through my trash? Stealing my things?" Her eyes bulged as her lips pulled back from snarling teeth. All semblance of her normal kind reserve had vanished beneath a twisted mask.

Fear trailed down Donna's spine. "No, I just wanted a quick look at—"

"Get out of my house, you hussy!"

She hesitated, her gaze darting between the door and the furious woman standing in front of it. She finally took a step toward the safer escape route that the front door promised.

"Drop that," Mrs. Abrams ordered. "It doesn't belong to you."

"It's just a paper!" Donna snapped as she tossed it onto the floor in front of her. "You threw it in the trash."

"You're exactly what I expected you to be!" his mother yelled, her voice strangely rough and twisted as she followed Donna toward the door. "Creeping around my house like a nasty little whore!"

"Jesus!" Donna barked as she flung open the front door and nearly jumped out, desperate to escape this madhouse. "You're fucking insane, you know that?"

"Get out!" the woman screamed, still following, her mouth pulled into a terrifying grimace.

She stalked Donna out the door and down the steps until Donna found herself moving backward as fast as she could, unwilling to take her eyes off the snarling woman on her trail. She needed to get the hell out of here.

"You get back up there and you stay put until Michael gets here, and don't show your nasty face again!"

"That's a fucking deal," Donna muttered before she finally took off at an awkward jog up the dark path. After a moment the footsteps behind her went quiet, and she glanced back to see the silhouette of Michael's mother getting smaller in the porch light.

"Holy shit." She raced all the way to her door and had closed it behind her when she realized she'd been so shocked by Michael's mom that she hadn't processed what she'd seen in the paper: Tori Bagot's tiny face in black and white just below that headline.

The girl was dead. Not gone home. *Dead.*

Oh God. Oh no.

Michael had been with Tori Bagot that night. She knew he had. There had been no doubt in her mind until he'd started talking, explaining, squirming his way free, lying the way he always did.

He'd driven to Lucky's, picked up Tori after her shift, and she'd never been seen alive again.

And now he was coming here. Wasn't that what his mother had implied?

Donna dug her fingers into her forehead, pacing back and forth across the small room.

Had Michael murdered Tori? Was he capable of that?

She didn't truly think so, beyond what anyone was capable of. But she'd seen flashes of his temper before, and she could imagine nearly any man becoming furious enough to do something stupid. Slap a woman or push her, causing her to fall and hit her head. Then he might panic and make everything worse.

Yes, she could picture that, especially if Tori had threatened to confront Donna. Or his wife. Hadn't he said someone was calling his house and hanging up?

"Jesus." Horror and fear twined into a sickening rope that pulled tight inside her.

Donna turned off the only lamp that was on, then sidled along the wall until she reached a window. She eased back the covering and peeked outside. There was no one visible near the main house, and no headlights coming up the drive.

What the hell was she going to do? Her isolated little cabin suddenly felt like a shack on Charles Manson's ranch. Or a room at the Bates Motel. An absurd comparison, maybe, but a shiver ran through her instead of a laugh.

She wasn't okay here. She was utterly, dangerously *alone*. She'd never even spoken to one of the ranch hands, and they'd certainly never spoken to her.

Donna let her forehead fall against the glass, but the coldness only made her shiver more. "You can leave," she whispered to herself, her breath fogging the glass into an opaque screen. "You're okay, you can just leave." But for a moment she was afraid to tear herself away, afraid she'd miss the warning brightness of headlights approaching.

Because what if Michael decided Donna was a threat too?

"Come on, girl." She lifted her head and let the towel fall back into place. What did she need? Her purse. A few pieces of clothing. Toiletries. She'd come with more than that, but that was all she needed for the night.

Donna gathered her things and pulled on a jacket, then checked the window one last time. Everything looked still. She grabbed her purse and dug inside for her keys.

And couldn't find them.

She checked the purse again, picking through each and every item; then she searched the whole cabin, thankful it was a small space. No keys. Not in the bathroom, not under her bed, not in the couch cushions.

Had she left them in her car?

She carefully opened the cabin door and craned her neck to look out.

There was no bright moon tonight. Clouds had covered the sky all day, and now the land stretched out in a blank expanse of velvet black. Scared to go out in the pitch dark, she reached to flip on the inside light. The flood of light from the open door wasn't much, but it seemed like a sunbeam chasing away the shadows.

She grabbed her bag and moved quickly toward the glint of her car to ease open the door as quietly as she could. The interior light revealed no key chain hanging from the ignition. Beginning to panic, Donna dropped her bag on the ground and crawled inside to pat around the bench seat and the floorboard.

No keys.

Icy terror began working long fingers past her spine and into her gut. Where were her keys? There was nowhere to lose them in that tiny little box of a house.

Was it possible . . . ?

She swallowed hard and popped back outside to turn in a panicked circle.

Was it possible his mother had taken them? After dinner? She'd been outside when Donna had crept in. Donna had seen her come in through the back door.

The hair all over her body stood on end as she imagined someone watching her. Eyes in the dark just a few feet away, waiting to see what she'd do. Donna closed the car door and raced back toward the beckoning rectangle of warm light. Her shoes skidded on gravel as she rounded the bumper, and something in her thigh pulled too tight, but she forced her legs to straighten and carry her toward shelter. Once she leapt over the threshold, she pulled the door shut and threw the bolt.

After she'd left that impenetrable darkness behind, she managed to pant her way back to calmness and started to feel silly. This wasn't the Bates Motel and it wasn't Charles Manson's cult. It was just one unstable woman on a ranch.

She flattened a hand to her chest and took a few more deep breaths. What was really happening here? If Michael had killed that woman, he hadn't told his mom about it. That was patently ridiculous. His mother shouldn't have known about Tori Bagot's existence at all.

So maybe his mother had overheard Donna on the phone, confronting him about the missing girl. If she'd heard Donna's side of it, it made perfect sense that she would be horrified and scared to see that the girl had been found dead.

That part might make sense. As for everything else . . .

"Think," she urged herself. What in the hell was happening here?

Okay. Mrs. Abrams had seen the story about the body being found. She'd been upset throughout dinner, and her worry had turned to panic because she wasn't sure if Michael was involved.

She'd freaked out, called him to demand that he come over, and then . . . what? She was worried Donna would go to the police?

Good thing to worry about, because Donna was going to the cops if Michael still refused to contact them. At best he needed to be interviewed and eliminated. At worst . . . well.

She shook her head and pressed her hand harder to her chest, feeling her heart flutter like a trapped bird.

No, this wasn't a movie. This wasn't some straight-to-TV horror flick. Her keys were missing, but she wasn't helpless. She had her own two feet and the cover of night. Whatever that woman had cooked up, she wasn't a ninja or a murderer. She was just a scared mother who'd gone off the deep end.

Steadier than she'd been before, Donna snatched up her purse. She pulled her license and some cash from the wallet and stowed it in her coat pocket before turning off the lights. Everything she wore was dark enough to camouflage her, and her Doc Martens were sturdy.

The door creaked when she opened it, though Donna was almost certain it had never made noise before. She saw nothing but blackness until her eyes slowly adjusted and she could finally make out a rectangle of lighter black between the door and the jamb.

I can do this.

She put one foot out into the night and took a tentative step forward. Then another. When she reached her car, it felt like the last barrier island in a vast sea, and she put her hand on the cold surface for a moment to steady herself.

But this wasn't her touchstone anymore. It couldn't help her. She raised her hand slowly from the precious metal and flexed her fingers. Then she put her palm to the strange, firm rise of her belly and stepped away from the car.

I can do this. It wasn't just her now. She had more to protect.

When something yipped from a near distance, Donna winced and froze. Just coyotes. She'd lived with them in the city, hadn't she?

"Shit," she cursed, shaking her head. She set her jaw and moved forward and made it ten more feet down the trail. Then twenty. When she got too close to the main house, she cut through long grass, angling past a curve to intercept the drive again. She couldn't scramble through barbed wire in the middle of the night. She needed to reach the gate.

It was always kept open, so she wouldn't even have to climb. It would be no problem at all.

She half jogged her way to the last big curve in the drive; then she paused, her steps slowing. The moon was rising, thank God. A pale halo of light glowed dully at the horizon.

This would be so much easier with a bit of light, and relief flooded her at the thought of being able to see her path. She took another step before the light changed abruptly, and she froze.

Not moonlight. No.

Headlights.

Fear kept her muscles immobile for a moment too long. She didn't know where to turn, where to run, and then there was no chance at all. The diffuse light became bright beacons, and then they turned directly onto her.

Donna stood like a strange, hunched statue, a model sculpted in the act of fleeing. Her only saving grace was that she had no bag, no belongings at all.

A car door opened ahead of her, though she couldn't see it. "Sweetie? What are you doing out here?"

It seemed as if the lights themselves spoke. She raised a hand to shield her eyes, but she couldn't see anything more than the hard square of the open door. Still, she knew his voice.

"Donna? Are you okay?"

She almost felt relief at the worry in his words, and that twisted up with her fear to shake her brain to Jell-O. "It's a nice night," she managed to croak. "I needed some air. Went for a walk. That's all."

"Don't be mad at Mom," Michael said, finally becoming a silhouette that moved closer, his shadow hands held up to comfort her. "She's under a lot of stress. I'm not sure what she said, but . . ."

"No, everything's fine!" Donna said too loudly. "I'm just stretching my legs. You can go."

"Go?" He chuckled and reached toward her as he finally drew near. "Why would I run off now that I'm here?"

"Ha!" She held still for his kiss but pulled back quickly, laughing again. "It's been a weird night."

"I bet. Hop in, I'll give you a ride back."

She hovered there, arms half extended toward him, mouth forced into a rigid smile. She couldn't run away. She hadn't been athletic before the pregnancy, and he knew these roads and ranches far better than she did. Worst of all, he had a car and she was on foot. The closest house with a light still on was at least half a mile away, and she'd have to take the road or she'd run straight into ditches or holes or pointed bits of wire.

She couldn't get away.

"Sure," she finally said, though everything trembled inside her. He walked her to the passenger door and opened it to guide her in as if she might break free with the wrong approach. His fingers curled around her elbow. Was that a murderer's hand pressing into her flesh?

She tried to hide the way she jerked from his touch by collapsing into the seat to free herself of him. "I'm really tired," she explained.

"Then why come out for a walk, silly?"

"It's . . . it's good for the baby." She'd meant to remind him of the baby to keep herself safe, but that had been a foolish impulse. The baby was the bigger issue, right? She felt as if a target had just flashed to life on her chest. *I'm here to ruin your life. How will you solve this problem?*

When he shut the door, she considered trying to make a run for it when he was settling into his seat.

But that was ridiculous. Hysterical. Whatever he'd done . . . if he'd done *anything*, it had been an accident. Michael was a self-involved shithead, but he wasn't a murderer. And he'd filed for divorce at long last. Their dirty little secret wouldn't be secret much longer.

"So my mom called," he said with a sigh as he closed his door. "And you were right. Yes, she's a bit irrational at times. But she does mean well. Surely you can see that."

"Yes," she agreed. "Of course."

"She got upset about something she saw in the paper, and she just . . . I don't know. She bottles up her emotions, and then they eventually spill out. What did she say?"

"Say? She didn't really say anything. Everything was weird and tense. I'm fine now. She's fine." She smiled. "It's fine."

"I'm glad I came by, anyway. If you were upset enough to go out for a walk in the dead of night . . ."

Donna swallowed at the word *dead*. "Yeah," she responded as mildly as she could, trying to keep her panic pressed down deep.

"I'll take you back to the cabin. Then I'll talk to her."

"Great idea." She sank into the seat as he turned up the trail to their place. She just wanted him to leave her alone for a moment so she could think. "Thanks for the ride," she added.

He glanced toward her as the car slowed, watching her even as he eased up the hill. "Sure. No problem."

When she offered another smile, his eyes narrowed. Why? Had she said something wrong?

Then she realized the issue. She was never this nice. Never accommodating. And now he was watching her carefully, thoughtfully, wondering what the hell was going on.

He switched off the headlights, plunging them back into the night.

"I'll go in," she said, trying for gruff, but her voice was still too high and cheerful, tight with her fear.

Michael opened his door without another word. He took the keys out of the ignition and slipped them in his pocket.

Shit. Another idea ruined. She stalled for a moment before finally opening her own door and joining him outside.

"What were you doing out there in the dark?"

"I already said I was going for a walk! Are you tracking my every movement now?" There. That felt more natural.

He opened the front door and turned on the light, glancing around.

A jolt of fear shot through her when she imagined him spying the bag. But the bag wasn't sitting in an incriminating lump on the floor. It was outside. He hadn't seen it in the shadow of her car.

"Sit tight, then. I'll be right back."

She gave a grumpy little wave, but her face tightened as soon as he left. She had to give him time to get down to the main house and inside before she snuck back out, and that was a blessing because she needed the bathroom, anyway. Peeing felt like her number-one hobby these days, and her nervousness was making it worse.

She sat down and squeezed her eyes shut, trying to think. Should she really run? Get the hell away and figure out the details later? Or should she wait and assume the best? Assuming the best had never been her default position, but the worst seemed like a fantastical nightmare.

The logical explanation was that he'd been sleeping with this waitress, and then she'd disappeared, and he didn't want to get involved for obvious reasons.

Except she hadn't disappeared. She'd been murdered.

Or hell, Donna didn't even know if that was true. This pregnancy was ruining her thought process. Maybe that girl had gone hiking and broken a leg and died of exposure. Donna hadn't seen enough of the article to know the details of her death. It could have been an accident. A car crash. Suicide. Anything but murder.

She blew out a long breath as relief shook her to her bones. Why had she jumped to the worst conclusion? Was she that afraid of accepting this new life?

Maybe it had been an accident. And maybe tonight Donna had lost her keys before losing her damned mind. This wasn't a mystery novel, and nothing was as bad as she imagined.

She felt better as she washed her hands and took a few calming breaths. She would negotiate these circumstances. She'd get the truth from Michael, and she'd support him or leave him. Did it even matter which at this point? She just wanted to have this baby and be happy.

And she did want this kid. That must be true, right? She'd come all this way, left so much behind, and that must be the core of this, right? Not her relationship with Michael, but this little alien growing inside her?

Donna tipped her head back and felt her blood settle and calm. She would sit here and wait for him, and then they'd talk. Like adults.

Her mouth felt dry, and she headed straight for the kitchen to get some water. Ever since she'd fainted, she'd been worried about dehydration.

And the water here was good. Cold and sweet, with a hint of mineral. She drew a half glass from the faucet and began to gulp it down until her eye caught sight of something that closed her throat. Then her whole body rebelled, and she was coughing, coughing, bent over and trying to get the water from her lungs.

Because her overnight bag sat on the floor a foot in front of the door. It hadn't been there before. She knew it hadn't. Michael had brought it in.

"Well, shit," she rasped, sliding the glass onto the counter. They were going to have an even heavier conversation when he came back. But at least she had her favorite pajamas now.

She passed the bag and reached for the doorknob to get an idea of his whereabouts.

The doorknob turned, but the door stayed still when she pushed. Heartbeat thudding, she turned harder and tried again. Nothing.

"What the hell?" She raced over to the window. Michael's car door was just closing; then his lights flared before he rolled away from the cabin. He'd been out there this whole time? Doing what?

Donna pressed her temple to the glass, then the whole side of her face, straining her eyes for a glimpse of the door, but she couldn't see it. Even if her line of sight could reach, Michael's car was taking the light with it as he moved away.

She lunged for the door and pushed again, straining hard. But he'd trapped her somehow. Wedged the door closed.

No, that wasn't what was happening. It couldn't be. Could it? Nausea rolled up, and she raced for the bathroom as all the impossibilities became suddenly real. She vomited into the bowl, her body heaving and sobbing.

Because what if her first instincts had been right? That girl had been in his car; Donna had seen her hand. Tori had been causing him trouble. And this blocked door was proof of something far darker than she'd ever expected about him.

And Donna . . . Despite all her tough posturing, Donna was just another deceived woman in an endless trail that stretched back in time to the first days.

Of course I love you. Of course I'll leave my wife. Of course I haven't been lying about everything.

"Oh shit," she sobbed. She'd wanted the same things everyone else did this whole time. Family and safety and love. Tears came as terror prickled through her body. She paced to the kitchen, then back, too scared to think. Too ashamed. How had she fallen for this? How had she given this man everything, then settled herself into a trap he'd lined with blankets, soft padding over steel?

He was going to murder her. He was off to reassure his mother, come up with a plan, and then he'd come back and kill her.

"Stop," she ordered herself past her tears. "Stop. Get it together."

One shuddering breath later, she pulled back a makeshift curtain to study the window. It seemed almost wide enough for her hips. She glanced down at her newly grown belly and winced, but she was pretty sure she could get the soft bits through.

She unlocked the window and forced it up. The frame stopped moving after half a foot. Squinting, she peered at the window, and for the first time she noticed the screws sunk deep into the wood. They were covered in paint, but they stood out just enough to stop the sash from rising more than six inches.

"Are you kidding me?" How had she not noticed them before? It had been cool, yes, but she'd never tried to open these windows fully?

She tried the second window, then the third. And each one played out like a reveal in a cheap horror film. The windows that would only open partway. The door that could be blocked from the outside. The mattresses that had been laid on the floor with random trash. Had they kept workers here to force them to work? Locked them in when they needed cheap labor?

Was Donna the cheap labor now?

She looked down at the curve of her belly, eyes widening at the thought. That was why his mother had welcomed her. A grandchild.

That was all she wanted. And Donna was just the sneaky hussy to deliver it.

The lights of the car had gone dark past the hill. Michael was at his mother's house. Scheming. But whatever wicked scheme he'd come up with, he hadn't counted on this bitch.

Donna scrambled over to the table and dumped out her purse. There in the center among all the other junk lay the red Swiss Army knife she'd carried for years. Her friend had stolen it from a boyfriend and slipped it to Donna. *I already have one,* she'd said. And Donna had kept it all this time.

She sorted through the tools, found the screwdriver, and got to work. She had to stop and scrape off some of the thick paint with the little penknife, but within minutes she was free. She pushed the window high and scraped her awkward, bulging body through the space.

This time she wasn't afraid as she looked out into the night; she was furious. She stalked away from the lights of the cabin and disappeared into the dark with two simple goals. First, get her body and her child safe. Second, make Michael Abrams pay.

CHAPTER 25

LAUREN

Lauren eased open the door of her grandmother's apartment, telling herself she was calm enough not to cry. If not calm, she was at least too drained. "Hi, Grandma," she called. "It's me."

"Lauren, my darling! This is a surprise. Come in!"

When she opened the door more fully, the sight of her grandmother looking so utterly normal brought the tears back to her eyes, despite her best intentions.

She sat in her cozy recliner, her black slacks ironed to a straight crease and her blue blouse crisp as summer sheets. A cordless phone lay cradled in her lap, but she held her arms up for a hug, so Lauren rushed forward for an embrace she desperately needed.

"You look so good," Lauren said tearfully, because her grandmother's face sagged only a little today. "Did I interrupt a call?"

"No, no. Are you all right? You look like you've been crying."

"Oh." Lauren rubbed her eyes and took a seat on the sofa, but she almost immediately stood again. "Things have been a little crazy."

"But your hair is a mess, Lauren!"

"I'm sorry." Lauren automatically touched her hair.

"Why don't you go brush it and then make us some coffee?"

She opened her mouth to decline. What she was about to reveal was too important to treat like a comfy little chat. But if she declined, she'd have to speak the truth—the ugly, life-changing truth—and the thought of putting that moment off felt like a lifeline she couldn't refuse.

She wanted to tell her grandmother about the wallet herself in the gentlest way possible so she wouldn't be faced with a shock from a stranger that might raise her blood pressure, and . . . God, all she could do was pray that her grandma would still love her, still want her, even after Lauren became the bearer of the worst news possible.

Cowardice prompted her to paste on a fake smile. "I'll start the coffee," she said too loudly.

"Thank you, my dear. I'm so glad you're here."

Lauren fired up the coffeepot, then escaped to the bathroom. The space was huge, big enough to easily accommodate the movements of a wheelchair, and the mirror was huge too, unfortunately. Her appearance truly was shocking, and she was surprised her grandma hadn't screamed at the sight of her. Her eyes and nose glowed red from her tears, and her hair stood out in wild clumps from drying beneath the hoodie. She looked like a walking nightmare.

And she was, wasn't she? She'd come to tell the horrible truth before she went to the police and they sent investigators out in every direction. *Brace yourself, Grandma, your world is about to collapse. Again.*

Her grandmother had obviously believed in her son's innocence. And why wouldn't she? Now after all this time, her own granddaughter was going to put him back in prison again.

Her grandma would hate her, probably, and Lauren's worst fears would come true. She'd be pushed away, out of this family that had been her whole world for so long. But maybe, just maybe, if she told her grandmother first, it would be less of a betrayal. Maybe she would even be proud of Lauren for doing the right thing no matter how scary it was.

Her dad had killed that woman and then manipulated the justice system to avoid paying the price. He'd manipulated Lauren too, and maybe that hurt even worse in her selfish little heart. All the subtle, awful things he'd implied about her mom. All the ways he'd wedged them apart and stolen Lauren's love. Her mom hadn't been crazy or unstable—she'd been right.

She must be so worried now, but Lauren didn't have the mental space to deal with that. First things first. Break the news very carefully to her grandmother. Turn the wallet over to the police. Call her mom. And then?

Then completely, utterly fall apart.

She filled her palms with cool water, then dropped her face into the pool of her hands and held her breath, not wanting to come up for air. But the water trickled free and exposed her again, so she soaped up her hands and washed her face. Then she picked up her grandmother's antique ivory-backed brush and carefully tugged it through her hair. It was the best she could do for now, but it was at least a fifty percent improvement, and she could smell the hot coffee even past the closed door.

This was it, then. It was time to face the hardest thing she'd ever do.

After planting a gentle smile on her face, she fetched her grandmother her coffee and pulled a chair close to her.

"Well," her grandma sighed. "I hope you haven't found any trouble with the pipes. That house has been good to me, but you always hear horror stories."

"No, everything seems good so far. But . . . I do have some bad news, I'm afraid."

Hornets buzzed in her gut, warning that she was in dangerous territory and about to be hurt. And she was. Half of her wanted to grab her purse and drive away, find a lake somewhere and sink the wallet and identification and all the destruction about to radiate out from them like a bomb. She wanted to throw them out as hard as she could, then run away, out of state, across the country.

But the other half of her knew it wasn't right. More important, it knew she could never outrun this.

"So I wanted to talk to you," she finally said, the last word cracking just a little.

Her grandmother set down the coffee and took Lauren's hand in her cool one. "What is it, my dear? What's wrong?"

"Well, I was working on the house, you know."

Her grandmother nodded.

"And I . . . I found something."

"What is it, dear?"

Lauren swallowed hard as the painful buzzing inside her got stronger and floated up into her skull. "It's that woman's wallet, Grandma. Tori Bagot, the woman who was murdered. Dad had her wallet hidden in the wall of his bedroom closet."

"Oh!" She raised her free hand to cover the O of her mouth.

"That means Dad was with her, Grandma. It means . . ." Her tongue stopped working for a moment until she swallowed and pressed on. "I'm so sorry. But Dad was with her that night."

Her brow dipped into a puzzled frown. "Well, we don't know *that*."

The way her grandmother's head tilted with confusion broke Lauren's heart, so she kept talking just to fill the yawning space between them. "I think we do. His lawyers claimed he'd seen her at the bar but that she was never with him. Never in his car."

"Oh, of course. Yes. I remember." She nodded, her eyes focused far away, and a wave of devouring guilt washed over Lauren. How could she hurt this wonderful woman this way?

She took a bracing breath and started again. "So if he—"

"But," her grandma interrupted, "he admitted to the police he'd been seeing her. He admitted they were lovers. She could have left that wallet with him anytime!"

"Oh, Grandma." Heart breaking at the eager confidence blooming on her grandmother's face, Lauren shook her head. "Why would he have hidden it, then?"

"Oh, you know how these things look." She reached out and held tight to Lauren's hand. "Regardless, that's all in the past. It's all settled. That terrible man admitted to killing that girl, and that's that. How in the world could some old wallet possibly matter?"

Lauren cleared her throat, trying to dislodge the lump of dread that had accumulated. "You . . ." She couldn't believe she was about to say this, but the words were rising up, anyway, still buzzing with danger. "You don't seem shocked. Aren't you surprised?"

"Surprised by what? We already knew he had a . . . a *relationship* with her."

"But the wallet . . ." The hair rose on the back of Lauren's neck, and she broke out in a sweat. Even the fingers still clasped in her grandmother's hand went slick. "You didn't know about that, did you?"

"Of course not! What a thing to suggest!"

But now it was all hitting her, the things she should have seen before. Her grandmother hadn't recoiled at the news of the wallet. She'd gone along with her son's scheme to keep his pregnant mistress hidden at the ranch all those years ago. And she was the one who'd paid off Kepnick to take responsibility for the murder. She *must* have been. How would her son have arranged for the money when he'd already been in prison for a decade?

His mother had been protecting him all these years, but more than that, she'd been *aiding* him the whole time. Making arrangements. Covering up.

"Oh, Grandma," Lauren cried as the truth crashed over her like a physical force. "Oh, Grandma, you knew. You knew he did it."

The papery skin tightened around her eyes, and her crooked mouth went flat. "I knew no such thing. Your father didn't kill that waitress, and it's despicable that you would imply something so disgusting." Her words suddenly sounded harsh as acid, a tone Lauren had never heard. "You've been talking to that madwoman again, haven't you? She's spent her whole life trying to poison you against us."

"Grandma—"

"How could you?"

She leaned back, surprised to feel herself drawing her body protectively away from this old woman. "This isn't what I wanted."

"Then stop this nonsense right now!" She slapped a hand against the armrest.

Lauren jumped in alarm, but the blood rushing to her grandma's face scared her more than the sound of the slap. "Please, please don't get upset. I don't want anything to happen to you. And I understand. I love him too, but I have to turn this over to the police."

"You have to do no such thing. Have you no decency? He's your father."

"I know," Lauren cried, her voice breaking. He'd been her hero. Her precious daddy. "I'm sorry." She started to get up, but her grandmother's nails dug into the back of her hand and pulled her back down. Where her skin had been sickly hot and sweaty just a moment before, an icy cold bloom raced to replace it. Whatever she'd thought might happen here, reality seemed to be crumbling around her, revealing nightmares.

"I gave you that house, girl. I gave you that name you wanted so badly. I gave you family and history and the kind of respectability your trashy mother will never have. And this is how you repay us? By stabbing your father in the back?"

Horrified at the snarling words and the twisted, hateful grimace, Lauren yanked her hand free, skin burning with the scratch of nails. "No. That's not what this is. I love you and Dad. You've been everything to me. I'm not betraying anyone."

"Then what do you think you're doing, young lady?"

Lauren shook her head, the motion sending her vision spinning, the world tumbling wildly in her thoughts. "This isn't my fault. He did this!"

"He didn't do anything."

She leapt up on shaking legs and tried to back away, but her foot caught on the leg of her grandmother's walker, and she stumbled backward. "I'm sorry," she stammered, wishing she'd kept her purse in her lap, but it sat next to the recliner, left there when Lauren had hugged her grandmother so hard. Hugged her. Before the woman had turned into a strange, snarling beast.

She edged closer. "I'm taking the wallet to the police. If he didn't do anything, then he'll be fine. If he's innocent—"

"He is innocent!" Her grandma's hand rose, clasped around the handle of her wooden cane. "Do you hear me?" She banged the cane onto the flooring with a crack. "He's innocent, and you will not ruin everything! You leave that wallet here, and go back home right now, young lady. I will take care of this."

Lauren shook her head over and over, denying the anger. Denying what it meant. If this was who her grandma was, then Lauren was losing both of her cornerstones at once. Could she survive without them?

"I'm sorry, Grandma," she said past her tears. She swiped her sleeve over her wet face and shook her head. "I can't go home. I'm going to the police, and if Dad did it, he'll have to pay the price for that. I only wanted to warn you first so you didn't hear it somewhere else. That's all. I love you. But a woman is dead, and if Dad killed her—"

"Your father didn't kill her!"

"You can't know that!"

"I can know it, you little idiot. He didn't kill her, because I did."

The cold sinking beneath Lauren's skin went away. So did every other feeling in her body, leaving her a numb brick, heavy limbed and slow witted. She stared at her grandmother's bulging eyes and twisted lips. "What?" Lauren whispered.

"I did it. It was me. So you consider that when you're making all these noble decisions. Are you going to turn me in?" She popped her cane against the floor again and swept a hand toward her ancient legs. "Do you want to send your ninety-year-old grandmother to prison, Lauren? Is that what you're going to do? Lock your grandma Abrams up?"

Lauren drew back, arms curling tight against her own body. "Stop it. You didn't do this. Stop trying to protect him. Please," she begged.

"As if I could. He would've ruined his life ten times over already without me. Your father is *useless*, chasing after his own pleasure like every other selfish man running around the world like he owns it."

Lauren frantically shook her head, but the words tumbled from her grandma's mouth, mushy with the stroke, but not nearly garbled enough to mistake for anything but terrible blows, each one landing more violently than the next.

"I told him not to marry an older woman, but he got sucked in by the money. Turns out he bought himself a dried-up old cow. But your mother was finally going to give me my grandchild. Finally! And of course he couldn't keep his pants zipped, so that idiot waitress was threatening to tell his wife everything."

"Stop," Lauren begged again, but her aging eyes gleamed brighter as they locked on Lauren.

"You wanted the truth, so here it is. I told him to bring that girl out to the ranch for a talk. And that was all it was. A nice little talk. But she refused to listen to reason. Things got heated."

"Grandma, please." Lauren's world pulled and bent around her, everything falling down. "Don't."

"Your father has never followed through on anything. He didn't file for a divorce. He didn't make the plans for keeping you. And he didn't kill that girl. He couldn't even hide her body the way he promised to. Then he dropped her goddamn wallet in the dirt outside my house and held on to it like a lovesick idiot instead of doing what I told him. He's a disappointment, just like his father, just like his sister."

Lauren's eyes fluttered, but she took a step forward, closer to her purse, and to the woman spewing terrible things.

Amazingly her grandmother smiled, an endearing half quirk of her mouth beneath those gleaming eyes. "You were the one I wanted, Lauren, and now you're here. My precious granddaughter. Isn't that all that matters? You're where you should be. Don't you feel that, my girl? You belong right where you are, on the land. You're an Abrams. You'll get married and have children, and you'll keep our heritage going."

And just like that, in that one transforming moment of horror, it all clicked into place. Her mother's invitation to the ranch, Carol's claim about an adoption, the murdered young woman. All of it fit together, and a sob coalesced in Lauren. It didn't float out of her. It built up, a low moan at first, gathering mass until it pushed up from her throat and finally fell from her mouth in a wordless, heavy cry.

"Calm down," her grandmother chastised. "This is a time for thinking, not crying." Had she said that exact thing on that night so long ago? Had she told her son to calm down and clean up the mess?

"You really killed her?" Lauren croaked.

"She wouldn't listen," her grandmother explained, voice calm and reasonable now, as if she wanted Lauren to understand. "She wouldn't stop yelling. And I knew she'd never shut up. I knew Michael couldn't control her. He couldn't even control himself. So I did what I had to do."

"And Dad knew?"

"Of course he knew. He was right there. I offered her a thousand dollars to go away, and she turned down the deal. What did she expect?"

A crack of hysterical laughter escaped Lauren's mouth, because her grandmother actually sounded confused. "I assume she expected not to be killed!"

"You're emotional," her grandmother responded flatly. "Leave the evidence and go home. I'll take care of it like I take care of everything. We'll burn the wallet. The case is closed. No one cares anymore."

Another wave of chills passed over her, shaking her soul. She said it so casually. *Go home. We'll burn the wallet. No one cares.*

No one.

Lauren frowned, goose bumps spreading over her skin. "Who's we?"

Her grandmother's eyes narrowed. "What?"

"You said, 'We'll burn the wallet.'"

Elizabeth's pale gaze slid toward the door for just a split second. Lauren remembered the phone that had been resting in her lap, and then she looked at the door too.

How long had it been since she'd called her dad? An hour? More? Oh God.

Her grandmother couldn't stop her from leaving, she wasn't physically capable, but her father was. And then what? Then what?

"I have to go," she whispered. She didn't realize she was weeping until a tear slid down her neck, tickling her skin.

"You're fine. We'll forget all this, and things will get back to normal." Her clawed hand moved down to her lap, and Lauren saw the long ridge of burgundy leather tucked into the cushion beside her leg.

Lauren looked at her purse, sitting right there at her grandmother's feet where it had been the whole time Lauren had been locked in the bathroom. She'd already taken the wallet.

Lauren reached toward it.

"Stop!" her grandmother snapped.

Lauren withdrew for a moment, horrified that she might have to wrestle this frail woman. Then she lunged forward quickly, murmuring, "I'm sorry," as she forced her fingers past her grandmother's knee and tried to grab the leather.

She wasn't expecting her grandma to let out a snarl, and she definitely wasn't ready for the raking fingernails.

"Grandma, stop!" she yelped, retreating for just a moment before she tried again. She didn't notice the cane rise in the air, but she felt the crack of it across her elbow.

The pain hit sharp as a hot nail as Lauren cried out and dropped her arm. She grabbed for her elbow, and the cane hit her again, catching the tips of three of her fingers.

She scrambled back with a whine, out of range of the swinging wood. Lauren shook her throbbing fingers and stared disbelievingly at the old woman who'd been at the center of her life for so long. The anchor that stabilized all her family dreams. That anchor was now a block pulling her down into mad despair.

Lauren glanced toward the door again, wondering what she would do if it opened and her father stepped through. Her whole life she'd been terrified of disappointing them and losing their love, but now she knew what real fear was. The fear that someone you loved might hurt you. Might kill you.

Would he kill her? His own daughter?

Her eyes widened as she turned back to gape at her grandma's twisted, angry face. Her own *daughter*? "My God. Did you kill MaryEllen too?"

Those brightly gleaming eyes went wide with shock, the delicate skin of her forehead webbing with wrinkles. "How do you know that name?"

"Did you kill your own daughter?"

Her clawed hands clenched to fists. "You don't know," she snarled. "You don't know anything about her. That unnatural little hussy! You don't know what she put me through, defying my every wish, taking drugs like some sort of gutter rat, running around with disgusting hippies. She was headed straight to hell no matter what—"

Lauren jumped forward, betting that between her quicker muscles and her grandmother's glassy-eyed rage, she could manage to snatch the wallet. The old woman lurched sideways with a cry and managed to catch Lauren's head with the cane, but Lauren closed her fingers over the wallet and pulled away.

The cane fell to the floor, and her grandmother lunged forward with a scream, and suddenly she was sprawled on the hard floor, wheezing.

"Help me!" she whimpered.

Lauren broke for the apartment door but halted at the threshold to look back at the broken old woman now helpless and writhing on the floor.

"Please, Lauren," Grandma whined. "My leg. It hurts. Help me up, darling."

Lauren wiped the streaming tears from her eyes, her scalp still stinging with sharp pain. This was impossible. This moment where she turned her back on this injured, crying old woman.

"Help!"

"I . . . I can't." This couldn't be real. It felt like a nightmare, so she told herself she'd wake up soon and carry on with her life. This would all disappear. Everything would be fine. It had to be.

But her grandmother's face went hard and twisted again. "You do what I say or you'll be out in the cold where you belong, you ungrateful little witch. Your father will never speak to you again either."

The reminder that her father was on his way was the prompt she needed to leave her grandma sprawled across the cold floor. She turned the knob and stumbled into the hall, leaving her grandmother screaming her name behind her, first in plaintive shock, then with increasing fury.

The door finally swung closed and cut off the sound of her rage.

Weeping, Lauren walked quickly toward the bank of elevators, but she was within twenty feet when an elevator opened and her father stepped off. He froze at the sight of her, but Lauren was already strung out on adrenaline, and she pivoted before her mind had even decided and started running the other direction down the hallway.

She was moving so quickly the doors blurred beside her. She couldn't be sure which was her grandmother's, so she hugged the opposite wall and raced for the emergency stairwell at the end of the long corridor, even as a nurse stepped out of one of the other rooms and let out a cry of surprise.

"Pumpkin!" her dad called out, like she was still his little girl, but she kept running until she burst through the fire door and into the cement-bricked stairway. A few seconds later she was at the ground floor and throwing open the metal door at the bottom.

She emerged onto an unfamiliar lawn that ended ten feet in front of her at a white vinyl fence, so she turned left and ran alongside the building until she saw a concrete parking lot ahead. Then she sprinted.

"Lauren!" His voice found her like a dart and hitched her breath with fear.

She needed her keys. Where were they?

Jesus Christ, she'd left her purse and keys and phone behind.

Lauren raced into the parking lot, sobbing now, trying to catch her breath as she ran toward the other end of the long building. There was an office there. Help.

But a big white truck was heading toward her, and when she tried to veer to the left side of the lot, it changed course and headed toward her. Had her father somehow reappeared to corral her from the other side? Or was it Kepnick's son hunting her down? Or—

She was about to scream and dive between two cars when the truck tires squealed to a halt and the driver's door opened.

"Lauren!" her mother screamed, voice high with panic as she stood on the running board and waved an arm. "Get in! Get in!"

A glance over her shoulder showed her dad emerging between two cars thirty feet back, mouth panting. Lauren lunged forward, yanked open the truck door, and dived in. "Mom," she sobbed as her wide-eyed mom reached for her arm and pulled her upright.

"I've got you, baby. I've got you."

"We have to go!"

Her father grew closer in the windshield, still running, still chasing. He was going to get her, drag her from the truck, make her—

Her mom hit the door locks, gave him the double finger, and threw the truck into gear.

Her dad tried to dodge, but she heard a faint clunk and saw him fall over.

"Mom!" She gaped in horror at the side mirror, but he popped up almost immediately, cradling his arm and cursing.

"Got 'im," her mom muttered. She pulled up to a gate at the far end of the lot and pushed a button that made it slide open.

"Mom," Lauren panted.

"What the hell is going on?" her mother demanded, voice shaking with worry.

"The wallet . . . I found . . ." Lauren collapsed into a ball and sobbed, unable to explain any more, unable to face it. Her mom's hand stroked her hair over and over, and Lauren wished she were small again, on the couch, protected by a worn old blanket and her mom's heavy arm holding her close. "How did you find me?" Lauren finally managed to ask past her tears.

"I knew you left your house. And your dad showed up right after—"

"But *how*?"

"I was worried about you, sweetie. I've been so worried! So I . . . well, I called up Carver Calhoun and asked him to keep an eye on you since you were living by yourself. After that email this morning, I had to check on you. I thought . . . Well, never mind what I thought. But Carver said he'd just seen you peel out of there like your ass was on fire. When he called back and said your dad had shown up, stomping around the front porch and cursing into his phone . . . well. I was already on the road by then, driving like a bat out of hell, and I asked Carver to follow your father. I just knew something wasn't right."

Lauren held tight to her mom's hand, wanting her close in a way she hadn't in so many decades. But the love she felt couldn't quite push away the awful guilt lurking there, a great dark form waiting just beneath the surface. "I'm sorry, Mom. I'm sorry about everything."

"None of that matters now," her mother said. "Are you okay?"

"No. Yes. I'm not sure. I found something. Something incriminating. Dad had . . ."

Her mom squeezed her hand. "So you finally know. I'm sorry, baby. I wanted you to know the truth, but . . ."

"It wasn't him, Mom."

She heard the breath leave her mother's body, but Donna said nothing and her hold stayed steady, gripping Lauren as tight as she could with one hand while she steered them away with the other. "I see," she finally murmured. "All right. That's fine."

"Grandma did it."

This time her mom's grip jerked, and she gasped in shock. "Lauren, that just isn't—"

"She admitted it," Lauren said, her voice strangely calm as she said it out loud for the first time. "It was her. Grandma killed Tori Bagot. She paid Kepnick to take responsibility. And I think maybe she killed her daughter too."

"MaryEllen?"

"You knew her?"

"No! No, I never met her. She ran away years before I arrived on the scene. Or . . . she disappeared, anyway. But your grandmother? I knew she was volatile, but . . ." She scrubbed her hand over her slack face. "My God. Her? You really think she did it?"

"I do. I thought maybe she was trying to cover up for Dad, but . . . no. You should have seen her face."

"I think I've seen that face before," she said darkly. "In fact, I know I have."

"You thought . . ." Lauren sent her mom a guilty look, relieved she had to keep her eyes on the road. "You told me she stole your car keys to keep you there. I didn't believe you."

"No one believed that part. Even I wasn't sure. That night seemed like a dream. Worst nightmare I ever had."

"I'm so sorry."

Her mother took a deep breath, shoulders rising to make more space in her chest. "I never needed you to believe me, baby. I just needed you to be safe. That's all. I just want you safe."

Lauren felt that great mass of guilt again, waiting. But not now. Not yet. "I am safe. Thank you for saving me. Again."

"I'll do it every time, baby, don't you ever doubt that."

Lauren let herself slump closer and rested her head on her mom's shoulder, amazed that she still smelled the same. Like Suave shampoo and Marlboro Lights. Just like she had all those years ago when she'd given Lauren everything she had, everything she could. Lauren had wanted more, and now it felt like she'd had the world back then and let it go.

Her mom pressed a kiss to her head. "It's up to you now, baby. Where do you want to go? Whatever it is, I'll help you. I'll break any law if that will bring you peace. I'll take you away from here, hide you in my house. I'll make an anonymous tip. Hell, I'll even help you destroy the evidence if that's what you want. I don't care anymore. Whatever you need, you say it."

Lauren angled her head to look out the window at the glorious hills that stretched beyond the streets of the town. She'd turned her back on her wild, imperfect mother so many times. She'd wanted a fantasy instead of reality, and her mom was nothing if not real. "I love you, Mom."

"Oh, baby." Her mom's finger stroked down her cheek. "I love you so much."

Lauren felt calm suddenly. Safe. She thought of her grandmother, too frail to survive a trial or jail or prison. Then she thought of Tori

Bagot, whose body had never been claimed by a family, whose cremated remains lay buried in an unmarked square somewhere. "I know it was a long time ago, but do you still remember where the police station is?"

A moment of silence. She heard the swish of fabric as her mom turned toward her. "You sure?"

She knew the calm would crack soon. She knew this would hurt more than anything ever had before. But right now, she could do this. "I have evidence to turn in. A story to tell."

"Baby, if you're willing to do that, I'm sure willing to take you."

"Do you think they'll believe me?" Lauren finally sat up and met her mother's gaze. She found grief in her eyes. And decades of pain. She wondered if she was seeing her own future there. But if she was, she saw endless depths of strength too.

Her mother sighed. "I . . . I'll let you go in alone," she finally said, and Lauren assumed it was resentment, despite the gentle tone. A punishment for all the years Lauren didn't believe her. That was fair, but it still stung.

But then her mother patted her knee. "I had my chance to convince them. They'll believe you if I'm not there to ruin it with all the old doubts. But you can do this. I know you can."

The calm rippled for a moment, and Lauren tried to hold back a sob, but it escaped anyway. Still, when her mom took her hand, it felt okay to cry. And her mother's hand held her tight the whole way.

CHAPTER 26

DONNA

The stone wasn't a grave marker. Despite weeks of searching by police, MaryEllen's body hadn't been found. The carved piece of granite that had been chosen from this land was more of a memorial, really. An acknowledgment that MaryEllen had lived here, a seventeen-year-old girl with a wide smile and a restless heart. She'd died here too, killed by her mother in a fit of rage.

That was the assumption, anyway. Elizabeth Abrams had never confessed with any detail. But Michael had flipped with the callous selfishness he'd always shown the world.

He'd confessed his role in disposing of Tori Bagot's body, though he'd denied knowing that his mother had planned to hurt her. She'd snapped and hit Tori over the head with an iron doorstop, and Michael had claimed she'd died immediately. Nothing he could do.

He'd pled down to time served for aiding and abetting, and he'd thrown his mother's last years right under the bus without hesitation.

Not that it mattered now. She'd been whisked out of justice's closing hands by another severe stroke. She wouldn't be punished, and she would never be locked away, aside from the punishment her own body continued to exact. She was locked inside her own flesh. Immobile in a nursing facility, unable to hurt anyone again.

Michael had claimed that he'd truly believed his sister had run away, because she'd threatened it several times in those last few months. He'd heard a wild, screaming argument the night she'd vanished. He'd even peeked into her room to see her stuffing belongings into a bag. That same bag had eventually been tossed into the shed to rot, as if even throwing it away was too much trouble for a girl like that.

He must have seen it. He must have known. But no one could prove a thing, and Michael's life continued as it always had.

Donna put her arm around her daughter and pulled her close despite the unwavering heat of the April afternoon. She tried not to touch Lauren so often that she became a pest, but she craved the contact after all those years of estrangement. And all the years before when she'd been too stressed and exhausted to show enough affection.

They stared silently at the stone together.

It didn't reveal much. Her full name. A birth date and the year she'd vanished. An etching of her face from a photo found in the attic. And one carved line: SHE IS REMEMBERED.

They'd spent months learning from her high school friends everything they could about this daughter who'd been so viciously, deliberately forgotten. How skilled she'd been on horseback. How much she'd loved music. How that music had pulled her into a new world of ideas and beliefs that had infuriated her mother. How much her friends had loved her for her wry humor and her quiet patience.

"I still think she's here," Lauren said.

"They didn't find any evidence under the cabin," she reminded her daughter gently, "and that was the only thing your father could remember being built right around her death."

"I know, but there was so much land then. I keep thinking of how Grandma insisted the new landowners only build on a certain spot. Maybe it was because she didn't want them digging."

Donna kissed her head. "Maybe MaryEllen is still out there some-where, alive. Maybe she really did get away and never looked back."

"Maybe."

Carver stepped closer, an ancient baseball cap in his hands. He still preferred his solitude, but he'd agreed to join them for a few minutes. "She was a nice girl. Polite and respectful. Only one I ever talked to over here. She loved to come play with my dogs when she was little, and she had a real gentle touch with them. I hope she's out there doing well."

They all stared quietly for a moment before he dipped his head in goodbye and turned to walk down the drive.

Donna watched his departure with a worried frown. "Are you really sure you're okay out here by yourself, Lauren? With all these bad memories?"

Lauren raised her chin. This new tragedy had transformed her. Hardened her. But it had also calmed her a little. She'd lost that bone-deep need to ingratiate herself with people. For the first time in decades, Donna could see herself in her daughter, though she wasn't sure that was a compliment anyone would want.

"It's mine," Lauren finally answered. "Even the courts have finally said so."

Despite her other legal troubles, her grandmother had immediately tried to snatch the land back from Lauren's possession. And after her second stroke, Michael had taken up the fight, one last betrayal of the daughter who'd loved him so much. But a judge had quickly ruled that the intent of the contract had been clear and that Lauren hadn't violated the terms of the loan. She'd been forced to take a more traditional mort-gage from a bank to pay off the money, but that hadn't been difficult based on the worth of the land.

"I'll finish the last of the renovations," she continued, "and then I'll decide what to do. But it's strange, Mom. I still feel . . . I don't know. I can't believe I'm even saying this, but I still feel grounded here."

Donna couldn't believe it either, but she tried to set her own feelings aside. "It is a beautiful place. Even I thought so, all those years ago."

"It is."

"But you should still sell it to a stranger just to spite that woman."

Lauren threw back her head and laughed, and Donna's eyes burned with tears at the sight.

She hadn't been a good mom, not in the traditional sense. After the trauma of the betrayal and the panic of her escape and then that awful, spinning stress of the trial, her new personal standard had been to lie low and never get close to anyone. Her entire existence had been survival and protection. She'd kept herself at arm's length from everyone, but in doing that she'd isolated Lauren as well.

But she'd kept her child safe. That had been her goal, and she'd done it. That was something, wasn't it?

The years of distance let her see all her mistakes in bright detail. The pain she'd planted so deeply in the one she loved the most. But she'd started to let her guard down in the past few years, and she loved her daughter so much it hurt.

She'd even started painting again, though she hadn't told Lauren. It felt too new, and she'd only painted trees so far. Faces felt so close, so risky. But she thought maybe, just maybe, she might paint Lauren's face sometime soon. Paint the new set of her jaw and her cautious, studying eyes.

"It might be good revenge to sell," Lauren said quietly, her gaze on the memorial. "But if MaryEllen is here, I don't want to leave her alone. Is that stupid?"

"No, baby," Donna whispered. "That's not stupid. And you're so, so strong."

"Well, I also have that very expensive new security system I had installed. And the DA assures me that Jeremy Kepnick will face at least a couple of years for helping his dad."

"Good."

Lauren smiled. "And I know you asked Carver to keep watching out for me."

Donna wasn't the least bit ashamed. "I sure did. And you do the same for him, please. His sister lives way out in Texas, so he needs you too."

She hadn't known his name thirty-five years earlier, but he was the man who'd answered her frantic knock that terrifying night. He'd called the sheriff and requested the car that came to escort her to safety. He was the reason she'd gotten out, and he'd been willing to help again when Donna had asked him to keep an eye on her daughter. His presence made her feel marginally better.

Donna finally forced herself to let her daughter go. "You're also kind, Lauren. Truly kind, and a far better person than any of us deserve. I'm sorry. You know that, right? I should have done so much better for you."

"Stop saying that. You did the best you could, Mom. And I understand now. I understand all your fear and paranoia and that *shell*."

Donna made a motion of knocking on her head, but before she'd even lowered her hand, the lightness left her and she let her smile fall away. That shell. It was still there, but she was growing weary of it, finally. Weary of holding herself so tight inside it.

Her husband stood a dozen feet away, waiting patiently for them to share their grief with each other. Donna sent him a small, grateful smile, and he smiled back. Oscar wasn't much of a talker, but he liked to drive down and help Lauren with electrical wiring when she needed it. Despite her newfound caution, Lauren wasn't built for coldness, and she'd warmed up to him already, fussing over his diet when he ate too much sugar.

"Don't be mad," her daughter suddenly blurted, and Donna groaned.

"Uh-oh. What now?"

"An old friend of yours tracked me down on Facebook after all the news stories. Tomás? We talked a bit, and he gave me his number if you want to call." Lauren held out a piece of paper.

Tomás. A warm wave of anxious nostalgia washed through her body.

"He really wants to catch up, Mom."

Donna's chest went so tight she had to force the breath into her lungs. "Oh, Lauren."

"He says he remembers me."

"I . . . I did go back. I tried. I slept on their couch for a while before the trial, but I couldn't get work. Then after you were born . . ." Donna gasped for air, but when Lauren's hand settled on her shoulder, she felt her touch like an anchor holding her steady.

Tomás. It had been so many years since she'd thought of her old friend. Of any friends at all, really.

"I was so broken," she explained. "I didn't know how to trust anyone after all of that. Not even myself. Especially not myself. I'd always thought I was so savvy, smarter than everyone. Hell, even after it all went down, I never realized Michael meant to stay with his wife and raise you with her. I had no idea until you told me. I wasn't so goddamn smart, Lauren, and I was so ashamed. Can you understand that?"

"I do, Mom. I really do. I'm a different person now, after all that. I know you weren't the same."

Donna took a deep breath and blinked back tears. "I felt like . . . I felt hopeless, and it took all my energy just to believe I could keep you safe. I never even hoped I could make you happy. And look what I did to you."

"I love you," her daughter whispered. "It's okay."

It wasn't okay, but it was what they had, and Donna burned with greedy love for all the time they were taking to build a relationship together. Finally.

Donna stared at the piece of paper in her hand. "I'll call him."

"Good."

"I might need a little time, but I'll get in touch." She glanced up at Lauren. "Speaking of getting in touch, your dad's not bothering you?"

"He hasn't called once," she said, and Donna was relieved that her daughter sounded thankful instead of hurt.

Lauren still didn't hate her father, but Donna had her back on that one too. Her daughter could practice peace, because Donna hated him enough for them both since he'd admitted he'd meant to take his newborn daughter to raise with his wife. He still hadn't admitted what they'd planned to do with Donna afterward, but she knew. They all knew.

Lucky for her, her new relationship with Lauren meant that she didn't have room for the boundless hatred she could have nurtured in her youth. Too much of her was taken up with joy and love now, but she kept that bright kernel of rage as hot as she could, just for the sake of justice.

At least the world knew the truth about him. And at least Lauren didn't have to squirm under his fickle attention, wondering if she was the one lacking. She wasn't. She was bright and warm and loving and beginning to value that about herself after all these years.

And finally, somehow, on this strange and twisted land, Donna and her daughter had both found their way home at long last.

ABOUT THE AUTHOR

Victoria Helen Stone is the Amazon Charts bestselling author of *Jane Doe*, which has been optioned by Sony Pictures Television, and *Problem Child*, as well as the critically acclaimed thrillers *False Step*, *Half Past*, and *Evelyn, After*. Formerly writing as *USA Today* bestselling novelist Victoria Dahl, she is originally from the Midwest but now writes from an upstairs office high in the Wasatch Mountains of Utah. After a career in romance that included winning the American Library Association's prestigious Reading List Award, Victoria turned toward the darker side of fiction. For more on the author and her work, visit www.victoriahelenstone.com.